No Time For Tears

JUNE MASTERS BACHER

HARVEST HOUSE PUBLISHERS
Eugene, Oregon 97402

Scripture quotations are taken from the King James Version of the Bible.

NO TIME FOR TEARS

Copyright © 1992 by Harvest House Publishers
Eugene, Oregon 97402

Bacher, June Masters.
    No time for tears / by June Masters Bacher.
    ISBN 0-89081-943-2
    I. Title.
    PS3552.A257N6   1992   91-37692
    813'.54—dc20   CIP

Printed in the United States of America.

To those who walked with me
through that decade of conflict
in the heartland of America—
without tears. Ours is the victory!

Contents

The heart has its reasons which reason knows nothing of.

—Pascal

Thus saith the Lord: Refrain thy voice from weeping, and thine eyes from tears; for thy work shall be rewarded.

—Jeremiah 31:16

*Let not young souls be smothered
     out before
They do quaint deeds and fully
     flaunt their pride.
It is the world's one crime
     its babes grow dull,
Its poor are ox-like,
     limp and leaden-eyed,
Not that they starve,
     but starve so dreamlessly,
Not that they serve,
     but have no God to serve,
Not that they die,
     but that they die like sheep,
     leaden-eyed.*

—Nicholas Vachel Lindsay
1914

1

Unexpected Collapse

"We are finished."

Like a thief in the night it came—the collapse of the country's banking system, the beginning of the Great Depression.

Those fortunate enough to own a radio might have heard the mournful announcement. One moment they would have listened to some unseen singing group crooning "Happy Days Are Here Again" above the crackling static, the next to the words of surrender of the outgoing President Herbert Hoover: "We are finished."

To the nine-year-old girl, with flaxen hair cut in a straight-bang Dutch boy bob flying in the breeze, the words were meaningless. Something was over. Maybe that was good. She paused only because there was a pause in the crooning, then went right on with her one-person game of hopscotch, once again keeping time to the song's rhythm: "Hap-" (hop) "py" (hop) "days" (hop)... the hopping helped her tired mind.

"Hello, Marvel. Have you heard?"

Mary Ann's voice startled her. The bare feet had made no sound on the Bermuda grass.

"I heard the president say—" Marvel paused, wishing she had paid more attention, all the while combing her thick, straight bangs with bare fingers. She tried very hard to concentrate on her favorite cousin's next words, but found it almost impossible. The wealth of blue-black curls Marvel would die for got in the way. Even now, in what must be a doomsday crisis, she marveled

9

at her birthday twin's beauty and sighed. No matter how reassuring Mother tried to be, saying, "You have a beauty all your own, darling—a part of it being that you are unaware." Unaware? Why, mirrors had no reason to lie. She was plain, plain, *plain*. So what if the high cheekbones showed promise of *great* beauty later and that she had inherited the Harrington blindingly blue eyes? If the situation were as desperate as Mary Ann sounded, maybe there would *be* no "later."

"You didn't hear a word I said," Mary Ann accused.

Guilty as charged. "I—I'm sorry—"

"I said," Mary Ann repeated, spacing each word far from the one preceding, "it means Daddy will be out of a job. Or don't you care?"

Marvel was jolted back to earth. So it was true, she thought dazedly—the "crash" she had heard people mention in hushed voices. Heretofore, Pleasant Knoll knew poverty only by hearsay. Now what had been as unreal as the Saturday matinees her family enjoyed had hit close to home. A few would know what it was like to be poor. What did the Beatitudes say about that? The cousins' Sunday school teacher, the buxom, kind-of-heart Mrs. Key, had quoted it often enough. Oh, yes: "Blessed are the poor in spirit; for theirs is the kingdom of heaven."

Care? Of course, she cared! She didn't understand, that was all.

"Maybe things aren't as bad as they sound—maybe Uncle Worth'll find another job—maybe Daddy can help." Marvel realized she was stumbling in an effort to find words of consolation. It always happened when she was scared. And she *was* scared—scared of the unknown.

Although the two little girls who had never known want or sacrifice were scared, the whole world was scared with them that chilly, gray March morning. Their confusion echoed the spirit of a nation caught by surprise. Three years had passed since the stock market's Humpty-Dumpty fall on Wall Street and nothing terrible had resulted, had it? Wall Street must be very far away, since few people had heard of it. So in the bigger cities they went on drinking from the river of earthly pleasures in the mindless "cafe society" manner of the Roaring Twenties. Behind it all there probably was a sort of desperation, a means of escaping warnings of the square-jawed president. And Pleasant Knoll remained just that: a small east Texas town of congenial middle-class, law-abiding citizens concerned only by the price of cotton and keeping their children shielded from the "evils" of big-city life they read about in *The Dallas Morning News* delivered by the daily train.

Mary Ann was shaking her wealth of curls in a sort of desperate way. "Daddy's not trained for other work. Banking is all he's ever known like the rest of the Harrington men—uh, except Uncle Dale."

"Uncle Dale" was Marvel's father. It was true that he was the only one of Squire (as he chose to be called) Alexander Jay Harrington's five sons (Dale, Worth, Alex, Emory, and Joseph) to break with tradition and choose farming over banking. Now the idea might be more wise than Grandfather had made it sound. Banking wasn't that different from, say, bookkeeping. Daddy could ask about a place for Mary Ann's father at the cotton gin where Daddy was assistant manager. But Mary Ann turned aside the idea. Banking was her father's life, she said, even though there could be no "gold watch of retirement."

There seemed little else to say, so Marvel went on with her hopscotch to release an inexplicable queasiness in her tummy. Soon Mary Ann joined her without invitation. There was no reason to doubt a welcome.

Suddenly Mary Ann halted in mid-hop. The sudden stop caused her to waver on one leg in such a way that they both laughed, breaking the tension—but only momentarily.

Mary Ann violated a rule by putting the other foot down and turned her white face to Marvel. "Now I won't be able to marry Jake."

Another laugh began in Marvel's throat. *Marry!* Mary Ann was teasing, of course. Only one look at her face said something quite different. Why, she was serious—dead serious. "Things are bound to get worse. His dad worked at the bank, too, and Jake was going to follow in his tracks—"

Marvel was scared again. Why did adults keep saying children didn't understand and keep secrets from them to "shield them," as they called it? But she said with forced calm, "That's too far ahead for us to worry about. Look! The wind's rising. Fanny came to do Mama's washing today. Look how the sheets are billowing—

like sails. Let's play hide-and-seek between them. Last one there's a pig's tail!"

The game ended as suddenly as it began. "There's Elmer! Let's go—quick," Mary Ann whispered. "He's the only cousin I dislike."

Dislike? There was no reason to dislike him. It was more that Mary Ann distrusted the bullying senior cousin—no, "feared" was the word.

"He struts around like he owns the place. Look at him—" Mary Ann said.

And well he might one day. Marvel wondered if Mary Ann knew Elmer's own father held a mortgage on Marvel's family's property in town. They had never talked about it. She herself had heard only by chance. Aunt Polly, Elmer's mother, whose florid face gave the impression of having run the few blocks separating her house from Marvel's, had asked Mother if they expected to beg that "the mortgages ride again," adding that it would be a bad mistake "but what one would expect from easy-come-easy-go Dale."

Something about her tone of voice was insulting. Mother was hurt. Marvel could tell from the way she answered, her actual words too muffled to hear. Defensively, Marvel rushed in to say, "You ought to talk it over with God before saying that!"

She would always regret that. But after all, she was two years younger then, far less *mature* than now. Mother, still lovely with her masses of gold hair retaining its elegance in spite of the stylish "shingle bob," paled.

"Go back to your playing—please, sweetheart." There was a note of pleading in her voice. Marvel had obeyed.

Once outside, she heard Aunt Polly resume her talking. "Honestly, Snow—that *child*." The way she said *child* made it sound like a bad word. "Why, she even has our Elmer thinking farm life is ideal—"

The window banged shut.

How could Fat Elmer (Mary Ann's secret name for him) be so stupid? And how could his mother be so hard-hearted? If the Mortgages needed a ride, it was right that they have one. She could sit on Daddy's lap if it was crowded. Wasn't that what the minister meant by "sacrifice"? She would ask Daddy tonight. His answer satisfied her—then.

"The mortgages aren't people, honey. They're something my stepbrother Frederick holds."

Fine. She hoped his arms got tired....

Now, suddenly, Elmer was there with the two little girls—not playing, of course. Being five years older gave him an edge. But it came as a surprise that he was playing the part of a grown-up— amusing but frightening. He was taller, thinner, and no longer walking with the limp caused, Marvel had heard Grandmother say, from an extremely difficult birth. (Mary Ann had sniffed and said, "That figures.")

"What are you doing here?" Mary Ann demanded. "This is no time—"

Elmer looked at her with disdain, then turned colorless eyes to Marvel in a way she did not understand—speculative, traveling up and down her small body as if... as if what? As if suddenly here was something worth considering. Then, without a word, he marched away as if satisfied. What on earth—?

"Ignore him—he's nothing to us." True, but why did he behave as if being here were a great favor he was bestowing... and something more?

After Mary Ann went home, Marvel sat outside in spite of the cold. The large house her family owned amid the vast cotton fields was little more than a faint memory, left behind several years ago when it was time for her to enter school and they moved to town so she could attend. She wished she remembered more. Somehow she knew it figured into their future, that they would need to talk about it, just as they would need to talk about mortgages and the perplexing "crash." It was a strange situation, one she wondered why she had never questioned. She supposed all children took things for granted just as she had—for that matter, Marvel thought slowly, the way the world had. Slowly she went inside.

Snow Riley Harrington paused in her late-afternoon ritual of turning on the ornate floor lamps, all flooding the living room with light in welcome to her husband's homecoming, and smiled. Mother must have been truly beautiful in her youth, for the signs remained. "Is something wrong?"

Her mother didn't know? "Tell me why we came here... why we left the farm Daddy loved so much... uh, why this house is mortgaged."

Mother seemed to hesitate before reaching a decision. "So you could have an education. Don't worry, little one." With a delicate lift of her shoulders, Mother dismissed the matter, looking a little wistful. But the dreams were back in her eyes.

Marvel was never sure, but it seemed that was the beginning of feeling responsibility for her parents, her time of growing up too fast... too soon.

She was right. Disaster sat on the doorstep. And nobody was prepared.

2

The Naked Truth

Typical of "heartland" weather, the sullen clouds slunk away as if they had been a part of the conspiracy to send its inhabitants to the poorhouse. Now skies stretching from horizon to horizon blazed almost as mockingly blue. Almost overnight dogwood and redbud burst into bloom along the few rises which as yet had escaped the plow. Just how deadly the thrust of that farm implement into the grassy breast of the virgin earth none had come to realize. Tilling meant cotton. Cotton meant money. Look at the bountiful gardens. And sharing the way they did among themselves, hard times would be over in no time—wouldn't they? Dry farming would still pay off, even though the price for the industry which had made them self-sufficient was dropping. Given another bumper crop or so would put the banks back on their feet. And again, well, wouldn't it? Or so they reasoned in little clumps around the hardware store. But the truth of the business was that all were shaken more than they cared to admit. Not that they had accepted the ugly padlocks barring entrance to the banks to which they had entrusted life savings as other than temporary. Not that they had faced the naked truth....

Marvel was listening to her father repeat these bright thoughts and trying to hope he was right. He always made her feel better, made any dark thoughts inside her curl up like a stinging nettle. That was it. Stinging nettles were treacherous. The fuzzy creatures were short-lived, their longevity only adding to their curse.

Their dried leaves were their weapons. Dried, they all but disappeared. One had to be on guard every second. Their favorite hiding place was between the cotton rows where she played with the happy, fun-loving ebony playmates—children of the pickers. They all screamed together for hours, the pain was so unbearable. And sometimes it would come back. Marvel shivered just remembering.

"What's the matter, sweetheart?" Concern showed in Daddy's Harrington eyes. Marvel saw herself reflected in their blue depths. But she saw, too, the fine lines surrounding them. The lines were new.

"How can we get our money?" she burst out. "How can we plant without seeding money? And," she paused to gulp, for ahead lay the biggest question of all, "Daddy, what *is* a mortgage? Can we—can we lose that place, and this one? Tell me, Daddy. *Tell* me—tell me all of it. I have to know!"

Marvel's voice dropped to an agonizing whisper. She hadn't wanted to cause him pain. She hadn't even intended to mention finances. What did a nine-year-old know? But she had to know who was right: the men on the shady streets of Pleasant Knoll or the now-hoarse voice on the radio.

He leaned slightly to her rightful place beside him at supper and planted a loving kiss on her forehead. "Wow! I always get a bang in the mouth," he said to make her laugh.

Marvel tried, but the smile came out crooked. Tears were too near the surface. He wasn't going to tell her.

"My, my, my, aren't we serious?"

"Have some more English peas and new potatoes that Mrs. Rogers brought us," Mother interrupted gently. "You always loved them—and Daddy can take care of us. I must bake Mrs. Rogers a cake, Dale."

Just like that? Mother could bake a cake and forget it?

Daddy was studying her face. Marvel could feel his steady gaze.

And then he sighed. "No—" he said with some hesitation, "our baby has a right to know. I—I never dreamed—"

"I'd wonder?"

"You're growing up so fast. Let me put that pretty little head to rest, honey. We have enough seed. It was a high-yield grade, very long-stapled bolls, so I saved the seed at the ginning. Heavy bales, too—remember how you and Mary Ann jumped from one to another? Feel better?"

"About the seed," Marvel said truthfully. "But—"

"Oh, that reminds me—I saved cottonseed meal for the cows, too. None of us will be going hungry. You didn't mention the cows, little businesslady."

Actually, she had forgotten the cows. They seemed less important than the land. "But if we lose the place—"

"We won't lose the farm. Why, your grandfather would turn his back on me completely. I shocked him enough in sticking with farming instead of taking to banking. My father never intended for his sons to earn their bread by the sweat of their brow—just hold onto the old home which has always been in the family."

"Now no more questions, honey. Sure you don't want another helping of these peas? They're delicious, Marvel. Oh, remember how you came to have that name? It's a gift from Daddy."

No peas. And she had heard the story of her name before. She waited quietly. No more questions, Mother said. But Daddy would tell her.

Only he didn't. The conversation was over—finished. Like hard times?

No, they would come back. Like the thistle. Like Elmer...

3

The Hopes...
the Fears

Mother planted her zinnias—the seeds which demanded little attention and made such a brilliant display—as a border down the short flagstone walk to the sidewalk. She was wiping her hands when Marvel opened the black wrought-iron gate. The gate the smithy made always squeaked a little—a flaw Daddy wanted Big Ben to correct. But Mother said no because the squeak let her know when their Marvel came home from school. It was a friendly squeak, a sort of "Welcome home!"

Today was no exception. Her mother straightened up to receive her daughter with a shining welcome in her always-undisturbed eyes. Marvel felt a rush of affection that came close to tears, a longing to protect her parents against the world. Almost fiercely she ran up the walk and threw her arms about the mother she loved so much.

The embrace brought a laughing protest. "Did you plan to choke me? I surrender! But careful, darling, or you'll have dirt all over. It's a good thing you have that stack of books in a satchel else they would have gone flying all directions. My word! Do you plan on studying all *those*?"

Yes she did. Marvel was going to study and study some more. Making the honor roll in fifth grade wasn't enough. She must prepare for high school and then college, "make something" of herself. Then she could pay off that hateful mortgage and...

"I want petunias as usual along the fence—and the sweet peas. But most of the neighbors are planning on seeding a few vegetables with the rows of flowers on the other side. What do you think?"

Marvel pretended interest, wondering if they would be here to harvest them. She would put no such thinking into words. Anyway, her mother was chatting away about having received two catalogs in one day—one from Sperry's Seed Company and the other from Sears and Roebuck.

"I always get carried away, you know, and want to order every seed and bush Sperry's features in color. They're *so* lovely...."

The words trailed away from Marvel's ears. She was watching her mother's expressive hands and wondering how they could have remained so lovely through all those years of rambling around in a covered wagon, going here, going there, always in search of a greener hill. And all the while her mother had had four younger brothers, one in diapers, to help care for. One would never know that her mother's background was so rootless except for one scar. The roving child of yesteryear had a passionate need for a home, security, and solid ground beneath her feet. And Mother was determined that her own offspring have what she had missed: a home and proper schooling. Fortunately, Grandmother Riley had attended a girls' boarding school and was prepared to tutor her flock—an advantage that the adventure-loving Leah Johanna Mier Riley insisted on without convincing Mother. Daddy, whose family had founded Pleasant Knoll so long ago nobody could remember when, was more impressed. It must be fun to travel . . . wasn't Grandmother Riley continuing?

And here was Daddy now, breaking into her thoughts without knocking. Dale Harrington scooped his daughter up in strong arms, singing out: "And how's my Marvelous?"

Yes, his *marvelous*, his marvelous daughter. Such a heartwarming thought. The Harringtons had had the experience of two heart-wrenching stillbirths. When the third child arrived screaming lustily, the father had looked down at God's miracle and whispered in awe, "Marvelous." The name had stuck—a derivative, anyway.

"Wow! You're getting too heavy for one man!"

Mother laughed. "Yes, I was just telling Marvel she must have some new dresses. Hers are all too short—"

"We could let the hems out," Marvel said thoughtfully.

But the suggestion went unnoticed. Daddy had swung Mother up in much the same fashion. "And how's my Snow White?"

Snow White—so named because of her coloring and all her brothers. It was too bad three of the dwarfs had died—small wonder under such conditions—and that the other four were scattered like the tribes of Israel. But it gave Grandmother an opportunity to ramble from her own mother who disapproved of her daughter's "gypsy" way of life, her husband included....

"Come on—tell us what wonderful things happened today! I always know when you're holding something back." Mother's eyes were shining with anticipation. Marvel felt her own heart pick up tempo. This was a game the three of them enjoyed together, a way of life.

Usually Daddy teased, made them wait and sometimes guess. But not tonight. This had to be important.

It was.

"I'm glad we've remained calm. It was panic that brought on closing of the bank—sheer panic. People who listened to the radio announcers rushed down and withdrew their savings. And newspapers gobble up this kind of thing. That's how they stay in business—feeding on tragedy. Can't you just see the kids on Dallas streets waving their newspapers on every street corner— even boarding the street cars to split eardrums screaming, "EX-TRA! EX-TRA! Read all about it! Banks shut their doors in failure!' See? It's only temporary!"

Mother clapped her hands in glee. "See, darling? I told you Daddy could take care of us."

It was too good to be true. Marvel obliged with a smile which she knew her father wanted. Then her smile broke in half. "When will they reopen?" she asked, wondering about their own money.

"Oh, soon—soon," Daddy said airily. "Oh, something else! There's talk of repealing the Twenty-first Amendment!"

For once Mother looked uncertain. "Would we want that, Dale?"

"We could put up with it—for the revenue. It would put the government back on its feet—"

"Yoo-hoo! Reach over the fence and get your just rewards for the lovely job you're doing out here. You have to be tired. My back ached just watching you."

Mrs. Autrey, who was forever "doing" for others, held out a cinnamon-scented, still-steaming pie. "Apple," she smiled, showing her dimple. "I read that men who used to hold fine jobs—you know, the big-executive kind—are selling apples on the streets."

"Sure enough?" Mother replied. "I want to thank you, Peggy—"

Margaret Autrey nodded absently. "Wonder why we're unable to find fruit here, exceptin' at Christmas? Got to have an apple for the toes of the little folks' stockings—but my, my, one to munch on between times would sure be nice. Joe bought these for a song from a vendor in Dallas because they were commencing to shrivel. Good for cooking, though. The newspapers claim farms are plum full of food, just no market. Joe next door heard talk that farmers were forming into angry mobs to stop foreclosures. Maybe—and I'm sure hatin' to say this—but just maybe we'd be smart going 'wet,' after all. What do you think?"

"I think," Dale Harrington said quickly, "we're lucky to live here, to have neighbors like you—and that I own a farm!"

* * *

Life was different now. Archie Newland, who tossed pebbles against Marvel's bedroom window as regularly as the sun rose, told her she was a "drag" when she ignored the gesture. The two of them had walked together since the day they entered first grade on shaky legs. Later Arch took to tossing the pebbles to wake her up so she wouldn't be late getting there, he claimed—and, still later, to get her to chase him. The other girls envied her. A good half of them wore his initials printed in their palms. He was so *cute*, they giggled. To Marvel, Arch was just Arch—a friend, but not a "boyfriend." As were none of the others. Neither Marvel nor Mary Ann had gone what their mothers called "boy crazy." The new Mary Ann was even less likely to bother. With Mary Ann it was different. Her walking with Jake Brotherton *meant* something. Nothing to go *ga-ga* over—just an understanding that there would be nobody else. The cousins never discussed it.

But they talked about everything else. They always had. And now they talked even more. Using a floorlamp as an aerial, they kept the radio turned low and listened to the news, beginning to understand.

The spring storms, which plagued east Texas roughly from March through May, interfered with reception, causing voices to crackle like walking on eggshells and often fade out completely. But the cousins heard enough to know that the Depression had deepened. "Industrial production has fallen to the lowest level ever recorded... railroads suffering financial loss... trains could stop altogether!" That voice trailed off. The one following confirmed the report, saying freight cars were running empty. "And," the announcer added, "banks continue to fail by the hundreds while the unemployed stand in the breadline for hungry families or stand waiting in the rain for a bowl of soup or free bed... nothing can stop foreclosures or give men jobs."

Palefaced, the cousins would turn to one another. "That hit us both in the middle—or has your daddy found work?" Marvel asked, knowing it was a foolish question.

"No work. It's getting desperate. And Marvel, he *did* ask at the gin. Not a chance. But I guess you know they're laying men off."

No, she had not known. Did that mean her own father might be let go? The Saturday-night paycheck meant more than food. It meant meeting the mortgage payment to Elmer's father. Marvel looked up to the May-morning sky where God was, half hoping to see His face—but there was a pillar of clouds between.

"What are you all going to do? I mean, how will you—?"

"Get by? I don't know. It's like," Mary Ann began, then paused to shudder, "it's like somebody died in our family!" She looked frightened at her own words. "People coming and going, talking so low Billy and I can't hear—and bringing food. Yep! It *is* like somebody's laid out right there before my eyes. And Billy cries a lot—he knows something's wrong. Mama and Daddy ought to talk to *him* anyhow. I try to keep him quiet—like it was a *real* funeral. It's not fair, but I guess it's good about the cakes and things—"

Mary Ann had stopped, embarrassed. Marvel understood. In fact, although she had always wished for a baby brother like Billy Joe as much as she wished for Mary Ann's storybook curls, maybe it was best that Mother and Daddy didn't have another mouth to feed.

It was good, too, that the state furnished students' textbooks now. Grandmother said people had to buy their own in her day. She scraped together enough to pay for one set. Mother and her oldest brother had to share the books the few times the family stayed put long enough to enroll in a real school. It was a poor arrangement because the two fought a lot and weren't on what could be called friendly terms to this day. The books were a good investment though, a help in teaching the children.

"I wish I could help," Marvel said miserably. "Well, maybe I can make a suggestion. We can study hard. I've already started—"

"Oh yeah? Thanks—and how're we supposed to eat?"

"I don't know. I honestly don't. But God will provide a way. You still believe that, don't you?"

"Yes and no—I mean, I'm not sure anymore. Look at the news. All we hear is misery—not just hunger—there's droughts and plagues and dust storms—and they lump them all together as acts of God!"

The girls had been sitting on a bench, shielded from view, in the town's small park. Marvel spring to her feet. "That kind of talk scares me worse than the news! I told you I'm doing outside reading for extra credit and such things are *not* acts of God. They're what geography calls *natural disasters*. When I said God would provide a way, I meant He'll show me. And I'll do whatever I have to!"

Shamefaced, Mary Ann said, "I'm sorry. God knows I didn't mean it—it's just—just everything—"

And suddenly they were holding each other tight and shedding the tears they had withheld so long for the sake of their parents—two little girls perilous times had forced to grow up too quickly.

When they regained control, Marvel wondered aloud how other children their age felt. She had been too busy with books to keep up with their friends. That was when her cousin told her about the horrifying game of Eviction. Some girlfriends were moving their dolls around like people, having them lose homes, live in rented rooms, then wander the streets.

Marvel was to be double-promoted at the end of the school year and again the next year. Meantime, much was to happen— some of it frightening, alarming. It began that day. As the girls parted, Marvel saw a strange set of tracks: a shoeprint on one side and a peculiar dragging line on the other. Her heart lurched. *Elmer* . . . he dragged one foot. . . .

4

Return of the Thistle

The banks did *not* reopen. Hard times were *not* over. In fact, they were just beginning in Pleasant Knoll. Consequently, Mary Ann's father had been unable to find work.

Dale Harrington tried to call his brother, but Worth had found it essential to have his telephone services discontinued. That evening Dale went to see Worth for the sole purpose of helping out the only way he knew how. School had let out now. It always closed early to allow boys and girls who walked four and five miles in from the country to help with spring planting. With no studying to be done, Marvel could go along and talk with Mary Ann. Mother would take her needlepoint and visit with Auntie Rae who undoubtedly would be mending or adjusting hems.

Auntie Rae was a family favorite. She had no family and, having grown up in Buckner's Orphanage, knew the meaning of "going without"—and that included most everything, including love. "Oh, they weren't unkind," she would say with a proud lift of her chin, "just too busy, overworked as they were and having to depend on small donations to feed too many hungry children. The teachers seemed stern—forbidding—in manner and dress, but they saw to it that we weren't ignoramuses, taught us the dignity of work—taught us to love the Lord, too!"

She was a little woman, but her manner and the masses of black hair (like Mary Ann's), piled high and secured with a fan-shaped comb, gave her the appearance of added height and a certain sweet dignity. Mother said her sister-in-law needed love and was so *acceptant*, taking her husband's relatives as her own family and adjusting to any way of life without a mumble. Rae Harrington (she was never told her maiden name, if anybody knew, so took the name of Buckner for herself) could be starving and nobody would know, according to Mother.

Marvel and Mary Ann sat out in the porch swing. It was cooler there, and Mary Ann had learned what the Twenty-first amendment was about—sort of. She had asked her teacher.

"Do you know what *prohibition* is?" Mary Ann asked now.

"*The* prohibition?"

Mary Ann's raven curls bounced as she nodded. "Whiskey and stuff, what makes men drunk—women, too, I guess. Can you believe it?"

"Yes, to both questions. But prohibition's the Eighteenth, so—?"

Mary Ann nodded again. "Well, some folks want it changed. There's a word Miss Cagney used *rat*—something."

"Ratified. I guess that's what Billy Sunday meant when he was pounding the pulpit and calling it a deadly sin and what we needed was an even stricter law—or more enforcement. I heard him preaching on the radio." Marvel paused to smile a little. "But I think we could have heard him without it. He was that loud—saying he would oppose that 'rot gut' till his teeth wore out, and then he'd gum it!"

"Do you think he's right?" Mary Ann looked confused and afraid.

"Yes," Marvel answered without hesitation, "but Daddy wonders if the government would make money—open the banks—"

Her cousin's eyes lit up. "Oh, anything for that! And it *would* stop this terrible bootlegging—"

"But encourage the gangsters in Chicago—call for more Gang Busters—G-Men. I don't understand. Nobody seems to."

The cousins sat thinking, watching the twinkle of lightning bugs in the thick, hot air.

That was when they caught snatches of their fathers' conversation. At first it sounded as if the men were quarreling. But no, Daddy was pleading, trying to convince Uncle Worth that he could at least *survive* on the farm, much as he disliked it. Good garden, the cows, and they could split whatever profit came from the cotton—if any. He could live in the family house...lots of room...Rae would like it...yes, the colored people and share-croppers were still there...and Uncle Worth could serve as overseer. What was that he said—till *he* came? *Daddy?* He lowered his voice, but Marvel was almost certain her father said that his own wages were cut.

The next words the girls heard had to do with Mary Ann. "What about her schooling?" There was a kind of defeat in her father's voice.

It was Mother who answered. "She's welcome to stay with us. She and Marvel are like sisters. She could come back in the fall—"

Was her mother's voice trembling when she suggested iced tea? Marvel wondered.

Auntie Rae's was not. There was courage in the way she said with characteristic frankness, "I'm out of tea—ice, too. But I have grape juice. Actually, I like it better lukewarm."

There was the sound of footsteps. The men were alone. And then it happened. Something that Marvel would never have believed possible. Something which tore her heart in half. *Uncle Worth began to sob.* It was an awful sound, beginning down deep inside and torn from him in the dry, rasping sound of a man who has never cried before....

* * *

Marvel was to wonder later if Elmer eavesdropped. Instead of an occasional unwelcome appearance, the stepcousin was forever popping up and was suspiciously well-informed. There was a knowing look in the pale eyes and a sting to his words. His very *presence* stung. Elmer, the stinging nettle. Given a choice, she would rather deal with the plant.

Fat Elmer (no, at 15 he had a good physique, except for the slight drag of his foot) tried to be—would the word be *lordly*? How silly—silly but fitting. Elmer looked down on all the "cousins," and seemed to hold Marvel in special contempt. Probably, Marvel supposed, because Frederick Salsburg was the son by a former marriage of her late paternal grandmother before she married the Squire. The man was very "well off" and "Uncle Fred" fell heir to his part. The stepuncle had a cunning mind and married the town wallflower, Pauline Wiggington, for one reason alone: money. Well, he had what he wanted: a mouthful of gold teeth; a long, sinister-looking black car; and that simpleton son, Elmer. Elmer's special superior attitude toward Marvel had to be the mortgage. If he hated her so much, what was the meaning of that unholy look? It couldn't be—why, she was only 11 years old now. Marvel shuddered and tried to stay away from dark places....

But Elmer had a way of sauntering up from everywhere to say, "Hello, Miss High and Mighty. You're in no position to be that way, you know." And he would look her up and down as if he owned *her* along with the mortgage.

"Go away!" she would say in fury. She would be sorry, he always said. And then the fear would set in.

Once he gripped her arm roughly. In panic, Marvel jerked free and ran. But Elmer's taunting words followed her: "We're gonna take your house, you know—foreclose." And his laugh was a frightening thing to hear.

5

A Gentle Acceptance

Worth Harrington moved his family to the farm. Marvel and Mary Ann clung in farewell but took comfort in knowing Mary Ann would be back in the fall. Exactly when depended on when cotton was picked and sent to the gin. They could talk often—at least, unless the lines were down or the batteries dead on the old crankstyle wall phones.

"Isn't it great—our having a telephone?" Mary Ann said, her eyes bright with unshed tears. "Farmers work together to keep it working. That way we don't have to pay—"

Marvel nodded, wondering if Mary Ann had forgotten that batteries cost money. "Just remember to ask Central for one long and two shorts," she reminded, referring to the rings.

"And you ask for *three* longs and two shorts. Oh, and we can ring each other out there on the party line direct—unless somebody is talking—"

The girls were only making conversation, trying to forget that they were parting. But if this was the way things were, they could face it.

There was a gentle acceptance throughout the county now, particularly in Pleasant Knoll. There was concern in the faces of all (downright fear in Marvel's when she was alone) but no bitterness in their hearts. The attitude was due to a deep faith— faith in the Father Almighty, and faith in one another. Together they would make it somehow.

"We've always neighbored," Mother said, "but we need each other even more now. There'll be no 'needy' the papers talk about in the cities. It's like Brother Greer said Sunday—you know, that God won't *let* it happen. He'll take care of us so there's no cause for concern. Right, hon?"

Mother was arranging an armload of daisies in a large jar. Her lovely hands kept busy with the dainty gold-centered flowers as she talked.

"Not exactly," Marvel said slowly. "Brother Greer doesn't hold *God* responsible. It's the world—" she bit her lip and stopped. One look at her mother's stricken face caused Marvel to change her words. "But you're right actually. His text said so in another way—I mean, it's a comfort knowing God knows our needs. The text about lilies of the field and birds of the air being provided for—"

But Brother Greer didn't say there was no cause for concern, Mother, Marvel thought to herself and then continued aloud, "And you're right—we do have good neighbors. Mrs. Autrey next door brought over some bantam eggs while you were at the Ladies' Aid meeting."

Why upset her mother further by telling her Mrs. Autrey's small pension had been reduced and that, wringing her hands, the widow had wondered how she could manage. Some housewives were swapping eggs for groceries at Benson's Store. But Wilbur Benson wouldn't take bantie eggs. That the pitiful hunchback, Maggie Reynolds, had begged for credit "jest 'til s'urp's in." When Mr. Benson had to refuse, both he and "Ole Mag" (as everybody called her) cried. And Margaret Autrey cried again when she told Marvel. "But I can understand," Mrs. Autrey had finished as she wiped her eyes, "it takes ribbon-cane so long to mature—be ready for the syrup mill. Poor dear should go to cotton. But nobody's paying Wilbur. He may have to close, too. Well, I'll do what I can for Ole Mag. She's proud, but when a person's hungry—"

Mrs. Autrey would try and help others? Oh, bless her heart.

"It's time for the revivals, Marvel—and we'll have to get our summer dresses starched and ironed. We'll go to all three, like always. It's good that differences in doctrine never kept our churches apart. Right smart of difference in one way, but we all worship the same God and aim to reach the same place. Is something wrong, baby?"

Remarkable how Mother could leave something she found unpleasant and go another direction without looking back. "I miss Mary Ann," Marvel said truthfully, "so I think I'll borrow some books from the principal's home library. He has some of the classics—wants me to do some home study to give me time for debating next term—"

Mother moved the daisies from the window seat to the entrance table. Daddy always emptied his pockets there (he said with a lopsided grin they had less in them every night). But there was a round mirror above the table which seemingly reflected the bittersweet fragrance of the daisies.

"Now we have *two* jars," Mother said with satisfaction as she backed away and surveyed her handiwork. "Are you sure you're not spending too much time with books for a little girl? But," she sighed almost wistfully, "I guess you're not little anymore—not *little* little."

"I don't feel little," Marvel admitted, wondering if her parents knew just how "big" her thinking was as she hurried out the door. Her mind traveled all over the world. Wrong to worry? Well yes, but all should be aware. God had said "Blessed is he that watcheth. . . ."

Marvel was not alone in her broad-scope thinking. Radio evangelists were emotionally declaring that the end of the world was fast approaching. Just read Revelation, all "doubting Thomases out there"! Then tent-show evangelists (accompanied by singing, swaying groups, string-instrument strummers, and sometimes other entertainers) took to the road to offer "one last chance." Sincere or not, these men attracted large audiences (took in enough money to let them move on) and filled the grassy aisles between folding chairs with hordes of converts.

Even Pleasant Knoll sat up and took notice when one of the more literate modern-day circuit riders unloaded his rickety, early-vintage truck (carrying all his earthly possessions) and hung out his sign: ONE LAST CHANCE—TONIGHT, IF THE WORLD STILL STANDS. Sobering words.

Preacher Dillsworth told how the Depression was spreading and how banks were closing all over the world. "They're murdering one another for a last bean in Europe—worldwide murder—their backbones and bellies rubbin' together. So their hearts have turned as black as the pits of hell, where they're headed!" He was right about one thing.

The very next day the new president, Franklin Delano Roosevelt, declared a national bank holiday. Pleasant Knoll was not alone then. Things were tough for the entire country...maybe for the whole world, like the tent-show preacher had said...like Hoover had said before his successor, controversial though both seemed to be. Herbert Hoover had warned the nation that it all commenced in Europe where the "economy is sagging," hadn't he? And that it was bound on spreadin'? But, a little shamefacedly, men on the corners admitted that "bein' a dyed-in-the-wool Republican like he was" had colored their thinking. There was one man in the county belonging to that party, and he was less than popular. Had to admire the Yank, at that. Old Ramsey Cook, the postmaster in Pleasant Knoll, had just cause to snicker, but didn't.

In fact, Ramsey Cook was as concerned as the rest of the little town. Suppose the new president saw fit to replace him as postmaster with a Democrat? It was a political office. He gave voice to his concerns when the men coming in for their mail seemed friendlier—even said he'd like to hear what Roosevelt had to say in this "Fireside Chat" announced on the newsreel at the Saturday picture show. Just show biz, but worth the dime to see the man—pretty calm character but seemed amicable about something he called his "New Deal" and dead serious. Too, did folks know he was *crippled*?

That information was news itself. Few attended the theater in the county seat anymore. You couldn't swap eggs for admission. But another exchange took place. The postmaster's news and "downright friendliness" bought him an invitation to gather with the community at Benson's Store for the radio speech. Wilbur Benson had better reception with his outside aerial. *Everybody* was welcome, the storekeeper said, and served lemonade—a real treat on such a sultry night.

Marvel enjoyed the chat, in spite of the air being so stuffy from the overflow crowd—and Elmer pressing his sweaty body against hers. He kept his eyes averted and pushed closer each time she moved. It was embarrassing, repulsive, and frightening. She tried to ignore him and listen.

"My friends," the resonant voice began, and the crowd felt that they were.

I want to tell you what has been done in the last few days, why it was done, and what the next steps are going to be.... A bank does not put money in a safe.... It invests it...bonds, mortgages...to keep the wheels turning...open gradually...the phantom of fear will soon be laid.... You must have faith...not be stampeded by rumors.... We have provided the machinery to restore our financial system; it is up to you to support and make it work. *Together we cannot fail!*

Excited cheers went up. President Roosevelt had made them understand the crisis and the solution. *Togetherness* would reverse the panic. Like he said in his inaugural address, "The only thing we have to fear is fear itself." Even Marvel felt a lift. If only she could handle fear of Elmer as easily....

6

Disastrous Response to Terror

Mary Ann was unable to call Marvel throughout the summer. The telephone batteries at the farm were dead. It was a bitter disappointment to both girls. Neither family could travel by automobile. Mary Ann's father had sold his Model A Ford for money to live on until the cotton was ready to pick. Uncle Worth looked forward to a bumper crop which would help them all out of this bind—if only they could hold on till then. What a blessing that the faithful black families—whom the original Harringtons had welcomed to consider the farm home—remained. The sharecroppers considered themselves lucky to have access to a mule and the farm implements—willing to keep the aging plows sharpened in exchange for a roof over their heads. They saw poverty as nothing new. They'd always known it. Just let them have garden space and use of the smokehouse to cure pork and, in poor toothless "Uncle Ned's" case (he never knew his last name or his age), to hang plaits of tobacco leaves to dry "fer chawin'."

All this Mary Ann wrote in her one letter to Marvel, ending with:

> This has to be my only letter. I can buy three postcards for the price of a three-cent stamp. That way I'll get to write Jake more often. He came out once, bargained for with Ole Mag—right glad she was to let Jake use the nag if he'd see that she had herself a

feeding. I know Daddy thought we ought to use the corn for meal, but he didn't say so. We all felt sorry for the old nag—just a bag of bones. Oh, it was good to see Jake! Mr. Brotherton can't find work either since the bank closed. He's looking into this "mass production" Ford's talking about. He's not handy with screws and bolts so couldn't keep up with that assembly line thing 12 hours a day, but hopes they need bookkeepers. But that means moving to Dallas. That's bad enough, but he says there are too many looking for work to hope—and, oh, Marvel, his dad's even talking about hitchhiking way out to California. I'd die, just die....

California! Marvel let the letter drop to the floor of her room. Why, that was hundreds—no, *thousands*—of miles away. And what would Jake's father hope to find there? Just last week she had heard one speaker go from bitter to sarcastic concerning what he referred to as "Tinsel Town" or "Celluloid Paradise"— meaning Hollywood, in "The City of Lost Angels." The faceless voice on radio said:

Nobody in this den of iniquity would know the rest of the nation is down and out. Hollywood's brand of heaven is an enormously successful effort to provide escape while they play dead. And for subtle sleight of hand, replacing the real, cruel world in need of fixing with make-believe, these corrupt glamour girls and boys with their long kisses, nude babies, profanity, and adultery are paid enough to reopen our banks. One such sultry vixen just bought herself and her lover a farm in addition to her Beverly Hills mansion. The rural love nest, reliable sources tell me, will cost 12 thousand dollars a year *just to operate....*

Marvel twisted her heavy sunlit bangs in concentration. Why add to her cousin's concerns? Mr. Brotherton was an adult—a very bright one. He would have to work in the bank. It was up to him, as head of the house, to make up his own mind. But wouldn't you think he would see some of the drifters who were beginning to pass through Pleasant Knoll and listen to *them*?

One man, on his way back to Arkansas hauling his family of 12 on a rattletrap flatbed truck, was forced to stop overnight when his overheated radiator burst. Fortunately, he could manage to mend it—as he had mended all other parts of the "ole crate" he'd said. But it took the remainder of the 40 dollars the entire clan had earned picking grapes near Fresno until work "played out fer common folks."

The men *had* to know. The women did. Marvel had told Mother and had been so proud of her. Snow Harrington called members of the Ladies' Aid, and those who could spare it took food. What they found was horrible: half-naked children with filthy faces and a paper-thin, sad-eyed mother too undernourished to nurse her baby. "I don' got no food," Old Mag told them (Marvel wondered how she even knew about the family), "but I got me a well full uv clean water, so bring them young'uns on out y'all 'n git yer'seves uh soak'n' in me warsh pot." There had been tears shed by the woman and her children, then tears by Mother's group when she said proudly, "Th' Lord'll be blessin' ya'll—us people's got to stick together."

Just remembering the incident brought a lump to Marvel's throat. No, she would make no mention now to Mary Ann. Neither would she tell about the two unmarried men right here who went to Dallas to check on a job with Ford only to find a well-fed man with rolled-up sleeves and face bloodred from yelling, "No! No! Nothin'—go home!"

Picking her cousin's letter up, Marvel finished answering it. Batteries were dead in their radio, too, so no news. What was happening to the Prohibition deal—the twenty-first Amendment, wasn't it?

Now that she *could* answer. It had passed in spite of the Billy Sundays and the church people's begging—actually getting down on their knees. So many hungry people couldn't vote. Some Constitution, wasn't it, that wouldn't let people so much as go near those silly ballot boxes without paying poll taxes? And hungry people couldn't afford *that*. "Our teachers say the majority's supposed to rule," Marvel wrote. "Majority? The so-called *majority* can't vote and..."

She had lifted her pencil then and, drilling her cheek with the eraser, thought back on something else she heard on the radio—just sketches, like part of a scary dream, but enough to know whatever the announcer for Light Crust Flour (who came on the air just before the Texas Dough Boys changed the mood with their joyful singing, "Roll your dough, boys, roll your dough...") meant by "economic debacle" in part. It must be mighty bad:

> The number of unemployed has reached 15 million and the unemployed have 30 million mouths to feed... hourly wages down... farmers get fives cents a pound for cotton and less than fifty cents a bushel for wheat. Desperate fathers battle behind big-city restaurants over rotten garbage... but when you've got children with bloated bellies... fighting like animals... and granted no more rights... unable to pay poll tax... can't meet residency requirements... wandering nomads looking for a day's work... some states banned welfare recipients... and, for all that, the surviving rich are blind as bats to the misery, claiming prosperity's bad, makes people smug and flabby.... They should know.... It's the millionaires talking.... "Just look," they say, "see how much more they appreciate us...."

Factory towns are bad off, too, Marvel wrote: chimneys not smoking, wheels not turning, railroad trains running empty— some places, anyway. But Uncle Emory found temporary work at the local station when the railroad's station agent broke his leg. Cotton kept trains running. Uncle Joseph and Uncle Alex, Jr. were less lucky. Grandfather wanted them to stay in banking. "Just how is never clear, even though he beats the sidewalk to pieces with his cane! He does the same because Daddy can't have our car fixed."

Oh yes, she forgot to mention that the radio announcer said the repeal wouldn't have passed if there had been what he called a "black vote"—black vote, strange way to talk about colored people. The bigwigs claimed the reason was that they couldn't read. Probably they were right... but to say they had *thick skulls* and couldn't learn? Well, they had sense enough to let liquor alone.

Marvel saw Jake on her way to the post office. He was wearing a starched white skullcap and had an enormous apron wrapped around his slim middle and tied in front and a glow on his face.

"Guess what!" Jake burst out before he reached her. "I'm working on Saturdays as a 'soda jerk'! Not a lot of business going on at Strong's Drugstore, but I sweep the floors between times—for two hours. Not much pay," Jake dropped his head, "but he says I'm lucky to be getting experience without pay—"

"Without pay?" Marvel was unable to hide her surprise.

"Well, pay in a way—a special way!" The glow was back. "Mr. Strong's going to let me treat Mary Ann to a double-dip ice cream soda! Now, you promise not to tell—it's a secret for her birthday."

Jake's gesture was touching. Marvel ached to share the sentiment of it when she wrote Mary Ann again, but a promise was a sacred thing. Anyway, something else that touched her even more had happened.

In response to her letter, Mary Ann had used one of her carefully doled-out penny postal cards to reply on the subject of the unfair way people talked about black people's skin having any bearing on their learning ability. God would hold us responsible for every word. What would He have to say about *those* words?

> I forgot to tell you I'm teaching Sula Mae and Casper to read along with our Billy Joe. They're soaking it up like floor mops. I wish my little brother would pay as much attention. I think Prissy and her brother they call Axle Grease would like to read, too, only they're too shy—just stand around grinning. They did ask me to come to a prayer meeting down in the bottom if I'd promise not to laugh. Laugh—*me*? You know I wouldn't. Anyhow, there wasn't anything funny. It felt kind of funny being the only white person. But they were too busy with talking to God in their own way to see me. It was sad, seeing them sway, hearing them shout (sometimes roll) as they praised His holy name—never once asking for more than they had. Even praised Him for all of *us*. I gave Sula Mae a red ribbon for her pigtails and Casper a cork for his cat-fishing cane. Oh dear, out of room. Love, M.A.

The words were so squeezed-together Marvel had trouble making them out. Then Mary Ann added two postscripts on the correspondence side: "Give Jake my love. Glad school starts soon and we can all be together." Then, "Be careful around you-know-who. He's bound on making trouble—got an eye for you. You'll see."

Mary Ann was right. It all began the very next day—the really serious trouble. Like the storm preceding it, the trouble had been brewing as long as Marvel could remember....

* * *

The new president put the alphabet to work, if not the people—at least, not all of them. FDR (as Franklin Delano Roosevelt came to be known), in giving shape to his "New Deal" platform, created a number of programs under his National Recovery Act (NRA). The program was met with some controversy and a lot of misunderstanding. A few warned that it was the "mark of the beast." A few faltering newspapers suggested bitterly the words really meant "*No* Recovery Allowed." But the majority went along with anything suggesting an end to the Depression and gladly displayed the colorful NRA signs in their windows...to offer new hope...restore confidence—and, in Pleasant Knoll, unlock the bank's door. "Sound banks" (whatever that meant) were reopening other places. Here, with traditional optimism—once having accepted hard times had knocked on their doors—they cinched in their belts and managed to shoo away the blues. So it would take longer. Together they would "make do." No need to "fear *fear.*"

But they welcomed the "guests" furnished by some of the programs. Mr. Roosevelt had done a good job in setting up the Farm Security Administration (FSA), sending out cameramen the way he did. They knew in advance and planned a "leisure-time" look in appreciation—a basket lunch in the park with horseshoe pitching and a barbershop quartet.

The photographers were not easily fooled, however. Taking note of the sparse menu, the dry gardens, and the padlocked bank, the crew decided this was not the common scene and went to document what the papers referred to as "rural poverty": barren fields...hungry children...and the beginning of dangerous misuse of croplands...taking away all the nutrients, they said, and putting nothing back... bringing too much under cultivation. This was dryland farming and some places were experiencing droughts....

Shortly afterward a Mrs. Sutheral had offered her services as home demonstration agent. As such, she would demonstrate the art of "shoestring cooking." The middle-aged widow was an immediate success. Why, the one-egg cakes were as good as the richer ones—a boon for both those who had to buy eggs and those fortunate enough to have their own hens. Now they would have more eggs for swapping for staples. And how that woman could save on sugar! Syrup cakes called for none at all—neither did "Depression pie," and both were tasty.

Two weeks later Mrs. Sutheral announced her plan to demonstrate "pea sausage"—a meat substitute, using dried peas, red pepper, and sage.

Mother was excited. "She says you can't tell the difference!"

An odd look had crossed Daddy's face. "Someday you won't have to pinch pennies like this, and my Marvelous can have some of those patent leather shoes—"

Marvel wanted to protest that shoes didn't matter. But that wasn't true. Anyway, she was afraid she would cry. *I'll help YOU*, she promised in her heart. Nobody could know how many hours she had spent on her knees praying. Surely God had heard and would help.

What was that Mother was saying—that he knew she did not mind—*that they'd been over this before*?

Marvel realized with a start that this was the first time she had ever thought of her parents' having a conversation without *her*. The three of them had such a close-knit family, what Daddy called "the three bears." Well, of course they did—they'd been in love before bringing her into the world. She felt more grown-up and proud of herself for feeling not a pang of jealousy. In fact, she felt closer to Mother and Daddy than ever before.

School would open next week. Time to return the borrowed books, maybe pick up more. Nothing short of death would slow her quest or zest for learning. The world needed human knowledge and spiritual wisdom more than it needed money. On the way out the gate Marvel noted the small cloud and wished it would rain. Mother's garden was dying. There had been so many promising thunderheads, but this one looked sincere. It was growing rapidly, blowing itself into enormous proportions, like a genie loosed from a tiny bottle. She quickened her step at the first brilliant zigzag of lightning. Daddy was at the gin; Mother, in the midst of the pea sausage demonstration. The eerie glow and unnatural stillness could mean a tornado. Shouldn't someone check on the storm cellar, air it out (she shuddered), look for spiders?

The dank air rose up to meet her as Marvel opened the door, using both hands and all her strength. She was panting as she eased her way gingerly down the narrow earthen steps to look for candles or lanterns. The steps were always slippery. The dampness made it a good root cellar. But it was so *dark*. Marvel was unable to resume breathing normally. Not a shaft of light. No ventilation. They dared use it only when the threat of a tornado was very real. The underground cell was dangerous.

Halfway down into total darkness, there was a feeling that she was not alone. Marvel turned sharply, aware only of eyes that gleamed like coals of fire before two hands caught her arms in a grip of steel.

"Gotcha!" a ghostlike voice whispered so near her ear she was forced to face forward into the gloom.

"Elmer!" Calm—she must pretend calm. "I'm finished—we can turn back—"

His laugh was more of a sneer. "Now what could you finish in so short a time?"

Oh, dear God, her heart cried out. Elmer was pushing her forward.

Premonition shook her very soul. *"Please, Elmer—*I only needed to let air down in case of poisonous gas. That is, the possibility—you know, the kind that forms in the coal mines toward Dallas—"

"Methinks the lady protests too much," he sneered, and then his voice turned harsh. "You know there can't be explosions without lighting matches! You're here to see about lanterns, so go on down—unless you're afraid of me? Why, you're shaking. You *are* afraid—"

"Don't be ridiculous!"

Afraid? Marvel was terrified, near hysteria. She had caught a strange, fruity smell on the wretched boy's breath. Liquor! She had never smelled alcohol, but instinct told her. So this is what the evil stuff did to people. But where did it come from? Legal, yes, but there was none available here...and Elmer wasn't old enough....

"Then down we go—where we can be alone." The hateful voice had grown husky, and he was fingering the back of her neck.

"Take your hands off me you—you pig!"

God must have heard her prayers. Else how was she able to whirl, strike his cheek with a strength that sent him reeling drunkenly and rolling to the bottom of the steps while she rushed to the top?

Though she ran with supernatural speed, Marvel was unable to outrun the words of fury which followed her. "I'll never forget this—never as long as I live—and you won't either, you little nobody—living off us like you do. *Oh, you'll regret this—I'll see to that!*"

Home! Even as she bolted the door behind her, Marvel knew that her safety was only temporary. Elmer would make good his threat...harm her...maybe her parents. If only she could share the awfulness of the afternoon with Mother. But they had never talked about things like that.

Mother! She and Daddy would be home soon, and the storm cellar door was open. Elmer was gone she saw through her bedroom window—and, thankfully, so was the cloud. Marvel ran out, secured the door, then hurried back to wash her burning face—all the while hearing the echo of that threatening voice: *"You'll regret this...regret...regret..."*

7

People Helping People

Mother came home pink-cheeked and elated. The pea sausages she brought with her were delicious. Daddy said he was proud of her. So it was a sort of celebration that Marvel tried to enter.

Still smiling, Mother said, "That's what it's all about, isn't it? People helping people."

Marvel tried to erase the ugliness of the afternoon with the beauty of those words. She had a feeling Mother meant more than learning to make pea sausage....

Mary Ann came back a few days later. There had been a terrible moment in deciding how to get her here. Daddy's car had broken down and he had shrugged the matter away with a grin. "We don't really need a car—and look at the dough we can stash away from gasoline!"

But now? It came as a surprise when Uncle Frederick benevolently volunteered to go to the farm and asked Daddy to go along. "I would like to look around the old place," he said. Frederick Salsburg never did anything without an ulterior motive, and the Harringtons' vast acres had never *been* "the old place" to him. The stepbrother had been an adult when his mother, whom the cousins had never seen, married the Squire. Marvel had only a faint memory of her paternal grandmother—the Squire's second wife. At her death, Grandmother Harrington willed her money to three of her sons (her husband having no need of it—then) and,

at Daddy's request, left him the farm. None of the others wanted
it.

"My blood-kin uncles' money seemed to dwindle," Marvel had
mused one day. "How does Uncle Frederick make his?"

"Dishonestly."

"Oh Daddy, stop teasing—you know what I mean."

He had frowned. His answer may have been close to the truth.
"Mortgages—foreclosures. I think everybody in the county owes
the man, and he has swindled most of the widows. Forget it,
honey. He befriended us and what I said was out of place, unkind."

Out of place? It may have been over her head at that time, but
was the truth ever *unkind*?

Now she understood. And understanding spawned a fear that
writhed around her heart like a live thing. *Was the farm mortgaged to this man, too?*

Daddy set her mind at rest immediately. "Absolutely not!" he
said almost angrily, then asked if she wouldn't like to come along.
Yes, oh yes! That was until she learned that Elmer was going just
to "look around." Then she said truthfully that Mary Ann would
need the space for her belongings and that she needed to finish
reading *Pilgrims' Progress*. But the fear was back.

Mary Ann talked a streak, but Marvel managed to hear
snatches of Daddy's animated report to Mother—enough to
know that they would be able to meet the loan on the mortgage.
Her mother cried—actually cried—in joy and relief and kept
repeating, "Thank God—thank God—"

"Crops in the big field dwarfed . . . shriveled . . . no rain . . . but
cotton in the bottoms . . . oh boy! Dale and Rae can survive . . .
our half will meet the payment—" Marvel added a silent "thank
God" to her mother's.

Mary Ann stopped unpacking. "I'm tired. Can't we walk—like
down past the drugstore?"

Had Jake told her about working there? Marvel spent no time
wondering. Instead she told about the terrible nightmare with
Elmer. Mary Ann was enraged.

"That creep doesn't have one mouse-lick of gumption. You
don't have to put up with such things. He's a no-good—worse,
he's *dangerous*. Stay away from that hateful piece of fish bait. He's
got no claim on you or your nice house. The nerve of him! Uncle
Dale'll fix *him*!"

"No," Marvel said hopelessly and told her about the mortgage.

Mary Ann looked undone, but only for a moment. "I knew about the debt, but not that it was to that ton of flesh we call 'Uncle Frederick.'" It was time to stop claiming kin.

"Anyway," Mary Ann finished brightly, "there's enough from the cotton to pay it off—"

"Not pay it off," Marvel interrupted gently, "but make the payment, thanks to Uncle Worth. Oh Mary Ann, look at your hands!"

Mary Ann put her red, burr-pricked hands behind her. *"Don't* look at them! We *all* worked—nip and tuck, but we made it. That's what counts." It was obvious that she had something else on her mind.

To Marvel's surprise, her cousin went back to Elmer. *No, don't talk about him!* she wanted to say as Mary Ann had said about her hands. Wouldn't it be better to repeat Mother's words in appreciation? "That's what it's all about—people helping people?"

But Mary Ann had begun already. And her words caused Marvel to feel faint... her hands and feet grew as cold as stones... her lungs filled up with the remembered damp of the cellar... for the words referred to Elmer.

"...and makes those gun-totin' robbers and murderers in the big cities *heroes*—said it took courage that most gutless Americans didn't have. The banks deserve robbing, he said with a wild look in his eyes. Just look what they'd done to *us*—" Mary Ann's words were spilling out as if she were unable to stop, and she was panting, "And he's going to get a tommy gun and help 'knock off' post offices—saw nothing wrong with that man—the one who kidnapped the Lindbergh baby—"

"Hauptmann."

Both girls shuddered remembering. When the ex-convict broke through a window and took that adorable two-year-old, every family's safety was at stake. The nation grieved with the Charles Lindbergh family when the toddler's still, cold body was found six weeks later. Murder... cold-blooded murder... and for 50 thousand dollars.

"And Elmer says the ransom was all right," Mary Ann whispered. "Anything for money—and nobody could put up a prison that he couldn't break out of. He's crazy, I tell you—crazy. *Oh, be careful!*"

They had reached Strong's Drugstore and, with a delighted squeal, Mary Ann, spotting Jake, darted inside. Marvel spun on her heel and started home, walking as fast as she could then, gripped by fear, running. Weren't there footsteps behind her? Hurry...hurry...*escape*...

"Hey, you! What'cha tryin' to do? Go uppity just because—"

Archie! Never had she been so glad to hear his familiar voice.

Marvel stopped and tried hard to appear calm. "Hi—and just why would I be uppity as you put it?"

"No cause. Just thought you'd become Miss High 'n Mighty when you learned you'll be double-promoted again—"

"Oh Archie, *really*? How did you find out? I didn't know."

But, sensing her interest, he shrugged (Boys! Sometimes they infuriated her) and said, "Th' principal," and then turned to another matter. Did she know agriculture would be offered to boys in "my grade," he said with pride, and something called "home economics" to girls? Oh, if only—

Then the "twins'" birthdays came. Mother invited the whole family. And the neighbors brought *six* cakes! No eggs, but delicious. And Mary Ann had her soda. Marvel felt a lump in her. throat when Daddy managed one sentence, "People helping people."

8

Dream Factory Versus Reality

The world was unable to stand the awfulness of truth. And so it sought an avenue of escape from the Depression-ridden world through what Marvel secretly labeled a "dream factory" of publications, at first intended for children but serving as a balm for their confused parents. What had happened to the trusted American standard called capitalism in which they had put so much trust? Well, questions did not bring answers, just as wishes had not brought measurable rain. Better dream a little... along with their children....

And so Sundays—after church and a lot of praying—found the entire family lying on their tummies on the floor or across the beds pawing through the newspapers (those who could afford the ten-cent publications) to seek comfort among make-believe heroes and heroines who still orbited in extravagant lifestyles. One family member would serve as reader for the group in order to hurry the cliff-hanging exploits along to another home. "Flash Gordon"..."Little Orphan Annie"...and hard-bitten detectives like "Dick Tracy"...or the teenage football hero "Jack Armstrong." It was less expensive than the movies considering that so much could be savored by so many....

To Marvel such trivia held no appeal. She preferred to read. Her parents preferred the game of "42," played with dominoes—more challenging to the mind since it involved counting, remembering what numbers had been played by whom, and keeping score. A lot more sociable, too, as it required partners—four to a

46

table. Sometimes they made it "84" and doubled the number of guests. The group moved from home to home. When Mother and Daddy hosted the group they included Daddy's brothers who brought their families. The cousins came along. That gave the younger ones an opportunity to talk about school and the older ones, their futures—a matter teachers were emphasizing more and more. Then there were refreshments which put to use Mrs. Sutheral's "common-sense" recipes. The ladies treated the matter lightly, not as if it were an absolute necessity. There was still iced tea, thanks to "Little Tummy Tucker's Igloo." The pint-sized man with gallons of humor had changed the spelling of his given name as another antic to keep Pleasant Knoll smiling. The "igloo" was a little building, insulated with sawdust, which he kept filled with blocks of ice delivered by the morning train.

Mr. Tucker in turn delivered by wagon. He owned keys to every house in the town, no doubt. Everybody trusted him. But then, he seldom had to use them. The doors were unlocked. People trusted everybody else as well. So "Tummy," by squinting, could see the square cards in the windows—the number on top indicating pounds needed. And, taking his heavy tongs, he carried the 10, 25, 50, or occasionally 100-pound blocks to the icebox. Sometimes he left lemons—a little shriveled but good for lemonade. What fun for the "42" parties then!

"I wonder how many owe him money," Daddy said once. And Mother had replied that mostly they shared food with the aging bachelor: "garden stuff"...homemade bread...quilts...and Ellie King knitted him a sweater.

This year the need for ice lingered. It was hot, so hot. School had begun as scheduled. And the foursome walked to school together as usual: Mary Ann and Jake (who could be called a *couple*), Marvel and Archie from force of habit, she supposed.

And Archie was right. She *was* double-promoted. The principal called her to his office the first day.

"I am expecting great things from you, Marvel," Mr. Wilshire said, pushing his glasses in place when there was no need, "so please don't let me down. I—I'm not sure the school board will approve, and I—"

Need to hold your job, Marvel finished in her mind. "I understand, sir, and I will do my best. I always have."

Mr. Wilshire looked relieved. He asked her then what her plans were for the future. "I'm not sure—not even sure I've made any,"

Marvel told him truthfully. "I want to see justice—more laws enforced, the hungry fed. Yes, especially that—"

"Some kind of social work maybe? I understand there will be some government grants. I don't know the details. I'll look into any kind of aid we can get, see what we're entitled to. Ever think about teaching?"

"No."

The man looked disappointed. "Too bad. I need some students like you, need 'em bad. People aren't paying up on taxes, money's scarcer—or is it 'more scarce'?"

Was he testing her? Marvel smiled. "'More scarce' sounds better."

"Good at grammar." Mr. Wilshire's pleasure was obvious. "Too bad about the teaching—state's cutting money for schools. County's got *none*, so there'll be no substitutes."

Substitute teachers, he must mean. "Oh, I could help that way. It would be good experience—working with children," she said eagerly, then told him what Mary Ann had been doing for the little ones who had never been to school. "And I just know she'd help."

"Very good—very good." Mr. Wilshire looked pleased with himself. This might be a good time—

"Sir," she burst out while her courage was high, "if you have time, I'd like to hear all about that new course for girls—'Home Economics' I think it's called. I'm *so* interested—if it's what I think."

The principal gave a short chuckle. "Time—time to tell you all about *that*? 'Domestic Science' is the proper name—as it came down from the government. Another grant, you know. Seems our president's *trying* to help us, in spite of all the criticism. It's terribly involved—includes canning, cooking, first aid to avoid doctor bills, taking care of babies, making over clothes. See what I mean? But why do you ask? It's for girls from eighth grade up—"

"But Mr. Wilshire, I *will* be in the eighth grade. Pardon me for interrupting." Marvel was flushed outside from excitement and embarrassment. She flushed *inside* and said a silent prayer. *Oh, please, Lord. Please—*

"Even a whisper He'll hear over there," the song went. Marvel knew from that moment that God heard even more. He heard *thoughts*. Otherwise, would the principal be saying this?

"So you will, so you will. I see no reason why not then—unless the teacher they're sending objects." He chuckled again, causing Marvel to wonder if the principal found much to laugh about in his job. "Next," he said with the facsimile of a twinkle, "you'll be asking permission to be on the debating team."

"Oh, could I—could I *possibly*?"

Mr. Wilshire's mouth flew open in shock. "You can't be serious—you *are* serious! I guess that surprises me most of all. Why child, that load would break your back. You'd have authorities on me for violating that child labor law. Oh Lord," he said tiredly, "I wish there could be more like you." He shook his head as if trying to clear it. "I don't think you could swing it. Let me think—"

"Please," she whispered, knowing she shouldn't beg. But it was *so* important: to her, to Mother and Daddy, to the *whole world.*

Marvel rose to leave. Extending her hand, she thanked him and then was unable to resist something else. "I hope, Mr. Wilshire, what you said was a prayer."

Was this usually hard-to-reach man going to cry? He had removed his glasses and was wiping them and nodding with his back to her. Somehow she knew she had won.

Jake, still determined to get into banking, jumped at the chance to keep Mr. Strong's books. If they could reverse things, show a profit—even a small one—he could pay him a little. Meantime, he could bring Mary Ann in for a soda—on the house, of course. Jake's father, fortunately, had replaced a teller on a part-time basis in Culverville, the county seat. He had been to Dallas and only a few banks had been allowed to reopen—not strong enough by the New Deal definition. Those "strong" few had a mile-long line of desperate-looking applicants.

Mary Ann, delighted with the invitation to help in the classroom, stopped in to share the news with Jake. Archie remained after school to ask questions about the course in agriculture. That left Marvel free to run full-speed for home—so fast, in fact, that she failed to see the eyes that followed her menacingly as she rushed through the shady stretch.

To her disappointment, her parents were not home. Of course. Daddy would be working yet—hours were long now. Mother was learning to slipcover at the home demonstration meeting. So, uninhibited, she hugged herself tight in congratulation and danced round and round, eyes closed, singing "Dancin' in the Dark..." over and over. When she stopped dizzily, her parents stood at the door, smiling with pleasure.

"Somebody turn our lights off?" her father teased. "That ditty must've been inspired by some guy who failed to pay his bill."

"Oh guess what—guess what—*guess what!*" Marvel laughed.

"Somebody shot the wolf on our doorstep."

"Stop clowning, Dale," Snow Harrington said, wiping her eyes. Daddy always made her laugh. If Marvel planned to marry at all, she would want a marriage like that of her parents. But marriage was out of the question—

"We gave up," Daddy said, his voice sober. "How long do we wait?"

Marvel burst out with all the events of the day crammed into one paragraph: the promotion, the teaching, the Domestic Science... and the possibility of getting on the debating team. "So what do you think?"

"Marvelous—oh, Marvelous! That's what I think!"

✳ ✳ ✳

The next week Pleasant Knoll's small local newspaper, hard put for news (and money), published an editorial by the principal:

> There were 126 pupils the first day and 211 enrolled now.... As cotton season is practically over and there is no other excuse for remaining out of school, enrollment is probably complete.... Teachers' concern is the double load on themselves and students' classmates that late enrollees create. All the work covered must be reviewed, using time that rightfully belongs to each class as a whole. We consider ourselves fortunate in having a few above-average students willing to assist....

One of the "few above-average," of course, was Marvel. And it was *she* who felt fortunate, as she did in qualifying for Domestic Science and—wonder of wonders!—getting on the debate team. It was like Daddy said, "Marvelous, marvelous!" The year sailed by on the wings of an eagle. And Marvel soared to new heights along with it—too fast for her to note that she was taking on a beauty all her own as Mother had promised. Too fast to concentrate on the Depression, see that it was worsening and putting her father's job in jeopardy. And, worst of all, too fast to see that Elmer was watching it all...waiting...biding his time....

Who needed the "dream factory" when reality was so *marvelous*?

9

Summer of the Circus

The circus is coming to town!

Pleasant Knoll was abuzz with excitement when the bill-posters arrived announcing that "The Greatest Show on Earth" (Ringling Brothers and Barnum and Bailey combined shows) would pitch its tent *here*—and at the peak of the season. Look at the business this "traveling city" of people and animals would bring in! Secretly, most were looking forward to the audience-captivating trapeze acts, the daredevil fire swallowers, the endless parade of trained animals, and the glamorous (if somewhat scantily-clad) showgirls who demonstrated grace and skill walking high wires without safety nets and jumping rope while riding horseback on a galloping steed. Pshaw! Let the few skeptics say it was a bad idea, that it could take *out* more than it brought in—and that there was precious little to take out!

Marvel was ecstatic along with the majority of the towns-people. Later she was to look back on it all with sadness, "the tear in the eye of the clown"—and worse. It would be a time she was unable to think about without a return of the terror it brought. . . .

But for now the child in her came back. She recalled circuses of the past, how she and Mary Ann had tried all the tumbling acts—their only real success being the tumbles they took when attempting to walk a sagging clothesline while balancing themselves with Chinese paper parasols (which, they reasoned, would serve as parachutes just in case).

The whole thing was as funny now as it had been then when the two of them remembered together. Skinned shins and smashed-flat noses had been worth the hours of giggling. Even now they curled up with laughter. Then, hugging each other, the cousins agreed that there were a million other reasons for celebrating. Could they so much as count all the school year's successes?

"Have I ever thanked you for mentioning my name when Mr. Wilshire asked *you* to help out in the primary grades, Marvel? Oh, I loved that—and being called one of the 'above-average' students gave me the nerve to ask if I could take Domestic Science."

"Wasn't it fun? And next year will be even better."

They talked about the well-groomed, soft-spoken Miss Marlow, guessing that the teacher came from Georgia. "Those instructors go wherever the government program finds a need—they have to agree to that when they volunteer," Marvel said, finding herself surprised at her own words. "I guess we're more *needy* than I thought. Remember those men who looked us over and took back a report?"

Mary Ann sucked her breath in. "Yeah—I guess I forgot that until now. But good for them. So what if I'm *needy* if it brings me luck like this—no, not luck, blessings, answers to prayers. Funny thing, I used to ask God to do this and that—organized it all for Him just like Jake puts Mr. Strong's books in order. Then when the answers came I didn't even recognize them!"

Marvel nodded. "He usually sends better than we ask for. Miss Marlow said something like that. She told me the night I stayed late to fix Mother's dress some things about her part of the world—called it 'down home'—and herself. She was lying in bed one night praying for herself when she remembered that a neighbor *walked* over 600 miles just looking for work, shoes fell off, feet bled—and came home without work."

Mary Ann shuddered. "And how did God answer *that* one?"

"I don't know—I honestly don't. About the man, I mean. All I can tell you is what Miss Marlow told *me*. She says He answered it all at once. That wasn't the end, just a beginning. The very next morning her own mother said at breakfast (all they had was biscuits and water-gravy because the cow was too poor to give milk—she says poor for skinny), 'You know, Clarinda—'"

"That's a pretty name."

"Isn't it? Add it to that name list you and Jake are keeping for your children," Marvel teased, then sobering, continued her story. "Her mother said, 'You know, Clarinda, I didn't git me much sleep—seems like I waked me up thankin' *Lordy, we're PORE.*'"

"Miss Marlow—and her so pretty? You'd never think—but what kind of an answer was *that*?"

"Like we were talking about, Mary Ann—you know, not recognizing God's answers. What her mother said and her terrible need gave Miss Marlow courage, faith in herself—"

"What I called *nerve*," Mary Ann muttered. "And I butted in—uh, interrupted. Won't I ever learn?"

"All you have to learn is to stop running yourself down. *Like* yourself. After all, God created you, gave you that super hair! The end of the story is that our teacher went right into town and there on the courthouse square stood that government man *looking* for needy teachers to teach in needy places. Now listen to this—*where there was still hope*! That's where *we* are."

"And that's how I hit it all so lucky—how it happened that I made over the dress Auntie Snow gave Mama—and how she'll have something to wear to the circus.

"Oh Marvel, I haven't told you, but Mama and Daddy are coming on *exactly* that night to get me. And they don't know. It'll be a surprise!" Mary Ann was growing more and more excited. "Oh, I'm glad you made over the dress for your mother...glad she gave Mama one...glad I saw what you did and copied you... glad Miss Marlow gave me credit for a 'home project' like your tomato vines...and glad Mama and Daddy'll be carrying in two cows to the auction."

Marvel laughed merrily, to which Mary Ann said reproachfully, "Poor cows."

"It's *carrying* I'm laughing about. I said the same thing, and it was Miss Marlow who said in the sweetest way, 'Now really, Marvel honey, did you ever try *carrying* a cow to pasture?'"

Mary Ann laughed then. "That's what we're in school for—to learn. I'm so proud of *you*. I'm not smart like you and—holy smoke!—not half as ambitious. Our plans are different anyway. But what I'm learning will come in handy—and oh, especially that homemaking course." She was growing excited again, "About the wagon—that wagon won't embarrass you, Marvel? It'll smell like cows, but—well, at least, if fat Elmer's papa offers to take me to our house to help I can say, 'Get lost'—and I will!"

Elmer! His very name made Marvel shudder. Was it memory or apprehension? Either way, she rapidly changed the subject, telling Mary Ann more of Miss Marlow's story when she would have preferred planning about the circus. Was her story true? The teacher vouched for it. How *awful*!

"A poor pregnant woman down home had her son fetch the doctor. He'd ushered half a dozen into the world for her without pay, but 'tweren't this po' innocent's fault—her's neither. So 'Doc,' she cried in her suffering, 'jest deliver 'im with all 'is parts 'n I'll *give* y'all this un."

Both girls cried. "Oh please, Marvel, let's talk about the circus!" Mary Ann said as they dried their eyes on a towel.

And they did, just as the whole town was doing.

Contracting agents came ahead of the "big top" people to arrange for space to pitch the tents, advertise, and purchase enormous amounts of supplies (mostly food). Just why the county seat would refuse to play host to "that mess" mystified Pleasant Knoll folk. Wouldn't you think they would jump at the chance for all that business? Why (and they vowed their eyes were "bugged out on stems"), it could put the town right back on its feet! Now, no one person could furnish any of the unheard-of amount. But together they could! Deacon Potts said, "Did ya'll say 200 *dozen* eggs? Gotta git these bloomin' ears checked on— ain't hearin' so good. Is thar that many hen fruits in th' *world*? Got me uh few good layers 'n I'll chase them other crazies till they git th' idee 'n do more'n cackle!" There was no bakery here, so housewives were struck dumb at the order for 2000 loaves of bread until—

"Now look here, ladies," Mrs. Sutheral said when she called an emergency meeting of the home demonstration class, "we're up to the task and here's our chance to show our worth. This is big business. *Men* in big business are going mass-production. Well, so can we!"

The ladies were all atwitter. Organize . . . make a list . . . bring whatever supplies they could from home . . . cut merchants in on the profits if they wished to donate ("Well, did you ever! You'd know Wilbur Benson would pitch in and try to help, but stores in the county seat don't figure."). Mixing, baking, and washing up could be done in the Domestic Science room. Miss Marlow was inspired. Here was an opportunity to give the girls some experience (and, needing the job as she did, help secure it). The "Ag boys" volunteered loud enough for the girls to hear that they would grind the 200 pounds of coffee from the burlap sacks of surplus coffee sent by the government. Farmers would bring in hay and grain. Were they sure they had no need for cotton or fish for the seals? Sure, they could bring that too—the black folks had a special knack for hooking catfish. Butter? Yessiree, that too.

The agents expressed a need for a ton—a whole *ton*—of fresh meat. Wasn't it a blessing that the auction was set for the same day? Yes, cattle and porkers. Mary Ann, who had felt sorry for Uncle Worth's two cows, never knew their fate.

And there were jobs! Boys went down to watch the unloading of the animals—1000 of them!—and the erecting of the gala-colored tent. Their parents were surprised to see them come running home to report: "Holy smoke! They've brought a whole *city*! Yeah, their own electric lights makers—plants, they call 'em (*plants* with engines?)—fix-it shops . . . and their hotels are on the trains where they live, cook, and sleep."

"Whoa there!" Aunt Eleanore (Uncle Emory's wife) said to Marvel's same-age cousin, Duke. "How in the world could our trains transport that much in such a grand style?"

"Oh, the Cotton Belt put on a special train. It's just too bad girls can't see such sights," Duke said grandly, casting a superior look at Marvel, who had brought a note inviting his mother to join in on the bread-making.

Marvel chose to ignore that and was glad for he dropped the affected air almost immediately. "I got myself a job and one for Thomas. We will feed and water the elephants. Not by ourselves though—too many. It'll take lots and lots of helpers. Will Summers is driving stakes right now—you know to secure the ropes the tent'll be tied to and—"

When Duke Harrington finished, Marvel went away with the impression that every boy in Pleasant Knoll would be working—those who wished to. And they all wished to. The reward for their all-day labor was a free ticket to "The Greatest Show on Earth"!

Duke's news set Marvel wondering how others would manage the price of admission.

That night she was to wonder about some other matters—first, at the supper table, and again at some upsetting words she overheard between her parents, even though they spoke in near-inaudible voices in their bedroom.

Mother, flushed and excited from the day's baking, brought home a fresh loaf of the Texas quick-rising bread made from Mrs. Sutheral's book of affordable foods. Miss Marlow's "girls" had helped weigh and measure, then were excused with a promise that they could deliver tomorrow.

"Nice departure from cornbread," Daddy said from the head of the table as he dished chili beans onto a plate. He handed it to Marvel to hand Mother who sat at the opposite end of the table. Next, Mary Ann (company) would be served, then Marvel, then himself last. Less food did not mean "less manners," Daddy had declared once. Marvel was glad it *was* only once, for it had made her want to cry.

"I like this arrangement," he was saying now. "Um-um, bread's yummy—and our lovely cook smells equally delicious, warm, and yeasty." He looked at his wife with pride and admiration.

"But not with a burnt bottom—" Mother stopped, horrified at what she had said. And above their laughter, she hastened to explain that was how she came to bring home the loaf...the bottom burned...it was going to be discarded...oh, come now, what she said wasn't *that* funny! And then Mother burst into laughter herself. Such a wonderful family, Marvel knew.

"Frankly," Daddy said suddenly, "I'm surprised that the circus is coming here, its heyday being back in the Roaring Twenties. Suppose they're trying to make a comeback, or giving one last gasp? They upped ticket prices at a bad time. I can see why—droughts causing feed prices to go sky-high. Still—"

Daddy paused. Mother looked thoughtful then said, "I remember now. The circus used to be called—what was it—'the poor man's amusement'?"

"That's right. Then came the Depression—not that it will last."

"Of course not!" Snow Harrington said staunchly. "The Ringlings, Barnums, and Baileys are smart enough to see that, too."

"And knowing they'll have motion pictures and radio programs to compete with, they're getting a head start, coming in person to pass the hat—"

He probably said more, but Marvel failed to hear. If people had given up movies and couldn't afford batteries for radios or even to replace batteries in telephones, how on earth could they scrape up the price of circus tickets—*even for tomorrow night's one performance?*

Mary Ann's face looked stricken. But she managed to chirp up brightly, "I have a feeling there'll be a crowd. We'll *all* be there."

Marvel smiled at her. Bless her. She was a Harrington through and through. One carried on—proudly. The mark of a thoroughbred, Grandfather said. And one *believed.* "Take no thought of the morrow...."

The frightening conversation between her parents later, of which she heard fragments, far outstripped concern over a circus ticket.

"Yes, what you heard's true, Snow...hear the railroad *is* on its way out of here...agent's back...Emory's finished...leave for sure...price of cotton's just too low...no yield." Mother's ragged whisper was too low to hear. Marvel pressed her ear to the door to hear her father's reply to what had sounded like a gravely important question. It was. "Yes, my darling...can't lie to you...be brave...work it out...not trouble *her*...cotton weighed here...less...and *if I'm without work*...God help us."

Marvel prayed for hours in the dark. Then, sobbing bitterly, she said what she knew she must: "Thy will be done."

10

When Worlds End

Dale Harrington was right—right about it all: the railroad, the cotton gin, and the circus. All their worlds were destined to end, and end even sooner than he thought. First came the circus, but not without one great performance....

The Dallas Morning News was to carry the sad story shortly afterward. The lengthy feature covered all circuses as well as the calamity surrounding the final show of "The Greatest Show on Earth." And to think that it was destined to happen here—right here in Pleasant Knoll. The account in part told about far more than the demise of a circus:

> The planned extravaganza, a comedy-turned-tragedy, which wiped out all hopes for a future of circus entertainment—so much a part of the American way of life—occurred in the small town of Pleasant Knoll, east of Dallas. The seemingly sudden death should not have come as a surprise as circuses had been on the sick list for years. Neither was it by coincidence that the end came in a small town since no city license would have been required....Expenses had been gnawing away at the heart of the Great Show like a hidden cancer for years....The vast one-time empire, like all other businesses, had been struggling for survival throughout the Depression, recovery failing to arrive on schedule...and without clear signs of a

total return to normal ... worsening in areas. ... A large part of the decline of the circus is a direct result of the Depression; the remainder, an indirect result ... being beyond the pocketbook of most families ... decline in railroad service ... expense of upkeep ... rumbles of "organized labor" bringing threat of strikes ... fires, always a threat to circus-life ... but who could have guessed that the "final blow" would be just that? Will there ever be another traveling circus? It is doubtful—at least in this generation ... and so it is with heavy hearts that a nation deprived of so much must become more so. ... And thus we bid farewell to a faithful friend.

* * *

The big day came—not bright and sunny as one might have hoped. But hearts of all in Pleasant Knoll were brilliant with excitement. And actually, they agreed, it was better this way. The sun had been merciless of late. And there was so much to do!

Mrs. Sutheral and Miss Marlow managed free passes for their helpers and families. Sheriff Weston and his appointed deputies the gatekeeper admitted without charge in exchange for the keeping of law and order throughout the three-ring performance. (Marvel and Mary Ann looked on with amusement when the men importantly pointed to their tin badges, then lifted their coattails to reveal pistols "in case one of them wild beasts" went on a man-eating spree.)

The show was to commence at sundown. The brightly striped tent was filled to overflowing hours beforehand, everybody vying for a good seat on the mile-high (at least, so spectators said) bleachers. People had flocked in from miles around, with the majority coming from the county seat. There was more employment there and people could afford the tickets. Besides, wasn't this educational for their young ones? But children showed more interest in the buffoonery of the grotesquely dressed clowns who honked their cup-sized red noses then reached down to pluck goodies from ears of the boys and girls. Most of them had never attended a circus before and, to the embarrassment of some of the more dignified mothers, literally rolled on the dirt floor beneath the big top with delighted childish laughter.

The adults were little less excited than their offspring. Something close to hysteria spread through the noisy audience. Perhaps the most excited families attending were those of the Dale and Worth Harringtons. Mother and Auntie Rae were "absolute knockouts," their proud daughters agreed in guarded whispers (and it was plain to see that they knew it!). They swept grandly down the aisle in their stylish made-over dresses with "uneven hemlines" of the thirties—exactly like those sold in windows of ladies' better stores—longer than dresses of the twenties in front and falling below the calf in back. They all entered just as the loudest brass band Marvel had ever heard struck up a stirring marching number. In fact, she thought when reviewing the awfulness that was to follow, the volume of the brassy notes accounted for the inability to hear the warning growls of thunder outside the tent.

Oh, the grandeur of it all! So grand it was that nobody noted there were far fewer performers and wild animals than promised. And, blinded by the spotlights of changing colors reflecting the shiny sequins and bangles adorning the aging velvets, laces, feathers, and glass beads, no one noticed that the costumes were worn threadbare and—in most cases—in need of cleaning. The stars might be dimming in the sky of the tented show, but one thing was certain (only *ifs*, of course). *If*, as rumored, this was a final reach for recovery... *if* it should fail... and *if* ever the circus made another try, it would have lost tonight's romanticism.

The band changed tempo, the lights dimmed, and a breathless silence settled—just enough to create suspense. And then wild applause began as all rings went into frenzied action. At the command of ringmasters in white tails and top hats, horses danced on their hind feet... muzzled bears roared in on motorcyles... jugglers wheeled in on unicycles while spinning balls and hoops with their fingers, arms, teeth, and noses... and a daring trio performed on the flying trapeze in midair without a net. Marvel wished for compound eyes so as to miss nothing of the glittering overture. It was all she was to see. And then the little-girl-again in her died a horrible death.

The band stopped dramatically at the lift of the maestro's stick. "La-de-eees and gentlemen!" the man shouted, "What you are about to witness takes seeing to believe! It requires absolute silence, else lives will be lost—"

At that moment came a fiery flash of lightning that lit the tent and almost simultaneously an earth-splitting rumble of thunder. That spelled a hit—and close. "Absolute silence" requested was out of the question—"loss of life" a distinct possibility. Another flash... another. The sky was on fire! And there was not a split second between fork-tongued flashes and the deafening reports. Thunder was a constant roar. And then a bolt struck the show's power plant and the lights went out. The immediate result was mass hysteria. Disaster was preordained....

The band leader tried to restore order by screaming "Stay calm... try to have it repaired... *calm*... CALM, I *beg*... I PLEAD!"

But his words fell on deaf ears, as did the band which struck up another march only to be trampled by the stampede of pushing, shoving, screaming spectators. No "crowd control" training of the officers could stop a stampede.

There was light made by the constancy of the lightning which exploded from the four corners of the earth. For a moment, Marvel sat frozen as still and white-faced as the painted statues which seconds ago had stood like marble carvings on a slow-moving turntable causing gasps of admiration. Then she felt the warmth of a firm, reassuring hand—Daddy, she knew without looking. Like the rock he was, her father calmly tightened his grip and pulled Marvel to her feet and close to him, then held her securely in a tight hug, his other arm about his wife. The three of them moved forward. Behind them came the Worth Harringtons. Uncle Worth had Billy astride his shoulders and hugged Auntie Rae and Mary Ann the way Daddy held her and Mother.

Somehow they made it—a miracle, a real miracle because moments behind their exit there was something akin to a tornado which, dipping down, lifted the flimsy top and carried it away, floating and flapping like the magic carpet in the land of make-believe. The bleachers were reduced to splinters. Screams lowered to moans.

Braced against the cyclonic winds, the two families stumbled over prostrate bodies, voices raised in hysterical prayer. "Follow us!" Daddy screamed, his words sucked up by the wind. Thank goodness, Mr. Benson managed a message to the sheriff: Come to his store, the walls were reinforced. Tummy Tucker offered use of the icehouse. Both men helped the sheriff in literally dragging those who had lost control completely.

Running as fast as the wind would allow, the Harringtons raced for Dale's storm cellar. Marvel knew without looking back that a crowd followed. She knew, too, that the clouds had taken on a green tint around the ragged edges. That meant hail. And hail could be deadly, both to people and the earth. What if—? No, there was no time to think of crops. Human life was irreplaceable. Hurry . . . *hurry* . . . HURRY!

Somehow Daddy and Uncle Worth managed to lift the cellar door. But it took help from other men to hold it open against the driving force of the wind. And there was a roar that all could hear even above the thunder and the wind. Faces reflected an eerie glow in the constant flash of lightning, as if all wore iridescent masks from another world.

"Women and children first!" the men shouted over and over. *"Now!"*

The inside air was stifling. And the overflow of people, jammed together so closely that none could sit on the crude benches lining the walls, sucked in greedily what precious air there was. But they had all reached safety and, in total darkness, prayers were being offered by Brother Greer. How had he—?

What happened next was so sudden, so unexpected, there was no time for Daddy to repeat the rules of safety. All would know, except strangers—

There was a sudden flare of a match, supposedly to light a lantern. And in the blinding light, there was time for only Marvel to see the face of Elmer Salsburg before the explosion that followed! There was no time to assess the damage—time only for the mocking whisper in her ear: "I warned you! And this is only a beginning. . . ."

11

Aftermath

The door of the storm cellar was gone. Hail, big enough to inflict death, came in sheets. Sheet-lightning continued, but the teeth-gnashing thunder dropped to a throaty growl. In the east a curtain of thinning clouds parted briefly, allowing a glimpse of a ragged, orange last-phase moon—a frightening sight...one which could have portended the end of the world, enlarged and painted with blood as it appeared.

The worst of the storm had passed, except for the hail which came from the ominous cloud seemingly hanging directly over the doorless storm cellar.

Daddy took over. No panic, just action, he said. They must get inside the house—*now.* "Cover your heads with coats, purses—anything. Watch your step there. No, no, don't look back—want to become a pillar of salt and be pelted by this storm?" *(Oh Daddy, even trying to joke them back to sanity!)* "*Run*—we'll get you all to safety. Marvel darling, *go*—go help Mother. And you, too, Mary Ann—*everybody*! Come on, ma'am—"

Inside, Mother and Auntie Rae were gathering blankets for their purple-with-cold guests...putting coffee on to percolate... consoling crying children...asking their daughters to do this and that.

The girls did as asked—and more. All the while their eyes and minds were working overtime. "The two north windows are smashed—" Mary Ann gasped at one time. "Rug's wet—I'll clean it up." Marvel nodded, remembering that *all* windows were shattered on their car. Just one last gasp from a victim of circumstances, she had thought with irony. "Cough drop," she said at one time (How much time had passed?) to Old Mag who was wheezing badly, asking herself at the same time if there were any in the house. But Old Mag resolved it nicely. "Don' be needin' no fancy stuff—teaspoon uv sugar and uh few drops uv coal oil'll do. But I do be needin' victuals t'put uh stop to this growl in my belly—cold biscuit sopped in 'lasses'll do—thicken th' blood, y'all know. Real peculiar so 'tis. Almanac uh sayin' hit's plantin' time. Shud be drankin' sas-sa-fras tea t'thin 'er—jest a-nother sign uv th' end uv this wicked world—"

The pathetic old lady was still mumbling when Marvel hurried away, tactfully avoiding mention that it was harvesttime, not spring. Now was the time to make use of Miss Marlow's "Quick-stir Drop Biscuits." Moments later she was popping pan after pan of the tripled recipe into the oven of the coal-oil-heated oven. One burner refused to light—probably in need of a new wick—but the other three, like the tripled recipe, worked fine. Undoubtedly, *everybody* was hungry. Uncle Worth and Auntie Rae had brought in cotton-blossom honey and home-churned butter. Mary Ann, seeing the project, was by her side at once buttering biscuits and spooning honey on the buttered halves.

"He's not here," she whispered between deliveries. "Elmer—he struck that match. I saw his face—and yours—"

Mary Ann, always sensitive to her feelings, had seen Marvel's eyes studying the crowd with fear. "Yes—and he *knew*—oh, Mary Ann, he *knew* it could kill us—kill us all—*and didn't care*—"

"Care? That fiend *care*?" she whispered fiercely. "How *could* he without a heart? Oh Marvel, you *have* to tell Uncle—"

"I can't—yes, Mother, we're coming! Don't you know it would mean foreclosure? We'd lose our home—melodramatic but it's true—but he's totally mad!"

A biscuit slipped from Mary Ann's nerveless fingers. "You've got to," she said desperately, ignoring the rolling biscuit. "We'll *all* be killed. He's not human—oh, the coffee's boiling over—"

It was then that Jake and Archie burst in the door. Their arms were filled with cardboard boxes marked Benson's Groceries.

Food. But they brought news as well—bad news, all of it. White-faced and out of breath from trying to run with the heavy loads, they panted (or were they sobbing?) out the horrible devastation beyond the relative safety of the Harrington home.

"Houses leveled...trees uprooted...Strong's Drugstore was no more...Mr. Strong badly injured—as was half Pleasant Knoll's population. Bleeding, broken bones...yes, there *had* to be some k-k-killed. Oh, it was horrible, horrible—"

"The churches? The livestock?" Uncle Worth's voice carried above the other questions. "We must go—"

"No, no!" Jake's protest was immediate. "Brother Greer and the doctors sent word to stay put. They'll need you later—"

"That's why the groceries—" Marvel took the box with shaking hands.

Archie talked on. The "Ag boys" would be making a washpot of stew—enough for everybody. Donations were already arriving. The tabernacle was gone—not even a shingle left. The grocery box fell. Cans rolled crazily.

Marvel's mind could absorb no more. The boy's voice floated away. Brother Greer gone and she hadn't noticed? Doctors? There was only Doc Wimberly here, and he had hung up his stethoscope years ago. He was older than Grandfather Harrington—had to be nearing 90. So who?

She must have spoken for Jake seemed to be answering her questions. "Three doctors braved the possibility of another twister and came together from Culverville—clear from the county seat in young Doc Elson's faithful old touring car. Five miles can be a far piece on such a night, if ever there was one! And animals—*wild* ones—are everywhere, all on a rampage! Now, stay—all of y'all. Stay, take care of each other, and *pray*. It's all that's left of Pleasant Knoll—just prayer. That's what Brother Greer's saying—"

When several attempted to bolt out, Jake and Archie barred the door with strong, young arms. "You don't even know if you've *got* a house. Obey or we'll be compelled to take the busy lawmen's time. *Don't you understand?*"

Marvel pulled a chair up to the dining room table and, hardly realizing what she was going to do, climbed up. And there, amid the contents of the box she upset (tin cans of sardines, pork and beans, cheese, and crackers), stood tall—looking for the world like an irate queen.

"Daddy! It's our house—and you are head of it. Somebody has to be in charge. God would want it that way. Come. Daddy, where are you? He's here—right here. Isn't God with us in—in time of trouble?"

Daddy's strong arms were warm and comforting as they folded her to his heart. And there, both weeping, they stood: father and daughter, the personification of love, as his steadying voice lifted in prayer. . . .

* * *

The aftermath spelled out the end of Pleasant Knoll as a small town—an end of a way of life that could never be duplicated. But like the human soul, the spirit of the faithful was to live forever. Its inhabitants would fight for it, die for it, but leave it they would not. It was in that spirit that they buried their dead and their past as well. Weren't they to comfort one another in time of sorrow? If this was the Lord's will. . . . Marvel and Mary Ann did what must be done, putting aside their personal convictions. *This was not the will of the Lord!* In the white daze of horror, they tucked away private sadness. Somehow they knew—both of them—that change lay ahead. For one thing, the cotton gin was gone. And gone with the same forceful wind was Dale Harrington's job.

12

A Time of Hope, A Time of Despair

Volunteers and a crew of Works Progress Administration (WPA) workers cleared the road of fallen trees so that Uncle Worth's family would be able to return to the farm. Later the WPA workers were to change the face of America—discriminated against though they were by the more affluent. They were sent in by the government, the men explained—a part of the new president's "alphabet soup," they tried to grin. Their faces showed telltale signs that here, too, were desperate men—and welcomed by the equally desperate Pleasant Knoll victims . . . at least, by most of them.

Daddy and Uncle Worth stood talking in low tones, their faces lined with worry as departure time, so long delayed, drew near. Marvel saw that Mother and Auntie Rae talked in desperate whispers and, turning their backs to the girls, wept the tears they tried to hold back—and then tried to hide them. It tore at Marvel's heart to see their thin shoulders shaking with emotion. Did they suspect as did their daughters that more damage would be waiting to greet them at the farm?

"You'll write, won't you?" There was pleading in Mary Ann's voice. "School will open even later, and you'll be my only contact—unless Jake can come. He has no job. But it's good the school stood up. Write?"

"Of course I'll write," Marvel assured her. "If Benson's radio works, maybe I can hear how things are other places—what else the new president's doing, all I hear about school—everything. I love you."

Mary Ann nodded, unable to trust her voice. And then they were gone, none seeming eager except the horses. The women waved handkerchiefs of farewell until the wagon creaked around the bend.

"I'll check on the mail," Daddy said thickly. "No job to go to—"

Before Marvel could finish making her bed he was back—back and out of breath as if he'd been running. "No mail—but news!"

The tone said it was good. And it was!

"I have work! Do you hear me? Work, *work*, WORK!"

Did they *hear* him? The question mingled with joy was just cause for laughter. Marvel gave way to the overwhelming urge. And then the three of them were slaphappy after the crazed days of a long nightmare.

Mother wound her arms about her husband, babbling senselessly. Marvel hurriedly wound her arms about them both. "*Tell* us."

"Give me air! There, that's better. Of all the unlikely places—I'm the new mail carrier on the Star Routes—have to be listed as 'sub' as I'm not in Civil Service. And it's temporary—the postmaster'll be replaced. Ramsey wonders why it hasn't happened already—the Democrat in the White House. But even a few days helps—right, girls?"

"Oh yes, Daddy, yes, yes—" Marvel stopped then, a big question looming in her mind.

Mother asked it for her. "Transportation, darling, How—?"

"Rest your pretty heads. He covered that, too. 'Now, you've been kind to me, Dale Harrington' (Daddy's imitation of Mr. Cook's Eastern accent caused Marvel to giggle), 'so it behooves me to befriend you in turn. Can't guarantee any automobile could make it over those whoops and hollers, slick red clay, high centers and the like. Sooo, better rely on my mare and buggy like the other guy did.' I'll have to take a snack of sorts: coffee, a boiled egg—you know what goes in a lunch bucket, Little Miss Domestic Science."

* * *

Life resumed a normalcy of sorts. Daddy's hours were long, but never a supper passed without a blessing which included an expression of thankfulness for employment. Mother volunteered her services in response to Mrs. Sutheral's call for help in feeding those left without a home. First, the ladies would issue a plea for the makings of the Ag boys' recipe for "Chicken Stew to Feed 100." Soon, she told Marvel, Miss Marlow would need her girls' help. "And," Snow Harrington said with a shine in her eyes, "we will be able to bring home the leftovers!" Yes, Mother, it was wonderful. And yes, she would help.

Meantime, looking neither right nor left at the clots of overworked men sawing, scooping away mud, and picking up debris (because the sight gave her too much pain), Marvel hurried to borrow more books. Her resolve to educate herself and prepare to serve others—her parents heading the list—had grown stronger.

Oh, there would be so much to tell Mary Ann—more than she realized. Because of her sudden impulse to stop by and thank Mr. Benson for his contribution of food during the disaster, he said, "You're a good girl—bound on going places in life, it's plain to see. Now, I'm not telling everybody, but I got me a powerful set of new batteries and a higher aerial for the radio so I can get— imagine!—foreign countries. But, of course, the storm just about finished breaking me—have to cut corners. But you're smart and have a need to know the news. So you just slip in. It's no waste of juice for *you* to listen!"

"Thank you, Mr. Benson," Marvel said demurely, wishing it were polite to reach right out and hug the merchant. "The radio's magic!"

Someday maybe there would be a way to get a record of the news exactly as it came over the air. But for now scribbling rapidly was the only way Marvel knew, so scribble she did. Mary Ann needed to know this latest news about the president:

The new president surprised us all. Before the election good thinkers considered him pleasant but unqualified. His critics have had to eat crow. FDR's quips and easy laughter reflect not vacuous amiability but buoyant confidence....Here's a tough-minded man, knowing exactly what has to be done. The nation had lost confidence in the government—in fact, in everything and everybody. Now, I guess he could burn the Capitol and we'd give a rousing cheer and say "Well, at least we got a fire started there!"

Marvel listened with both ears, read what newspapers she could get her hands on, and came up with her own conclusions. The president's so-called "New Deal" had turned Washington into a pulsating seat of power. Just like her own placid little Southern town, the whole nation—even the whole world—was jolted awake. *Times were tough.* But maybe hope lay in something the papers called "pragmatism," a game which called for quick, tough action. "Take a method, try it. If it fails, try another. But, above all, try something!" the papers quoted FDR as saying. They then added that included *relief programs*—now, and for the poor.

Such a game called for tough players. Such hardy souls, she read, as "Grumpy" (Harold Ickes of Interior), "Stinky" (Henry Wallace of Agriculture—farm boots knee-deep in barnyard manure and head in the clouds and looked up to by the Ag boys), "sheep in wolf's clothing" (hard-boiled but compassionate Harry Hopkins, relief chief), and "Old Ironsides" (Madame Frances Perkins of Labor, who made history by being the first woman in a presidential Cabinet).

"Cocky team," reporters wrote, "but FDR's the leader of this dangerous game—one he's hell-bent on winning! There's no choice. We fight or we *starve!*"

Mr. Cook, seeing Marvel's interest in keeping up with the news, offered to send the daily publication home with her father. Marvel was delighted and told the postmaster so. Now they could share the news as a family. Then she could clip out articles and mail them to Mary Ann. Her family could do the same— another way of sharing.

Ramsey Cook interrupted her thinking. "Got yourself quite a man for a father—yep, yep—good man to have around. Takes more interest in enforcing 'the mail must go through' clause than the Postmaster General! Roads still impassable several places— hail beat 'em to pieces, one being the old home place your Uncle Worth's occupyin', so no news in or out of there. Guess Worth went the long way around, steering clear of the bottoms. That's far as we deliver. Word has it them worthless beggars of this give-away president—you know, WPAers—will get to that road next.

'Course, who am I to be spoutin' off? In his bullheaded determination to railroad those handout programs through, that—well, I won't say the word for Roosevelt and his big-toothed, gadabout wife—he's overlooked dumping me. Ought to keep my trap shut, this town being all Democrats—"

Marvel bit her lip and chose her words carefully. "We should *all* be kind, the reason having nothing to do with politics."

He looked startled. Handing her the paper without reading it himself, he returned to work.

* * *

Marvel completed her lengthy letter to Mary Ann and received one from her the day she posted it. So those "worthless beggars," known as WPAers, had managed the impossible task of repairing the long stretch of country road. That was her first thought. Her second was to gasp at the bulk of her cousin's letter. Why, it should have come by parcel post! Stuffed inside were letters to Mother and Daddy from Auntie Rae and Uncle Worth. Marvel unfolded Mary Ann's to her, read only the first paragraph, then in shock let it drop from her fingers. There had been fire (lightning-set?)... burned granary... hail beat the corn and biggest cotton field to pieces... tornado sucked away the one bale of cotton.

13

To the Poorhouse in an Automobile?

The remainder of Mary Ann's letter had less to do with finances than with a terrifying mystery. Mother and Daddy gasped when they read the letters from Auntie Rae and Uncle Worth. Sober-faced, they dealt with the impact of the disasters privately—just as Marvel dealt with Mary Ann's account, and then her jarring question.

> At first we could find neither hide nor hair of the colored people and feared for their very lives. They were hiding out in the canebrakes, in sassafras thickets, between cotton rows...scared out of their wits. Sula Mae and Casper finally told me...not about the storm...the fire. And that a devil, a real-life devil, set it. Not the lightning at all, they said. *That devil.* Even had horns and a pitchfork—and oh, how he laughed and went dancing around the flames...then spotted them "cuz we wuz too scared t'run" and said he'd kill them...drive that fork through every last one of them if they breathed a word. Oh Marvel, something is going on. They wouldn't dare lie....God would strike them dead, you know....*Where was he?*...Ought we tell?

He. Elmer!

At first, the account sent Marvel's head whirling. Then the world came back into focus. Elmer had been in the storm cellar...struck the fatal match...then disappeared. But how—?

She finished her cousin's letter. The "devil" had ridden away at great speed on a horse as black as the cloak he wore. Crops were so short Mary Ann would be back early. That was good. She was discouraged and lonely. Marvel would please tell Jake she sent love.

The opportunity came that afternoon. Jake came to say that Mr. Wilshire wished to see her—and himself as well. Could they be there this afternoon? They could! Both knew something was in the wind.

Marvel, welcoming the opportunity to escape her dark thoughts, left a quickly scribbled note as to her whereabouts and went with Jake.

Both avoided the subject of the principal's summons.

"Has the station agent left?" Marvel asked as they walked.

"Oh yes—lock, stock, and barrel. Only way to catch the one passenger train passing through is to flag it down with a torch. Good news though for your Uncle Emory. He's staying on to clean up—"

Passing the bank building, Marvel saw that it was in the process of being torn down. She pointed and was sorry. Such a look of disappointment crossed Jake's face. Maybe one day they would build an even larger one, she said halfheartedly.

"We both know better, Marvel. I think this new president's sincere, but even he admits that the new government law can guarantee only a few banks to reopen. But like he says, we have to keep up our faith. And (brightening) I agree. He's suffered lots of defeats but keeps gaining ground. Like he says, our economy will come alive—slowly. Meantime, we have to look after each other. Take that old lumber—it's already being put to use getting roofs back on and the like. Rest'll have to make do with tents."

Marvel nodded approval and hoped the same would be done with any good timbers from the little town's only two-story building. Once it had housed a dry goods store downstairs and two doctors' offices in the upper story. The storm had made it unsafe. It was near collapse.

They had reached the school. The weathered brick had turned gray with age—an age which showed now that the wind and hail had stripped away all leaves of the ancient oaks surrounding the building.

"I'll come right to the point," Mr. Wilshire said after greeting his two nervous guests. "For reasons known only to the bureaucrats, Pleasant Knoll School has lost accredited status, which means that the state will lop off the top grade-level."

"And we can't graduate here?" Jake gasped. "Then we're faced with the choice of never finishing or managing to get to Culverville?"

The principal's lips tightened. "That's it," he said tersely.

"Will there be tests, tuition?" Marvel knew she and Jake were being impolite, but this was so important to them both.

"Fortunately, no. Just transportation."

Poor man. His job, too, might be in jeopardy. Of course, he would not discuss such a matter with his students. Marvel sympathized.

"But you must be wondering why I called the two of you here. We are fortunate in some other ways. There's a new government program—NYA it's called, meaning National Youth Administration. Then later there will be a hot lunch program using surplus foods for hungry children. We'll be needing help from the Agriculture and Domestic Science departments. This school qualifies for three helpers. There'll be lots of work and financial rewards will be nil—just experience and commodities."

Jake leaned forward. "I accept—that is, if you're offering—"

"I apologize. I don't seem to be thinking clearly these days— so much to think about. Yes, of course, it's a valid offer, based on scholarship, dedication, recommendations by teachers. You would receive foodstuffs, tools, and your school supplies for your two remaining years. Marvel, your pay—if one could call it that—would be the same except in place of tools you'd get fabrics for making into clothing. Both would be accountable to your teachers, probably put in charge—"

"Oh, wonderful, *wonderful!*" Marvel sang out, forgetting her dignity.

Something akin to a smile crossed the man's face. "I was allowed to choose only three—lucky to get that many." The voice was oddly husky. Any suggestions for a third recipient?"

Marvel and Jake looked at one another significantly, started to speak, and thought better of it. "It's up to you, sir," Jake said.

Mr. Wilshire nodded. "I think I understand." He rose, extended his hand, and said, "Thank you both."

"Thank *you*," they said in unison.

Two days later, after sharing their unbelievably good fortune at home, they learned that it was even better. The principal encountered Jake as he helped repair dangerous potholes in the street. He had offered the third NYA aid to another worthy pupil who gave him "what-for," said "death before a dole." So since their obvious choice was Mary Ann . . .

Before Marvel could get the glad news to Mary Ann, something happened that dimmed her enthusiasm. She should have been prepared, but is anyone ever fully prepared for devastating news?

The first of Mr. Roosevelt's "alphabet" measures had been creation of something called the NRA (National Recovery Administration). NRA's purpose, Marvel heard him explain in a "fireside chat," was to regulate wages, working hours and, indirectly, prices. The move was applauded by most. Bands marched. Songs emerged. And every available space was splashed with gaudy posters featuring a blue eagle symbol and below the monster (which many proclaimed to be "the mark of the beast") the words *We Do Our Part*. New Deal opponents continued a barrage of criticisms. Among them was Postmaster Ramsey Cook. Oh if only he had been less vocal, Marvel thought sadly. But in his bitterness he borrowed from an editorial in a Hearst newspaper as to the *real* meaning of NRA. Making a poster, Mr. Cook tacked it on the wall of the post office: NRA—*No Recovery Allowed!*

Lightning struck immediately. The Republican became visible and was retired with one day's notice. "Well, my darlings," Daddy said with a feeble attempt of a smile, "You know what *that* means. I will be among the unemployed—" His voice broke.

A kind of weight seemed to come down from above, a heaviness that gave Marvel the feel of wearing a tight-fitting cap. It was hard to breathe—as if the air held too much humidity, portending a storm. The three of them seemed to be balancing the world on their heads. Silence is golden? Not always. Marvel felt that if one of them moved, the sky could come tumbling down. And it would be her fault.

"Say something!" Daddy's voice was as sharp as aged cheese, which was new for him but encouraging. Life remained—a fighting spirit.

And the sky was still in place!

Marvel smiled up at him. "It would seem to me that there'll be a need for somebody to keep the place open—at least, until a new person takes over."

Mother came alive. "Of course! As I remember, the job requires an exam and that requires posting a notice. It could be *ages*!"

Suddenly they were all in each other's arms. They had life. They had love. And, Marvel supposed, even sadness could be a gift of sorts when it was shared.

But Mother's bubble, spun from nothingness in desperation, burst just as quickly. After a week's coveted work, a new man came in, selected from a long waiting list of eligibles.

*   *   *

Mary Ann was back. There was so much to talk about, each listening to the other solemnly...digesting every word...taking one another as seriously as they took themselves. There was good news and there was bad news. Mary Ann babbled away about Baby Zeke, the new baby brother Sula Mae and Casper had let her care for when they all came down with malaria...needed quinine...but who could afford it?

"Somehow white people manage credit—" Marvel paused, thinking of their own debt and wondered if that was so good, after all.

"I know," Mary Ann, taking no notice, sighed. "It's unjust and those black people would die for us—absolutely *die*—give you the shirts off their backs in a snowstorm. Giving is their way of life. Otherwise, you're breaking the law! It's God's law, so it's theirs!"

"I know. We're lucky, having neighbors like that—so virtuous and sharing. We all need each other. I think God planned it that way—"

Mary Ann nodded. And there went those glistening black curls bouncing and gathering sunlight. "Back to the narrow-mindedness of some with white skins, well, all I can say is that they ought to see Baby Zeke: fattest little dimpled legs, nose as flat as a pat of butter, headful of kinky curls, and a belly like a puppy's. He looks like an oversized caramel, good enough to eat." Again she nodded. "Yep, that describes him. And caring for him gave me some experience I want—" She flushed. "I need to see Jake and talk all about the good news you wrote me. Oh, how can I thank you?"

Marvel assured her that thanks were unnecessary, but insisted that seeing Jake could wait another minute. She needed to know if the malaria was dying out. "It could be handled, you know, by getting rid of those mosquitoes. That would mean draining the bottoms—like they're doing under the Tennessee Valley Authority Act, partly to build dams. I really know very little about it except what I see in newspapers. But it benefits people in other ways such as health—oh well, what am I mentioning this for? It would mean giving up the richest cotton land."

"Right you are—no need to mention *that*! In fact," Mary Ann frowned, "dollars to doughnuts—that's what our folks are talking about right now—giving up some cropland. Daddy brought a letter with him from some bigwig, telling about AAA, whatever that means."

"Agricultural Adjustment Act," Marvel filled in quickly.

"Daddy had us all read it. If he understands it right, the deal— New Deal, it's called, right?—actually wants to *pay* him to cut down on the acres of cotton he raises. Does that make sense?"

"Nothing makes sense anymore, but that's where the surplus foods are coming from—you know, those we'll be using for the hot lunch program we're to help on."

"*Cotton?*"

"Silly!"

The men's voices rose from the adjoining room. In the background was the heartbreaking sound of women crying.

"Bad for the land or not, cotton's our only hope, Dale. And look at the amount they're offering—a widow's mite, a slap in the face."

"More than we came out with this year. And now I'll be out of work—completely. I know we'd be giving up control of our land, but this man has a lot of faith in his programs. I guess cotton *is* sapping the soil," Daddy reasoned.

Uncle Worth's voice was rising. "Can a man be expected to look ahead to future generations and let his own family starve? One more bumper crop is all we need to set us on Easy Street—"

"E-asy Street, E-asy Street, I'm walkin' on E-asy Street—" Daddy crooned, bringing back the twenties with their raccoon coats and ukuleles and breaking the tension that had built up in the room.

"Forgive me," Uncle Worth said brokenly. "These are trying times, and a man gets desperate when he foresees hunger for the ones dearer than life—more precious than gold. Still, it's your farm—"

"I'm not sure anything's mine," Daddy all but whispered, "except the love and respect of my wife and daughter—and the respect part may dwindle like the fertility of the soil. How can they forgive me?"

Something in Marvel's heart seemed to topple like a wobbly chair that has groaned repeatedly to tell you of its misery and you were too wrapped up in your own problems to take note. *Oh Daddy, there's nothing to forgive. It's the times, not you. All this time I've wanted you to forgive ME, when neither of us failed. Kill love? God made it eternal!* She turned to Mary Ann. And suddenly both of them were weeping. This had to stop or their tear ducts would dry up like the bottomlands.

The Harrington brothers must have resolved their differences, if differences they were. "All right," Daddy was saying, "let's give it one more shot, old pal. I'm not sure I can meet my own mortgage, let alone go a note for you at a Culverville bank—"

"All I can do is try. Not that the cotton will be worth much even if I get the yield, but we'll hang on."

"That's the way to talk!" Mother's voice was too husky. "We'll stick together, share, scrimp, save—*anything* so that our girls can finish their schooling. Any sacrifice is worth that. Only two years for Marvel."

"Bless your heart, darling Snow," Auntie Rae burst out. "We'll get through this. With God as my Helper, we will!"

And there they were, Marvel and Mary Ann, feeling guilty again the way children do sometimes. It was all their fault. Marvel would make it all up to her parents. But Mary Ann was unwilling to wait. She burst in on their parents before Marvel had a chance to try and hold her back—not that she could have.

"Why won't you talk it over with *us*—let us know how you *feel*! Don't you think *we* understand?" she sobbed.

It was a touching scene—one which Marvel would tuck into her sack of tender memories, plucking it out at random and all those years between would vanish just like that.

"Oh my precious darling," Auntie Rae said as she dropped to her knees beside her daughter and then, as if for the first time realizing that Mary Ann was as tall as she, pulled her down in a little heap. "We wanted to protect you, shield you. How foolish when you two are bright and caring—and *wonderful*. Try and understand it's not easy being a parent—especially," she gulped, "especially in times like these—"

The men were moving about, making helpless noises. All the commotion had awakened Billy Joe who, although ready for school next year, had played himself out acting as Tom Mix (his movie idol) and fallen asleep leaning backward across the bedstead after shooting the last of a roomful of bank robbers.

Marvel moved in quietly and took him by the hand. "I know a new story."

Billy Joe, in his newfound independence, pulled away. "I'm hungry. I want a cookie!"

There *were* no cookies. Or were there? How on earth could Mrs. Autrey know? "Yoo-hoo!" she called, "I tried the ginger-flavored cookies we learned how to make—you know from biscuit dough—and they're downright tasty if I do say so myself. If somebody'll take 'em 'cross the fence—you all hear?"

"There you are, Billy Joe. Trot to the fence and bring us all a cookie," Marvel whispered.

"Now," she said brightly while holding back tears, "let's stop all the waterworks before we all drown. So we're a burden? You're only stuck with us 18 years according to the contract!"

"Eighteen!" Daddy's laugh sounded salted with tears. "Now, it's more like 21—" he beat Mother to where Marvel stood. "Make it more like a lifetime—and we love it—wouldn't have it any other way. Now, now, Snow darling, keep your distance. No more time for tears!"

Just as they joined hands and, at somebody's signal, went prancing around the room, Billy Joe opened the screen.

Some people can read lips. Marvel could read faces. Her wide-eyed little boy cousin said: "What on earth's the matter with *old people?*"

✳ ✳ ✳

"Walk a piece with me," Mary Ann insisted, still intent on meeting Jake. "Better put on your bonnet. That sun's still hot."

"And it's so dry. Everything's dying. How long has it been since we had a real rain?" Marvel asked as the screen slammed behind them.

But Mary Ann had no interest in the weather—not then anyway.

"I wanted to ask about Elmer. What do you think—and did you tell?"

"Elmer? I don't *think* where he's concerned. And no, I did not tell. Oh Mary Ann, don't mention *anything!* They'll foreclose and—well, will you look? Here comes Jake on the trot!"

Jake was smiling broadly, making his gray-blue eyes light up in a way which made him almost handsome. Breathlessly, he panted that Archie was right behind him and that Mr. Benson had let him deliver some bread and potted meat to Old Mag, living in a tent until her shack could be reroofed. "Not much—just enough to get her by until somebody could get her name on the relief roll. But guess what! He gave me a reward better than the quarter he said he didn't have. Said we could come—all four of us—and hear the president speak half an hour from now. He's some guy—said after all it would take no more juice for five listeners than for one. Good arithmetic, huh?"

Archie, who had grown even taller, hadn't gained an ounce and was as gangling as Ichabod Crane. But he was dependable and sincere. Marvel welcomed him with more enthusiasm than usual. His presence gave her a reason to turn away from her cousin greeting the man she planned to marry. That they *would* marry Marvel never questioned.

"You're looking fit," Marvel greeted Archie, noting his ruddy cheeks which she hoped came from his being outdoors a lot—not from her warm welcome. He must never, never get the wrong idea. Archie was a dear friend—always had been, always would be. There it ended. Anything deeper, forget it! Marriage did not fit into her plans—*not at all.*

Four abreast, they sauntered along, talking. Mary Ann and Jake held hands. Marvel and Archie kept step, shoulders carefully separated.

Jake brought up the subject of his, Mary Ann's, and Marvel's good fortune regarding the NYA grants. Still interested in getting into banking, he delved into the matter of the government's plan to make a shift in the U.S. Treasury. "You see," he explained to his audience who did not see at all, "the president can inflate currency by free coinage of silver, printing more paper money, or reducing gold content of the American dollar. Lots of farmers think cheaper money will up prices of their produce, help out on federal loans, lower interest rates, and let them keep their farms. AAA it's called."

Now they understood. Oh, not completely, but enough to be interested—each for a different reason. All began chatting at once. "Oh yes, like paying *not* to grow certain things, like cotton," Mary Ann exclaimed. "And," Marvel added slowly, "wheat and corn—maybe others." Yes, those were called "surpluses," Jake continued, and there would be others now, both because of the overproduced staples and as a sort of relief program for the hungry. Archie entered into the conversation then, excited over what all this would mean to the course in Agriculture.

Marvel drifted out of the discussion and into her own thoughts. The AAA, she remembered, had caused a lot of protests. Too drastic, some said. Help farmers? It was a move to rob them of their rights—give the government charge of the six million American farms. Next they'd be asked to give up their livestock, then their *families*! But, in the end, most seemed to be cooperating. They had a choice and it was better than being hungry. But Marvel's main concern was the talk of federal loans and what it would take to qualify. Maybe—

But there was no more time for thinking. The four had reached Benson's store. Mr. Benson hurried them inside and closed the door as the deep, reassuring voice of the president began:

Friends: Because of your cooperation and traditional optimism, our economy is gradually returning to normal. Our emergency measures are paying off. Those who have money have stopped hoarding it— and we are conquering the common enemy of fear.

Congress and your president have established mutual trust and respect. Together we have legalized the sale of beer which brings in new revenue and puts an end to the lawlessness of the Prohibition era. It is once again safe for our women and children to walk the streets. But I must caution you that the fight must continue. And, while our boys will never be called upon to serve their country overseas, we cannot ignore happenings in our Mother Country.... We must maintain our national defense.... And then, on the homefront, our job is unfinished. I see one-third of this great nation still ill-housed, ill-clad, and ill-nourished... and I wish to announce a different kind of program, the setting up of Civilian Conservation Corps designed to give some 2,500,000 young men meals, housing, uniforms, and small wages for working in the national forests and on other government properties... and give them dignity and pride to be a part of the CCC.... And for those pessimists who persist in the claim that we are heading for the poorhouse, let me respond by saying, "If so, we will be the only nation in the world to do so in an automobile!"

The rousing speech did exactly what it was designed to do: brought a rousing cheer, a new determination, a new hope. This was particularly true of one listener in Benson's store. Archie's face gave off more light than the inadequate bare light bulb dangling over his head.

"That's for me. I just feel it. My family needs money more than books. That's for me. That's for me." He kept repeating the words even before a commentator came on the air to summarize FDR's words and then editorialize a bit on his own:

Not even FDR's most bitter opponents of his New Deal policies can find much to say against this, in my humble opinion. Imagine accommodating two-and-a-half million of America's able-bodied young men— needy, in search of employment and unable to find it—and setting them to work on worthwhile projects. That's what the CCC program offers—and more! *They are to receive 30 dollars a month!* Now, a good portion of this will go to their families, taking a good many off the relief rolls.

My colleague here just handed me a note listing some of the things the president expects these boys to accomplish: participate in a reforestation plan; setting out new trees; bringing killer diseases of the trees under control—beetles, blight, blister rust; digging ditches for culverts to control flooding; building firebreaks to save the precious timber; terracing land in hopes of combating loss of soil where the dust storms hit; draining the mosquito-infested bottom lands—the list is endless! The entire nation stands to benefit: needy families, and maybe most of all, the CCC lads themselves! You betcha—looks good from here. Like the man on the hill said of his plan: "If a boy wants to become a man, here's his opportunity. *Work* is the name of the game!"

It was hard to tell which was more excited: the man on the radio or Archie Newland. "Mankind! Even uniforms—and it'll be like campin' out. You know, tents and stuff. I'm so glad I've learned so much about outdoor cookin' in Ag. And my folks are dirt poor. *I'm excited!*"

Mr. Benson grinned. "Never would've guessed. But don't go countin' your chickens before the eggs hatch. I wonder if you're old enough?"

Archie drooped, then brightened. "If I'm not, it won't be long. I'm older than my friends here—had to stay out of school to work. Elmer and me's the same age. Too bad that galoot's not *made* to go. He'll *never* be a man—a real he-man! But his old man owns half the land hereabouts and what he don't—doesn't, I guess—he *will*. He's got a mortgage on it, and he's accumulatin' more from folks who can't pay taxes."

Elmer. Marvel involuntarily shuddered. And then a strange feeling of apprehension crept over her—so strong, so real, it was as if somebody were trying to warn her. But of what?

"I need to get home," she said. "Mary Ann, you stay. You and Jake have had no time for that talk. No, don't come along, Archie—not now."

His tormented face tore at her heart. But she didn't feel like talking. Archie looked like a wounded puppy, but she mustn't encourage him.

Uncle Worth came home disappointed. No government loans to farmers other than owners about to lose their homes. But he did find out one bit of news: new creamery in Culverville . . . milk route to come by their house and up for bids. If a truck *did* pass, maybe they could sell milk or cream.

That night a tragedy rocked Pleasant Knoll, one which detained the Worth Harrington's planned return home.

14

When Life Becomes Too Much

Dinner turned out to be festive. Mary Ann came home bright-eyed and pink-cheeked. It must be wonderful to be in love. Just look at what it did for a girl so young. And it didn't end there. Take a second look at Mother and Daddy, or Uncle Worth and Auntie Rae. They adored each other, their love seeming to deepen with every anniversary. Marvel thought, as she set the table, that they all must have been born knowing what they wanted in life. All of them wanted love, a home, and a family—all except herself. She wanted an education, success, money to help her parents. Of course, that was for love, too, but one which had no room for the opposite sex. She had resigned herself long ago to being different. God had other plans for her.

"What are we having?" Mary Ann asked, folding the last napkin. "I'm late—but, oh Marvel, I wish the whole world could be as happy—"

"The world has a need for happiness," Marvel replied. "We're having waffles—a real treat. They take too many eggs—"

"Ooooh! I love 'em! Mother brought eggs—"

Mary Ann stopped, a little embarrassed. Because they were bantam eggs? Auntie Rae had swapped her white leghorn eggs for staples, but Mr. Benson did not take the little eggs bantams shelled out unselfishly.

"And she brought ribbon cane syrup and butter," Marvel said quickly to cover Mary Ann's awkward pause. "Yummy-good with waffles."

Daddy, busy measuring coffee, overheard. "We'd better make good of this meal. With the milk truck coming by, you'll be hoarding the cream, won't you, Worth? Oh shucks, I've lost count on the coffee."

Uncle Worth laughed suddenly. "That's okay, stub your toe! We'll make this a celebration. You know, I couldn't believe anything good could happen to us. Now I feel like the Lord took me by the shoulders and gave me a good shaking. That truck *is* coming—yep! for sure—and the cows are all good milkers, grazing in that tall grass in the bottom since the pastures are all being turned under."

Auntie Rae put her test waffle in the iron. "First one always sticks—lucky for Kaiser Bill, that scrappy tomcat of yours." Then, turning, she put her arms around her husband's neck. "Oh, I'm glad to see your change in mood. Of *course* we'll make it. It can't stay dry forever either, and cotton will shoot sky-high one of these days. Meantime we can eke out enough to pay that Shylock his pound of flesh—save this lovely house." She raised her face to receive her kiss of reward.

The crisis had passed. Uncle Worth's depression had lifted. And Marvel felt her own sense of apprehension sort of foolish in this atmosphere. "Waffles are ready! I'll have you know I mixed them, so we're all little red hens. I'm famished. Worth, get going with a blessing," Mother smiled.

"A short one, Daddy—make it short. I'm gonna eat a wagonload!" Little Billy Joe lifted innocent eyes to his father.

All laughed. All stuffed themselves. And celebration it was. Until—

There was a knock at the front door. Marvel asked Daddy if he would like to have her answer it. He said that would be nice, and so it was that she was the one to spot their unwelcome guest first. Red-faced and bloated, he stood there, seeming to block out all the world's daylight.

"Uncle Fred—" she gasped, wondering if she should so much as invite this man inside—a matter he settled for himself.

"Hello family!" he called out. "Do I smell waffles?" he wheezed. And brushing past her rudely, he dodged furniture and made his way to where the Harringtons sat. The nerve of him! Didn't he know he wasn't wanted here?

But the Harrington brothers, ever the gentlemen, rose and, without warmth, extended their hands in halfhearted greeting to

Fred Salsburg. The stepbrother pumped their hands vigorously and complimented the ladies effusively. What was he up to?

"Which of you lovely ladies made those delectable-looking waffles?"

He was actually drooling. Marvel turned away, sick.

And in that split second he had seated himself, taking up enough room for three. Everybody was juggling chairs as he tucked a napkin inside the front of his stiff white collar. Never had Mother's hemstitched linen napkins looked so small. The man needed a bed sheet!

Elizabeth Browning's beautiful love poem came from nowhere to lodge in Marvel's mind. Immediately she silently paraphrased it: *How do I* hate *thee? Let me count the ways....*

Immediately she was filled with remorse. *I'm sorry, Lord,* her repentant heart whispered. *I know I mustn't HATE... but, oh Lord, am I supposed to* love *him?*

Marvel would believe—no, *know*—forever that God answered immediately. His voice was so loud and clear that she almost dropped her milk glass. Surely the others heard! You *cannot alone, my child, but you are never alone. Find it in your heart to love him through My Son!*

In the moment's soft music which filled the room, she glanced from face to face. Disappointed, Marvel realized that nobody heard any of the miracle. Well, that was all right, too. It was between her and the Lord. And, she thought with more tolerance, how *could* anybody hear with the nonstop monologue of their unexpected guest? All the while he kept shoveling in food like he was pitching hay.

It surprised even Marvel that she was able to say, "Would you have preferred honey, Uncle Fred? It's cotton-blossom."

"Hey now, young lady, that sounds mighty nice," he said between bites.

"You oughtn't talk with your mouth full—and there's butter runnin' clear down to your collar!" Billy said loudly.

His mother looked horrified and stuffed an adult-size bite into her small son's mouth. That worsened the matter. "I'm too big to be fed!" he protested and was about to spit the food on his plate when his father took over.

"Then you're too big to correct your elders!" Uncle Worth's voice was firm.

"That's it, Worth," Fred Salsburg applauded—probably the only thing his stepbrother had ever done which met with his approval. "Make 'em toe the mark, I always say."

He then went on with his dissertation regarding finances. So that was what this was all about! Marvel felt the thrill of apprehension prickle her spine again. The only thing that saved the moment was Mary Ann passing by to offer another waffle from the second batch and pause to whisper without lip movement: "Claimed to be short-winded. I doubt that!"

Marvel repressed a grin and listened closely: "—made another purchase, too. Remember that big ranch with all the cattle out north—belonged to the Birminghams at one time. Never saved a dime in his life. So when the bank offered it for taxes, I couldn't let it slip. I feel no sympathy for birds like that. Good time to invest—maybe you understand now, both of you, why it's smart to put away for a rainy day. *Ahem!* By the way, here's hoping you are prepared. You know, I'd hate to foreclose—"

Daddy's face whitened. And, with fists clenched, Uncle Worth scrambled to his feet. His eyes were live coals of fury.

Then came the moment that was frozen in time.

It all happened so fast. And what followed was too fast and too horrible to remember.

Outside, there were screams of "Fire! Fire! Oh, God help us— it's the Baptist church!"

Marvel felt detached, lifted above it all. It was as if she were looking down on the three-ring circus again with so many acts in progress that there wasn't enough of her to absorb it all. Only it wasn't funny, amusing, or beautiful. Nobody laughed or applauded. And there were tears in the eyes of the clowns.

The Baptist church...her church...the only one she knew or had attended throughout her life, except as a guest...and Uncle Fred, his face ashen with shock, mumbling incoherently something about ownership of the land...that it did not go with the building, which alone was tax-exempt...and then that he must hurry...get home to Aunt Polly and Elmer...both were afraid of fire...it would *kill* them. Then he was gone. And somehow the rest of them were among the spectators.

It was gone. The oldest, most beautiful landmark of the rapidly disappearing little town was gone. One minute the church was there. The next it was a heap of evil-eyed coals, winking and blinking in satanic triumph. True, the church—like all other buildings, *everything*—was a likely victim to any spark under the tinderbox-dry conditions. But the people were right in their cries that it had simply exploded. Some were saying that they actually *saw* the beautiful carved pews and great swaths of the red carpet which covered the entire church fly like flaming-tailed comets in the air. And the great stained-glass windows simply blew apart. Then in seconds it was reduced to rubble. *How, HOW?*

Before Marvel could absorb the awfulness of the fire, she learned that Aunt Polly was dead.

Flatly ... without rhyme or reason—at least, on the surface—Pauline Salsburg, who feared fires according to her husband, was gone. Uncle Fred, stricken and dazed, found his way to where the Harringtons stood. "It can't be. It can't be—gone! It—can't—be—come—help!"

The following hours were a nightmare—a choking, grotesque nightmare. Marvel kept shaking herself mentally, praying to awaken and find it was all a bad dream. But she slept on. In the dream Frederick Salsburg was "uncle" again.

Men, all strangers, came in. Uncle Fred was overcome with shock. Mother and Auntie Rae coaxed the childlike man to bed. Marvel and Mary Ann made tea for him, while Elmer, who had remained strangely calm throughout the ordeal, answered the men's questions.

There would be an inquest, the men said, and then went away. Such matters could wait until after the funeral. Meantime, members of the family, the last ones to see the deceased's husband, were to remain in town. Circumstances of the woman's death were strange—very strange.

"So Fred is a suspect?" Daddy said sometime as he went about making the necessary arrangements that his stepbrother was in no state to make. "That is unbelievable. He's capable of many things—but *murder?*" Daddy, too, was dazed. That even an enemy could *kill?* He was amazed....

As was Uncle Worth. "We're not family. And do they suspect *us?*" He spoke disjointedly.

"We're the closest he has, and this is no time for letting our feelings show," Auntie Rae began, then burst into tears. *"Oh, how awful!"*

Mother was the most practical one. "Someone must help with final arrangements—" she stopped suddenly, her face changing expressions. "Where is Elmer?"

Elmer answered the question for himself. He had entered the room noiselessly, his face filled with great sadness. He was at the fire, he hastened to explain. There was something about fires which both repelled and fascinated him... but that beautiful old church.... Oh, it was too much for him to stand. So he had run away from the scene. Awful!

"You know how I feel, Marvel. Your face told me so. You did see me?" Elmer asked significantly—as if daring a denial.

Had she seen him? Doubt clouded Marvel's mind. Somehow she disbelieved his claim. But then, anything could have happened.

"*I* didn't!" Mary Ann said bluntly.

"You, my dear Mary Ann," the usually arrogant Elmer said with faked gentleness, "had eyes only for Jake. I doubt if you saw the *fire!*"

Mary Ann's eyes blazed. She was about to make an explosive response when Marvel shook her head in warning. They must be careful—very, very careful. Too much was at stake here to risk a misstep.

Elmer was the one who found his mother, he said miserably. It was such a shock. Pauline Salsburg was sprawled across the bed, according to her son's version, and "being very resourceful" (he said of himself), he had managed to drag his mother's body to safety. At the time he had supposed her to be overcome by fumes and in need of fresh air.

"But such was not the case," Elmer said convincingly. "Poor dear—she must have expired from fright—sheer fright."

"That is something the coroner must decide," Daddy said curtly.

Marvel doubted every word the deceitful stepcousin said. But there was no further time to think, sort out her feelings, and decide what she could—or should—do. Word of the terrible tragedy had gotten around and neighbors were everywhere at once. There was food, expressions of condolence. Bedding was hung out to air. Flowers, which came from business associates in Culverville in breathtakingly lovely arrangements by the skillful hands of florists, were arranged about the rooms. Women in dustcaps and talking in subdued tones tidied up the rooms. Let those "upper two-thirds" send their meaningless gifts. If it took being classed in the "lower third" to *care*, they welcomed the label. Didn't Jesus choose His 12 from the common men?

Time had lost its meaning. Mrs. Autrey brought a black dress, knowing that it was unlikely Auntie Rae would have brought one. "It's plum out of style," she apologized, "but fix it any way you want." Mary Ann took the garment, thanked her, and went to work nipping in the waist and cutting away the swag in back to even the hem.

Marvel finally located a black crepe dress in Mother's closet. "It'll have to have the hem lowered, dresses being longer now—mid-calf?"

Biting off a thread, Mary Ann nodded. Both were grateful to have their hands and minds occupied. "He wasn't there, Marvel. I—I dread the inquest," Mary Ann whispered. "Oh, don't go protecting him—you don't owe that devil. The children were right. That's what he is! You don't owe Elmer Salsburg *anything*!"

"Yes—yes," Marvel whispered back, "I'm—I'm afraid I—*we*—do. But that's not why I'll have to say truthfully that I don't know. None of us do for sure. Anything could have—"

Miss Marlow came to where the girls were sitting. "Oh, this is so dreadful. I have to admire the courage and dignity you're showing—both of y'all. I brought a casserole—after conquering my nausea. The fire all but did me in."

The cousins looked at one another. Neither of them had seen Clarinda. So—who knew? It occurred to Marvel then that Elmer's presence at the church fire may have been the worse of the two evils. . . .

Grandmother Riley came. How long had it been since Marvel saw her maternal grandmother? So long that she had forgotten how beautiful, truly beautiful, Leah Johanna Mier Riley was with her dark coloring, almost gypsy-like. And certainly her love for the nomadic way of life and talent in the field of music supported the illusion. Mother said that her own father, whom Marvel had never known, "could make any musical instrument talk." Marvel, noting that Grandmother had brought a violin along, wondered if she had taught Mother musical skills as she had tutored her in the three R's.

"Marvel, my goodness, how lovely you've become! A Harrington through and through. And I understand that you have a fine mind."

"Oh, Grandmother Riley! Thank you—and how dear of you to come."

"Of course, child. We're *family*—extended, of course, but family of sorts. Too," she said a little evasively, "there is some business—the boys, of course, did not know the Salsburgs. Tell me, my charming young lady, have you seen the Squire—uh, your grandfather Alexander Jay? I've seen the sons, but the Squire is making himself scarce."

Marvel promised to look for her grandfather and moved away. What Grandmother Riley said—both her question and comments regarding the uncles—underscored her realization that in crowds it was easy to miss faces. That included the thistle! She forced herself to think other-directional. Somehow her mind settled on the surprise she had felt that her maternal grandmother and paternal grandfather were acquainted—perhaps friends. Yes, there he was, the tall, stately gentleman with the distinguished-looking, closely cropped moustache and the cane which looked more like the men's accessory of the twenties than the necessity it was. The two of them were talking animatedly, looking almost youthful.

One by one, Marvel's eyes spotted the other uncles and their families. Uncle Joseph and Aunt Dorthea (and yes, the three girls) as well as the bachelor uncle, Alex Jr., were moving solicitously among the rank and file of the county seat. Testing the waters for employment? Getting back into banking was their sole purpose in life. Uncle Emory, to Aunt Eleanore's relief, was more compromising. Their sons, Duke and Thomas, were thrifty and willing to work, too. And there the two cousins were, making their way to where Marvel and Mary Ann were talking with their friends Opalene, Angie, and Clara Lynn.

Awkwardly, Duke greeted the girls while Thomas—younger and shy by nature—slunk behind his brother. Then, suddenly, overcoming the boy-girl awareness, all were talking at once. Did it strike everybody strange that two such dreadful tragedies would happen on the same night? Could there be foul play? If so (shuddering) there could be an arsonist wandering among them— even a *murderer*! Billy Joe wandered into the group unnoticed until in his six-year-old lack of judgment, he began to chant loudly, "Bang, *bang*—you're all s'posed to fall down. You-all are *dead!*"

Clapping her hand over his mouth, Mary Ann led him away. "I'll follow, if you will excuse me, and find Billy Joe a cookie. In fact, I should help with the serving—" Marvel told her cousin.

"We'll help. There are lots of people. And my sakes! Look at the food!" Dorthea exclaimed. "Want to come along, Angie—and you, Clara?"

Duke suddenly became a man. After all, he was 13, same as Marvel and Mary Ann—six months older, in fact. Straightening, he said, "And why am *I* standing here—for decoration? There's Old Mag—she needs a chair. Some of the others do, too. Let's get busy, Thomas, my man!"

There followed a confusion of faces, words, colors—all blurring together in Marvel's senses. Dimly, she acknowledged compliments for her efficiency—and, surprisingly, for her charm. Someone asked if both she and Mary Ann had white dresses for the funeral. "White is more appropriate for young ladies your age." Than black? But of course. Marvel managed to accept the suggestion as news. It was gracious to offer, she said, knowing that it was meant that way.

The next day Uncle Fred rallied miraculously. Dressed nattily, he seemed able to greet his business associates and become engrossed in what obviously were serious conversations.

Marvel was engrossed in her thinking, inwardly amazed, when someone walked up behind her, causing her to jump. Yesterday's milling and talking confusedly had dwindled into subdued whispers.

Careful not to make an exclamation of surprise, she turned to face, of all people on earth, Elmer Salsburg. Something in her mind noted that he, too, looked very jaunty in spite of his "great loss."

"I wanted to thank you, my dear. You have been a brick."

Marvel answered in like manner. "Thank you. I appreciate that."

Elmer edged closer. "You were wise to have spoken as you did. Thank you for that, too."

She stiffened. "I did you no favor," she whispered through clenched teeth. "I only spoke truthfully—not as a favor. You may *have* been at the fire. I—I could have failed to see you. That's all."

Elmer nodded as if understanding something she did not understand at all. "If you will excuse me—"

But he blocked her way and they must not create a scene—not here.

"Terrible about the church. Uh, have you heard who may have set the fire?"

Marvel jerked erect. "Who said it was *set*?"

He seemed satisfied. She was not. A deep suspicion was born.

"But the fire's not what I wanted to talk about. I want to talk about us." Elmer's voice carried an insinuation of intimacy.

"There is no *us*. Move out of my way. This is neither the time nor the place—even if there were. How *can* you? Your mother lies in state—"

Elmer actually laughed—low and careful, of course. "I can't be expected to mourn forever."

The statement was so ludicrous Marvel would have laughed under different circumstances. But what was he saying? "I must caution you, I'm serious. And I am not exactly a nice man—"

"With that I agree!" With a pounding heart, she hurried away.

15

The Wedding Dress

And then it was over. At least Marvel hoped that it was. One could never be sure, considering all the problems which her family knew lay ahead. Not that they were alone. But it did seem to her that Daddy, Mother, and she had more than their share. Perhaps she should follow Mary Ann's suggestion and tell her parents about Elmer and his frightening threats. But wouldn't that compound the problems? Or was she being fair—to have accused them in her mind, as Mary Ann had done openly, of holding back, treating them as children?

But the matter resolved itself.

Uncle Worth and Auntie Rae were compelled to remain in town until after the inquest. Billy Joe was unhappy. One minute he fretted childishly to go home. The next, suddenly a different person, he demanded to go to school. Marvel could understand his mother's vexation.

"I declare," Auntie Rae said, "I don't know *what* to do. The child is ready for school. If only there were transportation. He's a problem."

Mother could think of no solution. Auntie Rae had taught him all she felt capable of teaching. And Billy Joe needed contact with other children his age. Already he would have a major adjustment once he began.

"I wonder if—" Mother began and stopped, as if doubting herself.

Auntie Rae laughed. "He could stay with you?"

Then she, too, stopped—or *was* stopped. Billy Joe screamed, "No! I will not stay! I hate it here—I want my own mommy and daddy. Not you!"

He proceeded to fall on the floor, kick his heels in the air, and—in the words of Grandmother Riley—"cut a dido!"

It was she who picked him up and gave him a good shaking. "There will be no more of that, young man! Tell us you're ready for school? Why, any two-year-old would know better."

Wide-eyed but subdued, Billy Joe sat down and picked up a *Baby Ray* primer and began to read aloud: "Baby Ray has four ducks," pausing to eye suspiciously the woman who had dared lay a hand on him.

Grown-ups were strange. But, his eyes said, they were smart and knew how to teach little people how to be big people. One day he would be one. And she didn't hate him. In fact, she was smiling—and that made her kind of nice. Grown-ups could be nice—when you were good.

"There! That's better—yes, you will be ready for school!"

Billy Joe dimpled and stood six feet tall. His face showed that.

There was no time for further exchange. Who should appear but Uncle Fred himself? Marvel and Mary Ann looked at each other as wide-eyed as Billy Joe had been. Even the long, black car looked sinister.

"I've come for you—all of you who were there when—" he said, seeming less sure of himself. "The investigators are there—and—we'll all—"

"I'll call the men. They are repairing a window screen. The mosquitoes have been terrible. Are you ready, girls—Rae?" Johanna asked.

Auntie Rae hestitated. Grandmother Riley understood without being told. "Billy Joe will stay with me," she said firmly. "It's time he had some play. I know some sleight-of-hand tricks. Come to the breakfast nook. We'll need some handkerchiefs—"

"Oh boy!" he said without so much as glancing at his mother.

The two men, obviously officers of the law although dressed in dark business suits, were businesslike and to the point. They questioned Marvel and Mary Ann extensively. Because they looked guileless and would tell the truth? Did they see the deceased on the day of her death? No. Either her husband or son? Both. *Did they know of any reason why either should wish to kill Pauline*

Salsburg? Oh no! Their relationships were very good then? They did not know as they saw little of them. Was there any reason, in their opinions, why the woman's demise should occur at or about the exact time of the fire? No (Marvel felt herself tensing at what she anticipated the next question would be—and she was correct). *Did the young ladies see both husband and son at the fire which completely destroyed the Baptist church?*

"I saw Mr. Salsburg, sirs," Mary Ann said, "but I did *not* see Elmer."

Marvel felt her knees grow weak, threaten to buckle. Oh, what should she say—and how? She had seen the looks of surprise which crossed the men's faces which heretofore had been dead-pan. Immediately, they were immobile, without expression, again. But she knew that their ears were listening with new keenness. And *Elmer*—oh, heaven help her, she felt his eyes burning into her flesh, warning, daring.

Now those burning eyes were speaking: "Remember the episode in the storm cellar, Marvel? I do not forget easily, and I remember that stinging blow of rejection. You have yet to pay for that—you poor little creature, at my mercy, you and your family. You are afraid of me... afraid... *afraid.* ..."

The words pounded against her eardrums. Afraid—*yes*, she was afraid. But, lifting her shoulders, Marvel determined that she would not lie.

"Stop harassing my daughter! You have no right!" Daddy's words sounded far off. She needed to warn him before it was too late, but her tongue clove to the roof of her mouth.

"I am sorry," one of the men said with surprising gentleness, "but we must get at the truth. Would you like a glass of water?"

Marvel shook her head. "Thank you, sir. I am all right. It's just that it was all such a shock that I am unable to tell you those I saw or did not see. And believe me, I would tell you—tell you at any cost—"

There were other questions then, more probing ones. When her part was finished, Marvel was shaken, completely exhausted. She must get away. "Please, gentlemen, if you are finished with me—"

"You may be excused," the other man said curtly. "You and the other miss both probably belong in school—"

"School begins tomorrow," she murmured, "but we are working."

The men thanked Marvel and Mary Ann for their cooperation and reminded them to be in touch if they should think of any additional detail, no matter how small. The cousins promised and hurried toward the closest door leading out.

Marvel was aware that someone was following, so quietly that it might have been her shadow. Her shadow was Elmer. "Now we can become more friendly. You know *how*. Else I must prove that I am making no idle threats. *You will pay*—"

"*You* are not excused, Mr. Salsburg—get back in this room. You are a key witness. You found your mother's remains!"

Marvel found herself actually running. Mary Ann was right. Elmer was more than dangerous. He was insane and capable of anything. There was no limit to what that demented mind would do.

"He *is* crazy," she sobbed.

Mary Ann placed a comradely arm about her shoulders. "Don't cry, Marvel. Sh-h-h—want Miss Marlow to think Uncle Dale and Aunt Snow've been beating you? That lunatic's not worth your tears. He's more than dangerous. He's possessed of a devil. That's it—*devil*. Oh Marvel, none of us are safe as long as he—if devils have gender—is around!"

The next day the police officers were back. The verdict, based on all evidence, was *suicide*—death by Pauline Salsburg's own hands. The coroner had found enough sleeping powder (prescribed by her doctor) to kill a dozen persons.

"But why would any physician prescribe so much?" Marvel questioned.

Both men shrugged. "That is not our business, miss. You are all dismissed. Case closed."

Marvel was both relieved and perplexed. She would have supposed that the investigation would have dug deeper at this point. But then, it was good to be free. She was only too glad to be led away by Mary Ann.

Then, shockingly, Elmer was dispatched to Annapolis.

"Annapolis?" Marvel gasped when Daddy told the news. "For military training? How on earth—?"

"Clout—nothing more. Except the almighty dollar. They amount to the same. Easy to have pull with the bigwigs with money behind you." His voice was edged with bitterness. "Unfortunately, in America *class* is based on a man's worth—"

Grandmother Riley sniffed. "Hogwash! Well, the inverse is most assuredly not true—which is to say that a man's, a *real* man's worth does not determine his class. Gold does not a gentleman make. Look what class Fred Salsburg showed in wheeling and dealing right there. Oh well, the saints preserve me, I might do the same if I were stuck with an idiot son like Elmer—a chip off the old block, unless I miss my guess. I saw him, Marvel—saw him with my own eyes trying to make time with you, and you remained a lady. Now there's *class*. My, my! How I do carry on! Forgive me, Dale dear, they are family and I—"

Mother reached over to pat her hand. "It's all right. They are what you used to call 'shirt-tail relatives,' if that. It's only that they had nobody else—"

"*Touché!* But mostly," Leah Johanna Mier Riley, whose background linked her with royalty (Europe's definition of "class"), confessed, "I hungered to see you three. Then too (she coughed discreetly), I needed to talk with your father, Dale."

Her son-in-law met her eyes questioningly, causing Grandmother to laugh. "Don't hesitate to ask. It's obvious that you're curious."

He grinned. "All right, dear lady," Daddy teased. "Are your intentions toward my father honorable?"

Everybody laughed when Grandmother, who obviously wasn't expecting that, became as flustered as a young girl. Managing a quick recovery, "an eye for an eye," she said tartly. "Only in your case, it's a shock for a shock! Ready? The Squire and I own the large plot of ground on which the church was built—*and* the taxes are paid. Let Salsburg try and get his claws on *that!*"

Yes, that was a shock!

* * *

Uncle Worth, Auntie Rae, and a reluctant Billy Joe had gone home. The little boy, too young to realize that his parents faced goodness-knows-what, had fallen in love with "Grand'mere" (the French word Grandmother Riley had taught him). He loved her stories, her violin-playing (the instrument "wailed like the wind," he said)—and yes, he loved her strictness. And so, to prove himself grown up, he held his crown of curls high and obeyed when she said: "Now this is no time for tears!"

Mary Ann had squeezed back her own tears, put the past behind her, and readied herself for school. "This will be an eventful year—I feel it!" she'd said hurriedly to Marvel. "But thank God, you have fat—fat-*headed*, anyway—Elmer out of your hair!"

"Yes, and thank God indeed! He'll be there a minimum of two years."

By then or long before, Marvel supposed, those in charge would have discovered that he was a far cry from what Annapolis sought.

By then I will be away from here. I have to be. The thought, seeming to come from the limitless stretch of cobalt-blue above, startled Marvel as much as Elmer's return. Leave *here*? That would be impossible. God would have the answer when the time came....

✳ ✳ ✳

There was a touch of Indian summer in the air and the skyline was aflame with color every direction Marvel looked. Oh, how good to be back on schedule. School had been in progress a month now. And today was special—the day Miss Marlow was to show the fabrics made available for qualifying (deprived, really) schools because of the oversupply of cotton. *And oh*, her heart sang, *Mary Ann and I may be able through the NYA to receive a bit of our pay for keeping teacher records!*

"We have to talk about patterns and things," Mary Ann said, shuffling her feet in the colored leaves. "I—I'm going to ask for a wedding dress."

"Are you out of your mind? You know there'll be no luxury fabrics. And a wedding dress *now*? I'd laugh if you were less serious!"

But Miss Marlow thought differently. Clapping her hands in childlike glee, the Domestic Science teacher exclaimed, "Perfect—just perfect! Honey-child, you are an answer to prayer! *I* have promised to marry Clyde when my contract's finished two years from now—the silly thing restricts me from marriage until then. Sure enough, it does. But," she sighed, "it's a blessing that wedding dresses know no style. Why, it's sweet to wear your great-grandmother's and practical to borry—borrow—from friends."

In minutes, it was arranged between them to Marvel's amazement. Together, her cousin and her teacher would select material—bisque because dead-white makes a bride look bilious and in need of a "round of purgative" and what bride needed that on her wedding night? (They were giggling.)

Under Clarinda's guidance, Mary Ann would do the actual stitching, in return receiving NYA credit. And Miss Marlow herself would buy enough for two. Mary Ann was right. Coming up: a strange year—stranger than they could possibly envision....

16

Wanted Dead or Alive

Grandmother Riley was a dear. Marvel grew more and more fond of the many-faceted lady, the most endearing quality being her ability to bring out the best in everyone. She was the essence of simplicity, while at the same time very complex and intriguing. And her wisdom and understanding of Marvel's generation was amazing.

"How could I feel more at ease with her than with my own mother?" Marvel asked Mary Ann, the question directed more to herself. Immediately she felt guilty. How could she have given voice to such a thing when she loved Mother with a passion? Almost fiercely, she said before her cousin could answer, "Forget it! That's not true—and I shouldn't have said it!"

"Of course, you should, silly. And it's true. She's *your* grandmother, but I feel that she's mine, too. And I feel the same way. Maybe I'm the one who ought to be sorry, and I'm not one bit! We're shy around our folks, right? Sometimes I feel it's my fault to have been born. Figure that one out!" Mary Ann sighed. "But that's wrong, too. They love me. I know that. But something holds them back, ties up their tongues. I've got it! I think it's the responsibility they feel. While Grand'mere—I love that name and am going to use it—well, anyway, she's raised her brood and can *be* one of us. Make sense?"

It did.

In fact, it made so much sense that it saw the two of them through the trying times ahead. There were things crossing the invisible line between childhood and young womanhood girls needed to know about life. And Leah Johanna Mier Riley was only too willing to discuss their questions with delicacy and charm. Being the model of discretion, Grandmother would never stoop to tattling. "Someday, mark my word," she said during one session, "marital relationship—even, I would go so far to say, *planned* parenthood—which would let children grow up *knowing* they were loved, wanted, and planned for, will come. Until then—alas!—I wish more parents would tell children the beautiful truth."

The girls nodded in agreement, saying it was a lot better than all this snickering over half-truths, making it all sound *dirty....*

Mary Ann's words helped, too, when Marvel heard raised voices in the kitchen where she knew Mother was having disagreements with her own mother. Once she would have been hurt and confused. Now she understood, could even smile in her newfound wisdom. It smacked of reality.

But Marvel's serenity was to be short-lived. The subject mother and daughter were discussing was disturbing.

"You know what having a home means. I can't live without one!"

"Snow Riley—"

"Stop calling me that! Is it so hard for you to realize I'm a grown woman and—"

"Then act like one! You need a roof over your head, but that's only a house—not a *home*—and certainly not a shrine."

Marvel, amazed as she was, could picture Mother—her gentle mother—defiantly facing her own mother.

"*Shrine!*" Mother's voice was rising. "Just because you lived the life of a nomad, with no thought of our needs, thinking only of yourself—sacrificing our security for your own selfish urge to ramble—"

"Now you listen to me, young lady! You keep a civil tongue in your head. You owe me nothing except respect, and I demand that!"

Suddenly Mother was sobbing. Marvel, unable to believe her ears, longed to rush in and pull Mother close, tell her everything was going to be all right, comfort her as she would comfort a child.

But, she realized, her mother was not a child. It was not as much between the two women as it was one generation against the other, struggling to understand and unable to, resorting to words to cut through the distance between. A little poem from one of her nursery-rhyme books came back then:

> Keep a watch on your words, dear children,
> For words are wonderful things:
> Like the bees, they can create honey
> Or, like bees, they have terrible stings.

True. But wait! Why were they discussing a house versus a home anyway? The low, soothing words which followed answered the question.

"Now, now, baby-mine," Grandmother almost crooned momentarily, "we both got carried away. Just as we were both right—and both wrong. A child never understands until becoming a parent how many tears we shed, how many misgivings we have, how uncertain and afraid we are at the time—while pretending for your sake to be invincible. We want to give our offspring a shoulder to lean on while, to tell the truth, we are leaning on yours."

"You were a wonderful mother—and I apologize. I still need your advice, guidance, inspiration. It's just that I *do* need a home—"

"And you are entitled to one, sweetheart. You have put your child ahead of your wishes, however. And you've lived by the Good Book and taught her to. Admittedly, you and I are different, but let me remind you that my blood flows in your veins. And I only meant to reassure you that you'll measure up, bear up, and even find your experiences a blessing in disguise when the time comes. For you're right, that man is an ingrate—a Lucifer who'd qualify to be kicked out of heaven. Never mind *your* kindness in his hour of need—although that 'need' may well have been faked, just a smoke screen. He'll not take that into consideration. He'll foreclose, and I wanted to prepare you. So buck up. You'll manage—just keep a pair of my vagabond shoes handy!"

Foreclose...*foreclose*...FORECLOSE. Grandmother was right. Frederick Salsburg would take away this lovely house. A short time ago Marvel would have thought, "Let him try. Daddy will fix *him*!" But she knew the inevitable was near at hand now. She, too, must prepare. But—*Oh, dear Lord, help me*, her *almost* grown-up heart cried out piteously—for now, she could be a little girl again, briefly. So, pressing her hot cheek against the soft blue wallpaper with the gold-centered daisies which she and Mother had chosen for her bedroom, Marvel wept her heart out. Then, lifting her head, she whispered, "Thank You, dear heavenly Father, for giving me the strength to move on."

* * *

The rapid-fire shots with which events took shape allowed for those talks. Grandmother, who was a firm believer in taking life as it came, welcomed the opportunity. The air grew cold without further prelude. A stiff wind blew in, known as a "blue north'er" in east Texas, to announce that winter had arrived early. Not exactly time for June brides....

"Excellent!" Johanna Riley said, "and what a cozy arrangement we have with the two big fireplaces back-to-back. We'll just move our belongings into the dining room and not disturb the 'old folks,'" she smiled in a cunningly conspiratorial manner. "I'm glad that little Miss Georgia Peach allowed for this arrangement. Let me strike a match to this fire while you girls tell me again just what happened."

Miss Marlow and Mary Ann had selected the fabric, the pattern, laces, and notions, they summarized again. Then, quite agitated, the young Southern-belle teacher called Mary Ann into her office to tell her tearfully that the Board of Education had decided that the making of satin wedding dresses could be misunderstood—yes, even though Miss Marlow had paid for the materials. They must be very, very careful with funds earmarked by the government for the needy. One crooked step could do it, you know. "Big Brother" out there was on the lookout for anything that smacked of fraud, misuse of funds. Well, they hoped Miss Marlow understood. Miss Marlow, in turn, hoped *Mary Ann* understood.

It was Mary Ann who suggested turning the dresses into her home project. Why not? A home project was required. And, fortunately, at this point a home project could be anything. There were no regulations.

Miss Marlow had stopped wringing her hands, her agitation gone. Oh, how clever! But of course. And would Marvel like to assist as *her* project? Of course (with just a hint of secrecy) there could be some—er—leftovers, you know, from the required cotton dresses? Fabrics, foods (they *would* try out some recipes at home, too, and share findings?). And so it was that Marvel and Mary Ann received an entire bolt of fabric (enough for themselves, their mothers, and Marvel's grandmother) to have a dress. With a little imagination, which they all possessed, each dress could be a different "designer's model." There would be remnants of various colors, buttons, and the like. That gave them access to all other patterns . . . a hoop of cheese . . . rice . . . flour . . . not to mention the leftovers from dishes prepared in demonstration in class. Oh, and of course, their own dresses were to be made and modeled, along with the other girls'! Wasn't it wonderful?

"Wonderful is a weasel word! It's a basketful of love straight from heaven. Truly, 'God is good'! And we're going to have ourselves a ball!" Johanna Riley said.

Life took on a needed sheen after all the recent happenings. Grandmother had a special way of bringing out the best in people. Yes—and more. She had a talent for turning work into play. She knew when to talk, *how* to talk, and when and how to listen as well. Marvel knew that she and Mary Ann were receiving more than sewing instructions. They were learning about life and how to live life at its richest. . . .

And then came that special evening when the entire world around them changed. Grandmother Riley bargained for what must be the most beautiful radio set in the world! Marvel had difficulty holding back her tears. This meant that the gracious lady had to be making the ultimate sacrifice financially. Of course she made use of the installment plan. Even so, the payments would gobble up most of her small pension. But here was a proud lady, one who lived by the better-to-give formula spelled out so clearly in the Bible. And as to the receiving—well, the whole group of them would be the receivers! So scolding her would be improper. Better-to-give could mean a big hug!

Giving her that bear hug, Marvel added a bonus. "Oh, I love you, dear Grandmother!" She squeezed harder. "Say, 'calf rope,'" she giggled.

Mary Ann followed her lead with one difference—the use of "Grand'mere." The shine on Johanna Leah Mier Riley's face was almost holy.

Was it the burnished sheen of the walnut veneer console-style radio cabinet in the glow of the open fire which made the voices on programs sound as if all concerned used golden mikes? Somehow that illusion made the news booming into the Harrington household more bearable—the console's beauty, yes, and the beauty of the two wedding dresses which brought visions of a new life, a happily-ever-after one right in the here and now in the midst of the present darkness in a bizarre world. As if hunger and downright squalor were not enough, now this....

Heretofore the world of children orbited around a set of heroes and heroines whose extravagant lives were chronicled in a rich new range of media, the "Sunday funnies." But Marvel and Mary Ann were not *children* by any standard. Besides, who could afford newspapers, however inexpensive? Nevertheless, Marvel could smile at snatches of conversation she overheard from the few who managed an occasional paper to be pawed through before church and the rare programs she heard on radio, such as the latest exploits of Flash Gordon or the pet expression of Little Orphan Annie—"Leapin' Lizards!"—taken up by even those who had been denied the privilege of seeing them or hearing them via the media.

Now, through the magic Grandmother Riley's pension had brought, these dream-weavers walked right into Dale Harrington's living room to cushion the blow of harsh reality which hung overhead like the dark cloud just waiting. Ignore it one might. But that could not stop the inevitable spewing out of its wrath.

Meantime, Marvel listened to the children's programs along with the children. In spite of the blatant barrage of sales pitches for trinkets, toys, and breakfast cereals—right at the cliffhanging moments of the breathtaking adventures, there was a comforting preservation of the American way of life, a gentle persuasion to the Depression-ridden parents that makers of the commercial products were promising good times would return as long as they maintained faith in good old capitalism. Despite their unblushing probusiness dogma, such programs had their value—even though they clutched at straws. They created the common ground on which these heroes and heroines stood: virtue...good, clean living...hope. And, added together, the programs held rewards unlimited. They provided an inexpensive and wonderful world of make-believe during the hardest of times this nation had ever known, when to children the real world out there seemed no fun at all, and to the grown-ups around them it was downright frightening.

As those beneath the Harrington roof listened and laughed and cried together, the beautiful bisque satin slithered almost sensuously across the knees of the eldest and the two youngest of the group. Marvel and Mary Ann had finished the machine-stitching of the lovely gowns. Now, they could sit with Dale and Snow Harrington in the living room and whip on lace, bind the raw seams, and thread rows of dainty seed pearls around the sweetheart necklines. Grandmother, determined that no detail should be spared on the precious garments, delighted the girls by daintily embroidering the names of the brides-to-be in baby-blue on the underside of the hem. Oh, they were storybook models!

And part of it all, Marvel realized, was inspired by the magic of those evenings and the fairy tale stories to which they listened. Carried away, Mary Ann listened in fascination to descriptions of the *Big Little Books*, some which had pop-up cardboard replicas of Tarzan or Flash Gordon; others, cutouts of Shirley Temple and Buck Rogers.

"Did you hear? *Did* you?" Mary Ann exclaimed, almost dropping her sewing basket in excitement. "Imagine 400-page books for a single dime! Remember, Marvel, that at one time the principal said there would be some small payments in cash through NYA if we met all the requirements?"

Marvel remembered. "I'm a jump ahead of you. You want to get one or two for Billy Joe! He'd love them. And you know what? I'd like to somehow start a children's library—"

Her cousin gasped. "You! Why, I thought you didn't plan on marriage! I was going to say, some for my brother and—and—some for our children—mine and Jake's. Now stop laughing, all of you!"

They all stopped. But not because of what Mary Ann commanded.

Until now the children's programs chose as their settings the Old West, the American football fields, outer space, or the jungles. Now suddenly, the announcer said in hushed tones that a new series was beginning. The background would be the slums of gangster-ridden cities.

Gangsters! The very word made shadows, which briefly, had slunk away, come from their hiding places as if to gloat.

Before the controversial program began, the news media took up a needed crusade against it. Such was not intended for the ears of children, the radio announcers protested, causing the sponsors of a new chocolate drink called Ovaltine to drop "The Daredevil Crooks" like a hot potato. America would *not* wave its flag for a criminal army already on the march, they said. Parents cheered in admiration and bought more of the product than the makers of Ovaltine expected.

Jake and Archie were listening with the Harringtons the first evening the radio spelled out the situation more clearly:

Well, folks, are you ready for the sordid truth? It is not enough that we should endure the ghastly reports of men who lost every red cent of life investments they thought they had tucked away safely—some blowing their brains out as a result. And, in a little aside, let us tell you that there are sources which warn that the worst is yet to come. Or, as "Amos and Andy" would tell us, "Yuh ain't seen nothin' yet!" Keep your ear to the ground for the rumblings on Wall Street. . . . Say what you will concerning radio's political priest, you'll not be alone. Coughlin's views are under pressure from all quarters. In this country, one simply can't get by with calling the president the Great Betrayer or screaming out in angry tirades that tightfisted Jewish bankers are responsible for failure of the U.S. banking system. As a matter of record, this station will cease to air this man's fulminations from the Shrine of the Little Flower at Royal Oak, Michigan. But now, ladies and gentlemen of radioland, we have with us crime of a new order, so deceptive it is eating our insides like an undetected cancer: *crime!* Not just the usual type of crime which has always been with us—where the offenders are caught, given a fair trial, and punished accordingly. No, a different kind of crime: *organized!* And our nation's citizens, impoverished and embittered by the Depression, actually find a certain justice in the mounting number of bank robberies. "The *real* bank thieves," some defend, "were the bankers themselves. . . . Didn't they take away all we had? Let these men do what nobody else has been able to do for us—*get it back!*"

"I can't stand anymore," Mother said with tears streaming down her lovely face. "I can't. *Oh, God help me*—I can't—"

Without a word, Daddy strode to the radio and turned the knob to "off."

For a moment, all was silent. Disbelief was written on every face—and then all began talking at once.

"This isn't new," Jake said soberly. "I've been keeping up with the crime scene. I've had to do research for Ag, you know. That includes reading *Farm and Ranch* magazine, as well as newspapers and all the Government bulletins—"

"Me, too," Archie broke in eagerly, "but for a different reason, you know. And I'm here to tell you this CCC business looks better all th' time. Next best to enlistin' in the army—"

Marvel was surprised when Daddy interrupted with something akin to a growl. "The army's the *last* career a young man should consider, what with all the goings-on overseas. Depend on our getting involved like we did in World War I! I call it *I* because we're bound on a II!"

"Dale!" Grandmother Riley scolded gently. "Tsk, tsk (she paused to bite off a thread). You wouldn't want us to be isolationists now, would you? I sincerely feel that God chose this new world to set an example—help the rest of the world. Let Europe hang onto the past. Our *future* is far more important."

Her son-in-law did not reply. And Marvel felt like reminding her grandmother that there might not be any future. Then, shaking herself mentally, she reminded herself that she must cling to her faith.

"I was gonna tell you I'm leavin' soon. Yep, I qualified. So let's all give a big 'whoopee!' Sorry to feel so up in the air—" Archie began.

"Don't apologize, my boy. So, one-two-three, all together, 'Whoopee for Arch!' " They obliged. "Now, if I may have the floor, let's allow Jake to fill us in. Obviously, he knows more than he had a chance to share." Daddy looked at Jake Brotherton.

All nodded, still dazed. Until now, WANTED: DEAD OR ALIVE had had no meaning.

"The announcer was right," Jake said then. "Hard times brought on a marked boom for one profession anyway: *crime.* And he's so right in voicing a strong objection to that 'Daredevil Crooks' program. Take that swash-buckling Dillinger criminal—claiming to a vulnerable public to be a modern-day Robin Hood, and actually becoming a folk hero. Do we want our children growing up to become *trained criminals*? Stealing and robbing are that, nothing more, by whatever disguise. 'He don't rob pore folks,' the more illiterate man-on-the-street declares—yes, right here. Then "Pretty-Boy Floyd"! That pretty grin and his so-called generosity don't keep him from being our nation's number-one desperado packing a handgun and—get this—a submachine gun! He'd stop at nothing—even broke out of a so-called escape-proof jail in Indiana, took two hostages, then gave them that innocent-looking grin and handed them four bucks for streetcar fare home!"

Jake paused to catch his breath, while the eyes of his audience begged for more. "How the public can be so blind baffles me," Jake shook his head. "How can they say 'good ole Johnnie' about Dillinger, take his money, and manage to overlook that the man has gunned down ten men already."

Mother looked dangerously pale. "Where is he? This killer—where does he live?" she managed to whisper. "This 'good old boy—or *who*?"

Jake's laugh was no laugh at all. "Don't lawmen wish they knew! John Dillinger escapes them all—lives on the run. He can be anywhere. I'm probably talking too much, but I am sitting here with people I love and," he gulped, "this desperado can be anywhere—anytime. None of us are safe. Now, stay calm, but stay on the lookout, too—he's especially apt to hide away, get lost casually in small towns. Like all bandits, he—well, in plain English, he is just a cold-blooded thug."

They all said good night in somber tones, and tried to go on.

In the days to come, Marvel, hurried home from school just to listen more carefully at a time when others would not be more upset than they were already.

While legitimate businesses continue to close and more and more farms lie barren, so many Americans are moving to the shady side of the law they out-number carpenters with nothing to build by four to one...grocers, with nothing left to sell by *six* to one...and now, hear this, doctors whose patients can't pay and have nothing left as a medium of exchange since the drought, by *20 to one*! These criminals dodge the lawmen: robbing, kidnapping, murdering.... In large cities they are going underground...raking off millions through extortion, prostitution, and auto theft...then in fast-moving cars move on to small towns, hit them and hide out...."Daredevil Crooks" indeed. We are stunned and scared.

17

A Closer Closeness

The wedding dresses were finished and, after stroking them lovingly as one does a cuddly kitten, wrapped in tissue and folded before storing for that Someday. That day would be with the advent of better times, when with cumulus clouds of veiling they would march triumphantly down the aisles to give their hearts to the men they loved. Mary Ann went so far as to mention orange blossoms. And the others let her dream—having no idea how close to the truth she was.

"Now," Marvel said practically, "we must get busy with the cotton dresses for ourselves, our mothers—and (lowering her voice) I do believe that with careful measuring we can turn the fabric so that we can make one for Grandmother. Remember, we hoped we could. We'll try."

Mary Ann was delighted. "Oh, Grand'mere would love it. And you know what? Both sides of the material are the same so that it's—what's the word?"

"Interchangeable—"

"And her button box is running over with the most *beau-ti-ful* buttons. There are some mother-of-pearl ones—just like her ear-bobs."

Marvel laughed. Then reminded Mary Ann that their English teacher had told her that word was a no-no. "Ear*rings*," she had said firmly.

And so the evenings around the fire continued—with one change. A major one!

Mother had come home from home demonstration class one evening fairly aglow with pride—and something else. "Guess what's for dinner: 'mock apple pie!'"

The *faux* fruit filling (which the family admitted later *did* taste remarkably true-to-life) explained her pink-cheeked glow. And the pie itself, with its golden-brown, fluted pastry and lattice-woven top, was a thing of beauty.

Those who shared the pie wanted to tell the excited cook that her "pinch-penny" dessert was delicious. But about all they could manage was a chorus of "Mmmm's" because Mother dominated the conversation.

"Now, if you were unaware of the ingredients (which they were at that point), you'd never, ever guess it wasn't the real thing, would you? Another name for the creation is—imagine, if you can—'cracker pie'—takes crackers, you know, which none of us had. But you know what? Mr. Benson got real generous. You know how frugal that man is, a 'Scrooge' really. But—well, promise this will make no difference? I mean—it's truly awful. Mrs. Sutheral had trouble telling us, but it could happen in anybody's kitchen, and we all got laughing—" Mother giggled in recollection, then went back to her talking before anyone else could speak. "You girls' friend, Angie Stone—her mother, that is—started chanting, 'What? You naughty kittens have lost your mittens, then you shall have no pie' because that was a *mouse* pie—and it looked *exactly* like this! Well, Mr. Benson—"

This was too much. Dale interrupted his wife. "Wait a minute, Snow! No, don't talk, *listen*. Do you meant to tell me—my stars—"

Mother burst out laughing again, wiped her eyes at the look of horror in the eyes of the diners, and asked, "Are you *sure* I am to keep my tongue bridled, or do you want an answer? Don't worry, my pets, you've already gobbled it up. Nope, no mice! It's just that a mouse—poor hungry little critter, rodents get hungry like us—got caught in the cracker barrel—caught by a customer, I mean—and the fainthearted lady keeled over in a dead faint. Said she'd report Mr. Benson to some agency President Roosevelt's appointed to see that our foods are clean. Now, tell me, if that woman hadn't had a sharp eye, do you think that tightfisted merchant would have *donated* the whole barrel to us? The shopper saw the little mouse jump into the barrel, so it couldn't have been there long. No reasoning with her though—*dared* him to sell one more cracker—"

Grandmother Riley was the first to collect herself and find the story amusing. "Laugh and the world laughs with you, so come on family."

Oh, it was good to laugh again, Marvel realized. What's more, it was good to have Mother so happy. Let her babble on. Nobody really cared that the delicious pie contained cinnamon, cream of tartar, more crackers, and lemons. Lemons? Mrs. Sutheral had a skimpy little budget and could buy the lemons. Letting her mind wander, Marvel—remembering Mary Ann's promise to herself that she would have an orange-blossom halo on the cap of her wedding gown—let herself drift into the fantasy of plucking lemons from one's own tree ... oranges ... grapefruit which here only a few knew existed. ...

She was jolted back to reality when she heard Mother saying that she had more to say. So that accounted for the additional glow.

It all boiled down to this: Mrs. Sutheral told the ladies' group (and Miss Marlow would be soliciting help from the girls) that it would be both helpful and wise to compile these recipes born of hard times—"need being the mother of invention"—and print up the collection. They even had a name for the book: *Stretching to Survive*. Newspapers sometimes did the printing free, in turn keeping money from businesses which wished low-cost advertising—and who didn't?

"We're all so excited!"

"I never would have guessed," Daddy teased, having digested the last of his "mouse pie." "There's certainly a need. This Great Depression, as it's commonly called now, has hit hard at dinner tables all across America, forcing families to skimp and save. Maybe one day we'll find a way to distribute the books—just a thought."

"An excellent one," Grandmother applauded. "I was thinking back to my own generation when a different need existed—when we were traveling, you know, as so many are now. I guess," she sighed, "we were and still are looking for greener pastures. A chapter in *Campfire Cookery* would be helpful, Snow dear, and *I* can help with that!"

Now that the family was excited along with her, Mother was finding it difficult to regain the floor. That she had more to say was obvious—only nobody looked her way.

"We're getting into the subject of how to feed our families. I mean, later—" Mary Ann said, a flush of color beginning at the hollow of her young throat and rising to the round forehead. "I'm talking about vitamins and minerals—stuff I never heard of before, and how to balance diets and make them nutritious but low-cost—you know, stretching soups. Marvel, didn't Miss Marlow say butchers would give away soup bones?"

Marvel nodded. "Interestingly, peaches are just as tasty canned without sugar. Other fruits, too, I would guess—if only we could water those fruit trees on the farm. It used to be like the Garden of Eden out there: figs, walnuts—of course, the black walnuts grow wild, but our ancestors put out English walnuts. Oh, that's something else! We learned that nuts furnish as much protein as meat. Daddy, why did we stop growing peanuts? Jake and Archie say their Ag teacher says cows give sweeter milk from that kind of feed, and we could use our coffee mill to make our own peanut butter. Oh, I'd love that!"

Daddy looked puzzled but pleased. "You young people are just too smart these days. I'm all for that, but be hanged if I can answer some of your questions. I don't even know why we stopped raising peanuts. You make me wish I were out on the farm again. Hindsight's good, you know—easier than looking into the future."

"We'll need to include all this, Snow," Grandmother said, seeming to grow more and more excited. "Oh, I see you are," she said, noting her daughter's pencil was flying. "And Dale, both looking backward and forward are important when put in proper perspective. Take this cookbook. I'm looking over my shoulder at how we substituted molasses for sugar, made stale bread into puddings—right good with spiced-up sauces, just water thickened with flour. And we used to pick dandelion greens, wild mustard, and what about poke salet? Then, there are wild persimmons—cooked down they require no sweetening. Snow, I can see you have more to say, but don't interrupt—not yet. Dale, I'm looking forward, too. Mark my word, there's a great day coming when the seven lean years turn back to the seven fat years—and we'll have learned to do what the Lord wanted us to do all the time, like stop being pigs and have sense enough to look up to see where all those acorns are coming from. Then, unless I miss my guess, there'll be folks who get a hankering for some plain old Depression-style food. Yes, this is the time to glean from grass-root cooking, so now's the time for preserving it! See? I told you, Snow, you've a lot of my blood in those veins. I told you you'd measure up! End of speech. Now daughter, you may speak."

"—Hard Times Cabbage—Pea Sausage—Biscuit Cookies Peggy made—oh, pardon me, Mother—yes, whatever you said was right. Now," she said, laying down her pencil and suddenly looking uncertain, "I—I have something important to ask—or suggest—no, *ask*. So lend me your ears—"

"One minute, your majesty, while I prepare for surgery," Daddy said lightly. He reached into his pocket and pulled out a pocketknife. "I hate parting with this ear, but it's for a good cause."

"Oh Dale, be serious!" Mother said, but she was laughing along with the others. Daddy had a way of helping her relax. For the millionth time Marvel promised herself that in the unlikely event she should change her mind, she would settle for no lesser husband than her father. But then, there would never be so ideal a marriage. . . .

Mother lifted her dimpled chin and burst out bravely, "The ladies must have a meeting place, and I thought that if they could come here—well, we could work on this project."

"I'm a step ahead of you!" Daddy said enthusiastically. "And listen to the radio—right? Well, *how—about—that?* All in favor say 'aye!' All opposed, keep your mouths shut!"

"Aye!" they all shouted at once. The girls could go on with their sewing. The men could bring their bookkeeping, whatever. And couldn't Jake and Archie bring their harnesses and rope ladders for home projects? Yes, *yes*, YES—as long as they were as quiet as mice. *Mice?* The kind you put in pies? They were giddy with joy. . . .

And it kept up. The room bulged, so some sat in the bedrooms and craned their necks. They popped corn in a wire popper over the open flames of the fireplace . . . they worked . . . they *listened* . . . and they prayed together. A new closeness developed. God was not finished with them yet. They dared believe in the future together again—a time when hard times would be overcome . . . tumble down like the walls of Jericho.

Marvel would forever believe God was preparing them for a future that held trials and tribulations undreamed of by mankind.

18

The Unexpected

School was going well. Most students if given the load Marvel carried would consider the burden to be too much. For her it was no burden at all. It was a joy, a challenge, and downright exciting. The secret, known by no one including herself, lay in her fine mind—photographic, as if there were a camera tucked away in her brain enabling her to turn pages rapidly and take pictures. Her excellent memory was the second asset. It enabled her to recall at will. Whatever she needed to remember simply floated back like Wordsworth's "Daffodils" at her bidding, as if she had pushed a button or turned a knob. Highly motivated, she attacked it all with an unshakable faith that she was following the will of God. He had need of her service, whatever it was. Not knowing was an important and exciting mystery. She would know when the time came.

Principal Wilshire shook his head in disbelief, disturbing his heavily oiled and combed back, graying hair and causing it to loosen. "I don't see for the life of me how you do it, young lady," he said, attempting to repair the damage to his hair with his hand. Then, shaking a starched handkerchief to loosen the folds, he wiped his hands. To remove the excess oil or avoid her gaze? "You're taking twice the normal load—all solids—except the Domestic Science. And the way you attack that makes it a solid, too. And yes, here I see you're experimenting at home with recipes. And now you want to add public speaking to debating?"

"Yes, sir. I do. But I *want* to do it."

And then she told him about the recipe book. "I will include my findings in the collection for all to share."

"In addition, you're helping your cousin—oh, go ahead. There's no stopping you. You're bound to be the best this school ever offered Culverville High," Mr. Wilshire said with pride. He met her eyes for the first time. "I will give you the highest of recommendations there—and at college as well. I suppose that comes later?"

"Yes, sir—and I thank you." Marvel smiled then and dared tease this too-serious man, "Please don't be concerned as to whether I'm taking time for fun. It all depends on how we define it, I suppose. *Yes*, I'm enjoying myself—in my own way. Boys are not a part of the picture—not that you would ask. I thank you again."

Marvel offered her hand. He took it uncertainly, seeming incapable of speech.

She walked out thinking: *You don't know half of it, Mr. Wilshire.* Some things are better left unsaid. How she spent her evenings was one of them.

* * *

Those evenings were precious even in present tense. Just how precious would dawn soon enough. For, almost without warning, they were drawing rapidly to a close. But for now miracles were happening.

Grandmother said halfheartedly that she should be getting on to the next of her "dwarfs," as she still called them when speaking to her "Snow White" daughter.

The very mention of her leaving drew waves of protest (when *one* protest would have kept her put!). She must stay and help with the cookbook. Grandmother must help complete the dresses. Then, Grand'mere couldn't leave—simply *couldn't*, Mary Ann cried out and, without thinking, revealed the secret.

"How could we piece together a dress for *you* without you here—oh, me! I've done it—let the cat out of the bag—" and she burst into tears. "Forgive me. I could die, just die—"

Leah Johanna Mier Riley's rich laughter, shining with unshed tears, filled the entire house. "Oh, you wonderful, wonderful family! You make me glad to be alive. I praise the Lord for you!"

The crisis had passed like a summer shower. Grandmother excused herself to make a quick exit to blow her nose. When she returned, in her hand was her violin. Tonight there would be music!

"I'm glad you made me feel so welcome," this surprising lady said. "There's more I need to do—several things on my list. I guess I should give priority to talking with the Squire. He—well, he and I have some unfinished business. Any chance, Dale?"

"Of having my father here? Of course! Now, why haven't I thought of asking him? And come to think of it, Snow, would you have any objection to our including my brothers—or would it be awkward?"

"Why would it be awkward?" Mother wondered aloud. And then and there another miracle was performed. Two nights later Uncle Emory and Aunt Eleanore, together with Duke and Thomas, joined the group. Marvel and Mary Ann covered any hesitation there might have been by talking of school at once. Marvel seldom saw Duke as taking the prescribed number of courses. He had remained behind in Mary Ann's class.

"My, how you've grown!" Marvel said, meaning it. "What have we here—a prizefighter in the making?"

For some reason the idea threw the younger brother into fits of laughter. Thomas rolled on the floor, holding his middle.

His father failed to find it funny. "Get up from there," Uncle Emory ordered. Then answering Marvel, "Duke will go into banking, of course—"

Marvel believed he was about to say something more when he was interrupted by the arrival of her bachelor uncle, Alex Jr. Was it because he was older, having no family himself, felt awkward around children, or a shy personality which made him appear distant? She had never grown to know him very well. But tonight Uncle Alex seemed different—friendlier, eager. It was as if he had a secret—the kind that simply must be shared.

All this she was thinking when Uncle Joseph and Aunt Dorthea with their family crowded through the door. And the entire family seemed to be talking at once. The "entire family" included Squire Alexander Jay Harrington and Leah Johanna Meir Riley, although the two sat apart from the others completely absorbed in each other.

It was like a family reunion—no, a large reception to celebrate their being together, for the entire community was there surely.

Snatches of the conversation began to find its way through the din of voices to reach Marvel's ears. "Congratulations—both of you," Uncle Emory was saying to his brothers. "You did manage to find work at the bank in the county seat? Which of the two banks? I wouldn't have supposed anything was open, but maybe the contacts at the—er—funeral—What's the matter—did I saw something wrong?"

Very wrong apparently. Both men's faces were chalky. They had shifted their gaze as if to study their shoes and, although the uncles were tall men, they seemed to shrink in size.

"I was about to say my son would go into banking—follow my footsteps—when the others here came in," Uncle Emory said. Uncle Joseph laughed bitterly. "Follow *my* footsteps? God forbid! I—I am ashamed—*very* shamed that I—I—"

"Whatever you're doing, Joe old boy," Daddy said warmly, "you have no reason to be ashamed. Any work is honorable. Buck up!"

"That's right," Uncle Emory said. "We're all in the same boat. Yes, we're working in the bank—but not the way you'd expect. Joe here's working in the vault—never seeing the light of day. Might as well be in the coal mines! Me—well, I'm polishing the floors—and feel guilty as all get-out at that. If I'd had any idea they would let the old man—black, of course—go, just to make room for me...And it's leading nowhere," he lowered his voice, "so I might as well give up. I can see now why all those men took one final flying leap off the Empire State Building when the crash came—"

"Gentlemen, take heart," Uncle Alex managed to say casually, although it was obvious that he was having difficulty restraining his excitement. "Russell Brotherton, remember him? Against his better half's wishes, maybe his son's as well for all I know—that's the problem with families from what I observe—no, don't object, men! I should be allowed to tell you this." Then, spacing his words carefully apart, as if to let each one absorb, he continued, "Russell Brotherton hitched a ride to California, keeping it to himself—and—landed—a—*job!*"

Mary Ann had come to stand at Marvel's side unobserved until she breathed an appalled, "Oh no!"

"Doing what—picking cotton? Hitting the fruit harvests?" One of the men asked with a shade of sarcasm.

"Working as a bookkeeper in a bank! The government re-opened banks there—rich because of Hollywood and all the other things that don't have to do battle with nature. For that matter, so's Oregon, our frontier state in a sense but flourishing because of the ports."

Jake appeared out of nowhere. At the sight of Mary Ann's face, he said softly, "I didn't have any choice but to keep still, honey—so please don't be upset. I wouldn't hurt you for the world, but my father made me promise. And I'm not going! Come on, tell me it's okay—that nothing's changed between us. Oh Mary Ann!"

She turned a stricken face to him, her mouth quivering. Then, for the first time, Marvel saw her cousin reach out and embrace the man she planned to marry.

It was hard to concentrate after that touching scene. But Marvel had to hear what her own father was saying. "...so I get desperate sometimes, too. I'm—well, doing janitorial service too—keeping the post office clean, with only an occasional chance now to carry the rural mail. But it's not enough, and there's no word from Worth. The mail still can't get through out there...milk truck can't run...no transportation...Mary Ann, poor kid...keeps a stiff upper lip...but..."

"Can you meet the mortgage here?" Uncle Alex asked.

Daddy's simple one-word answer split Marvel's world in half. "No," he said simply.

Someone had turned the radio on. Immediately, all talk stopped. Oh, what an evening to hear the terrible words of the announcer:

We interrupt this program of Stamps Quartet hymns to bring you this special report. Word just reached us that Bruno Richard Hauptmann, the most hated criminal of our time, the German ex-convict who allegedly entered the upstairs nursery by ladder and kidnapped the infant son of our aviation hero, Charles Lindbergh, has been apprehended and sentenced to death by execution in the electric chair. The nation, which was stunned by this heartless criminal...It is almost frightening to note that our citizens register a sense of satisfaction in news of his forthcoming death. Those of us who continue to cling to the idea that the taking of one life does not justify the taking of a second must ask ourselves if we, in the throes of the terrifying Depression, are becoming heartless—particularly in this, the heartland of America? On the other hand, the heinous crime committed by the alleged kidnapper violated every home in America. And, unless there is a change in our laws, our justice system, *something*, none of our homes are sacred.... We, therefore, must caution that all parents guard their children... double your watch... lest your own child be snatched from your arms... ransom paid... the child's life taken regardless. Repeating: Bruno Richard Hauptmann...

Brother Grady Greer hurried to the console radio and switched the knob to "off." "Let us kneel in prayer," he said.

Archie came in and, noting the situation, dropped to his knees. When he approached Marvel to say, "I need to talk with you," she hardly heard. Nothing would ever be the same. Too many unexpected things had happened.

19

Sacrificial Love

In retrospect, the pieces of the puzzle fit perfectly. And it was good to know the truth. Dale and Snow Harrington were not alone in their financial bind. The other Harrington brothers, although seeking different goals, were losing hope rapidly in a sound future here. Change was inevitable. Just how or when none of them were ready to say. There was so much to consider. But how they could talk...be open with one another...unashamed. How could they have thought otherwise? All this Marvel gathered from their conversation. There was a certain beauty in truth that nothing else could rival.

Mary Ann had heard fragments and Marvel filled her in on the rest. "And before you find fault with Jake—his making no mention of his father's going away—please try and understand the difference. A promise should never be broken, or a sworn secret revealed—"

"I *do* understand," Mary Ann answered softly. "It's just that it means—oh, I don't know what it means! I can't stand the thought of Jake leaving me—"

"Jake isn't leaving. He told you that. And even if his family goes to the Northwest, it will be a long time from now."

Mary Ann nodded. "He *promised*, didn't he? You know, I'm learning a lot—a whole lot. It seems just yesterday when I would have gone into a tantrum like Billy Joe!" She grinned. "Still can't keep my mouth shut though, can I? I mean, I up and let the cat out of the bag to Grand'mere—you know, about her dress? Oh say, I have the funniest little feeling that she wants to look special—I mean special-special. Business, she says—you know between her and our grandfather. They acted so—I don't know how to say it—"

"Don't mince words! They seem to be enjoying one another's company," Marvel laughed. "Yes, there's a kind of mystery."

"Oh, say," Mary Ann changed subjects again, in her usual way. "Do you think your Uncle Alex *is* going to California or 'way up to Oregon or farther? If he does—oh, it scares me—would you?"

"We have no idea what the future holds, Mary Ann. Don't worry about it. God will show us the way in His own time. By the way, did you hear the minister volunteer to help me with some questions on the Bible? Wow! Mr. Wilshire would skin me if he knew. He thinks I overdo."

They both giggled. Subjects closed—both of them: the now and the later of life. The dresses must be finished by midterm. And hard to believe as it was, that was drawing near. The mother-daughter banquet came beforehand. Could Christmas be that close?

Yes, it could. The fact was brought home to Marvel first by way of a sermon by a radio evangelist whose name she had failed to catch. And later the season of winter blew in by way of a "blue north'r," freezing, merciless winds which had no compassion for anything in their path. And those winds spawned the silver-thaw ice storm which closed all the roads again. But much was to take place between the two.

Marvel was busily jotting down questions for Brother Grady Greer after a grueling day at school. The background of uplifting popular songs smoothed away her cares: "Heigh Ho," "Whistle While You Work," and "Some Day My Prince Will Come." Her lids grew heavy and she laid her pencil down on the library table in the living room where she was working and listened to the announcer give the background of the music, which came from the fairy tale but held so much meaning for the Riley family. Just wait until she could tell Mother and Grandmother *this*. Their empty pockets would be filled with joy!

Only Hollywood could do it, ladies and gentlemen. This news is sure to lift the spirits of all who hear—

regardless of our desperation. Perhaps it is exactly what we need, an escape from the awful reality surrounding us—and that which we know one day we must face in dealing with the crisis building in Europe.... We *must* indulge in a bit of dreaming, even fantasizing... and that opportunity comes from Walt Disney's daring, even in the face of scoffers, to put on the silver screen the world's first feature-length cartoon.... Did you hear *cartoon*, but such a beautiful one: *Snow White and the Seven Dwarfs*. Disney has a legion of animators working full-time on completing this magical production, offering a retreat from reality! Meantime, you have just had the privilege of hearing some of the songs featured in this unbelievable production, released for financial reasons—quite simply to promote this fairy-tale movie. They predict that when it is finally unreeled, those of all ages, the young-at-heart, will flock to see it.... Break the piggy bank if you must, but be there! Now we proceed with our regular programming while you out there "Whistle While You Work"!

Marvel picked up her pencil, smiling. Then, thoughtfully, she wrote down the questions which to her seemed some of the most difficult for the layperson to understand. There were people in the great Somewhere outside the realm of Pleasant Knoll who knew nothing of Christianity. Knowing carried a responsibility— the ability of responding in an understandable, concise manner. Brother Greer could help her.

Now how did one answer a question like "How do you know God exists?" or, "Isn't the Bible self-contradictory—one part canceling out the other?" or "Does science dispute the Bible?" Marvel paused. What she had written was fine for the inquiring Christian. But these questions were not the heart of the matter. As the rich young ruler of the Scriptures asked, the basic question was *"What do I do to be saved?"* "Believe... accept Christ as your personal Savior." Yes, but—and suddenly it was clear, so clear that a voice might as well have spoken: *"Without the resurrection, the cross would have no meaning!"*

But there was so much more she needed to know. How and when she would make use of these answers was the unknown, as were all the other subjects she insisted upon learning more about. She recognized only one thing: One day she would use them as a balm to help heal a hopeless society. The greatest problem, in spite of material needs, was the longing for peace. There was despair in the human heart.

And so it was that Marvel Harrington was well-prepared when she commenced her probings with the help of a baffled but able minister....

So absorbed had she become in preparation that the nameless radio announcer was speaking before his mention of the holiday season brought her back to the here and now:

> And as the holy birthday approaches, we are reminded daily of how fragile the balance of world peace is. What a disappointment it must be to the Prince of Peace and His Father Who sent Him. There can be no lasting peace throughout this troubled world until the Prince of Peace returns to establish His kingdom. Christian friends, you will remember that the shadow of the cross hung above the manger then just as the dark shadows hang over our small corner of a troubled world, while the evils of hunger and homelessness gnaw away at the weakening fibers of our faith. But, there was eternal hope in that shadow ... for 'twas the cross which brought promise—promise of eternal life! "Peace I leave with you," our Savior said in farewell before ascending to heaven to prepare for us a place. So be of good cheer, spread the good news—here and abroad! Spread the hope of it to Europe where a madman by the name of Hitler is persecuting Jews and other minorities...to Italy which is under the thumb of Mussolini...to Manchuria...China proper ...as the shadow of another world war deepens. Give the greatest gift of all, the gift of love....So it is a wary Christmas? Obscure those shadows that would cloud the happiness of the great day ahead, for His light still shines and will do so eternally if we share our hearts!

Oh, praise the Lord! The man was right. Some things never change. Christmas was coming—a time when families draw together, when petty differences melt away under the warmth of the day. But there must be love—sacrificial love. And there would be.

20

"For We Know in Part..."

The long, shiny-black car—looking almost sinister—slunk noiselessly by like a monster looking for its victim. At the corner of Elm Street where Marvel (once accompanied by Archie), Mary Ann, and Jake turned toward school, the creature turned, too. And the second time around, it halted in front of the Dale Harrington home—almost—oh, what was *wrong* with her?—as if it had a mind of its own, its victim chosen! Oh well, it was not her concern.

Marvel had hurried home as usual—not to study, however, but to add finishing touches to the four dresses. They *must* be ready for the mother-daughter banquet. Oh, how lovely they were. *How* lovely! Grandmother's, of course, would be her Christmas gift. Did she imagine it, or was it the very loveliest of all? *So* much love had gone into it.

Deep in thought, her needle working against the clock, making the dainty stitches Grandmother had taught her, Marvel was oblivious of the spectacle outside her front window until the back door slammed and Mary Ann rushed breathlessly into the living room.

"Who—what—oh, Marvel, I was scared out of my wits! I was afraid to come in the front door. *Look!*"

Marvel's eyes followed the direction her cousin's shaking finger pointed. What she saw amazed her. So the elegant vehicle *did* concern her. It was parked in front of her home.

Her first reaction was one of curiosity, replaced immediately by a feeling of uneasiness. Something whispered of trouble.

Marvel inhaled deeply to shake off the feeling of apprehension.

"Who is the driver?" she all but whispered. "We know nobody owning a car so menacing-looking."

Mary Ann cautiously moved closer to the window to stand hidden behind a side drape. The new vantage point let her see from a new angle.

"Good grief! I—I can't believe my eyes! Why—what?"

At the sight of Mary Ann's colorless face, Marvel moved to the opposite side of the window, knowing it was rude and hoping they would not be detected. Before she could focus her gaze, the two grandparents emerged in style.

The car was parked in a manner which allowed the Squire to appear first, having occupied the side next to the house. The tall, stately man moved with agility usually reserved for men half his age. He leaned on his cane, Marvel noted, as he stepped on the fender and then to the ground. Afterward, however, the cane *tap-tap-tapped* on the short stretch of concrete and around to the opposite side of the vehicle in a near-prance. Marvel half-smiled, recalling his snort when a contemporary said his windowsills were lined with medications. "Leave just one off and I'd be a goner—you *would* serve as pallbearer?"

Johanna possibly spotted her escort's approach and allowed him to open the door for her. She could be sly on occasion. At any rate, the two of them came back together, her hand tucked lightly through the loop of his free arm. Grandmother's cheeks were pink, her eyes smiling into those of her escort as if he had said something very amusing. They stopped at the driver's window, blocking Marvel's view.

But Mary Ann could see. "Oh, he—the driver—is rolling down his window. *Great day in the morning!*" she gasped, as if having seen an apparition. "It's that—that man you call 'Uncle Fred'!"

Frederick Salsburg.

"What on earth made them do it—go with that crook, that pompous *hypocrite*?" Mary Ann sputtered. "Can you see? Crane your neck and try. Can you see if—if anybody's with him—if he's—"

Marvel's heart began to pound. *"Elmer?"* The very mention of his hateful name caused the gooseflesh of fear to prickle her skin. How foolish. To her cousin, Marvel said, "He can't be—we both know that. He's miles away in that academy—military training—"

Mary Ann's eyes registered surprise. "You should know that animal's capable of anything. He could gnaw his way out of any prison—and that's just what it is. He's just there to escape punishment. You know exactly what I'm talking about."

Yes, she knew—knew only too well. But there was no need in borrowing trouble. Besides, the scene before them had captured her full attention again. Grandmother had turned slightly, enough to reveal that her face had gone from pink to red and her eyes were flashing danger signals. And Grandfather, whom Marvel had never seen angry (although told of his being capable of fury), was shaking his cane like a dog bent on killing a rattlesnake.

The scene ended with lightning speed. Rudely, the window glass rolled up and the car roared away, leaving the two elderly people staring after it in shock.

How rude of him, how crude. But how typical!

The pair who had been the object of Frederick Salsburg's disrespect handled the matter with more grace than Marvel was able to manage. For a moment, they stood like statues. Then Grandfather Harrington lowered his cane and began talking. Grandmother Riley looked up at him almost raptly, nodding in agreement. And their wrath subsided.

When they turned, the warmth of the open fire wrapped around her just to see the glow on the faces of two persons she had come to love so dearly. Momentarily, she—along with Mary Ann—could forget the ugliness which lurked nearby, the *why* of the two grandparents.

"Quick—get Grand'mere's dress out of sight! She hasn't seen it, just knows it's coming for Christmas—" and in mid-sentence, Marvel whisked it away.

Just in time, too. Without bothering to knock, Johanna entered as if propelled by a little breeze and took the Squire's hat and cane.

"Oh, we have the most wonderful idea. You tell them, Squire," Grandmother all but purred as she hurried to hang her guest's belongings on the mirrored hall tree. Marvel noted that she paused to look at her reflection and pat an imagined stray hair in place.

Grandfather smiled almost shyly. Then, as if making a toast, he boomed, "I hereby propose an early Christmas—a time when we return to the real meaning of the word—a time when the holiday was not a commercial orgy...so glitzy...so frantically last-minute...but a time to lock out the false, reaching back into a generation Johanna and I remember—a time to share our time and our love with the people we cherish! Let us not wait until this planet is swallowed by the jaws of greed, the hopelessness of depression, the awfulness of war. Here's to Christmas *now*—now while there remains time!"

Mother and Daddy had entered noiselessly. All were so enthralled by the beauty of the moment that nobody took notice until their voices joined in the chorus of "Here, here!"

The world around them took on a strange feel of unreality. What did it matter if they knew only in part the meaning of all this? For now, it was enough, Marvel decided, to join Paul the apostle and accept that "For now we see through a glass darkly."

Talking rapidly then, the senior members spoke only of the lovely plans they had made, bringing back the delectable torment of wondering just what mysteries and surprises awaited as they "opened packages" verbally and one by one stripped away all the ribbons and bows of meaningless gifts. Their enthusiasm was contagious, making the helplessness of the net of reality from which none of them could escape easier to bear.

"One package is on its way," Grandfather began. "With or without the help of a carrier, the mail must go through! The recipients are none other than your parents, dear Mary Ann. I met Santa in the flesh today—a roly-poly milkman! His name is Bumstead, I think, but you'll remember him as 'The Captain'— remember?"

Yes, she remembered the next-door neighbor on the farm who drove a rattletrap truck when he could afford the ten-cent gasoline. But it was news to her that the Captain had made the lowest bid on the milk route which would begin at the corner connecting his nonproducing farm to their own and traveling to the communities farther away, make a 40-mile swing terminating in Culverville. 'Twas true, Grandfather vouched. He'd made his first trip out today, the road leading straight into town being impassable all this time. But it, too, would open next week.

"You mean—oh Grandfather, you mean—" Mary Ann gasped.

"That's what he means, my child," Grandmother soothed. "Now we all know how lonely it has been for you—and you've been a rock, bless your heart. But this is no time for tears."

"I—I know," Mary Ann said, giving way to a tidal wave of tears. "But—oh, thank you for letting me blow, Grand'mere. These— these—may I blow again? Thank you—you—you're—*hankie again*—you're the one that—who—taught me—about tears— of—of—joy!"

Grandmother was rocking her to and fro in her arms. Marvel decided it was best not to interfere.

"I lost my audience!" the Squire boomed again. "Ah, the mystery of women, wonderful creatures that they are! Dale, will we ever in this world understand them? Here this one doesn't even know what she's crying about. Attention, please!" His eyes were on Mary Ann.

There was silence.

"Much better," he approved. "Now I can tell you that I sent a new set of telephone batteries to Worth and Rae. So keep your ear tuned for a call as soon as that man gets back from his route."

"On a dead 'phone?" Daddy asked, dropping his head.

"*Dead?* Your instrument wasn't dead, just sleeping," his father said, laughing at his own joke. "Make yourself useful. Where's the package, Jo?"

"Here, your majesty!" Grandmother handed him the bundle nobody had noticed. "On second thought, Dale son, *you* take them. Make yourself useful. It's still your house—"

Still? That implied something different, something Marvel put out of her mind. She thought instead of the two sets of telephone batteries. Small, but putting hearts in touch.

All was bedlam then—a lovely kind of bedlam. The men were talking about the government loan which allowed construction of a creamery at the county seat. Now the cream would no longer have need of train service ... good since none was available ... better anyway, as the schedule had been uncertain and the cream, often exposed to the merciless heat of the sun, was spoiled by the time it reached its destination—mostly the ice-cream parlors. Pay would not depend on butterfat content, either. The creamery would accept milk ... income better. ...

Mary Ann conquered her attack of weeping. Now, in a state of near-frenzied excitement, she talked with Marvel of her plans to

sacrifice her precious mite earned from overtime in the principal's office through the NYA. With it, she dreamed, there would
be the cut-outs mentioned on radio—her surprise for Billy
Joe—and (excitedly) for Grand'mere, her Aunt Snow, and her
mother. Yes, they were available by ordering through the newspaper as mentioned on radio. Marvel pointed out that the style
show would be over and the dresses would then be ready, the
surprise part being the finishing touches.

Oh, the idea of an early Christmas was Spirit-filled!

But what was Grandmother saying? The entire family here—
but what about food? Oh, they'd find a way, she and Mother were
agreeing. And with Rae's additional food brought in... Come to
think of it, why not let everyone participate? Each could bring a
dish....

Their voices drifted away and Marvel let her mind see the
remembered sparkle of snow, listen to its crunch, feel the warm
light of candles, and smell the green scent of pine. Surely they
would be able to find an evergreen... and mistletoe... and there
were boxes of worn ornaments... a big Yule log... and all of
them singing carols....

But not to the accompaniment of a violin! What on earth was
Grandmother saying? *A piano!*

"The old upright was in the Baptist church—you surely remember it, Snow?"

Yes, Mother remembered. But how on earth?

"One day we'll go into the details, but *not* until after this early
celebration we plan," Grandmother said firmly. "Just know that
somehow Frederick moved the instrument out before the fire—
almost as if—well, he knew, or smelled fire in advance. I have my
suspicions, but the Squire and I have taken an oath to bridle our
tongues until the time's right. Salsburg claimed he planned to
buy a new one, wanted to store this one at the ranch. No! It's
coming *here*—now, no questions!"

21

Peace—in the Icy Hand of Uncertainty

Auntie Rae called the next day. Always cheerful, she practically curled the telephone lines with her shouts of glee now. Marvel, who answered the telephone, wondered if Mary Ann's mother gave way to wild abandon in an effort to hold back the tears. The long stretch of time she had endured the isolation, the being separated from her daughter—the world, in fact—had to have been trying, almost heartbreaking. Near tears herself, Marvel handed the receiver to Mary Ann.

Mary Ann, laughing and crying simultaneously, caught her mother up on all the recent happenings. Then, as one by one Mother and Daddy talked with Auntie Rae and Uncle Worth, excitement grew. Oh, tell Father Harrington how much, how *very* much, they appreciated the gift of the batteries, Mary Ann's parents begged. And Mother was to tell Grandmother how great it was to have an early Christmas! Yes, it was true—the main road was open now. A giant tree had fallen, knocking out a bridge, but they could ride in with the Captain on his milk route. He had room for the ham Auntie Rae would bring, and for the other goodies, too. And oh, wasn't it wonderful! Mother said later that she honestly thought Auntie Rae could be heard *without* a telephone when told that there would be a piano, but—

And there she stopped. Something was wrong—very wrong. Marvel sensed it. Questioned, Mother said in a puzzled way, "I'm not sure. Her enthusiasm just seemed to give way to something—well, like fear, when told of the circumstances."

"Did she say more, Aunt Snow? *Did she?* You're holding something back. I can tell," Mary Ann said. "It's better to know—"

Mother hesitated. "I believe we agreed to postpone talking about any of this until after the fashion show—and our Christmas," she said, casting an anxious glance over her shoulder at her husband who was talking now with his brother.

"That was only about the piano. And Uncle—no, I will *not* dignify him with that title ever again! If it's going to upset Mary Ann, take away some of the shine of our plans—" Marvel began.

"You're right," Mother said firmly. "We will ask Mother to come right out with the truth. After all, we're all grown up, including you girls who—who (she paused as if to choke back tears) have had circumstances causing me—to lose my baby!" Looking at Marvel, Mother sighed.

Grandmother stepped from her bedroom. "Now, now—don't go sentimental on us, Snow. The Squire and I made a mistake in thinking you all might have trouble handling it. How silly of us—how pompous, self-important. All that and more—to think ourselves capable of—well, chalk it up to thinking experience gave us the corner on wisdom. We should have known better, just two old—"

"Stop berating yourself," Marvel smiled. "The only thing you're guilty of is eavesdropping. You heard every word."

"Of course, I did," Grandmother said, her head held high. "So you want to know about the piano. Well and good. Bear in mind, however, that I can tell you only of Frederick's unpardonable behavior. I cannot explain what's behind it—nothing good, rest assured."

"Tell us!" Mother said almost angrily.

Johanna Riley licked her lips as if half-enjoying herself. "Anon, anon—and, meantime, daughter, you keep a civil tongue. The man's behavior was contradictory, misguiding—well, *you* figure it out. He treated us as if we were made of china. I admit I was impressed, while experience warned of danger. And I think danger *is* lurking nearby.

"Beside the point: you want facts. He took us for a bit of a spin around the town, coming to a stop, naturally, at the site of the fire. That's when he told us about the piano—then became nervous *and* nervy! First, we must ride out to Dale's ranch with him as the piano must—absolutely *must* be taken *there.* When the Squire told him the roads were impassable, he refused to believe it—said we'd try, and began wheedling like a child. Wouldn't we enjoy surprising Worth and Rae? Help them choose just the right place for the piano? Then he'd hire a truck. Well, we were prisoners, absolute *prisoners*. He was going and we were going along, and that was that! All right, let the idiot *try* to get that long, low car a piece of the way. Let him make a total fool of himself!

"Of course, the chance never came, as the workmen stopped him long before we got there. Would you believe (she lowered her voice as if to keep the men, still on the phone, from hearing) he *threatened* those laborers—WPA workers, they were. Said he had a handgun in the side-flap of the door—and I don't doubt it one bit! *But* nobody ran, his bluff was called. So what a time he had trying to turn that monster of an automobile around—had to eat crow and accept help of the very men he'd threatened. Alexander—the Squire, that is—forgot our apprehension and enjoyed his having to eat his words!

"All the way back, he ranted senselessly about having to get that instrument out of sight, then asked if he could bring it to *this* house temporarily. Later he would make other arrangements—get it out to the farm, and it had to be *soon*! So there you have it—oh, except that he changed tactics then, drove back to the church, questioned us to see if we had *any* idea how the fire started, eyeing us strangely. No, we didn't. So he went to work trying to buy the property where the Baptist church once stood. Both of us refused. You saw the rest, I know you did—how he drove off so rudely. But why does he want to get the piano out of his house? Almost like he's *hiding* it. And I still wonder how he came to have it—"

Mother's face was ashen. "I—I don't know," she whispered. "But something fits together here. I just feel it. You wanted the truth, Mary Ann—you've a right to it. Your mother says—oh, this is hard to say—but she says the children out there, you know, Sula Mae and Casper, kept up their stories about the devil until Billy Joe was having nightmares. She was ready to take them to task when she saw the strange creature with her own eyes—and—and he was ready to light a fire, spotted her and ran away with an unearthly scream, disappearing down in the bottoms. Oh, I don't know about any of this—who, how?"

Daddy had hung up the receiver, obviously having heard none of the conversation. But something else was troubling him. Marvel could always tell by the way the little blue vein on his left temple enlarged and pulsed more rapidly. She waited, hoping Mother noticed, too. She did.

"What's wrong, darling?" Mother asked outright.

Given no time to think after talking with Uncle Worth, he blurted out the truth. "No parity. Worth decided to leave off the number of acres allowed—those devoted to cotton under the program. Said cotton prospects looked so poor anyway—rumors saying 'Cotton is no longer king—' "

"So?" Mother encouraged continuation.

"So without the parity—almost no cotton prospects without rain, just the bottomlands—there's nothing. No hope—"

"Stuff and nonsense," Grandmother interrupted. "There's *always* hope. You have a job. Oh true, not to your liking, but we're all making do these days. It's only temporary. So perk up, Dale, son. One thing's certain: That man in the White House knows what he's doing. He'll make sure nothing like this happens again. We *will* learn from it!"

"That's what we said when the world war ended. And now while we are haunted with today's starvation, the prospect of another one, maybe bigger, hovers over Europe—and we'll get involved."

Grandmother stoked the fire needlessly, sending up a shower of sparks. "Now, now," she said crisply, "that doesn't sound like the man my daughter married. Where's your faith?"

"On death row."

Mary Ann was sobbing noiselessly. "There's—th—th (she tried to say between hiccups) m-*milk*—ex-cuse me—route."

"Not enough for your folks to live on," Daddy gritted out. "Oh, forgive me, all of you. It's just that it all gets to be too much sometimes. I guess we danced too soon!"

"We did not!" It was the first time Marvel had spoken. "You lost the job Grandmother was talking about. I heard you tell Uncle Worth. But we planned a nice Christmas and *we're going to have it!*"

"Come here, infant," Daddy said softly. "Come here and let Daddy give his girl a big bear hug."

"And wipe your noses—every one of you!" Grandmother commanded. "Want red noses to make you look like Mrs. Claus

Wednesday night for the fashion show? We have a million things to do before then. And Dale, you men are going to have to buckle down and help. We need some strong arms. *Then* we're ready for that early Christmas!"

Oh, it would be a glorious one, they all agreed. There would be evergreens . . . a tree . . . and just wait and see what Rae was bringing from her overflowing storm cellar. . . .

Storm cellar. "Oh, dear Lord, help me!" Marvel's heart cried out in terror.

Then she squared her shoulders. Peace! They could and *would* have it. God offered it and they must accept His gift by rising from this valley of despair to stand on the peak of His love!

22

Medals, Scars, and Unhealing Wounds

The Harringtons, Pleasant Knoll, east Texas in general—in fact, the entire state—was not through learning. Time had not finished with its trial by fire. Instead, it had assigned to them the cruelest of all teachers: experience. They had seen only the beginning of horror. But God, in His infinite wisdom, knew the end from the beginning—and on their side He placed the gold medallion of love.

The media did its best to emphasize the government's great strides in attempting to alleviate mankind's suffering—no longer making mention of the ghost towns and the once-solid citizens who now, haunted by fear of starvation, had become the unwanted, the avoided, the modern-day lepers. The announcers had accepted it in stride—perhaps accepting the financial crisis as a way of life. They concentrated instead on life the way they wished it were, not the way it was.

And so the beautiful carols filled the living rooms of those who had radios, and the commercials carried the undertone of triumph as if Wall Street had never been and the good old days were back to stay:

> To the countless number of us who grew up in a stagnating world—knowing no difference because our parents before us were too inexperienced, too young, or too blind to teach us—we can see now that the crash on Wall Street was inevitable ... that it had

to come in order for us to get our values straight. What's more, we must see to it that such a thing never happens again, that there are no more fickle times like those of the so-called Roaring Twenties—and we *will*! Why? Because we are wiser, more sophisticated, and have learned from our mistakes. One might say, then, that the Humpty-Dumpty fall of the stock market was not without value. In fact, it carried a magical catharsis—yes, a real purification! Look at the black-and-blue of the initial shock in comparison to the red-green world of Christmas around you and see the stars of accomplishment to further our rejoicing. Franklin Delano Roosevelt has not only set America on its feet, in so doing he has found a way to make it more productive, more sanitary, and more beautiful! You *know* what the CCC is doing to make men out of boys...and some of you have had the opportunity to participate in the marvelous opportunities offered through PWA, another ingredient of FDR's jokingly called "alphabet soup." Through this, those qual-ified—or we might say gifted—find a dignified way in which to offer the fine arts of their skill to those who have missed such luxuries. Yes, millions of us fall into those masses. If you feel that you are among those who could share your talents, say, by teaching music—any instrument—teaching art...

Marvel, putting the finishing touches on the last wreath, missed the announcer's instructions on how to apply. Wouldn't you know that on the fifth circle of pine greens (with cones), mistletoe, and wild holly (every minute twig strung by glowing, red-cheeked berries), she would prick a finger, drawing blood as red as the berries? With an "Ouch!" she stuck the finger in her mouth, bit hard, and—alas!—that prevented her from getting the entire story. Grandmother with her music (and she sus-pected her mother was equally skilled), Auntie Rae's beautiful punchwork—oh, so many things...there was so much to tell. What a beautiful gift right here at Christmas. Marvel paused. Not that she agreed with all the man said about the national econ-omy. "Get thee behind me, Satan!" she ordered, speaking more to herself than to the forces of darkness. "This is Christmas!"

Voices told her that the entire family was home from the grueling schedule they had kept since Mary Ann's family arrived of filling the house with foods, packages, and yes, laughter! They had been in too much of a hustle-bustle to waste time on negative thoughts. The phrase came back as it had so often: *no time for tears*. And this time it was literally true.

"Well girls, let's get supper going quicklike! Tonight's try-on time here at home, then the big dress rehearsal at school!"

Grandmother's reminder brought a squeal from Mary Ann. Marvel had never seen her more excited. Silently, she prayed that nothing would spoil that mood.

Making her own voice sound happier than she actually felt inside, Marvel pointed to the wreaths. "All finished!" she said. "And the streamers are wound and ready. Daddy, where are the big, red fluted bells we used to have—the ones that open?"

"Up in the attic," he said, holding a hand to his back and faking a moan. "Here we go again, Worth. I'll need a hand—*two* hands," he grinned, "and a ladder."

Supper was of simple fare, mostly leftovers with Grandmother's crispy-brown cornbread sticks. No time for dessert. Let cornbread and sweetmilk do. Fine, fine. Nobody cared. Excitement—not food—furnished their energy. They weren't going hungry yet. And when the wolf did come—although the likelihood was shut out temporarily, inevitable as it was—food was as close as any neighbor's back door.

Marvel went back into the kitchen to bring a fresh supply of cornbread. The others were too busy talking to miss her. Too busy, too, to hear the rattle of the back screen. Mrs. Autrey had hurried between the two houses. Quick! Did Marvel have an extra "poke" (her word for a brown-paper sack grocers used to furnish)? Her new neighbor would be embarrassed if he knew she was here, but they couldn't help finish preparations for the big style show without—without something to serve to keep his feet off the ground, half soles being beyond their reach right now.

"I can do better than that," Marvel said understandingly. "What about cardboard? Mary Ann's folks packed some things in old shoe boxes."

The woman was pathetically grateful. She hurried back home after asking Marvel to please keep this between the two of them. Peg Autry need not have asked that of her. The last thing Marvel wished to do was make even a tiny suggestion of the closing in of the Great Depression. Understandably people were unable to afford doctors and dentists. But innersoles for shoes? It was frightening....

"Well, thank goodness, we got the men from underfoot," Grandmother said as the last decorations were on their way to the school. "Now, where are the dresses?"

"Spread out on my bed waiting for your inspection. Oh Grand'mere, just wait. *No*, don't wait! Hurry!" Mary Ann was too excited to finish. Instead, she all but flew to fling her bedroom door open wide. "You first!"

"Me? But I— you—the rest of you go on. The style show's for you."

But her protest was feeble. Anybody could see she would split at the seams if she didn't do as she was told. "Oh, my goodness gracious sakes alive! I never in my born days...oh, oh, oh!"

And with tears streaming down her face, Leah Johanna Mier Riley grabbed her finished dress, pressed it to her face in a genuine embrace, and ran her fingers lovingly over each detail. Then, as impetuously as a girl in love, Grandmother held the dress next to her still-shapely body and whirled about the room, stopping to admire her reflection in front of the full-length mirror. "Oh, I love the color. I love the way the ruffles caress my face like tulip petals—and the pink is just my color. And I love all of *you*! Oh, it has been years since—say, what do you think the Squire would think? Oh—"

Mother, Auntie Rae, Mary Ann and Marvel burst into laughter when the older woman clapped a hand over her mouth. The laugh brought her out of her state of euphoria. She was all business, brusque in manner in order to hide her embarrassment.

Clapping her hands for attention, Grandmother ordered: "All right, we've wasted enough time. Get into those mother-daughter dresses and let me see you walk. Keep it natural, walking the way you'll walk down that ramp. Shake a leg and get yourselves into those glad rags!"

Shake a leg? Glad-rags? Amused, the others obliged. Imagine Grandmother Riley using that modern slang.

"Straighten up, ladies! Lift your shoulders, tuck in that tummy and buttocks. Now walk like that. Marvel, relax the shoulders just a bit, honey. There, you have it. Mary Ann, once more. Wait, I believe you'd better try walking with this book on your head. Very good, very good, winners every one of you. So remember to walk like winners! Better yet, think of yourselves as queens. That's what the good Lord intended—queens of our households. So get your crowns straight. Oh, beautiful. Oh, I envy you—I—I—forget that. I'm happy just to be a spectator."

Marvel understood. Then and there she made a decision.

* * *

The night of the style show would stand out in Marvel's memory forever just in fragments—almost frighteningly beautiful impressions—so real and yet so unreal that they folded into a mosaic of sounds and color. It was a moonless night, but the air was so clear and crisp that the stars seemed to hover close to earth. Someone was playing a violin softly to the accompaniment of a player piano turned to "soft" that without anyone's aid automatically near-hummed the well-known carols.

Marvel recalled in her red-and-green-touched recollections thinking that perhaps Grandmother was the only person around who could have played the upright piano left at their home. But she was unavailable!

Residents of Pleasant Knoll sat up to rub their eyes in disbelief when Mother Snow Harrington and Daughter Marvel Harrington *and* Grandmother Leah Johanna Riley were announced by the narrator, Eleanor Harrington, who had agreed when invited by Mrs. Sutheral. Tonight Aunt Eleanor *was* pleased. After all, here was third-generation of the community. And while she may have wished a daughter for herself, two sons were quite an accomplishment. She had wondered, of course, who made the delightful arrangement.

Marvel read the thoughts in the face of Uncle Worth's wife. Then there was no time remaining for thinking. Only she and Miss Marlow need ever know of the small conspiracy between them....

The quiet beauty of the extravaganza was broken by the startling shock of a cane pounding on the auditorium floor, its measured beats rivaling those of a drum. Silence. Then Squire Alexander Jay Harrington lifted his cane as well as his voice in a

"Bravo! Bravo!" at the exact moment Grandmother walked down the ramp, bowing and smiling at an admiring audience.

The audience, following the highly respected gentleman's lead, rose for a standing ovation. It was as if, carried away on the wings of fantasy, this were a celebration indeed. The crowd had become revelers. Singing along with the background music happily, all seemed to be drifting into another world. Candles flickered... and the scent of evergreens was almost intoxicating. Let strangers come, but not to change them.

These were their people—a part of themselves at their best. And they were proud, *proud*, PROUD. Marvel felt the miracle of it all ripple along her spine. And a vision came—or was it a memory of something that happened so long ago she was unable to remember it clearly? Here was America's heartland, not as it was, but as it should be: rolling green hills of natural grassland dotted by contented cows chewing their cuds lazily beneath the native sweet gum trees aflame with color. *One day...*

More cheers! The third-generation group had won first place, with Mary Ann and Auntie Rae a close second. Medals... *and* each to receive a bolt of goods. But Marvel's eyes had lost their vision, seeing instead two faces. Oh no!

23

The Kaleidoscope of Shifting Emotions

"Where did you disappear to?" Mary Ann, smiling rapturously, asked.

"Oh, you noticed? I thought you had eyes only for Jake. I needed to be here on hand when all of the family comes. And besides—"

"Besides, you wanted to be ready for your own admirer! Oh, I saw him in the crowd. You know he's in love with you. Oh Marvel, this is the happiest night of my life. Yes, of course, Jake's coming—is here, in fact. The two of them came together. You *did* see him? You look so startled. What's wrong, Marvel? Why do you look so strange?"

Mary Ann was genuinely concerned.

"You mean Archie?" Marvel managed, hoping it was instead of—

"Who else? Silly! Oh, I think I understand. You weren't expecting to see him. Of course not—that was the point, his wanting to surprise you. And I can see he did."

Had she even known he was gone? Marvel couldn't remember. Maybe he had told her. If so, she had forgotten. So much had happened.

She inhaled deeply. Obviously, Archie had wanted to be here for the mother-daughter banquet. And from the sheer shock of seeing that other face, she had come home without waiting for the big meal the Agriculture class was to have prepared. Was she the only one to have seen that face—that other face—in the audience? Oh, she couldn't have imagined it. Elmer Salsburg was there! He was cruel, ruthless, selfish—and, like an animal in wait, biding his time to have revenge. He, she realized with a jolt, was like his father.

What was Mary Ann saying? That the stoves did not work? That instead of the banquet at the school, neighbors would be bringing their food here—including the boys in class? That's what Jake was attending to, putting all the chicken stew in big granite pans. So her cousin could understand the need to get home. She would put the tables together. By then the boys would be inside...and, oh Marvel, she *knew* how excited she must feel....

Marvel turned to the kitchen. "I'll get the fixings for half-moon pies—use some of Auntie Rae's green tomato mincemeat. I—I think Miss Marlow sent along raisins. They would add flavor," she said, hoping that her voice did not shake as badly as her hands.

"*Dee*-licious," Mary Ann bubbled. "And let's make some of those old-fashioned peanut patties. They melt in your mouth, but we had to wait (she paused to giggle) until the 'goobers' came. That's what Billy Joe calls 'em—got that from Sula Mae and Casper. These were brought in from Oklahoma."

"My goodness, look at all that food—all packaged. Was it all a part of the so-called awards? Well, how gracious—and we'll share it."

"Here they come—all of them!" Mary Ann became so excited she caught up the skirt of her new dress and wiped a plate free of possible dust. "Oh, my sakes, what am I doing?" she gasped, almost dropping the dish in her excitement to pull Jake inside with Archie on his heels holding the great containers. "Right on in the kitchen. Oh, come in, come in!"

Suddenly everybody was inside. And again the evening took on a dreamlike quality. All Marvel could remember distinctly afterward were the din of happy, excited voices, the grabbing of both her hands by an Archie she would never have recognized, and her own anxious watching of the windows wondering: *Could I have been wrong about Elmer?*

"Yes—yes, of course, I will see you again, Archie," she promised. "You said two weeks—then join us here for Christmas," Marvel said. "Early Christmas."

The idea of an "early Christmas" held everyone spellbound. It was preordained from the beginning that it was intended for all of Pleasant Knoll. A "family affair"? Wonderful! They were *all* family. Invitations were unnecessary. It was more a matter of who would take what—like one of their regular get-togethers, only better. It was *Christmas*, a time for celebrating the holy birth, a time for *love*, brought from a Savior who sacrificed His life for our sins— the greatest gift ever given to mankind... a Light in this world of darkness.

So suddenly it was Christmas once again. Early December was just right. Wasn't love such as His intended for always? It all seemed very logical, especially this year. For there would be no frenzied shopping, no madness of baking holiday cookies when there were no ingredients, no frantic making of Christmas lists when they had no money with which to purchase gifts, no standing in line to mail cards and packages either. Just making-do and sipping from their overflowing cup of love.

And just as suddenly, Marvel felt lifted aloft to that other world along with them. There was no snow, but she could hear its remembered crunch—out on the farm, wasn't it, when seemingly she had had all the time in the world to share with Mother and Daddy? There was no hurry-hurry, just a blending of the generations—as there was tonight. There had been no economic pinch then. And now she found herself not allowing it to matter. It was into a world of want and need that the Baby Jesus came to seek... and to save.

This moment seemed sufficient unto itself, and that was as it should be—especially at Christmas. This group had seen the "star," and in their own way were making their way to Bethlehem of Judea. Grandmother, looking much like a pastel angel, was coaxing out Christmas-touched, mystical notes from her violin. Accompanying her at the piano was another Christmas miracle: *Mother!* And one of the neighbors had joined in, her fluty soprano trilling on the high notes.

"A community sing!" Grandfather demanded, standing near the piano. Never had the carols sounded so beautiful in Marvel's ears. She listened with appreciation before joining.

A kaleidoscope seemed to shift and all the colored particles fell into a different pattern. The room was filled with spice and laughter. And the serving table, when she looked at it, overwhelmed her. Why, there was a feast spread before them—foods born of creativity, all recipes coming from the cookbook the ladies were putting together. Marvel moved to help, bringing out her own half-moon pies, here again by popular request, and readied the coffee.

"Brother Greer, will you ask the blessing for us?" Daddy, the gracious host, asked.

Grady Greer obliged with a brief, but touching prayer.

After a chorus of "Amen's," Dale Harrington shouted: "All right, fall in and feed your faces!"

From that moment, the noise became deafening. And not one complained. In fact, each seemed to attempt to outtalk the rest—and to add to the confusion of sounds, someone had turned on the radio. The announcer's voice wafted through a crack in conversation to reach Marvel's ear, his tone as bubbly as the product he offered:

So—go pour yourselves a glass of Pepsi, the drink of tomorrow! Compare prices, compare ounces, share that news, and share that cola refreshment. There's more in that bottle than one person can hold! Go ahead—make sure it's straight from the ice box. Ummm, taste that goodness? You have done more than *seen* the future, you've *tasted* it! Now, not *back* to the news but *on* with it. For better times are coming—you can taste it, you know—yes, radioland, a time when you say to one another, "What depression?" I can see a reverse of migration as our people flood no more into the urban areas but go home to their heritage in the smaller communities or, the lucky ones, to their farms and ranches! It is rich with promise, that land—a place where a man can be his own man, a place where Americans can reap from what they sow, enough for themselves, enough for this country, enough to feed this entire world. A place to regain identity, commune with nature, find pleasure in life that our founding forefathers found before us, that indeed the best things in life are free, or nearly so. Let's repeat the headlines regarding the militant labor unions who are threatening to sit down on their jobs unless the demand is met to create a five-day workweek and the

> exciting news that oil has been discovered in east
> Texas—another inducement to the rural areas—

The exuberant voice trailed off. Nobody heard more of the labor unions' "foolishness." No man in his right mind would refuse to work once he landed himself a job! But now, this oil business—well, it was worth looking into. Mankind! That black-gold might be just waitin' to slosh down the middle of Pleasant Knoll. Or, was it best to keep mum? Was money *that* important... bringing in, well, all kinds? Look at the crime in big cities.

Marvel's mind was subdividing a million places at once, some of her ideas sending chills along her spine, while others held her heart in a warm clasp. The overall feeling remained: a certain pride in her own—a knowing that come what might, Pleasant Knoll would remain the "Hometown, America" the announcer had described. It would retain its traditions, one of them being eternal optimism which sprang from hope, faith, *belief* in themselves, in each other, and in a risen Lord. Nothing could alter that. Hadn't they proved that in the present situation? It was all hard to understand. Why try when even the men who called themselves "experts" were confused? Oh, nobody bought new cars or fancy clothes. But the clothes made no difference. She found herself thinking that it would be nice if their old car were repaired, gasoline cheap as it was. Oh well—

Maybe an auto repair shop would go in one day. Meantime, she forced her mind back to reality. How comforting that the people surrounding her had allowed neither Depression-time blues nor the government's attempts to patch up the wounds it was supposed to have cured, only (according to some) to make them deeper. Tough years? Undeniable. But they themselves were tough in fiber, with an ingrained peace that went along so well with this beautiful season....

"Marvel!"

The sound of Mary Ann's voice jolted her out of the world of thoughts. "Oh!" Marvel said, almost startled to find her cousin, Jake, and Archie still at the side table where the four of them had decided to take their trays. "I was just enjoying a moment's quietude."

"In this babble? That would be a strain on my imagination!"

"That's why she's so smart—thinkin' like she does," Archie defended Marvel's statement to Mary Ann. "An' still readin' I betcha," the boy directed the last words to Marvel.

"When I can work it in. It has been a busy year. Mr. Wilshire will vouch for that. I must speak to our principal. I see him being nice to Old Mag. Have you had a chance to talk with him, Archie—tell him all your accomplishments, just let him see how you've muscled out? You look so nice with that short haircut and the forest-ranger-colored uniform."

"Olive drab's the color. I wonder what a ripe olive looks like on the tree and what the tree looks like. We just might be goin' out of state. But it'd be just like 'em to send me back to Oklahoma where all that dust is blowin' everything away—'dust wind' the farmers left breathin' enough t'stagger out tell us. And me wantin' to go to California. Still, I'm guessin' them Okies'll be goin' there."

"*Okies?* Do they like being called that, Arch?" Jake asked.

Archie's face colored above his olive-drab shirt. "Ain't likely. But they're used to it, I'm guessin'. Ever'body calls *us* 'Tex.' Never got around to likin' it, but," he sighed, "just kinda got used to it."

Marvel, feeling empathy for him, reached out and touched his calloused hand lightly. "Don't mind too much, Archie," she smiled. "Several of the cowboy singers who are forming groups are taking the name of Tex-this-and-that. But I understand how you feel. While those fellows wear the name with pride and select or compose songs about our state, it's different being—well, lumped together—"

Archie's eyes brightened. "Yeah," he said, "like we was the cattle—that's it—cattle, ready t'stampede. I can feel one comin'—nearly taste th' dust."

"Be happy, Archie," Mary Ann said with a hint of a plea in her voice. "It's Christmas, and everything's going to work out. Just look how happy everybody else is—even planning for next year."

There was a pause in the conversation. It was long enough to hear someone asking Grandmother and Mother if they had heard about that new government program to teach music? If so, most all of the ladies wanted to take lessons. And, oh yes, there was pay for it!

While the womenfolk talked about music and other things this wonderful man in the White House was doing for "culture," their men were planning ahead for a community garden. Wells were getting low due to lack of rainfall, but they would share water to give plants a drink. It would be a good idea to find who had saved which seed from times when gardens had more nutrients. Fertilizer? Nothing better than barnyard manure. Farmers would share—

"See?" Mary Ann said triumphantly.

Archie saw. From then on, he talked of all the skills he was mastering. Some people thought that the CCC guys only learned about the forest, but there was so much to learn. Some of the camp bosses had learned that he had a skill, called it an "apti—apti-aptitude" for fixing motors, engines, and all that. He could get Mr. Dale's Essex goin' in no time a'tall. Fact was, he just might think about puttin' up an auto body, fender, radiator shop—besides just engines. He could do the whole works providin' he could find a pardner.

He looked inquiringly at Jake. But Jake shook his head and said with a grin, "Sorry, pardner, and thanks for the compliment. However, I still have my own personal dream. We come from a long line of bankers, you know. Now, settling *here* appeals to me. Mary Ann and I love and understand the community. But I am willing to go almost anywhere, as long as we can be together and I can find my life work."

Mary Ann looked as disappointed as Archie. "But couldn't you just think about the advantages? You remember that song about fortunes always hiding? I remember the name, I think. Isn't it 'I'm Forever Blowin' Bubbles'?"

"Bubbles bust," Archie said, almost sullenly.

Mary Ann nodded and sang what she obviously felt was proof:

> They fly so high they nearly reach the sky,
> Then, like a *dream*, they fade and die. . . .

Marvel, hearing a knock, excused herself and stepped to the front door and, standing in the shadows, opened it with a smile on her face. That smile faded like her cousin's dreams.

For there stood Frederick Salsburg. She was stricken dumb.

"Not enough," he hissed through gold teeth, "to know I'm the uninvited guest. Now you refuse to invite me inside. My son's right. You're a snob like the rest of the Harrington clique. And here's one branch of them living in *my* house, might as well face it. Well, the more I see of this family, the more I realize that I am more of a friend to the Almighty than to mankind—*no* friend to human beings actually!"

"I would question that such a thing can be," Marvel whispered. "We have had this conversation before. I don't know why you're here."

"Why, to bring you a gift! Fireworks are a tradition," he said in mockery, thrusting an explosive package into her hands. All seemed to ignite....

24

Discoveries

Marvel managed to stand beside her parents and shake hands or accept embraces from their departing friends. She even managed a smile to go along with theirs, while self-consciously holding the so-called "gift" (so frightening and repelling, the hateful package was) behind her. Maybe nobody would discover her secret. Then what on earth could she do with it?

Meantime, would this evening never end? Neighbors were in no hurry to leave the party and seemed to linger on as if to stop the clock, hold this warmth, savor each second. Jake and Mary Ann were in deep conversation in a secluded corner of the living room; and, Archie, under the pretext of waiting for his friend, was among the last to take leave. At last he made his way to where Marvel stood.

"You look tired—plum tuckered out. And no wonder!" Archie sympathized. "I—I wanted to—well, ask you to—uh—take a walk."

Archie looked down at his shoes and was unable to go on.

"This was a busy time, you're right. You said you would be here two weeks. There will be another evening and," she smiled, meaning the words, "a walk sounds nice."

"But I had a present—"

A present? He shouldn't have. Still, there were his feelings to consider. "Not too much—we'll see." Then she added, "But it was thoughtful. You must excuse me now. I must say good night to some other people. And Billy Joe is tugging at my skirt."

"And what a pretty skirt!" Embarrassed, Archie rushed away.

Marvel exhaled in relief and turned quickly to her small cousin, fearing that he had hold of the fireworks. "Don't you want to play? There are some other children by the tree."

"I saw 'em—I want to see *you*. You didn't see my *Little Books* and they're magic! See how they pop up like—like this. Open and see there? A dwarf came to life," the little boy giggled, "like a jack-in-the-box. An' there's a mean ole wicked witch—"

There was no way to dismiss Mary Ann's brother and he was sure to demand attention if she tried. Billy Joe was tired and apt to get loud. That would attract more attention. But how?

The question was answered. Someone else would dispose of the package for her. For suddenly it was removed from her nerveless hands—slowly, gently—almost, Marvel thought for a panicky second, as if to do so without her knowing.

And then she heard the familiar voice. In a low-pitched tone it was hard to hear what Grandfather Harrington was saying. "I guess that no-good thought he could pull one over on me! Well, I'm not in my dotage yet—not past outfoxing the likes of that rattlesnake, taking advantage of a young lady. But then, how *can* a rattler be a *gentleman*?"

"What does it mean?" Marvel whispered back.

He was silent until the thinning crowd was gone. The house was emptied except for immediate family—namely, Mary Ann's folks and her own. Mary Ann, still starry-eyed, led a protesting Billy Joe to dreamland with the promise of a story. Mother, Grandmother, and Auntie Rae were clearing away dishes left in the living room. Daddy and Uncle Worth were talking soberly before lending a hand.

Grandfather, who remained beside Marvel, picked up the conversation where they had left it.

"I think you know the answer to your question. While it has been our tradition—once was, back when we had money to throw around—to have fireworks at Christmas, Frederick Salsburg brought these as a reminder that your father, supposedly, is as poor as a church mouse! And, speaking of church, I heard Salsburg claim friendship with the Lord! A mockery, a real mockery—he'd be the Almighty's worst enemy. Claiming indeed, as he did to your lovely grandmother, that he planned to build a magnificent church where the Baptist church once stood."

Alexander Jay Harrington snorted, rapped the carpeted floor with his cane (thankfully deadening the sound), and continued. "I despise virtuous villains!"

"What are you saying?" Marvel managed, suspicion beginning to roll in like a quickly forming cloud bank.

"That he came to serve notice to vacate to Dale and Snow, saw me making my way to you and, like the coward he is, made haste to disappear. A gift? Pig's eye! Why, that robber, that thief—and worse! I have never doubted that he murdered his wife, burned those buildings, and— You look shocked. Your face is stricken. This can't be news—"

"I'm confused—not sure. And there's no proof he—"

"No *proof*!" Grandfather's voice had risen. "No proof, but we *know*. Maybe he didn't do it, but he masterminded it all, and will slip through the fingers of the law and go free—like that simpleton son he had to do it for him! I'd kill a rattlesnake, and I—"

Daddy was beside them. "What is it? What's happened?" He put his arms about Marvel's shoulders, but she was unable to stop shaking.

Marvel willed Grandfather with all her heart to keep the unwelcome visit to himself. But he told every detail while she listened in disbelief.

When Daddy spoke, his voice was flat and expressionless. "Did you tell the man he was trespassing?"

Marvel shook her head.

"In a way he isn't—" Grandfather acknowledged, his voice subdued. "He'll make good his threat and—"

"That doesn't excuse him!"

The two of them talked on. Marvel wished it were all a bad dream from which she would awaken. But the conversation continued, Uncle Worth joining in. They would have to be prepared. It was good, her father was saying, that they had talked about the possibility of their sharing the house on the farm. Only there would be so much to work out—that is, if it were possible—

Marvel, still unable to speak, felt another's presence And there stood Mother, her face fixed with fear and loathing.

"We can't. You know we can't. It's out of the question!" Marvel had never heard her mother's voice sound like that. It was as sharp as broken glass. "Marvel is *not* going to be taken out of school. Nothing in the world can make me move away! Say it isn't so—*say* it," she shrieked.

"How can I promise, Snow, my darling? Don't you know it's tearing my heart out?" Daddy looked at each of them helplessly.

Marvel's heart bled for them. Oh, what could she do? What could she say to comfort them? That is, if she could speak. *A sacrifice of love!* The words came back to haunt her. She could agree to the move if that would help. But she could not build a school.

Everything happened quickly—so quickly there was nothing, absolutely nothing, she could do to stop it.

Daddy had promised Mother that somehow they would manage without a move. Grandfather was telling of the horrible part—all about his suspicions, and then the entire group was involved... talking... *talking*... TALKING.

Mary Ann came back from tucking Billy Joe in bed. She must have left the door open and heard every word, for now the worst of all possible things happened. Her cousin blurted out all about Elmer....

* * *

The plans seemed unfinished when the Worth Harringtons left—unfinished and unclear. The parting was an emotional one. What was there to say? The fact that December twenty-fourth and twenty-fifth were yet to come made the good-byes harder.

"How did we manage without tears?" Marvel asked Grandmother as the two of them stepped aside from the remaining Harrington brothers and their father. The entire family had come to see Uncle Worth and Auntie Rae off in the Captain's milk truck.

"Long years of practice, bearing up. 'The hard grip of steel,' this thing called organized labor calls it—not that we in these parts can go along with that bushy-eyed rabble-rouser, John L. Lewis! We do face up to our problems and take them on in the same way—you understand? Like a handful of Goliaths, we meet the giant-sized situations and see beyond them. And then, dear Marvel, we're the victors! You're a born thinker. Experience has done the rest. So you understand?"

"I—I guess so," Marvel said, wishing she did.

"Of course you do! Well, they're out of sight. How kind of Mr. Bumstead to drive by here. They made it. No tears. Now breathe deeply, and feel happiness. Smile just for the sheer exhilaration, excitement, and balance between mind and body, human beings and our Creator—for survival."

"And survive we will!" Grandfather declared, as he joined the two of them. "I anticipate a change, yes, but in the long run it's going to be for the better. You girls wait and see! I can foresee my sons getting back into banking where they belong. And look at *me*—fit as a fiddle thanks to your grandmother here, Grand-daughter. Remember all that foul-tasting medicine? Gone—all gone. Who needs medicine? And when that Salsburg—my step-son I hate to admit—comes to this house, I'd like to meet him myself! He can do this thing *legally*, but morally?"

"Who ever accused Frederick the Great of possessing *morals*?" Grandmother asked tartly.

"He'll wish he did by the time I'm finished with him. So get that medicine back out for another patient! Yep, just wait until Alex-ander Jay Harrington, Esquire meets him—"

"I'll meet him myself!" Daddy growled. Then he lost the sud-den show of bravado. Wilting like Mother's flowering moss in the hot sun, he said helplessly, "But what is there to do?"

"You can meet him!"

"Yes father. I can meet him."

But when the papers were served the following day, Frederick Salsburg was nowhere in sight. A stranger, identifying himself as an official representing the county (and proving his identifica-tion) served the notice to vacate. A process server, the ID called him.

Marvel prayed for a long time that night that her father would make the right decision.

* * *

Mary Ann was unduly quiet the next day. Perhaps her unnatu-ral silence was due to missing her parents. Or it might have been that she was afraid of being scolded for telling the secret the two of them had vowed to keep, Marvel thought. If so, her cousin was worrying needlessly. After all, this was best, the right thing. The family had held a kind of truth party, opened up about pent-up emotions, concerns—everything *any* of them had kept hidden. *We asked our parents to stop protecting US!* Marvel accused herself, realizing that she and Mary Ann had done the same thing. But wait a minute—

Startled, Marvel realized that while these thoughts were correct, there was another possibility she had overlooked. Why, how small her thinking had been! Moving—and the odds were that move they must—would have the same effect on Mary Ann as herself. She, too, would be taken out of school! There was little in life one did alone, wasn't there?

"You and I must talk." Marvel approached Mary Ann when an opportunity came. "This house is like a morgue."

Mary Ann was putting her books away. When she turned to face Marvel, she was shuddering. "Don't say that! It—it reminds me of that awful time when—well, you know when—after the fire and the supposed suicide. How easy it is for some people to forget. I mean, we tried to be kind to that terrible man, and what do we get in return? Kicked out, that's what!"

It was good to see Mary Ann show anger. Anything was better than shriveling inside. There had to be some fight left, something Grandmother called *righteous indignation*!

"Well, you're right about the man we once called *uncle*. But we knew it was coming. You know what our job is, yours and mine? It will be up to us to try and get through this—and something more."

"What more could there be?"

"Lots more, so stop talking like a martyr. But what I had in mind was that it's going to be up to us to help our parents—keep them from feeling guilty about something they are unable to help."

Mary Ann nodded. "I've thought and thought about that."

Marvel let her think some more. And when Mary Ann spoke again, Marvel was prepared for what she said. In tears, her cousin confessed, "But I guess I'm worrying about how to tell Jake. He has to know—"

"You'll think of the words. When do you see him again? And why haven't you told him at school—avoiding him like you were steering clear of me?"

"Answering your last question first, yes, I guess I was. Only our schedules *were* different—sort of—and he's been looking at Uncle Dale's car with Archie. It's down at the old garage building, you know. They're going to fix it up—the car, I mean. At least, they think they can. Then you asked when I'd see Jake. Oh, please don't be mad at me. You know I've been walking around in my sleep and forgot to tell you—"

Mary Ann stopped, embarrassed.

"Go ahead, I promise not to be angry."

Marvel was not angry when Mary Ann blurted out the news. Shocked and startled, yes—disappointed as well that Archie made arrangements to see her the following night without her knowledge. Of course she *had* promised to see him, so halfheartedly she told Mary Ann it was all right, having no idea that another decision lay ahead. At least others would call it that. For now, *angry* was hardly the word.

The boys arrived early, even though they had taken special care with their grooming. The four of them started walking as if by mutual consent toward the school. The route led them past where the Baptist church had once stood. All of them fell silent as they drew near the heap of ashes. Something made them pause—a relief to Marvel, as the loudness of their footsteps echoing on the hard ground and bulging concrete stepping-stones had bothered her.

Marvel shuddered. A tight hand had taken her heart and squeezed it—hard. The cold sense of apprehension!

"This place gives me the creeps," Mary Ann said, her teeth chattering. "It's like ghosts—or maybe I'm seeing you-know-who—"

"Elmer?" Archie said the dread name aloud. "Do you think he done it? Rumor has it—"

"Never mind rumors," Marvel said quickly. And before she could say more, Mary Ann made a suggestion to go—a suggestion Marvel agreed with.

"Let's you and I go by the school. I have something to talk about." That was Mary Ann's way of saying she wanted to be alone with Jake when she talked about moving.

But it was Archie who answered. "An' me, I want to talk with Marvel," he announced to the group. Then, taking a flashlight from his overcoat pocket, Archie turned its beam on the cemetery gate and propelled Marvel toward it. "I'm guessin' you got family 'n come here lots. Me, I'm common—"

"I haven't been here for such a long time—except on Decoration Day," she said as they made their way through the mounds. "I do have family."

It was a moonless night, the darkness unrelieved by stars, with a breeze among the nude trees whispering of snow. Marvel welcomed the help of Archie's flashlight. It was easy to find the ornate statuary of angels which marked some of her ancestors' graves. They looked too elaborate among some of the later mounds with simple headstones and the sites flattened by time and identifiable only by rectangular metal nameplates. Who were they all and what had each contributed?

She was startled when Archie broke into her contemplation to say, "I'm real proud to let you know I'm finished with fixing th' Essex. I thought ya'll would be kinda glad to know. An' I'm gonna put in that shop like I planned, so we'd be well-fixed—if you'd wait for me—"

At first it was the sound of his voice that was startling, not the words because they did not sink in. They couldn't.

Her silence was misleading.

"Me—I'm not good with words, and I know this is not a good time—an' a downright funny place—but, well, I just had to up 'n say it while I had th' chance. I'm thinkin' it was all right—I mean us bein' here 'n all. You not answerin' shows me you're givin' it some considerin'. Then when you say a *yes*, I'll know it'll mean you mean it—"

Was Archie proposing—actually, asking her to *marry* him? Oh, he couldn't be. He just couldn't be.

His next words told her differently. "I'm not teasin' 'n if you're thinkin' we're young, 'course I ain't meanin' tom'mor, we can wait 'til I git outta CCC's and get set up. 'N my gift's uh ring—too cheap—"

Archie, who was fumbling with his hands as he had fumbled for words, managed to turn the strong beam of light toward himself. She saw that his eyes were alive with an unnatural brightness that spelled hope.

Trying to hide her astonishment, Marvel said quietly, "Archie, you do me a great honor—"

"You mean you will? I—I don't know what to say. I mean, all my life, I'd planned on how 't'say it 'n—"

"Archie, Archie, my dear, dear friend. Listen to what I'm trying to tell you. No, no interruptions. You must listen. I am trying to tell you how much you mean, but that marriage is out of the question. Somehow you have read the wrong thing into our relationship."

"You're sayin'—you're turnin' me down—" he whispered hoarsely.

"Let me explain. It's for none of the reasons you might think. It has nothing to do with age, family, education—none of that matters, so don't torment yourself. There's nobody else. I don't plan marriage—*ever.*"

She could tell by his voice he was crestfallen. "Oh," was all he said.

25

Where There's Smoke...

When Marvel told Grandmother of Archie's proposal, the older woman nodded with understanding. When told of her sympathy for him, there was another nod. But this time her grandmother spoke.

"You, being *you*, would have compassion. But in the long run," she said as she stirred stew for the evening meal, "you did the young man a favor to tell him outright. You can't marry a man because you feel sorry for him."

They spoke of other matters then—about moving and how they wished Dale and Snow Harrington would talk more openly, about school and how well Marvel was doing, and then about Marvel's feeling of apprehension when viewing the ashes of the church. Did Grandmother think there was the faintest possibility that Elmer Salsburg could have done such a terrible thing?

"Well!" Grandmother burst out, giving the stew a more vigorous stir than it needed, then slamming down the long-handled fork. "Look what that thorn-in-the-flesh did to you! And remember that, as the saying goes, 'Where there's smoke there's fire!'"

Marvel thought about that as she readied the table for supper. Grandmother said Southern Beaten Biscuits would be nice to go along with the vegetable stew except that the flour bin was mighty low. Then, as if regretting mention of shortages, she switched on the radio.

Ironically, the Lightcrust doughboys, to advertise the product they were pushing—Lightcrust flour—were singing, "When It's

Springtime in the Rockies." When the song ended, the news came on.

The announcer talked first about organized labor. Despite the Depression, some of the corporations (nobody seeming to know exactly who owned them) were reporting minerals taken from the earth's bowels of profits up in the millions of dollars (nobody knew for sure the exact figures, either)—tons and tons—perhaps a million—of coal, limestone, and ore to mention a few. Add on the by-products, and he reckoned it would take a fleet of ships or more railroads than the United States and Canada had to haul 'em all.

But who does the dirty work, folks? You know the answer: the *little* man, the common laborer! And his condition's mighty grim and mighty hopeless. But he says there's no choice, what with all this unemployment. And conditions in the automobile industry— all big industry, in fact—are just as tough. So what's a man to do when he's got a sick wife needing a doctor, kids to keep in school, one of them eating on stubs, his teeth rotted out from effects of typhoid and malaria, and can't afford a dentist—and still, there's a roof to keep over their heads and empty bellies to stop from growling because of hunger? Men like that have got to have a *voice*, be heard, be listened to—whether you like the fearful John L. Lewis or not. He does go after big business, try to get them to see clearly that, much as men need money (and that means work!), they have other needs, too. Still, when they get work— say, in the mines—safety conditions are as bad as wages are low and uncertain. They die off like flies with carbon monoxide poisoning, explosions, black lungs, exposure, fire with them trapped "down under." Bad? It's inhuman! So you out there on the farms and living in the rural communities, be happy . . . stick this drought out. For lucky you, if you are among the country dwellers.

A gust of cold air announced Dale Harrington's homecoming.

Marvel, caught in the spell somewhere between hope and despair, ran to meet him. "Oh, Daddy—Daddy!" she said, burying her head against him. "Did you hear what the man said? Maybe it won't be so bad living out there on the farm after all!"

"I know, I know," he comforted. "No wonder men are mobbing the White House—even taking their wives and children along! A man has to keep his dignity. Not that that's right either. It's all very confusing. But what *is* right?"

"That's what the child's saying, Dale son," Grandmother said gently. "Marvel is willing to go. Now that's the sacrificial love we talked about such a short while ago."

Daddy groaned. "It would kill Snow. You know how she feels about keeping our daughter, our jewel, in school. But wait now, I promised her—and maybe just maybe we won't *have* to move, my pet."

There was no victory in his voice, just submission.

"What are you saying?" Marvel whispered.

"That I had a thought and so did what those men are doing. Which was all I could, under the circumstances. I went to see— Oh, here comes Snow, Mother Riley. Please, *please* neither of you say anything about the possibility of our staying put," he said hurriedly.

When Mother entered, she had concerns of her own.

"Oh, that brother of yours—" she gasped while trying to remove the heavy, woolen scarf Grandmother had woven for her as a Christmas gift.

Daddy jumped to attention. "Here, darling, let me help with that before you suffocate," he tried to joke. But his voice held no laughter. Hurriedly he said, "Uh, wh-what about my brother?"

"He's so wild about banking. He has a fixation. He's sick."

"All right, you have him diagnosed, Snow," her mother said briskly. "Now would you tell us who the patient is!"

Marvel longed to comfort her father, tell him that Mother had said brother—*not* stepbrother. For somehow she knew that the man he had gone to see was the owner of this house and that it was no longer theirs no matter how they felt about it. The official who pushed the notice to vacate into her hands had spelled out the inevitable.

"Alex, Alexander Jay, your father's namesake—and I'd reckon right about now, his pride and joy! A chip off the old block, all right—loving banking the same way," Mother spat the words out bitterly as she struggled with the buttons on her coat.

Her husband reached again to help. Marvel heard his sigh of relief.

It was Grandmother who spoke. "Now, now, daughter, keep a civil tongue in your head! Exactly, what is the nature of your brother-in-law's crime?"

"Imagine," Mother said as if talking to the living room walls, "Alex's listening to Russel Newland—someone out of the family—and following him to California as if he were the Pied Piper."

There was silence—not the golden kind...a gloom-filled silence. Marvel remembered her own sense of apprehension. But what, if anything, did that have to do with Uncle Alex, Mother, or any of them?

"The Pied Piper sounds like the title newspapers nicknamed Huey Long, that man who mesmerized the poor people of the bayou country. You've heard about him, Mother? The 'kingfish' who sold himself a dream of being president and believed it so much he wrote a book called *My First Days in the White House*." Marvel had tried to say the words lightly to dispel the gloom. When it seemed only to thicken, she added, "I read it—and talk about woolgathering writing. But," she swallowed, "I guess he pumped hands, maybe twisted arms—and that doesn't sound much like Jake's uncle."

"Sounds exactly like him," Mother insisted. "Mary Ann feels just the way I feel, too, about being tolled away."

"You aren't being tolled away, sweetheart," Daddy said.

Grandmother cleared her throat as if to remind her son-in-law that the agreement was to say nothing of the possibility of remaining here.

"Well," she said, "Alex has no wife, but it's most likely she'd go along, like it or not."

"That's not fair. Women have equal rights. We can vote."

"So can the Negroes," Leah Johanna Riley said tartly, "and they're a far cry from being treated as our equals in spite of being courted for their votes by such lurid grafters as Eddie Crump, called the 'ring-tailed tooter' down Memphis way. He got to be mayor like that. Which has nothing to do with the honor and privilege of being a wife! You know how the Bible defines the good wife. But even more important is Christ's view, calling the church His '*bride*'. Hard for us mortals to think in such terms—a serious responsibility, a holy one."

Marvel excused herself quietly and took leave. Making coffee was better than crying about everything. As she took the coffee from the shelf, she spotted the cheese Miss Marlow had doled out. That would be good with the stew. And Grandmother *had* made the biscuits.

Thinking didn't drown out the conversation in progress. "I know—I know what a good wife is, and I want to be one."

"You are a wonderful wife, the best!" Daddy declared. "I'm the one who's a failure—"

"Stop berating yourself, Dale son," Grandmother broke in. "Neither of you has failed. Times are trying, that's all. Overlook me if I meddled, both of you. No, no, don't protest. Mothers have a way of interfering because," (there was a catch in her throat) "we care so much. Oh shucks, let's face it. I'm just a sentimental old woman. But Marvel and I were listening to the news and, un-ladylike as it is, those women marching with their men on the White House in protest—well, I'm trying to say that men *need* their women! Don't worry, Snow White, about who goes where. Just remember what I said before—that if the times comes, you'll follow Dale and adjust to anything!"

Two days later, just two days before the "real Christmas" (at least, the date set aside for celebrating the birth of Christ), matters came to a climax. The time for peace and good will was one of desolation and despair. . . .

Grandfather rapped sharply on the door as Daddy, Mother, Grandmother, and Mary Ann were making small talk over dessert. Although what happened after that was blurred, details of the prelude were etched sharply in Marvel's mind: the delicious odor in the baking of the six-layer cake, the satisfying goodness of the filling, even the beauty, the luxury, and the recipe. The peanut butter used in both the batter and the filling were a part of the packages allotted to the four ladies ("More surpluses, you know," Mrs. Sutheral and Miss Marlow had said). They said the same for the sack of flour and the ten-pound bag of sugar.

How lovely the rare treat looked on the Spode dessert plates with the dainty violets and gold rims. Marvel, feeling festive (or was she chasing away shadows?), lighted red candles.

Grandmother was charmed. "It's so lovely, girls—"

"And so yummy-good," Daddy added. "You know, we should have asked some of your young friends, girls—maybe all the family—except that I'm selfish. I want enough left for tomorrow night."

Only there would be no tomorrow night here. Time had run out.

When Alex Harrington's cane announced his presence, he did not wait for an invitation to come inside. He burst in with a breathless announcement. And there was terror in his face.

"Outside, quickly! All the family's gathered in the yard. It's fire—*fire*. Has to be a dwelling. Flames light up the entire sky—"

They rushed outside to find the uncles, aunts, and cousins in such a turmoil that it was difficult to understand their words. But they were pointing. *Oh, dear God, no!* They were pointing toward—

Mary Ann must have thought the same. When the telephone rang sharply and insistently, there were no longs and no shorts—just one consistent ring. That signaled fire. And it was Mary Ann who raced back into the house to answer.

Marvel stared in astonishment as the flames reached higher and higher. The whole night sky was crimson. Mindlessly, she could only stare—hearing nothing, feeling nothing.

Mary Ann's scream jolted her back to reality.

"It's my house—I mean, Uncle Dale's. It's gone. Do you hear me—gone!! Everything's lost. That was my mother, calling from—from Captain Bumstead's. And Billy Joe was crying. Oh, I want to go home—I mean, *your* house. Something awful's going on. Oh *please*, let's go!"

Marvel reached out her arms to her cousin, wondering what she could say to Daddy. He had loved the great old house, and she guessed she had, too. *Down deep inside, I guess I wanted to go back*, she realized. But what was Mary Ann whispering hoarsely, desperately?

"It had to be him—just had to. They saw the tracks even while they rushed out—and there was one that dragged. He's done it again!"

Elmer! "The devil," Sula Mae and Casper had said.

"Unbelievable! How—it can't be—"

"But you know it is. I'm so scared! And I was trying to put away all grudges. All I can do is be thankful Mother, Daddy, and little Billy Joe are alive. Can't we *go*—somehow?"

Jake appeared suddenly. "The Essex is ready, Mr. Dale. And Tummy Tucker's here with his flatbed. Try not to worry. You know how good people are to donate when there's a fire."

* * *

It was true—all of it. The big house was gone. So were the surrounding trees and all else that had made it a beautiful landmark. All that remained as a monument was the lone charred trunk of Great-grandfather's English Walnut tree. Once upon a time that tree had dropped its burden of nuts in the autumn-time. Now, mockingly, chunks of charcoal broke loose to echo and reecho among the ruins, the sound dying away for lack of an answer in the dismal bottomlands.

And over all hung the smell of carnage—a collection of nauseating odors cast off by the carcasses of farm animals which had perished in the fiery furnace devouring the house and the outbuildings and the drowning-in-mud catfish, suffocating for lack of oxygen in the lowering sloughs. Once those no-outlet bodies of shallow water had served as sources of water for the farm animals. They were especially valuable when the manmade pools were drying one by one due to no rainfall.

In Pleasant Knoll the family had talked too much. Now they were too silent, as if visiting a tomb. From respect, Marvel supposed. Her father had witnessed a death—the death of a dream—while they grieved as one mourns the death of a stranger, knowing a part of humanity was gone.

Marvel felt a grief all her own—a grief for what was and what might have been. Fragments of memory transported her inside the Harrington home, once a near-mansion: the old paneling carefully chosen for its grain... hand-hewn furniture... brocades... the butler's pantry (had any Harrington ever kept a butler?), complete with speaking tubes and a call box she and other children (faces dimmed by time) used to play with... and laughter. Someday it might have been restored. But most of all, Marvel had hoped to restore the land... its inhabitants... crops—make it a heartland, a heritage.

That night she heard low sobbing in her parents' bedroom. It

172

was no surprise that Mother was remorseful. Then Daddy, in an effort to console, said desolately, "Either way we'd have lost it. I—offered to trade it to Frederick for the mortgage, but no chance after the fire."

26

Moving Out, Moving On

Moving out took one day. It happened suddenly, but could there be one among them who had not foreseen it? Marvel had known that this house would be lost from the moment she heard mention of the hateful mortgage. But where they would go was another matter. Had she secretly entertained the *hope* of returning to the farm? Certainly not under present circumstances—not with the house gone, and not as an escape from greater tragedy. They must escape...somewhere...anywhere! Remaining here was to risk their very lives.

Of course, moving on would take more time—a commodity they did not have now. The future would take care of itself. There was just this day; and they must hurry, *hurry*, HURRY....

Uncle Worth and Auntie Rae came in with Uncle Joseph and Aunt Dorthea last night. Marvel suspected that none of them had any more sleep than she, Mother, and Daddy, because they were all gathered on the front porch when Grandmother opened the door to let them in.

It was all decided, even between Mother and Daddy. They had no place to go, Uncle Worth said, unless Dale would allow them to move into one of the places occupied by the sharecroppers and field hands. Of course they were welcome, Daddy had said tonelessly. Then, if they would consider coming back, too (Uncle Worth spoke breathlessly, his voice sounding as if he'd been running uphill)—well, the whole family would pitch in and help.

173

Captain Bumstead had offered to help them all move and neighbors "out there" (meaning the farm) would bring in wagons with sideboards. Well?

It seemed to Marvel that packing was in progress before anybody answered. Neighbors from "in here" surrounded them. How they found out was an unknown factor, the "x" in geometry that could mean anything, she thought foolishly as she furiously began wrapping dishes. Dishes—they would have to have dishes, even though there was a question as to whether there would be food to go onto them.

Grandmother was whistling. Sure enough, the tune was "Whistle While You Work." Marvel caught her eye, and her grandmother winked! Her jovial approach was contagious among the people who had known what want, loss, and foreclosures meant. It was no sin to be poor. And suddenly, all of them were singing the lyrics along with her—perhaps to hold back their tears.

Fortunately, there was no time to think. Daddy seemed suddenly excited. "I don't know where on earth all this will go. I mean," he grinned, "where we'll find a place for it. I *know* where it's going!"

"You'll find a place, Dale son. You know, this brings out the gypsy in me. I'm used to packing in a hurry and making-do with what there is to do with. I almost wish there were room for me—" Grandmother said.

"What do you mean?" Daddy was sincerely shocked. "There's *always* room for you. Why, this household would never be the same without *you*. Besides," he whispered, "you'll have to be tutor—the way you did on the road. Remember, it's Marvel's schooling that troubles our Snow—that and—and—" he paused to swallow, then whispered, "that and a home—"

"Fiddlesticks! Home is where the heart is. Dale, I know my daughter will adjust. She'll measure up, I promise. And you—you will build back. She'll have that house. 'The darkest hour is just before dawn,' as the saying goes. Well, you don't have to work at convincing *me*. Your saying I'm needed means I *am*. Here, move this carton. Oh, here comes your father—"

"And Jake!" Mary Ann shrieked, stumbling over boxes to meet him.

"An' me! Here comes *me*!" Billy Joe, who had been ignored as long as he could stand it, found his words very funny. "An' *me's* glad, glad you're coming—glad, glad. Oh, Gran'mere, you have to come. *Me* has to have help. *Me* has to learn everthing all over—"

"I should say *me* does need help. Now," Grandmother said briskly, "behave yourself and open the door for your grandfather!"

Marvel stole a glance at her mother's face. It was without expression...pale. But there was no desperation.

"This piano—where do we put it, Mrs. Harrington?" Jake asked tactfully. "I have enough men here to load it in if it goes."

"It goes!" Uncle Worth said determinedly. "There's a single-room building not in use. We can sing again with Grand'mere."

"Yes, we can sing."

Oh, thank You Lord, Marvel's heart was singing already. The voice she'd heard was her mother's.

The first truck pulled out. Then one by one, the other vehicles followed—with some hugs, promises to write, to call, to visit... and an enormous box of oatmeal cookies. Also came a quilt with each of their names embroidered on an individual block and— oh, how lovely—in the very center a field of bluebonnets, so real there was a feeling that one could reach out and pick a handful of the dainty, blue-purple flowers.

How had it happened? How on earth had they managed? Marvel wondered as, seated with Jake and Mary Ann in the protesting truck filled with cartons, she realized that they really were headed in the direction of the farm.

The Lord alone knew what lay in store for them. But He would provide a way. Marvel felt thoroughly confused. And yet, in a peculiar sort of way, inside her there was a strange sense of exhilaration. God moved in mysterious ways. But He had provided a way of escape—escape from the sinister Frederick Salsburg, whose lust for money knew no boundaries, and his sick-minded son who would stop at nothing to get revenge. "Vengeance is Mine." A rumble of thunder echoed God's warning.

This was not the end. It was the beginning, an unfolding of His will. Faith would see them through...perhaps sending rain this day....

* * *

Sula Mae and Casper, alerted by the sound of the trucks, were on hand when the loaded vehicles stopped. A flash of color darting into the persimmon thicket which had yet to be cleared said others had fled.

Sula Mae's eyes were enlarged with wonder, her pigtails seeming to stand straight up. Chewing on a forefinger as if it were food, the black girl looked shyly at her bare feet.

"Remember me, Sula Mae?" Marvel asked her onetime playmate.

Sula Mae nodded but did not look up. "You'se Marvel—Missy Marvel ah'm s'posed to call y'all—bof uv y'all, Missy Marvel 'n Missy Mary Ann. Ah'll be 'memberin'—shure 'nuf will—"

Mary Ann reached out and removed the girl's finger from her heavy lips, then patted it gently. "You have forgotten something already, Sula Mae. How to speak slowly and clearly. It's important to look at the person you're addressing, too. But you are *not* to call us Missy. Does the same go for you, Marvel?"

"Absolutely! We're one of you now—and we'll be needing your help, beginning right now!"

"Kin ah he'p, too?" Casper was less inhibited. "Cain't ah, big sis?"

"Yeah, you'll git—get to he'p—help—me h-help them!" big sis said.

Marvel and Mary Ann clapped in applause.

Proudly, Sula Mae squared her shoulders and took charge. Placing the right forefinger and middle finger between her lips, she pierced the air with a shrill whistle. Children of all ages surrounded them.

The houses were more like shanties: some missing windows because of the hailstorm...all in need of having roofs patched... and one of them slanted crazily. There were no toilet facilities, just buildings "out back" (the better ones protected by rough-plank doors—one creatively decorated by an oversized star and undersized half-moon). Marvel looked around her and felt a wild desire to laugh. The other outhouses had only burlap taken from feed sacks hanging across the entrances to guarantee privacy.

She opened one of the better toilets gingerly, only to be greeted by an indignant "settin' hen," according to Sula Mae. " 'N dem don' take a hankerin' t'strangers," one of the other children said (Marvel had yet to learn them all by name). So, she supposed, one must share "squatter's rights" of that building, as well. Mary Ann giggled along with her. But Sula Mae, being accustomed to the ways of the poor, was dead serious. "Better'n— better than some's got it," she said solemnly. Then Casper explained that they just "got behind a bush."

"We didn't know half of it—those of us who remained in town. It's all so different now—such a shame," Marvel whispered to Mary Ann.

"I know, don't I just? But I'm sort of used to it," her cousin said. "Still think we can manage?"

Mary Ann's voice was frightened. She needed reassurance.

Well, the Lord would have to help them, Marvel thought quickly, making it into a quick prayer. Then, squaring her shoulders, she said, "Of course! I'm not saying it will be easy, but remember what we promised ourselves? That we must help our parents, especially my mother, adapt? Oh, will you look—there's Fanny, who used to do our wash!"

In the saffron light of approaching darkness, Fanny could have been a figment of Marvel's tired mind. But when the ebony-skinned woman spoke, there could be no mistaking her identity.

In low, musical tones Marvel remembered from childhood, Fanny said, "My, my, how grown-up you-all are, both of you," she said. "Now 'course I been seein' the other missy—but yuh, Miss Marvel honey-child, well, I never in all my born days. Oh, baby— mah baby anyways, seeing that I used to love the way them purty blue eyes would look up into mah face an' make me feel real humble-like when I sung lullabies and watched them go shut like your mama's four-o'clock blooms, come that time. Now, ah'm still hereabouts an' still you-all's servant—"

"Oh Fanny, you are *not* a servant, and you are not to call me 'missy'—no title at all—just Marvel. Servant indeed! You're a godsend, that's what you are!"

With that, Marvel reached out to her and Fanny—dear, blessed Fanny—hungrily folded her to the remembered warmth of her breast.

Godsend she was in the days to follow. "Is there no end to what those hands can do?" Marvel asked in wonder.

Fanny laughed her deep, rich laugh. "Well now, they cain't be turnin' white, hard as I've been scrubbin'," she said and went on shoving heavy furniture about, making mile-high beds, and capably unrolling rugs and shifting them to cover the worst places in the rough, bare floor.

"There's one thing for us to set straight though," Marvel said in no uncertain terms as, following the woman's lead, she moved about quickly to offer assistance. "And that is this: You are to enter by way of the front door—get that straight."

Fanny shook her wealth of kinky, midnight hair. "Now, Miss— uh, Marvel hon, *there* you got yo'self something I cain't do fo' shure. Why, th' Lawd God of Israel would plum strike me dead!"

"You know better than that, Fanny. You're not ignorant and superstitious. Our Lord is a God of love, and He would not want you fearing us white people. So front door it is—and that's final!"

But what the woman had said gave Marvel an opening to ask about the "devil" which had the children so terrified. There was every reason to be afraid, Fanny assured her, and went on to tell of some sightings of her own. And yes, that awful creature was on hand the night of the destructive fire. Old Uncle Ned who knew a "right smart" 'bout everything said, " 'Tweren't no 'polter-geest' what went round shakin' dishes 'n pullin' pranks,' no'm—nothin' t'be tee-heein' 'bout, right real sho' nuf wuz—evil, bent on doin' fo'ks in, packin' 'em off to e'rly graves." Same way with Hezzie, th' preacher-man, Fanny said. "Hezzie was a man bent on tellin' th' truth. An' he'd swear on his Bible—oh, how he wish't he could read hit—that devil was uh real flesh-'n-bones critter—nothin' escapin' th' graveyard er th' furnaces uv hell. More like he'd run away from uh madhouse!" And Fanny said her "Ain't Heliotrope sez they's—uh, they both be right as rain (Oh Lawdy, wouldn't rain be nice? Just take a lissen to dat—that—thunder, honey child!), uh real piece uv human flesh putten together by th' Almighty Hisself, 'cuz He's th' only 'un whut can be uh doin' dat, but po'sessed uv the seben devils lack th' Good Book dun be tellin'."

How long had Fanny been here? "Come," she said, when work played out. Then on to another task while Marvel asked more questions.

Then did she see tracks that night of the fire?

Yes, with her own eyes. The ashes wiped 'em clean away. Saw him—it, whatever—too. And Fanny was "of a mind" that it was human.

"What do you make of it?" Marvel asked Mary Ann the first chance she had.

"Elmer, of course," her cousin answered without hesitation. She pushed back her raven curls with a grimy hand, leaving a streak of smudge across her face. "I'm too tired to think, but this I know: We *have* to tell our parents. Surely, there can be no doubt left."

No, there could not. *Sometimes evil is so dark only innocence can see it.*

From the first exhausting day, the people of the bottomlands and the sharecroppers' wives (all having grown up here and begging to stay on, this was the only home they knew, the Harringtons their only family) brought food. And, simple fare that it was, never had food tasted so good: dried beans and salt pork, corn pone, grits, collards and hawg jowl... dried persimmon puddin'... gallons of "sweet milk" with co'nebread fer crumblin' in it... gravy fo' soppin'... so'gum pie... and once "Watkin's vanilley mouse" (questioned, it was discovered that, having an abundance of cream from cows allowed to graze, the women listened to Sula Mae and Casper haltingly read the recipe in the little cookbook the Watkins man gave along with the flavoring, and made the "mouse" ah, er, wuz hit mouses seein' as they'd been more'n uh measly *one*?

The Harringtons suppressed their smiles of amusement. Mouse pie had another meaning to them—one they weren't sure their dark friends would understand. Gently, they corrected the pronunciation and praised the delicious concoction highly.

It was the night of the mousse-for-dessert that the girls told every detail of Fanny's hair-raising report.

None of it was as surprising as Marvel would have expected. Even Mother seemed resigned. But then, Mother's calm acceptance of the almost impossible situation had been most surprising. Grandmother, whose sewing machine had whirred around the clock for days, hemming curtains, making over drapes brought from town, and adjusting throws and spreads, was right about her daughter. Snow Harrington harked back to the sterling Mier stock of the *Mayflower* (although Grandmother's husband, Chauncey Riley, rest his soul, used to say that ship would have sunk if all those making claim to having been aboard were passengers). Naturally, her Snow White would measure up when the test came.

"Why? It makes no sense. But then," Uncle Worth paused to sigh, "what does these days?"

"Worth, darling," Auntie Rae chided gently, "we've a lot to be thankful for. We're all together out here, not exactly under the best of all circumstances maybe, but *together*. Right now we're all bone-tired and it's hard to think straight—"

"Not hard for me!" Daddy's voice boomed like the thunder overhead. "With the house gone, the land was worthless in Frederick Salsburg's mind. And he delights in cornering one of us Harringtons—you know that. In his feeble mind, you and I were both caught. I was gullible enough to think he might—just might—exchange the two places, freeing me of the loan, fool that I was to borrow from him. Not that he'd be caught dead on this farm—"

"Well, he'll *be* caught dead if he or that half-wit son of his ever sets foot on this place!"

Now Uncle Worth, too, rumbled like the thunder. Marvel could almost feel the floor shake. Not that it would take much....

Marvel looked around the house her family was to occupy and noted how cozy it looked: walls freshly kalsomined in a jersey-cream tone, Mother's full-length mirror enlarging the quarters, expensive paintings hung at eye-level, and ruffled priscilla curtains lending a cottage-like look—modest and unpretentious, but completely charming. She felt a strange peace stealing over her. *I'd have said it was impossible*, she thought, *but nothing is impossible with God.* "Oh, ye of little faith!" Marvel scolded, as her head drooped sleepily....

✻ ✻ ✻

By the end of the week, the transformation was complete, inside and out. Dale occupied the largest of the three houses. It had three bedrooms, giving space for Grandmother. Worth said he could manage with two if Mary Ann and Billy Joe would share. Of course, of course—it was all just temporary anyhow. The extra house (the one in the worst condition) would be used for storage. Grandmother looked ahead and wondered what the Squire would do for quarters when he came—not *if*, but *when*.

"That's easy," Marvel said quickly. "Grandfather's welcome any time at all. You and I will share my room." What a joy to see the shine of her grandmother's eyes.

On Sunday there was company. Neighbors called, bringing butter, jellies, jams, relishes, and vegetables from their winter gardens which had survived several spells of freezing temperatures. The womenfolk offered seeds, bedding plants, and cuttings for houseplants. It was common practice, they said, to swap eggs with those whose hens went into a molt, for milk with those who were waiting for their cows to freshen. Cream, now, that was a different matter. It went into town along with regular milk (easier, especially for those having no cream separator). Now and then, they admitted, they indulged—just plain forgot about budgets—and had ice-cream socials. The Captain was bringing blocks of ice from Culverville for people on his route. Otherwise, the only way to keep milk from spoiling was to lower it in sealed syrup buckets down in the well. Thank goodness, wells were not lowering—a blessing. No, no place to worship— well, a place, just an old building where young people met for Sunday night singing. Real nice on account of there being a piano for the note-singing classes in the summertime. Would you believe the Stamps Quartet (yes, sure enough, the men who sang on radio) came clear from Dallas to teach—and sell songbooks, too, of course? But it had been a spell since a preacher had come. Not that you could much blame them. After all, they had to make a living, and farmers were pretty hard hit as far as cash was concerned. Of course, the colored folks had a church house—a preacher, too. But then—well, you know—"

"No, I do *not* know," Marvel said firmly. "In fact, Mary Ann and I have every intention of visiting. We've been invited."

There was silence. What was there to say? Marvel and Mary Ann asked the two girls (Ruth Smith and Annie Pruitt, as Marvel recalled) about school. The visiting girls were evasive. There was a little school about four miles away—Hills' Chapel which once served as a combination church and school. Hard getting there though, roads so rough and muddy in "books time." Some went if they had horses to ride. But, they admitted, attendance was irregular. Boys had to start late, after cotton was picked, then quit early for plowing time in spring. There was talk though— just talk, mind you—that maybe one day there would be transportation.

When?

They didn't know.

What was the delay?

They didn't know that either—grants, they believed, but from where? County, state, maybe—or could be the government. It was all up in the air. Better not plan on anything these days, they guessed.

They'd be afraid to go, scared out of their skins, the girls admitted, so they gave it little thought. Wouldn't it be terrible-awful if the law *made* them go?

Marvel tried to erase their fears and assured them that, while all who entered the big-city schools would feel apprehensive and, yes, somewhat out of place (downright "outclassed," Mary Ann interrupted), in spite of it all, just think what an opportunity!

Ruth and Annie had given only skimpy information, but it was enough to send Marvel's heart to soaring. *Dear Lord... dear Lord, please...*

The guests had taken their leave early. There were pigs to slop, cows to milk, and chickens to coop up. Owls had been terrible of late, just terrible—and talk about being bold—no fear a'tall of people.

Obviously, they had enjoyed their visit. All were in a jovial mood, the men talking of a "roofing day." Oh, sure, between them, there would be plenty of shingles left over from their own roof jobs. And the good ladies would fix a fine meal—always did on such occasions.

The next onslaught of company was different—surprising... exciting... life-changing!

From the time the vintage Ford drove into what passed as a driveway and parked with a backfire, there was a confusion of faces, voices, laughter, and tears. Jake... Grandfather Harrington... Brother Greer... Uncle Emory and Uncle Joseph... all riding in Mr. Wilshire's car. *Mr. Wilshire* the principal! Marvel was conscious of a great weariness....

Her mind drifted away in a fanciful daydream. They had all come for a special event—a marriage feast... *always a fine meal on such occasions.* Those joined in holy wedlock, the Queen Mother and the Squire, by Brother Greer; groomsmen, the latter's sons; while the dowager-bride's ladies in-waiting...

Jolted from her childish daydream by a question, Marvel realized Mr. Wilshire had posed it: "So would you like to come back and finish school under those circumstances, my dear—you and Mary Ann?"

"I must think," she managed through numb lips. "Talk with my parents, as you will understand." Oh, if only *they* had listened when she failed!

"Yes, of course! Remember there would be no board and keep. You'd share quarters with Miss Marlow. Best you move on, you must!"

27

The Miracle

The air was heavy with a portending storm. People fanned themselves with handkerchiefs or, if privileged to have an electric fan, kept the blades noisily busy. At "Ma" Armstrong's Boardinghouse, Pleasant Knoll's only remaining claim toward anything resembling a "home away from home," guests sat on both the upstairs and downstairs screened porches, hoping for a breeze and a tad of good news. The downstairs radio was turned high enough so that those below (as well as neighbors) could hear the news.

The announcer had been touching on a revolution in faraway Spain, admitting that a child suffering a dog bite would get more attention, when suddenly he interrupted, asked listeners to give him a moment to get organized, then burst out:

> Yes, here it is, folks! Word has reached this station of the appointment of a director of the FBI. We have been hoping for just such a man as the Federal Bureau selected, his name being J. Edgar Hoover, dedicated to nabbing all these daredevil crooks who have taunted the law, terrorized the world—some even claiming to be Robin Hoods, taking from the rich and giving to the poor, while others killed only for the joy of seeing the flow of blood. Frankly, I guess what we waited for was a leader, a hero, a hope! Hoover's very appearance qualifies him. One look at his six-foot height, his

football-player's sturdy build, his jet-black, penetrating eyes, his heavy dark hair and square jaw supports that. And to listen to his words is even more reassuring: "I am dedicated to cleaning up this rotten mess," he says in a crisp, no-nonsense voice that comes out in a barrage of staccato bursts, like the rattle of a tommy gun. And, lest you get the mistaken notion that he's bluffing, be informed that Director Hoover has already hand-picked himself over 600 G-men (meaning government men) to rid us of crime, his slogan being: *Crime does not pay!* There's no hiding place, he promises, and one look at this clean-living top cop, watch him walk in that brisk and military manner, leading his army, says nobody is safe from that long arm of the law....So, folks, we can rest a bit easier from now on with young Mr. Hoover and his army in charge...*if only he does not burn himself out.*

"Reassuring—that's what our parents were so concerned about when we left to come back to finish the year: crime, I mean...Elmer, you know," Mary Ann stated. "And it's funny—funny-*strange* that we've seen neither hide nor hair of fat Elmer's no-good daddy. I'm guessing he—they—have skipped out, but this kind of man is bound to find them. They're swindlers, murderers in my mind, thieves, and—what's the word—pyro-something. We had that word in spelling, remember?"

"*Pyromaniac:* One who has an impulse to start fires. It's not a common word, but we're in advanced spelling—just a few of us. Whew, it feels like somebody set fire to the whole world!" Marvel said, with an attempt at lightness she did not feel. "Good news, yes, about this Mr. Hoover."

Mary Ann pushed back her heavy curls and muttered something about one of those boy-bobs. Then, pencil between her teeth, she turned a page of her tablet. "This pre-algebra's killing me—it and all those evil spelling words. I'm not smart like you and Jake. What that announcer said about this all-American boy—sounds like he ought to be selling cereal. No, I guess not. Jack Armstrong wouldn't burn himself out like they thought the FBI man might do—and like you're apt to do the way you keep pushing like a freight train! Why do you do it? Ugh, I smell cabbage again."

"Cabbage?" Marvel managed a laugh. "I thought you liked Mrs. Armstrong's stuffed cabbage—no relationship to Jack."

"I do like it, but not on a hot night like this—too hot for the middle of May. Well, Mary Ann," she muttered to herself, "get with it before this slave driver cracks the whip. Oh, I just remembered something else I heard on the radio. This hardworking hero has a passion for corned beef and cabbage, good old Depression food we're all famous for. Maybe that's why you work so hard—thinking we'll rise above the situation?"

"Partly, I guess," Marvel said quietly, "or at least help our parents to—and thinking ahead to future generations. Then, there are other reasons, too. Relax, Mary Ann, school will be out soon."

Mary Ann looked at her with tears in her great, dark-fringed eyes. "I'm a spoilsport, that's what I am—saying one thing then turning around and contradicting myself. I should be thanking you for all you've done—and don't think I *don't* appreciate it, Marvel—all you've done—and Miss Marlow—the principal—everybody. I don't even want school to end. See what I mean about switching tracks? It means I'll be leaving Jake and you. Oh Marvel, it means you're finished with school and no school out there. Go on, scold me!"

"No, no scolding. I understand. But look at the bright side. We'll be with our parents. There's a lot we're prepared to do to help others: teaching that'll pay Sula Mae, Casper, and all the other children for the catfish they keep supplying us with. Do you realize that they walk with those poles and bait all the way to Rock Creek?"

Both girls went back to work. Adjusting to the heavy burden of studies, plus the office work of the NYA program, and all they participated in to help Miss Marlow had been difficult. But there was more, much more. They gave Ma Armstrong a welcome hand with preparing for the evening meals then doing dishes afterward in exchange for their own meals. Miss Marlow shared her quarters, but the Harringtons were a proud lot—no charity. They would accept nothing for which they did not pay or earn in another way. Then there were the private lessons with Brother Greer for Marvel. Somehow the Lord had given her strength.

Why worry about tomorrow? She was preparing for it, although only He knew what it held or what He would demand of her.

Weekdays were filled to the brim. On Friday nights they had arranged to go back to the farm, returning early Monday morning. With them, on the jolting, bone-shattering ride in the protesting truck, they carried food (declared "surplus"), fabric (donated by the government aid program), and money! Now, their parents could have the Captain bring them ice to cool their parched throats and buy such luxuries as a can of salmon or potted meat from the peddler—even buy fresh meat on the rare occasions when someone butchered and "peddled" the cuts all over the countryside in an effort to make the "critter pay for its raisin'."

The families were pathetically glad to see them and treated them like guests. There was so much to tell, so many questions to ask that it was time to say farewell before they had finished greeting.

"Come see the crops," Daddy always insisted. Marvel would walk with him over the tired, thirsting acres and offer words of encouragement. The corn did look surprisingly lush, but cotton prospects were dismal. There was no stand even in the patchy places which had come up. What little there was gradually surrendered to the thriving Bermuda grass, which was begging to become pastureland again. If only it would rain. But the very heavens seemed to have dried up.

"Is it this dry everywhere, Daddy? Is that what's causing the Depression?" Marvel wondered. "Much as I study, you'd think somebody would have come up with some answers."

"Nobody knows," Daddy had said. "Oh, I forgot to tell you that there's a new office of agricultural services—part of an emergency measure provided by the government. The new county agent has been out and is coming back—has some real good ideas. But back to your question: yes and no. Times are worsened by the prolonged drought—I guess you could call it that now. It's not responsible directly for hard times, but added to it makes tough going. The county agent said Texas, Oklahoma, and Kansas are affected the worst, although some other states are right on our heels. Seems we've all been planting wrong, taking more from the soil than we put back into it."

Mary Ann overheard. "I thought the land was supposed to support *us*, not the other way around. Oh Daddy," she cried out in her little girl "fix-it" voice, "you don't plan to be a farmer forever, do you?"

Uncle Worth tried to reassure her without sounding ungrateful to his brother. They were all victims of the times, Marvel thought tiredly. Then, with a puckish smile said, "Come on, let's sing the blues away, 'Oh, it ain't gonna rain no more, it ain't gonna rain no more! Rabbit on the hilltop kickin' up his heels, it ain't gonna rain no more'!" Daddy laughed and joined in, making her feel good.

Gardens were looking good, considering, the women told the girls. There were radishes and green onions, and they could only hope that the butter beans and black-eyed peas would mature. Of course, poke salet flourished around the stumps—had to be careful of those stinging nettles, naturally. One had to be on guard against thistles.

Stinging nettles! Yes, one had to be on guard. Oh, little did they know.

Thankfully, Grandmother turned to other matters. She had replaced Mary Ann in assisting Sula Mae and Casper with their reading. In turn, they were helping all the others. She had sought out neighbor's children, as well (among them Ruth and Annie) and coaxed them to study under her tutelage. Mother and Auntie Rae joined in then, expressing their joy over their own children being in school. That meant everything, *everything*! Did they know how vital that was to them?

Yes, they knew.

Sometimes the entire group of adults made an effort to come up with a plan for the following year. Mary Ann was *not* to return to Pleasant Knoll alone, and that settled that, her parents declared. And, as for Marvel—well, Mother and Daddy had learned that a boy from one of the "backwoods" schools kept hacking away at furthering his education. His parents were somewhat progressive (who knew how?) and he was checking around to see if other students would want to share expenses and share a ride to Culverville. It wouldn't cost much... of course, it was an old touring car, open air... and you had to put up curtains when it rained. Not the best, but...

More than we can afford, Marvel longed to cry out. Surely they knew the idea was quite out of the question. No, they didn't. They were not realists. They were dreamers. Well, one needed a dream in order to survive, so she listened and tried to make believe that it was possible . . . or was it faith that kept them all going?

* * *

The principal called Marvel into his office a week before school was to close. "You have won every possible award," he told her. "They will look good on your record when you transfer to the county seat. You are a credit to this school, and we are all proud of you. We'll be expecting great things of you. I can't thank you enough."

"Don't thank me, sir," Marvel said humbly. "All of you deserve the awards. But I promise not to disappoint you. But Mr. Wilshire, if you're thinking of public recognition—an assembly—I must decline!"

The man looked startled. "It was to be a surprise, and here you go surprising me. Well, not really. You're hard to figure, but most refreshing. And I suppose you'll want to bow out quietly—no parties. I'll speak with Miss Marlow. Somehow, I expected this, knowing you. I've prepared a course of study for you to follow during the summer, something which will strengthen you for the coming year."

Mr. Wilshire adjusted his rimless glasses and looked at her as if awaiting an answer to some unasked question. Marvel thanked him and sat waiting. There was more to come, she was sure. But she could never have guessed its magnitude—never in a thousand years. *Never!*

"A miracle has happened!" he burst out. "There's going to be transportation into Culverville provided by the state—not much, but a way!"

28

Flaming Sunrise

Although the remembered trees had fallen prey to man's axe, the farmlands of home looked deceptively green. Chinaberry trees lived up to their other name: umbrella trees. They served as welcome shade for panting hens who dusted themselves while the strutting roosters scratched unsuccessfully for food by day. By night, after the fowl had sought an early perch, adults and children alike sat beneath the trees and fanned themselves, listening to the whippoorwills down in the bottoms and watching the fireflies as they darted among the branches.

Gardens were wilting already in the relentless rays of the sun. Wells were lowering, and those who tilled the soil were gravely concerned about drinking water for their livestock. If this drought kept up, they agreed, there would be no water for filling the troughs. Just as there was a shortage on feed. The maize had dwarfed, and most of the corn had been a disappointment. At least there was fodder stored away with the pea vines. Wasn't it gratifying to learn from the county agent that peas (legumes, he called them) were among the plants considered good for the soil? Contained nitrogen—if one could put stock in such talk. Yes, one could, both Daddy and Uncle Worth assured them. The boys studying agriculture in school had learned that. Yes, they had it on good authority. Jake Brotherton was a friend of theirs— and there were others. There was a friend of Jake's, lived next door to the Dale Harringtons come to think of it, now was in the CCC's, Archie Newland—

Archie! Mention of the boy's name reminded Marvel that she had given him no thought, no thought whatsoever, since his proposal. She hoped Archie would find a girl who would appreciate him. He deserved that much. She hoped he had forgotten her, too.

All of the men occupying the other houses expected to help out as they always had and repeated over and over how grateful they were to Mr. Dale and Mr. Worth. The two men shared what they had. At least the root crops were bountiful, which meant onions to dry and both yams and Irish potatoes to store. Just maybe the squash would bear. They were usually pretty dependable, and they kept well when packed in straw. The colored folk had planted peanuts, saying hit made no diff'rence to them what dat white man, Mr. FDR, good though th' mister was, there wuz not allus a-gonna be more'n 'nuff uv 'em. The Harringtons voiced no objection. Peanuts were a good staple, very versatile, and were fun to parch over the flames of winter's open fire. Mrs. Sutheral had shown the ladies so many things to do with them. Then the livestock went wild over the sweet vines. Daddy added that the county agent approved. They were legumes . . . good for the land.

May melted into June, and the gardens were gone. Mother found one pinto bean vine still green among the dried ones when they were picking in preparation for threshing and putting away for winter. Covering her seriousness with a laugh, she recalled that there was one volunteer pea vine where the maize had been. What a creative dish she could make by combining the two. Billy Joe meant his laugh. It was funny, real funny, and he made it so.

"Pass the peas and beans please!" he said repeatedly at the supper table. "Isn't this a dainty dish to set before the king?"

"Good to see the child laugh," Grandmother said in a little aside to Marvel. "He's far advanced for his age and is very upset with us all—sees no reason why he shouldn't be in school like you and his sister. Aggravating and goes against the grain with me, but he will no longer buckle down with me. It's a problem, has me worried. But his parents don't need another problem— none of us do."

Marvel glanced at Grandmother, bemused by her attitude. It was the closest she had come to being discouraged. "You've done your share and ten times over, Grandmother dear," she said reassuringly. "To quote a wise lady by the name of Leah Johanna Riley: 'You can lead a horse to water. . . .' You know the rest. He'll snap out of it—just a phase."

"Snap out of it applies to Leah Johanna. You left out Mier— Riley, too. Canning season came to an abrupt end, except for the berries the little ones are picking down in the bottoms. Oh, I do wish we had enough sugar for jelly—"

"Jam! Jam with the seeds left in it so we can chomp!" Billy Joe broke in. "And chomp and chomp and chomp and keep on chomping."

"Billy Joe, come pick a bouquet for the table," Auntie Rae broke into his chant. He was wound up for the day, his mother knew.

"The old maids are all there is—and they look like they're made outta straw like Casper's mattress. No wonder they're old maids. Nobody would have a straw *woman*!"

"Get going," his Gran'mere ordered. "Then you can pick the figs."

"I'll get Casper to help and tell him we can catch june bugs. He likes to pick tater bugs off the potatoes. Oh, get going you said."

"Enterprising, but see what logic he uses?"

Marvel saw.

Before she could answer, Grandmother had gone into other matters—mostly about her school clothes. Her only grand-daughter had to look proper in that city school. There were bolts of the cotton fabric from the grants and awards. Sears Roebuck had not mailed out their fall catalogs, but these summer styles would hardly be outdated. Notions they could pick up the next time the peddler made his rounds.

Mary Ann overheard. "I guess this means getting me ready, too." Her voice was unenthusiastic. Marvel felt a pang of irrita-tion mixed with sympathy. On the one hand, here was a chance of a lifetime. On the other, she could understand her cousin's not wanting to leave the school where everything was familiar. She would miss her old friends—as would Marvel. Only the school held nothing more for her. But of course, there was Jake. Mary Ann lived only for him. Hard to understand—

Grandmother must have read her thoughts. Without stopping her scissors as they skillfully snipped away at the dress she had envisioned from the Nile-green cotton material, she made a comment Marvel was to recall later.

"I hope you will meet the young man of your dreams at this new school."

"I have none!" Marvel said quickly.

"Well, sometimes the dreams come afterward."

Mother and Auntie Rae joined them. From then on, heat forgotten, the sewing machine was kept busy. The monotony was broken by the radio, its music, and its news broadcasts. Of course, they could use it only when the sewing machine was not in use. Otherwise the static made it impossible to hear.

They managed to gather that J. Edgar Hoover was living up to all his promises. He'd captured "Ma" Barker, the matronly killer, by personally strapping on his .45 and heading his troops. First nabbed her onetime paramour, Alvin (Old Creep) Karpis, then arrested the notorious woman.

"What's a 'paramour'?" Mary Ann, turning impatiently for a hem, asked.

"Lover," Marvel said in disgust. "No wonder such a man tired of his mundane tasks like uncovering federal bank frauds and pursuing prostitutes! I think he and I would understand each other."

"Yeah, and you're both going to burn yourself out the same way. They say he never sleeps. He's married to his work just the way you're married to your books. He's married to that job."

"Ambition is a jealous wife," Grandmother muttered, her mouth full of pins.

The mothers made no comment. Mention of Hoover's work with getting to the bottom of bank frauds had caught their ears—particularly Auntie Rae's. "Oh, if only, if *only* things could open for Worth—"

"Keep looking God-ward," Mother said wistfully, confirming what her daughter had always known. Snow Harrington would like to live "back in civilization." But given a choice, she would stay wherever her one and only Dale was. Marvel vowed again that she would never marry unless she could have such a marriage. Safe to say for there would never be another....

Mother's reference to trusting God reminded Marvel that they had promised to visit the black folk of the bottomlands and attend their church. Here it was July and the promise just hung there in the sultry air like the drooping sunflowers which no longer found energy to lift their tired heads. Everything of beauty was gone. Maybe a bit of beauty lay in worshiping together. She needed something to revive her wilting hope.

She mentioned the matter to Mary Ann and was delighted when the entire family decided to come along. The service was indescribably touching about the whites and blacks worshiping together. Marvel felt near to the heart of God in that little lean-to with dirt floors as the uneducated but pure-of-soul Brother Hezekiah spoke emotionally of loving one another in this world in preparation for a better world "up yonder" where there was no hate, no hunger, just joy in that glad tomorrow. There was a chorus of "Amens," and soft, sweet crooning. Marvel envisioned the flaming sunrise of that glad tomorrow . . . and felt a newborn hope.

29

Change of Heart

The family came away from the humble building feeling much the way Marvel felt. Moved by the Spirit which prevailed there, Fanny, flanked by Sula Mae, Casper, and their endless chain of siblings and associates, bravely came forward to introduce "Uncle Ned," Heliotrope (her "ain't"), and Hezzie (the preacherman). And suddenly the entire congregation gathered around their "bosses" and responded to their warm greetings. Love knew no color.

"How refreshing," Grandmother said, touched by their simplicity. "I feel as if I've had a change of heart. Don't ask me to explain."

It needed no explaining. It was enough to *feel*. And there was not enough energy to do more. Even the light of the full moon, shedding molten silver over a wasting land, felt hot. It was enough to breathe.

But *change* was the word. There were changes ahead nobody would have dreamed possible. One thing was certain: *change*. Nothing remained the same—except God. Oh, blessed be His name—the same today, tomorrow, and forever. Marvel held fast to the reassurance....

School clothes were completed, as were Marvel's research papers, reading of recommended English novels, Dickens' works, and the indepth written reports—each paper so advanced it resembled a term paper. She felt secure and, although there was a fluttering of apprehension, she was well-prepared for the swiftly approaching school year.

Summer had passed midpoint, but the electrical storms—usually tapering off in late spring—lingered. Some called it "heat lightning," but all hoped that one of the storms would bring rain.

And one of them did. There was a lightning storm which struck with such force it might well have heralded the end of the world. All who had storm cellars sought refuge underground. The Harringtons had the largest one around. In its immensity, the cellar resembled a cave with several rooms. There were benches, cots, and a few emergency provisions in case of a disaster. Walls were lined with canned fruit and root vegetables. There were countless containers of jams and jellies, and along one wall was a line of pottery crocks filled with kraut, mincemeat, and aging pickles.

But the dank air was sickening and the uncertain flames of candles brought back memories which added to Marvel's nausea. She prayed that nobody would make mention of the horror Elmer Salsburg had caused. Nobody did. It all happened so long ago. Not that she could forget.

Outside the wind howled like a banshee. Then there was a deathly silence as if the group had been trapped inside a grave—buried while still alive.

And then the rains came—came with such force one would think the very sky had split in half. They all clapped, but there was no sound above the raging storm.

Billy Joe whimpered in fear. Auntie Rae tried to soothe him, as did Mary Ann in her own way. "Someday," she muttered, as the storm tapered off, "we'll move. I hate storms. We could go to California."

Nobody paid attention—or was Marvel the only one who heard? The others were pushing out to dance in the rain. Only the mouth of the earth was thirsty and seemed to have swallowed it all.

"I doubt if it did much good," Daddy said in disappointment.

"Crop-wise, probably not, but the air smells so clean and sweet," Grandmother said. "That's a welcome change!"

Daddy looked at her with appreciation. "Gives a man reason to hope that more rains will follow. I'd almost forgotten that it *could* rain!"

Soon afterward the county agent came. Nattily dressed in khaki knickers with matching cap and wearing gloves and tinted goggles, Mr. Inman looked more like a pilot than a farmer. However, he was all business when he set his crew to work after discussing the procedure with the Harringtons.

"East Texas was never meant to be cotton country," he said flatly, confirming what Marvel had suspected all along. "Too bad man tampered with nature. Even the Indians knew better! Well, gentlemen, we can't put the trees back any more than we can say a few magic words and see natural grasslands with cattle grazing like the buffalo once did. It would take more time than we have. Second best is replenishing the soil, feeding it. It's not only thirsty, it's hungry. Commercial fertilizer's too expensive—artificial, too. Government studies show it's best to select plants rich with nutrients."

Daddy wiped his sweating brow with the back of his hand. Marvel, looking out the window with the Harrington women and children, noticed how frayed his chambray work shirt had grown and how faded. Once blue, the cotton fabric was bleached almost white. The overalls he wore were in the same sad condition.

She was not surprised when he said, "I'm sure what you're saying is true, but under the circumstances—well," he hesitated and then asked bluntly, "just how do we live?"

The county agent nodded with understanding. "We've taken that into consideration. We have to make the land pay as best we can."

He went on to outline the plan. It all made sense. They would try and preserve the soil. Already the little rain they'd had had washed away some of the topsoil and the land was bone-dry too soon. Come those evil winds like Oklahoma and Kansas were experiencing and all of it would blow "from here to kingdom come," leaving nothing but hard-pan...bedrock. The outlook was grave.

The plan was to terrace the vast fields, zigzagging the raised beds in an effort to make small windbreaks. Hitching the teams of draft animals to well-sharpened plows, they would turn the soil upward in curving rows. The good news was that the terraces could be planted with melons and other vine crops in an effort to let productive crops serve as groundcover. Corn would be grown

for both table-use and feed for livestock, shipping being out of
the question. There would be no feed—and with natural pastures gone, no more hay baling...a grim picture. But corn, like
cotton (which would continue to dominate the bottomlands and,
with barnyard manure, the land would produce more than the
drier sections), was soil-depleting. Suggestion: plant velvet
beans at the base of stalks to feed the soil and intersperse with
peas and alfalfa crops which were kind to the land and could
tolerate "support crops" like oats. All this would create a food
cycle: the land would feed the stock, the stock would furnish
farmers with dairy products and meats and then furnish ferti-
lizers. And the ladies would be happy to learn that Mrs. Sutheral—
he was right in assuming that they were acquainted?—would be
out to show all neighborhood women some new ways of utilizing
this new way of living. The winds were coming, and Mr. Inman
wanted the people to be prepared and know how destructive a
drought could be. They would be prepared as best they could.
Otherwise, curtains!

Marvel did not trust herself to look at Mother. This must all be
frightening to her. And there was no way to escape. One of the
books Marvel had read and done a paper on had been on this
very subject. But why add fuel to the fire? She had digested the
facts in silence. Looking back hurt, as did looking forward. But
the words remained.

"Drought" is a dreaded word. And the one on the horizon
holds the greatest threat. During the droughts which occurred in the world war, prices remained high, affording
dry-land farmers a good living.

Beginning in 1930, however, a new dry period set in, this
one accompanied by low Depression prices. Added to crop
failure, the situation was grim enough. But another has
struck, like a tornado touching down to suck up all hope....

Everyone suffers when drought comes. The great drought
in progress is shaking a dusty fist in the faces of those who
till the soil to feed themselves and the rest of the nation. It
finds us now with a surplus of food stocks raised earlier.
The carryovers have saved the nation from total starvation.
But these very blessings are threats in disguise. They depress
farm prices, in turn impoverishing farmers and lessening

their ability to cope with drought losses. The bottom has dropped out of prices. But, in like manner, the bottom has dropped out of production. It has become a vicious circle. A rise in prices would do no good when farmers have nothing to sell.

Farmers are not alone in their suffering. Higher food prices have heaped coals of fire upon the heads of city dwellers, many of whom are unemployed. And they hurt in another way as well. Impoverished farmers cannot afford city-manufactured goods. Thus, everybody loses when drought strikes. There are no winners, except the anonymous rich who, like scavengers, feed from the flesh of those who perish.

Drought hurts the land. The greatest injury of all is done to the land itself, because starving soil will affect more than the present generation. Never more appropriate than now was the warning of the Scripture, Deuteronomy 5:9, "God, visiting the iniquity of the fathers upon the children unto the third and fourth generation."

Lands subject to drought usually have a natural cover of grass, which acts as a natural protection. Although it may be dying down, grass roots hold together and protect topsoil from being washed away by rain or blown away by wind. When moisture comes in the future, roots revive, or dormant seeds sprout, and the grassy blanket is restored.

But once the plow has removed that natural blanket, drought can strike a deadly blow. Dry-land methods used in the past have pulverized our soil to a powdery fineness, an easy victim of winds. Erosion occurs and land is rendered unproductive for years to come.

The part which had been most frightening to Marvel concerned the pages regarding her own home:

Wind erosion has stripped earth from thousands of square miles of once-rich farmland and pasture. The region under "Siege Perilous" at present begins in the Texas Panhandle and spreads ... so severe it threatens to "dust out" completely millions of acres. Wind-driven topsoil has become heaped elsewhere ... these *loess*, as they are called, become compacted into excellent soil...leaving a barren trail of desolation. Grazing lands are ruined and, if a stockman overgrazes, he furthers the danger....Underground grassroots (fed by the water table below the surface) are damaged...and when rain comes again, it increases the damage. Man has violated nature too long.

The government has recommendations but no guaranteed cures. Farmers are urged to search for drought-resistant plants until a better solution can be found through trial and error. Too, they should take advantage of the government's efforts to train them to rotate crops and seek free assistance from agents who, having suffered losses themselves, have learned firsthand the advantages of *listing* in terraces. Such contour plowing is accomplished by means of combining disks and plows...pulverizing...and heaping up in horizontal furrows in curves extending the entire length of each field. These furrows catch soil when it begins to blow as well as catching and holding water when there is rain.

And there is one final word of warning. Farmers are urged not to undertake too ambitious programs or contract debts which cannot be paid off by continuously good crops. Too many farms have been lost already. And strive as your government will, it is unable to devote its efforts, during this Depression, to more than the most immediate and pressing of hardships. Then, however remote it may seem, should there be war...

Oh, no! Marvel had never been able to read beyond that point. There was more than the heart could bear at present. Why borrow trouble?

But now that the county agent had come, she was glad that she was prepared and understood. She was glad, too, that Daddy and Uncle Worth listened to Mr. Inman. Grandmother, who had seemed to retreat into a world of thought of late, took it all with typical grace—as did Auntie Rae who was as flexible as a willow. Mary Ann took no more interest in the proceedings than she took in her assignments the principal had outlined for the girls. Marvel had given up pushing her. She must decide for herself. And, she supposed, there was a kind of logic to her cousin's rationalizations: "I can see the use of fractions, I guess," she said repeatedly. "A homemaker needs to know how to divide recipes—in proper fractions, that is. *Not* in those silly improper ones. Even their name tattles their uselessness! But for the life of me, I can see no use in figuring how much a gross of pencils cost when people have trouble scraping up enough to afford *one*. And as for Angle A equals Angle B, who ever enlarged a dress pattern by *that*?"

Why argue? Mary Ann's mind was made up. Her goal was set. And so was Marvel's own. Maybe they were both right ... or both wrong. Somewhere there was a happy medium. Married women sometimes worked—some from choice, others from necessity. Perhaps there were no jobs out there. But there were *needs*—needs she could meet. And something pushed Marvel on no matter how difficult—how impossible—it all seemed.

"Mary Ann," she said, suddenly remembering something Mr. Wilshire had said. Marvel was surprised when Grandmother, Mother, and Auntie Rae turned toward her. It was only then that she realized all the women had been watching wordlessly.

Stumblingly then Marvel shared the incident. One of the boys—was it Archie?—had questioned the need of an education if a person only planned to dig ditches. The principal had answered seriously, "He can dig better ditches!" Mary Ann yawned and switched on the news.

The anecdote probably fell on deaf ears. Fanny had brought the children from the bottomlands and they all watched in the sizzling sun, which was almost invisible at times as the wind picked up the powdery soil and formed it into "dust devils" which whirled—picking up everything in sight—and danced away in hot-breathed glee. Only Marvel saw.

"Did you hear? *Did* you? Marian Anderson, the well-known—"

"*And* well-educated!" Marvel interrupted, a little piqued with Mary Ann. It was very unlike her, and Marvel mumbled an apology. "Go ahead, tell us what you heard on the radio. We're interested."

"She's going to sing—actually *sing* before the president!" Mary Ann was as breathless as if she'd been running in this heat.

"You mean the Negro contralto who has toured Europe?" Grandmother asked, equally surprised and pleased.

"*American* Negro," Marvel added by way of identification.

They all agreed that it was wonderful and about time, too. Imagine, after touring Europe, and last of all being recognized by her native land. A triumph all the same. And with a "better late than never," they looked at the time and said they must be preparing the evening meal. Those men would be exhausted and, they hoped, hungry.

"Oh," Grandmother turned to look at Mary Ann. "Did you tell us when this is to take place?"

"Tonight!"

"Then indeed we *must* rush. I am presuming, of course, that all of you agree we should invite our Negro friends in to hear this take place. It's a triumph for their race."

"It's a triumph for us all," Marvel said quietly.

And, of course, they would invite Fanny, Sula Mae, Casper... all of them ... and if the house overflowed, *Praise the Lord!* They could watch through the doors and windows. And they would turn the volume up so that the beautiful voice carried all over the bottomlands, blending with the whippoorwills.

It should be the song of the nightingales, Marvel thought. "A voice like hers comes once in a century," the great Arturo Toscanini had said. The nation would never be the same. This was a historical step in history.

Had she said it aloud? As she and Grandmother worked together in the kitchen, slicing tomatoes, pouring the steeped tea, and inventorying the supply of ice, Grandmother said, "I'm glad this happened now. I mean I'm glad that I can watch the happiness on those faces before things change—uh, for us personally—a change, you know."

30

"The Only Thing
We Have
to Fear..."

The voice of Marian Anderson still echoed through the bottomlands where cotton bolls were beginning to open, bearded and white-locked with ancient promises they could not keep, when the greatest change of all took place—so suddenly, there was no time to plan, to think the idea through. Sudden at least to Dale and Snow Harrington and, most of all, to their daughter.

Mrs. Sutheral came calling as Mr. Inman had said she would. When the stylishly dressed lady parked her red coupe, she paused to wipe at the dust now coating the shining surface with a small, dainty handkerchief while dust, still whirling behind her, seemed drawn as if by magnet to the new vehicle.

As everyone rushed out to greet their guest, Daddy laughingly said in a little aside to Marvel, "Hopeless—about like trying to mop up the ocean with a sponge!"

The dust was clearing and the passengers were visible. Grandmother was the first to make a positive identification. "Look! What do you know—if it isn't the Squire himself!"

Grandfather, his face beaming, walked spryly between the two borders of wilting daisies. The space between served as a walk, just hard ground and swept clean by broom and wind. It was easy to see that Alexander Jay Harrington, Esquire harbored news. What could it be to put such a bounce in his once-faltering step?

Mrs. Sutheral, once called simply home demonstration agent, had a new title, she announced proudly once she was seated in the living room. She was now *county* home demonstration agent.

"That means I'll be traveling to the rural areas, training a select few who will, in turn, organize women within the community. I thought of you ladies immediately—you especially, Snow—you being the most apt to stay put," she said, almost in one breath.

Marvel caught Mother's eye and saw the same question there that had occurred to her. Was there an unvoiced meaning to "stay put"? But their thinking was cut short by their guest's next words.

"You'll be paid—not much certainly, but a bit—besides the opportunity of distributing, after taking your fair share, the surplus goods. Which reminds me, I came bearing gifts!" she smiled.

"They'll be welcomed," Mother assured her. "Would you like some help bringing them inside? Anything perishable would be certain to surrender on a day like this. Would you like a cool drink?"

"A cool drink would be wonderful, yes. And, yes again, I would appreciate having help. Perhaps the drink afterward."

The foodstuff was the proverbial pot of gold at the end of a rainbow: rolled oats, raisins, rice, peanut butter, flour (white and wheat), sugar (white and brown), and mysterious unmarked packages in large paper sacks securely tied with cord string.

"Now," she smiled, "I have something new. Take the keys, girls, and open the turtle box. There's canned beef—too many cattle to feed, you know. And there'll be more. The best part is that canning facilities are being prepared by the government. Your center will be Culverville, and there you'll be able to use *tin* cans! There'll be an opportunity to market your produce or exchange with others. Sort of a common storehouse, you know—even better since the government will be bringing in food from other places. Kind of like Christmas, isn't it?"

Marvel felt an unexplained sense of discomfort. Good as the news was, it took a bit of getting used to. Was there a difference in this kind of program and well, standing in a bread line? What had they done to earn the food and the services? And somewhere buried deep within her was the nagging question: *Are all our rights being taken from us, robbing us of our freedom?* Freedom was America's heritage. It was every citizen's duty to preserve it. She sighed deeply, remembering that Mary Ann said she read too much. *Thought* too much would be more accurate. And for now she must listen.

"It's wonderful what all these government programs are doing," Grandmother said brightly. "I suppose that's how you came by that eye-catching automobile—not intending to ask personal questions."

"Oh, I'm *glad* you mentioned that!" Mrs. Sutheral said with sincerity in her voice. "It's just a loaner, but who cares? It oils my ego just to drive it. A real beauty, isn't it?"

Marvel joined Mother in the kitchen to assist with the grape-juicing. Fanny had brought the last of the muscadines and "possum grapes," along with the first ripening persimmons and a message that hickory nuts were beginning to fall "down yonder in th' bottom groves."

When they returned with the tinkling glasses, Mrs. Sutheral and Grandmother were talking together in low voices. Their conversation stopped once Snow and Marvel entered. They were joined shortly by the men who drank thirstily, pausing only to say repeatedly, "Um-*ummm*! This hits the spot!" Thirst satisfied, they excused themselves to have a close look at Mrs. Sutheral's car.

Grandmother laughed indulgently. "There's something about men and motors—a kind of love affair that makes us women a little bit jealous. Still, I'd like a look myself as soon as the men—"

She was watching closely through the window as they inspected the red car. Biding her time, Grandmother darted outside—conveniently, just as Dale and Worth Harrington came inside. Their father remained. And together the two older people inspected the car, talking, *talking*, TALKING.

Something was in the wind. Marvel had felt it since Mrs. Sutheral and Grandfather arrived. No, before that. It had begun when Grandmother mentioned being happy that she could be here when Marian Anderson sang. Something had sounded temporary....

Grandfather and Mrs. Sutheral politely refused lunch. They needed to make preparations, as did Dale Harrington, his family, and Mrs. Riley. Preparations? The answer was to come soon—very soon.

The dust was still swirling and eddying behind the county home demonstrator's red coupe when Grandmother dropped the first shoe.

"No need bobbing a dog's tail joint by joint—causes too much repeated pain when one whack would do it once and for all. So the news is, we're going back into town."

"Who's *we*?" Daddy who had paled beneath his sunburn, asked.

"Me, for one. Worth can take it from there."

Worth Harrington, dropping his eyes to his work shoes, stumblingly said "we" included his household. His father thought there very possibly would be work for him. Rae had a chance to teach some classes in quilting and other handwork (she'd have to explain) under the PWA program for fine arts. Admittedly, some called the president's New Deal hogwash, the opponents saying it was "creeping socialism" or "business fascism" (Hearst newspapers referred bitterly to all the "alphabet soup")...but it was working! More people were on the payroll...more artists, writers, and musicians were changing the complexion of America while "singing for their supper."

Mary Ann began talking excitedly (not seeing an inch beyond her nose, Marvel thought in resignation). Marvel did understand, didn't she? About school—and everything?

"Everything" meaning Jake, of course. But Marvel nodded.

"Yes, I think I do," suddenly finding that she did. "But my understanding has nothing to do with it. You don't need my approval."

"Or mine," Mother said weakly. "But Mother, what will *you* do? Where will you stay? I suppose with one of the boys somewhere? I'm not even sure I know where my brothers are, I'm ashamed to say."

"Don't be!" Grandmother chirped happily. "I'm not going to try and locate them. None of them have gotten in touch with me—probably have troubles of their own. But, to answer your question, I plan to stay at the rooming house. That's where the Squire and Mrs. Sutheral live."

"Oh, and Miss Marlow!" Mary Ann's voice had risen several octaves. "Maybe *we* can stay there, too! Marvel and I did—and Mrs. Armstrong always needs help with her cabbage! Oh, it's nice there, and there are electric fans—"

Billy Joe was jumping up and down senselessly, having no idea what all the talking meant. Marvel wasn't sure either.

"I'll miss you," she said to Mary Ann. "I—I'll use your books and workbooks helping Annie and Ruth out here. School will be opening in Culverville soon now, and I'm hoping they will go."

If her cousin answered, the words were lost in the jumble of a million others. Auntie Rae was explaining to Mother that it was strictly for Mary Ann's school—and, of course Billy Joe would be entering "primary." And Grandmother hoped everybody understood that "Gran'mere" had been toying with this idea for quite some time—she and Father Harrington (meaning Grandfather).

Uncle Worth was simultaneously explaining to Daddy that they would have to "look around" for a house—a problem, he realized, until he could find something to do. Grandfather held fast to his going into banking, and he couldn't wait to get back— but, well, could they just leave the furniture until they could get settled?

And Grandmother was explaining that her pension would keep her. Also, she could teach violin lessons. Mrs. Sutheral had made that clear. "You'll have the piano so you could teach. I'll leave the radio—"

She stopped suddenly. "How could I have forgotten?" she said so loudly her voice carried above everybody else's. "The Squire and I have found a way, with the help of a good many others, to rebuild the church! There's a grant—WPA workers doing the work and PWA doing the decorating: making the pews, painting murals on the walls, even stitching the curtains that separate the big auditorium into rooms for Sunday school. Architects, under the same program, are at work already. Now tell me that isn't exciting if you have the courage. Go ahead, I dare you!"

There was more talk, but Marvel's mind had turned her mental calendar backward. "We have nothing to fear but fear itself," Franklin Delano Roosevelt had said of the Depression in his inaugural address. They must all be strong, expect the best, and work to achieve it. And, above all, hold onto faith. "We can. We *will*. We *must!*" She lifted her eyes God-ward and saw a host of clouds. They could work together, cooperate, and bring rain. The family must do somewhat the same. Success—no, call it *victory*—would come. . . .

Everything was packed and ready when Jake drove out to pick up his passengers in a touring car he had repaired. He brought a letter along from Archie for Marvel to read.

She skimmed it quickly, noting that he spoke of reenlisting for another six months for the second time ... "but I git this awful pang of homesickness sometimes, been workin with dynamite blastin them big heavy rocks, blowin rocks so high there ain't no sun. And sometimes pieces come down like shots, killed one man when him and me had planned to coon hunt the next day. Makes a man think, you know, wonderin' if it's worth it, bein' away from family and all. I caint re-up nohow. I got a job back home. Gotta prove need, y'all know. Ain't much choice, is there, buddy? So 30 bucks is 30 bucks. But mankind, I shore miss all y'all. Does that girl know how lonesome I git? I gotta school pitcher I jest look an look at till I cud cry...."

Poor Archie—wearing his heart on his sleeve. Being "that girl" wasn't easy. Marvel handed the letter back to Jake, shaking her head sadly. He nodded his understanding. He pitied their friend, too.

Time passed quickly. There was little talking until the last minute. Then all talked at once. Promising to write, to call, even (rashly) to visit. Marvel and Mary Ann clung together. Mary Ann's lips were quivering, but there were no tears. Jake tactfully started the engine. Parting was never easy—

Then, surprisingly, just as he shifted gears and turned the switch from "battery" to "magneto" (which would generate power and save the "juice" of the batteries), Uncle Worth called to Daddy:

"The good Lord looks after fools, they say— If this f-f—, well, *man* I like to call myself—should be so lucky as to find work, would you want to think about this?"

Daddy said a flat no, then turned on his heel and hurried away. Mother followed, letting tears spill over. Marvel alone waved them out of sight. Then, without trusting herself to pretend bravery another minute, she half-ran to the solace of the persimmon grove. There in the leafy silence, she closed out the rest of the world and gave herself over completely to the wonders of nature.

How balanced and uncomplicated life seemed in that undisturbed corner of the world. One day, all too soon, it, too, would fall prey to what mankind called "progress." Gone ... forgotten ... without anyone learning the lesson that fruits which ripened without outside help took their own required time and patience. But oh, the goodness of the wild, sweet delicacies hiding there for eyes willing to seek and find and hands willing to harvest. The miracles of God's handiwork were there throughout the years, but never more visible than at harvest time...so ready to share....

Now with the tender-sweet season of spring gone, and summer promising to surrender to fall, the air would grow more brisk, the colors more vivid, and all the maypops, wild plums and grapes, dewberries, blackberries, huckleberries, and blackhaws would be but youthful memories. Explosively beautiful and sweet to the tongue and nostrils as the preceding seasons were, Marvel preferred autumn-going-on-winter in the wetlands. In this thinning grove, it was easy to remember life as it had been: undisturbed, wild, having its own way...a Garden of Eden.

Once upon a time there had been deciduous hardwood trees—hickories, oaks, and sweetgum—and their colorful leaves carpeted the ground in thick piles of bright orange, sunshine-yellow, and pink-shading-to-scarlet. The flamboyant leaves had piled knee-deep to the children who took time to *live*—a part of living being the search for buried treasures of fallen hickory nuts, black walnuts, and chinquapins (wee, sweet chestnuts—all gone now).

And then there were the wild persimmons, the only reminders of the unspoiled long-ago remaining. The slender, stately trees reached high above the heads of all the other trees to garner the sun to sweeten their golden fruits. Sweeter and sweeter they were as the leaves were stripped away by the winter winds.

Marvel remembered helping Daddy fill gunnysacks with fallen nuts and how—always—the two of them, impatient for a mellow-ripe persimmon, would pluck one of the golden treasures ("forbidden fruits," Daddy called them) before they were mellow-ripe. She smiled, remembering the result. Their mouths began to draw and pucker. Daddy would make a game of guessing which was manufactured from underripe persimmons: quinine or alum. And then he would say, "This time we've learned a valuable lesson." But they never did.

Well, she knew now. Tempting as the fruit looked, it had not matured. Fully ripe, persimmons were squishy-soft and could be sucked from their skins or put through a strainer for jams, pies, cookies, or holiday breads. But the ripening process required patience—and faith.

A sudden snapping of a dry twig caused Marvel to jump. And then she relaxed. Barefoot children were fishing nuts from the slough.

"Fanny! You startled me." Marvel knew then Fanny was their escort.

"You hadn't ought to be here Miss—uh, Marvel hon. I'm not sayin' it's not safe, but my people don't feel right down here in the shadows. That creature—devil or whatever—put a fear in us all of fire. And it does come, lightning or foxfire maybe, but a big ball—"

"St. Elmo's fire, it's called. But I'll go if you'd feel better."

"I would, honey child. And we got sweet tater—potato—pie for you."

"Bless you—this land is ours. I see you love it, too. Remember how it used to be? One day it can be again, unless we fear *fear.*"

Mother looked relieved when Marvel returned but asked no questions. She had opened a can of the beef Mrs. Sutheral brought and put it into a cream gravy to pour over hot biscuits. "Hello baby," Daddy said. They seemed happy to be in charge again.

31

"Keep a Dream in Your Heart!"

The first persimmons had ripened to a molasses-like stage by the time classes began at Culverville High School. Mother made a dreamy dessert of the gooey pulp studded with hickory nuts the night before registration. She topped the pie with mountains of whipped cream—an extravagance since it should have gone to the dairy.

"Enjoy it, darling," Mother said gaily as she served a generous slice to Marvel. "This is a special occasion."

But Marvel noted that her mother's hand was unsteady. They were all tense, parents feeling—as parents had felt since time began—that they were "losing" their daughter. She was entering a world in which they had no part. Daughter feeling—as children had felt in past generations and would continue to feel in generations to come—that she must exhibit a courage she didn't feel.

To cover their anxiety, Marvel, Mother, and Daddy engaged in small talk, their voices trying to sound light. The weather remained hot, but a good rain would break the heat. What would Marvel wear tomorrow? Mother had laid out the tan crash dress with brown buttons and bound buttonholes matching the wide-stitched linen belt—so tailored and becoming, so *right*. Marvel smiled and said it was just what she planned (which was true, as it was simple and understated). Daddy said she would be beautiful no matter what she wore, his eyes carefully avoiding the single bale of cotton representing a year's work.

"I have enough gasoline to take you, honey. Are you sure you don't want your mama and me to come along?"

"Thank you again, Daddy, but I've arranged to go in with Mr. Bumstead. The milk truck goes right past the school. I'll be finished by the time he comes home with the empty cans."

"It'll be so dusty," Mother said with concern. "You'll be wilted. That truck is so hot. You'll feel dirty and tired—"

"The bus will be no better, Mother. I wish you wouldn't worry."

Her father agreed. The school buses were a "disgrace," he'd reported after talking with the county school superintendent, Bob Bowden. They had been personal friends since high school days, Dale Harrington explained. Mighty nice Bobby landed that position. Just showed what an education could do. The way Daddy said that made Marvel wonder if he had some secret regrets about life. This Depression had caused many people to reevaluate values, have second thoughts, even indulge in some if-I-had-my-time-to-live-life-over—

Maybe it was the timing. At any rate, Daddy suddenly chose to go into a background that Marvel had never suspected.

"Bobby went on to business school—wanted me to but, well, I had other ideas. If I could have foreseen the future—"

"But you had eyes on this land, didn't you, Daddy?"

Daddy finished his pie, complimented Mother, and laid his fork aside before answering.

"Well yes, I always intended coming back here sometime— wanted to, anyhow. But I had eyes on a certain young lady, like all the other fellows around town. Winning your mother's hand and having you come into our lives are the only great accomplishments I can claim. Otherwise, I guess I'm kind of the black sheep."

"Don't *say* that!" Mother cried out. I won't have you putting yourself down just because they do it! All of them do—even Worth. Oh, he tried to handle it and was fairly successful, but I could *feel* it. Banks, banks, *banks!*"

Mother's voice had risen in a way Marvel had seldom heard it do before. *Strange*, she thought—with pity in her heart for the two she loved so much—*how we live around people, feel we know everything there is to know about them, only to find we know nothing at all.* Marvel knew then that the three of them were adults together. Somehow the realization made her feel stronger.

Appetite gone, Marvel folded her napkin, pressed the creases carefully, then said, "Go ahead please—both of you. I need to hear this. Some of it I have felt, now that I think about it. Tell me—"

Daddy did not hesitate. In fact, he seemed relieved. "My father meant well. He was just the family patriarch, felt he should make all the decisions, and none of us were to question. My brothers were no weaklings, but I sometimes wondered if they didn't feel that going along with Alexander Jay Harrington's plans for them was easier than objecting. I was different, something I can't explain—maybe it was hard-headedness like my father said. Anyway, I despised everything about banks and bankers. Still do, in a way. Maybe they feel it—those bigwigs sitting there with greased hair and puffing fat Havana cigars. Could that be why I'm not a successful borrower? That they feel my resentment? Or act envious of their black leather chairs rolling around on marble floors that they order mopped every time a customer steps on a white square? *Ordered* is not a strong enough word! The way they yell at those poor, cowering black men—cowering there, at their mercy, saying, 'Yes suh, boss!' Or—" Daddy's voice had risen with emotion, but realizing he was out of control, he softened his tone, "it's more likely that I act inferior, which is how I feel, I guess—having to crawl like those men cleaning—to *beg*. Well, it won't always be this way. With God as my witness, I promise!"

"Oh, my darling—" Mother was weeping. "My poor darling."

"Don't cry, Mother. Daddy's right. This isn't the end. I'll study. I'll make you proud of me—just as I'm proud of you, just as you are. Don't apologize, Daddy. Let your feelings out."

Daddy straightened with pride. "I have everything a man could wish for, and here I am licking my wounds. You two make me *feel* like a man, give me something to live for. But I got off the subject—though heaven knows how I got on it. But you wanted to know your background and, believe me, you can be proud of your heritage, our sweet Marvelous—and you *are* just that! So here goes."

Disappointed with his son's "lack of ambition" and still determined to dominate him, Alexander Jay Harrington had decided that military school would give him proper discipline, as well as prestige. The name carried weight in high places and he knew the "right people," he said. So, without consulting his son, he made the contacts for entrance in Annapolis. Daddy, who loved baseball almost as much as he loved farming, had made a name for himself. But never did he entertain even the remotest hope of making sports a career. It came as a total surprise when a scout spotted him as he hit his third "homer" in the vacant lot where the teenage boys played on Saturday afternoons. After the game, his side the victors, Daddy had experienced what every boy dreams of when the scout asked him a few questions then told him to expect a contract from the American League and named a sum which rendered him speechless. Running home faster than he'd covered the distance between bases, Daddy had panted out the wonderful news. Wonderful? To whom? Dale Harrington only.

"Looking back, I'm ashamed. Our relationship might have been different if I'd swallowed my pride. But well, doggone it, I *was* disappointed." He paused. "Did I say that word? I know: telltale language, poor usage. I know, Marvel—might as well hark back to dog-tired, dog-poor, and all that!"

Mother and Marvel had laughed, breaking the tension. "Why not?" Marvel shrugged. "It's all right to use dogtrot and dog-eared. I asked Mr. Wilshire about something being correct and his answer surprised me: 'What are the educated people using?'"

"But I'm not *educated*—except by the school of hard knocks! Which brings me back to my story. I guess it had to happen that way, father and son standing their ground. Right or not, I balked."

Mother smoothed his hand. "Nothing wrong with that, precious. You'd have hated military life—all that regimentation."

"Maybe. It seems to be agreeing with Elmer. Any news on that loser, Marvel? I can see by your face that you'd rather not talk about him—good judgment. And he'd better not come sneaking around here. Forget that I mentioned Fred's son. This was to be *your* night."

"Oh, it has been, Daddy, you shared your dreams."

"Just pipe dreams. Empty. Useless."

"Dreams are never useless, Dale," Mother said softly. "Your life wasn't too different from mine—your feelings at least. I was a disappointment to my mother and she was a disappointment to hers, remember? We simply can't impose our thinking onto our children—and I guess dreams aren't inherited. We each have our own. In some strange way, I guess dreams are useful."

"Oh, they are! They are indeed! I'm glad we had this talk. You will never know *how* glad—either of you! We can be ourselves now and share our dreams. What you both have told me about yourselves and your dreams are secret reflections of *you!*"

Mother and Daddy were happy now.

"Keep a dream in your heart, Marvel darling," said Daddy.

32

Brave New World

The great two-story high school was packed and nobody seemed to be able to cope with the situation—including the teachers who were attempting to register the students. Consolidation was a new experience for them all. Teachers were weary. Students were frightened. And all were hot.

Marvel, apprehensive but not scared, looked around her as she worked her way up to the front of one of the countless lines. Her heart went out to all around her. It was safe to guess that most of the young people coming in from the rural areas would be dropouts. Already they looked defeated, outclassed both socially and academically. They were eyeing those they supposed to be "town" students and comparing themselves unfavorably without taking into account that they had been denied the same opportunities. "See this as an opportunity to make up that difference," she longed to say. Only that would be improper.

Their failures, which were almost inevitable, would be no fault of the teachers either. They would be overloaded, their schedules making individual teaching impossible. They wouldn't intend to neglect or ignore the very ones who needed a bit of encouragement. It would just happen. She wondered for the first time what happened to school-age girls and boys of migrant families. Were provisions made for them?

"Next!"

Marvel moved forward and sat down quickly. The man's voice

had been impersonal and brisk, with an implied "Let's get this over!"

"Name and school you came from, please," he said now, without looking up.

"I'm Marvel Harrington," she said to the top of his head, careful to keep her lips from turning upward with amusement.

"*Harrington!*" He looked up now with interest. "Are you related to *the* Harringtons?"

"I suppose you might say that. We are the only family by that name in the area—at least, that I know of. I am Dale Harrington's daughter."

He was younger than she had thought, and when he removed his glasses and massaged his eyelids he looked even younger. "Dale—I don't seem to recall a Dale. Is he the son of Alexander Jay Harrington?"

"Yes sir, *one* of his sons."

"In the banking business, I would suppose?"

"No sir, my father farms. We have the home place. As to my school—"

"Ah, Miss Harrington, your records from Pleasant Knoll precede you—and the name, of course, is very well-known. That will help."

Marvel cringed a little inside. Why should that make a difference?

It shouldn't. But it did, as time would tell.

There were certain required courses, she understood? Yes, she understood. Would Miss Harrington wish the college prep? Yes, yes, of course she would. Miss Harrington would.

"But please call me Marvel," she said simply. "And might I know your name, too, please?"

"An oversight—I beg your pardon. I am Mr. Anglo. Unfortunately, I will not have the privilege of having you as a student as I'm to oversee an experimental class beginning this year—sort of a business opportunity class for those terminating education with high school. They'll need jobs and work is scarce. This will provide on-the-job experience. Well, it doesn't concern you—"

"Oh, but it does!" Marvel said quickly. "I mean I'm glad to hear it, Mr. Anglo. But I mustn't detain you. Here is a list I prepared." Reaching into a small clutch bag, Marvel drew out a sheet of paper showing the subjects she wanted to take and handed it to the teacher.

Mr. Anglo scanned the list and, looking baffled, moaned as he shoved it across the table to her. "This is impossible—utterly out of the question!"

"Why sir?"

"Why? It would go against all our rules. We run a tight ship, have the reputation of being a no-frills school. Already you will be carrying a heavier load than you're accustomed to."

"I doubt it, sir. Take a look at my records."

The teacher examined the material Mr. Wilshire had forwarded to him, noted the long line behind Marvel and, with a sigh, said he was unable to make this exception. In fact, he doubted that it would do any good to see the principal—

But it did. Mr. Phillips was all business but willing to listen. "Do you realize this kind of work load would give you no preparation time at all? No study halls, and all these subjects are solids except the home economics class. Well, actually one could put it in the same classification the way Miss Whitcomb conducts her assignments—lots of outside reading, home projects, and you may be unfamiliar with our facilities. The cottage, built like a real home for understandable reasons, is about a mile from our school and students have to walk—in your case, *run*. How in the world would you manage?"

"If running is essential, I'll run!"

Mr. Phillips' snapping black eyes seemed to pierce her soul. Marvel felt uncomfortable under such scrutiny but did not allow her own eyes to falter. It was blue against black, a sort of testing. There would be no more chances—just this one.

"*Please*, Mr. Phillips—it is very important to me." Marvel's voice was so soft she could hardly hear her own words.

"Very well." Pushing his swivel chair around, the principal began to write out a permission slip. The scratch of his pen was deafening in the silence of the stuffy office.

"Oh, I can't thank you enough. I promise you won't regret this. I'll study at night. I don't date boys the way some girls do, and my parents will cooperate. They'll see that I have space and time—"

Realizing that she might be talking too much in her excitement, Marvel stopped in mid-sentence and sat with her sweating bare knees pressed closely together. Looking at Mr. Phillips' dark business suit, white shirt, and conservative tie, she felt a first embarrassment with her white ankle socks. True, all the other girls wore them. But supposing he didn't approve? She was glad now that Miss Marlow had stressed the natural look, forbidding any makeup for young girls except for a pale pink lipstick manufactured by *Tangeé*.

"You will need to show this slip to each teacher. Have each initial it and return it to me, please, Marvel," he said, turning to her.

Marvel rose quickly. "Thank you again, sir—so much."

Stuffing the slip in her small bag to avoid smudging the wet ink with her sweating palms, Marvel rose and thanked Mr. Phillips again. She was turning to leave when he detained her.

"Just a moment. If you wish to drop one or two of these subjects, nobody could find fault with that. It's poor scheduling. You need a study hall following home ec. That's a long walk, sometimes in rain or snow—or, just the opposite, heat. Well, I need tell you nothing about the weather here. Girls are often late."

"I see no problem, sir."

"There *is* a problem! The only way I could juggle your classes around to accommodate all you ask for demands that geometry follows home economics. Missing any instruction in that area puts you at a disadvantage."

"I can understand that, Mr. Phillips."

His face was unreadable. "I teach all junior and senior math. I demand punctuality!"

Marvel met his gaze levelly. "Then I will run a little faster!"

* * *

Mary Ann called that evening. "I can't wait to hear all about your day."

Marvel gave her cousin a quick account, suspecting that there was more than interest in her report behind Mary Ann's call. There was an undercurrent in her question, even in her listening without comment. "Enough. Sometime I'll tell you about the new on-the-job training program," she finished.

But Mary Ann's plans changed when Marvel mentioned the new class. She wanted to hear more—hear it right now! "I don't know much about it," Marvel said. "It doesn't concern me."

"It concerns *me*," Mary Ann interrupted eagerly. "I will need a job. That course fits the bill for me—oh, and for my Jake. I guess he'd like to go on to school, but that takes money. This world makes no sense. Have to *have* money to *make* money—go to school so you can make money, but it takes money to go to school. Am I making sense?"

"No, but I understand what you mean."

"But you don't approve—I can tell by your voice! I know you want me to go to college, but I'm not going. I don't want to."

Marvel was tired all right—"dog-tired," she smiled to herself, remembering Daddy's words. She was tired, too, of trying to make her cousin see the value of an education. Why bother? Take care of *now*.

"So what's new with you, Mary Ann? I miss you lots."

"I miss you even more. I wish things were the way they used to be—and someday they will be," she said mysteriously.

"What's up, Mary Ann? Something, I can tell."

"A lot of somethings."

Everything was going to be fine with them—really it was! Mary Ann was working with Miss Marlow again. Auntie Rae had more than she could do and loved it. She was teaching stitchery under the PWA program and the classes were jammed. Besides, she was working on the church drapes. Oh, Marvel should see the church—more beautiful than before the *fire*. (Some good things had come from that, after all. Not that the culprit with big hands and pea-size brain meant any good, but wait till she finished—just wait!)

Mary Ann gushed on hurriedly. So much to say, and it *had* to be said. Marvel, being married to books the way she was, would have no time for anything—even listening—once school got in swing. Marvel listened—interested yes, but feeling that she would cave in from exhaustion and hunger. Why, no wonder. She'd eaten nothing since five o'clock this morning. But she must hold up. She *must*. Eventually, Mary Ann would get back to—to—(*Come on, Marvel, say the name!*). But Marvel was unable to force the syllables.

"Marvel, are you there? Oh, here's the main part!"

The main part indeed. Why then would her ears go deaf? No, no, not her ears. The problem lay with her heart. It was caught in the steel grip of a vise being squeezed tighter and tighter until, finally, there was no blood remaining. Only bits and pieces of Mary Ann's important words penetrated Marvel's brain—

enough to spell out the beginning of some unforeseeable disaster. Enough for that, yes.

Grandfather? Fine...and part of the overall plan. Only too glad to even the score. Frederick Salsburg outfoxed him...took advantage of his grief when the grandmother the girls had never known died of dropsy. Moved in for money which should have gone to the Harrington heirs (even though he'd had his share of his natural father's money when she remarried). Marvel did understand? Well, something awful was going on—there being two kinds of awful: awful *awful* and awful *wonderful*. Strange things going on...faint lights in the house Marvel's family had owned once...but nobody there...noises, too, like the place was occupied by *ghosts*! Scary, all of it...and the same thing going on in the Salsburg house. Everybody scared with all the talk of hoodlums hiding out. About ready to summon one of Hoover's G-Men...those crime busters still moving at a full gallop running down desperadoes...making good J. Edgar's warning: "Crime does not pay!"...real hero, that man—powerful. Might outrun FDR for president. Out after more than gun-totin' gangsters and racketeers...including "shyster lawyers," "sob-sister judges," and other legal vermin...*all* "criminal jackals"— men operating just within the law but robbing, *murdering, burning*. Salsburgs would be a target.

"You're right," Marvel managed to say faintly, "but can you come to the point? Does this tie together somewhere?"

"Yes, oh yes! In a two-kinds-of-awful way! The *awful* part centers around the thistle! Oh, the horror stories—talk, nothing anybody can prove, but now everybody's more scared of *him* than the badmen of the underworld! Hiding out from the law— escaped convict—deserter to be shot on sight—runaway mental patient—all that and more! But the one scaring me most is that he's been shot, left for dead, only to live—minus one leg. Being a kind of 'Peg-Leg Jack,' the mystery man leaves a kind of trail— like he was dragging that peg leg. Ring a bell? It *does* sound like Elmer. Oh, Marvel, be careful!"

Marvel's heart was pounding. Mother was trying to fry chicken in this heat, knowing it would please her. But the heat from the wood stove swirled around her, robbing her of her last ounce of energy. Even the smell nauseated her. She simply had to terminate this endless conversation. Unfinished? Oh no, she couldn't!

"Now on to the awful *wonderful*," Marvel suggested as lightly as she could. "I can't wait."

"All right!" Mary Ann's voice was triumphant. "Frederick Salsburg's panicky, in need of cash, running scared—who knows? He's put most of his property on the market. Nobody has money and wouldn't want the houses anyway after all the talk, so it's down to almost nothing. Remember Ramsey Cook, the Republican postmaster? He thinks there may be a new administration and the post office may reopen, and a *bank* or so come back, maybe on the shares. Daddy's willing to chance it, so we're all going to buy from Salsburg—maybe *all* of it. Right now just your house. It's a steal but, like Grandfather says, he stole from *us*. We'll move in, and Daddy doesn't mind working with WPA since it's so temporary. Sort of a straw boss at the church—"

"You sound busy and happy. Don't do anything foolish. Never mind about the future. Who knows? But for now, promise me you'll stay in school. *Promise!*"

"I promise. That was the reason behind our moving, but it was all for the best. You can see that!"

Marvel could not see it. In fact, she was terrified at what Uncle Worth and Auntie Rae were doing. True, better days would come sometime. She *had* to believe that and prop it up with prayer. But it would take time and patience. Nobody could force change by idle wishing. Try biting into an underripe persimmon and you get your lips puckered.

"You've not answered." For a moment Mary Ann sounded petulant, then her voice softened, "You're not mad about the house, are you? After all, it was yours."

"It never was. But yes, I do have reservations about it—not wanting your parents to get into the same trap. And after all you've told me, I feel it's *you* who should be careful of—of *him!*"

There was a flash of lightning followed by a growl of thunder. The line snapped and crackled. Mary Ann might as well have been calling from Mars. She said something about Grand'mere's happiness . . . but, of course Marvel knew. She called Aunt Snow, didn't she? Still helping Billy Joe . . . loved school . . . one day that wedding dress . . . *Eeeck!*

The strike was close. *Not a fire—not a fire, Lord, please!*

Mother called dinner. Marvel hung up the receiver as if the black instrument itself were the bearer of frightening news. She debated about sharing the disturbing conversation with Mother and Daddy and decided to postpone it. After all, it was mostly rumors and blind hope. Besides, her parents wanted to know all about her experience.

"Well," Marvel flashed a brilliant smile at her waiting parents, "your daughter entered a brave new world today. I'll need your help. But right now I want the biggest piece of white meat in that platter!"

33

Dare to Be Right

Daddy was shaking her gently at the improbable hour of 5:00 A.M. when the telephone rang. "Who on earth at this hour?" he muttered.

Marvel fought off the temptation to pull the lightweight coverlet over her head, inhaled deeply the delightful aroma of frying bacon and percolating coffee, and sprang to her feet. It was a special day. Even the Rhode Island Red rooster knew, his shrill herald to the new day announcing the sunrise. Of course—the first day of school! Good Mr. Bowden called Daddy and told him the tentative bus schedule.

"Hurry, sweetie," Mother called needlessly as Marvel pulled on the clothes she had laid out the night before: a pale orchid-floral cotton dress with quaintly dropped yoke, short puff sleeves, and demure high collar which could be opened with one, two, or three of the giant mother-of-pearl buttons. Grandmother had taken such pains with that dress, puckering her brow over the "new" styles in the Sears and Roebuck catalog. "New, my foot!" she had scoffed. "This was the style when Heck was a pup! Solomon would know better that there's 'nothing new under the sun.'"

She felt a twinge guilty at withholding details of Mary Ann's chat—no, chatter was more like it. But there was no time now.

"Who was *that*? Is everything all right?" Mother asked anxiously as she poured the coffee. "It's hot weather for oatmeal, darling, but you need something to stick to your ribs. No? It's a

224

long time 'til noon. I made you a sandwich and put in some molasses cookies and raisins. You'll find a place to snack, won't you? We haven't talked about it. My goodness, how I do go on. I always do when I—I'm concerned. I'm more concerned about school than you are, Miss Bright Eyes! You look lovely. That dress makes those big blue eyes of yours look purple. Well, Dale dear, out with it. Who and what?"

Daddy grinned. Everything was all right then?

Only it wasn't. Something was up. Something bigger than they were. Bigger even than the state—and that was whopping, seeing that Texas was the biggest of the 48 states. It was—Daddy almost strangled on his coffee—something which involved the entire country and the whole world!

"Tell us—please do, Daddy. I must be on time, especially today."

"Sure baby, I know. The man making that ominous call was in—hold onto your chairs!—Washington, D.C. Didn't take the time difference into consideration. Just boomed out with 'Do you know there are only a few days to save your country?'"

"What on earth—?" Mother gasped.

"Meaning the election! I guess people either love FDR or hate him with a passion. Voters have always had strong convictions, and these tough times have turned them into radicals. Some see the man as—blasphemy though it very well may be—what they declare to be their personal savior. Those who have bettered themselves, you know. While Wall Street has declared him to be the very devil—and give him what-for. That was somebody from the *Tribune*, saying I *had* to pay my poll tax. What with, I wonder? If not, he almost threatened, we'd be under fascism, socialism— even communism! Sounded like he was going to horsewhip me. No problem seeing which side *he's* on!"

Mother refilled the coffee cup Marvel would have no time to finish while posing the question of how the anonymous caller came by their name. That, Marvel thought, is the world's most poorly guarded secret. It was the Harrington name, of course. The name would open all doors—even get Daddy into Annapolis. Alexander the Great! She loved Grandfather. It was the shallowness of people's values that went against the grain.

Daddy had said something she missed. Mother was saying they had a right to vote however they chose if they were qualified. It was a free country.

Daddy finished his coffee. "So we're free to be poor, I guess."

* * *

Marvel ran part of the way to the designated corner where the bus was to pick up a handful of students. "Annie—Ruth," she greeted the two girls breathlessly. "I'm glad you're here!"

Both of them were apprehensive. "Can't rightly claim *we're* glad—me anyhow. Papa said I didn't have no—any—choice," Annie stammered.

"Me neither," Ruth said. "Us country kids is bound to get uh cold shoulder, not havin' much schooling. Well, them books of your cousin's helped—only we didn't understand 'em all."

"I'm sorry I was unable to spend more time with you, but I'll make up for it. Just stay in school and I'll help every way I can."

They were right, Marvel knew. Sad to say, they would face impossible odds. It wasn't fair. But that's the way it was. Period.

Somewhere in the distance a struggling vehicle backfired—the bus undoubtedly. The county school superintendent had prepared Daddy. It was a disgrace, he said. They'd probably be the laughingstock of the school, but it was transportation. They were fortunate to have *anything*. What was that saying—oh yes: "We are only rich when we realize we have nothing at all." Well, they were rich—very rich, she thought a little bitterly. Money had nothing to do with her thoughts, just injustices.

"Hop in all of y'all!" a jovial voice called through the cloud of dust. Glancing over her shoulder, Marvel saw several other boys and girls had kept their distance purposely. She'd had no chance to speak. A word of encouragement might have helped.

Now they all pushed forward. Marvel was the last to climb onto the running board and step inside. The delay had given her an opportunity to look at the homemade body of the bus, mounted on what was undoubtedly a used frame and engine. Smoke from the exhaust was mingling with the dust, causing her to cough and her eyes to water. The cheap tin body, painted a garish yellow, was lined with lidless eyes: windows, crudely sashed, which swung outward—the only visible means of ventilation. Ventilation? They'd suffocate in all these fumes.

"Move on back—clear back. Gotta make room fer lots. Get a move on. We got 40 miles to'go!"

Forty miles? When it was only five miles to Culverville? Marvel was to learn that they would go to country schools she had never heard of—all the "chapels" Annie and Ruth had spoken of— twisting...curving...backtracking in impossible heat, incredible cold (with no heat, of course)...and enough rain to cause an untold number of accidents. The boys would push when the vehicle was hopelessly mired to the hubcaps. The girls would get out and walk to lighten the load. They would be caught in storms with bolts of lightning setting the world on fire and winds twisting limbs from trees and blocking the road...causing them to arrive late, rumpled, miserable, and too frightened to concentrate. Such conditions, together with a heavy curriculum, was enough to try the very souls of the youthful riders.

But for now she was aware only of the crowded surroundings. She, along with the others, strained to hear instructions. Unpadded plank seats lined each side (boys on one side and girls on the other). Then there was an island of back-to-back seats running the entire length between the other rows. The reason for separation according to gender became obvious almost immediately.

"Scrooch up. Set yourselves close together. That's it, pack in there like sardines!" the driver ordered, then added the horrifying order to "put y'all's knees in between—y'know? Left, right, left, right—alternatin'. Git th' picter? Sorry, foks, ain't no other way in th' world we kin pack in here!"

It was a terrible arrangement. Small wonder they all complained. Cattle going to slaughter had better accommodations. And, Marvel sighed without comment, in a very real sense that's where most of them were headed....

Conversation was impossible, but there were those who attempted to shout to each other above the grind of the bus. All the while they were compelled to jam themselves more tightly so that other passengers could board. Marvel would have liked to take a look at the countryside, but it was useless to try. Too, there was nausea to fight off brought on by the endless curves, the jolting bumps, and the smell of cheap cologne, hair oil, boys' "plow shoes" in need of airing, and lunch sacks mashed flat and contents possibly spoiling.

It was a bad dream—one of those in which one is trying to awaken and can't. A dream—yes, it had to be a dream. This was impossible.

It was no dream. Instead, the bus rocked on...and on...and *on*. Until at last—stiff...aching...exhausted—they reached their destination.

As Marvel was preparing to step out of the "yellow peril," her secret name for this thing called a bus, the driver leaned over to touch her hand. "Marvel—uh, Miss Marvel?" The voice was uncertain.

There had been no opportunity to look up during the trying trip. Now she found herself looking into the face of Archie's father.

"Mr. Newland!" she exclaimed in surprise. "I never dreamed— You must forgive me. Things were a little confusing. And it's Marvel, of course—just plain Marvel."

"Beggin' pardon, Marvel, but they ain't nothin' plain 'bout *you*."

Marvel smiled her appreciation of what the man obviously meant as a compliment, asked what time the bus would be leaving in the afternoon, and made an attempt to hurry on. It was late.

"I'm gonna try real hard not t'be so late agin. But, like you say, t'was confusin' today. Still 'n all, I gotta tell this 'cause I'm real proud t'say I hepped on that bus. Right proud t'have me uh job, too. It'll be leadin' t'more—wait 'n see— Good when a man's able t'do with his hands like the boy 'n his ole man. Shure is now that folks—even them with money—quit changin' cars ever' coupla years. Gonna be more 'n more need fer auto repair shops—jest 'bout double th' business—"

"Yessir, I'm sure you're right. 'Bye for now. I *must* run!"

And run she did. At the door, a girl who seemed to know her way around directed incoming students to the auditorium for an assembly. Marvel joined the long lines pushing hurriedly up the stairs and eased herself into one of the desks in the back. The principal was just taking his place on the platform to give an endless list of instructions. Students were in no condition to appreciate his quote from Longfellow:

> Heights of great men reached and kept
> Were not achieved by sudden flight;
> But they while their companions slept
> Were toiling upward in the night.

"Then in closing, let me remind you about morals! *'Dare to be right*, dare to be true: *You* have a work none other can do'!"

Marvel rose stiffly, the words echoing in her ears: *Dare to be right… dare to be right…* for yes, she had a work none other could do.…

34

Toiling Upward

Marvel adapted quickly and well to the new school environment. But that is not to say it was easy. Many were the times when she was to recall another phrase of the poem Mr. Phillips had read aloud on opening day. "Toiling upward" indeed! Every day presented another glass hill to scale—hills others feared to so much as attempt. Rural students gave up without trying, seeing themselves as failures from the first day. The on-the-job-training class was too new to be of benefit as of now. Until there was a change they would be compelled to take a heavy load of "essential" courses.

"There is no excuse for failure," the principal declared. "All it takes to succeed is concentration! Be aware early in the school year that failure in any one subject constitutes failure of the entire grade. There is no such thing as 'make-up' work or returning the following year to play around with an easier load. Our country is in need of well-developed minds and we are here to see that any student graduating from this school will have one!"

Oh, Mr. Phillips, Marvel's heart cried out, *what about the others: the dropouts, the losers, the "failures"?* They would have no chance to toil upward—ever—unless somebody cared. Breadlines would lengthen....

The high-school junior was unaware at that tender age that she would be that "somebody" and that what she took to be personal thoughts were not her own, but the Voice of God preparing her for the work He planned for her....

Classes were overcrowded. Desks were wedged so closely together that there were no aisles. Windows were closed against the heat but also kept out the air. It was difficult to breathe— there was no oxygen. Students were restless, unable to concentrate. Marvel could feel her clothing wet against the hard surface of the fold-up seats. Teachers, red-faced and fraught with frustration, had little choice but to use a scattergun approach. All students received the same assignment and were expected to complete it on a given due date. All were to read the same books and take the same test. And all either passed or failed with no opportunity for making up assignments missed, lost, or misunderstood. It was like trying to board a train: Either one held a ticket or one did not. Only it was worse because surely no train had only one destination with no opportunity to get on or off along the way on a long, long journey. Small wonder so many jumped out the windows, so to speak.

The worst part of the trying situation was that the assignments were designed to meet the needs of well-prepared students— namely those teachers had taught previously. That boiled down to "town kids" being those to whom assignments were geared. Teachers had pressures, too.

Miss Robertson, the quiet-spoken spinster who taught English, spotted Marvel almost immediately. "You are one of the more promising students," she said as she detained her between classes. "I would like you to try for an exemption. Based on daily performance, tests, and outside reading, students averaging an A are exempt from midterm exams." The teacher spoke rapidly now as members of her next class filled the room, "and—and— *take your usual places, please*—your name would be on the honor roll, of course."

Surprised and pleased, Marvel thanked Miss Robertson and asked quickly what she should do now. Check out a copy of *Moby Dick*, Miss Robertson said—only two copies in the library. Best hurry!—be wise to borrow a notebook from a former student and see how it was to be turned in—a future assignment.

Marvel nodded, afraid she would be late to her next class. She was about to hurry away when the English teacher said, "Just a moment, dear. The name Harrington—are you related to Alexander—"

"His granddaughter, yes ma'am."

Word traveled. And she was "in." Not that she wouldn't have to claw her way to the top, burn midnight oil to achieve great heights, and then continue to climb without pausing to breathe. But it helped to gain recognition. Otherwise she might become one of Thomas Gray's flowers, "born to blush unseen, and waste its sweetness on the desert air." Remembering that it took the patient craftsman seven years to polish his "Elegy Written in a Country Churchyard" for market, she took heart. God had filled this world with riches—some for the taking, others worth striving for. And strive she would!

Math was difficult, but no more so than she had expected. Mr. Phillips was exacting, demanding the best his students had to offer—and then some. He was fair, but life was a straight line with no detours.

"Here, I'll need your help, Daddy," Marvel pleased Dale Harrington by saying. "Math is not my favorite subject or where I do best."

"I used to excel, but there's a lot I've forgotten," he warned.

But he did help. Even his warm support helped when she became a frightened little girl now and then.

And she helped him. Only Marvel had no way of knowing that. She would have been amazed had she known that the very day she asked for help, her father had had one of his greatest blows yet. Oh yes, his pride was wounded. He'd learned to swallow that a long time ago. But his concern for his family had driven him into a state of desperation.

Daddy told her about his most recent humiliation at the bank. How terrible! It was not unusual for farmers to borrow money to make a crop. There had to be seed and sometimes commercial fertilizer for the tired soil. Then families had to buy staple foods, no matter how well they provided for themselves, filling their larders with canned fruits and vegetables, salting down or sugar-curing pork, and threshing dried peas, beans, and grains. This year, of course, was more difficult. There had been precious little to preserve. Didn't bankers understand that?

"To be fair, I guess they have to save their own skins. It would be all too easy to end up like most of the other banks and have to close their doors," Daddy admitted reluctantly. Then, as if posing the question to himself, "But do they have to treat us like dirt under their feet?" Daddy's mouth twisted in an odd way.

Marvel, hurting inside, encouraged him to talk about it.

"The truth is that we have 30 dollars to cover it all—and I had to grovel to get that much. Any minute I expected that vampire to say, 'Roll over, doggie, if you want a loan. Good boy, shake hands, wag that tail to show appreciation'!"

"Oh Daddy!" Marvel said with a laugh. "Nothing could be that bad."

"Worse, sugar," he said through clenched teeth. "I might as well tell it all, now that I've burdened you with it. I'm sorry about it all, but there's not a lot I can do. I wanted to throw it in the man's face when he said I was lucky to get anything for those worthless livestock."

"Livestock? You mortgaged our mules—our horses—our *cows*?"

"For 30 pieces of silver. *Now*, what do you think of this father of yours? This half a man—this *failure*?"

His tone scared her. The words were those of a half-crazed man. And men, stripped of all pride and left with no direction to turn, were desperate men. And—God forbid—some committed suicide.

Marvel pushed the geometry book aside, causing paper and pencil to fall to the floor, then impetuously climbed into the warmly familiar lap and threw her arms around his neck—a little girl again.

"Oh Daddy, you're not a failure! I hate that man for making you feel that way—hate him—*hate* him!"

Those were childish words—words the real Marvel could never say. And certainly words she could never mean. But they were torn from her throat in sudden white fury at the cruel person who put her wonderful father in such a position.

And they worked a miracle then and there. Her own misery turned the man's attention from himself to his child. A bystander would have seen the change. He was a *man* again—a man with everything to live for. Dale Harrington could hold his head high, enter the lion's den, and not be afraid!

They were able to talk then. They would follow the county agent's rotation plans as nearly as possible, planting only enough cotton to pay off the loan, put the rest into corn alternating with legumes, and plant the terraces with watermelons and cantaloupes. Those were good Jersey cows, so it was worth gradually increasing their herd. The dream was back. He'd show Elijah Cohane, his socialite wife, and snobbish—by all reports—daughter.

"Daughter!" Marvel gasped. "That would be Amanda Cohane in my geometry class—the only one who never speaks to me face-to-face."

"That's right," Mother said from the doorway, "her grandmother's name. Snob is the word! Now how about some hot cocoa, you two?"

"Wonderful, my queen of hearts. Then back to the books with a vengeance. Got ourselves a hill to climb!" Daddy said with a smile.

35

Fireside Chats

The year rocked on. One day the world was ablaze with color. The next, it was dull and lifeless. Trees, resembling black skeletons in a dark dance of shadows, stretched out their barren limbs to sway in the out-of-season hot winds.

There was no further mention of money. Talking would do nothing to chase the shadows away. Thirty dollars wouldn't go far. Aware of how pitifully inadequate the loan was, Marvel stretched her school supplies as far as possible. "Waste not, want not," Grandmother had always said. Maybe. At any rate, not a sheet of notebook paper must be wasted. So without comment she disciplined herself to write small, careful to make no mistakes. Watching Amanda Cohane crumple sheets carelessly, then flaunt herself down the aisle to toss them in the wastebasket, Marvel thought it would be an enlightening experience for the indulged girl to be in her situation even for a short time. No, even then the banker's daughter wouldn't understand. The two of them came from different worlds and, in a way, Marvel pitied her. Amanda Cohane was the one handicapped, not Marvel Harrington.

As Thanksgiving neared, Mother and Daddy had gone into a new routine, filled with small surprises—and dreams. Idle thinking? Bubbles destined to fly into the stratosphere, bursting, fading away? Not for them. In their dreams they stood at the threshold of a wonderful future where nothing was too good to be true! Weren't the happenings of today proof positive of the tomorrow?

Mrs. Sutheral had made her promised appearance. She brought the usual rations which Mother and Daddy refused to see as "relief." The county home demonstration agent suggested that perhaps Mrs. Harrington might like to cook dried peas and beans—especially appealing to the palate with a smattering of salt pork. City folks enjoyed common foods sometimes. In the exchange program it was six of this for six of that. And it was good for rural families to have a change—variety, you know. A group could come to the cannery, make use of the equipment for putting up foods in tin, plan balanced meals, and the like.

"If you don't have your group organized, there's no time like the present. Grab a parasol or straw hat, Snow. This heat's enough to bake the brain," the woman said, fanning her skirt to and fro. "These stockings are sticking to my legs. You know, I hear there's a new fad in Dallas. Women going bare-legged— very practical."

Going from one farmhouse to another and introducing the plan put the program into action. That was how Mother came to know the mothers of some of the students Marvel had met. Becoming acquainted proved helpful later, both in organizing church services and encouraging the students to stay in school (in a few instances, it worked).

The meetings opened a whole new world to the rural women. They all had more in common than they had realized, and were more alike than different. At first the name of Harrington intimidated them, but it was a barrier overcome quickly. They fell in love with Snow and felt sorry for her, in a way. It must be right smart of a comedown living like that, after the luxury she was used to. And then there was all that talk—she had to know it— about that brother-in-law of hers being the daddy of that firebug! And there was bad blood between 'em—that Salsburg robber being a half brother of her husband's. *Shhhhh!*

Mother gave no indication of hearing.

On one of Mrs. Sutheral's regular visits she brought a good supply of remnants: mostly silks, satins, and brocades or velvet. There was to be a demonstration on making Christmas gifts at home. But one of the remnants, larger than the others, she held out to Marvel.

"I understand you girls are making underwear in home economics?"

"Oh, yes—yes indeed!" Marvel said happily. "This pale pink nainsook is exactly what I need for tailoring a slip. And oh, Mrs. Sutheral, you *knew*! You've even brought thread. And you'd know laces are not for me! You have no idea how much I appreciate this—"

Realizing that tears were near the surface, Marvel turned away to refold the soft fabric needlessly. With her back still to their guest, she said as lightly as she could manage, "By the way, it's no longer home economics—it's domestic science! Doesn't that sound impressive though?"

"About time somebody realized how important our job is. Homemaking is a science, all right! And you needn't be *too* appreciative, my child," Mrs. Sutheral said softly, dropping her brisk all-business manner. "I'm just as grateful. You people make it possible for me to have a job, you know. It's not the best of times—or is it? This may be our most shining hour. We've all grown closer, more compassionate.

* * *

Mother had lots to share with Grandmother but said in disappointment that she seemed in a hurry to terminate the call. "Either that mother of mine's holding something back or trying to hide something. But what could it be? I know she cares, but—"

"Now, now, don't go borrowing trouble, my Snow White! Mother Riley's undoubtedly too busy like that daughter of hers and—" Daddy smiled, "granddaughter, as well. But here I go, not practicing what I preach. I've wondered why those brothers of mine never call."

"Mary Ann, either," Marvel said. "It *is* strange, isn't it?"

They were not imagining it. This they decided after Brother Grady Greer's visit.

"Still willing to help organize church services out here?" their former pastor asked the moment they had seated him.

They were.

Well then, how about the week after Thanksgiving Day?

Fine. And did he have some literature and used hymnals?

He did.

"We can get everybody's attention immediately if we make use of what they enjoy so much: singing!" Marvel said. "They *love* to sing. The Stamps Quartet used to come out and hold singing schools, and these people know music."

"Oh excellent! That was my news. How did you manage to get the jump on me?" the man so dear to their hearts grinned. "They published new books this year, and with budgets cut back the way they are, it follows that sales are down. They need help. Too bad," Brother Greer shook his graying head, "but it works in our favor. Stamps will give away X-number just for the advertising, just if we make mention to the other communities."

For some reason they all fell silent. Something needing to be said just hung there. Each waited for the other.

When the minister spoke, his words concerned what his hosts had hesitated to put into a question. "Speaking of music—"

"Yes?" Mother encouraged eagerly.

"You should hear your mother's protégés perform! How that woman finds time is a mystery to me, with all else she's doing—and some family worries."

"There's something wrong. I knew it." Mother's voice was resigned.

"Well yes—in her mind, at least. But I'm not the one to tell more. I hope you'll see them all at Thanksgiving."

"We will now," Daddy said. "Meantime we'll pray."

"No time like the present," Brother Greer said in a pleased voice.

That evening Mother telephoned Auntie Rae. It was a party line and it was easy to know when there was an audience.

"With so many listening in, it was hard to hear," Mother reported. "But I know she'd been crying. I could tell by her voice. If it were anybody besides Rae, I might shrug it off. We all have our moments. But she's so easygoing, so bouncy and able to bend with the wind."

Nobody could deny that.

"I couldn't ask her anything. If only we'd been able to talk alone! In fact, that's what Rae said to make me know for sure my suspicions were true. 'I need to talk, Snow,' she said. That's when she told me there would be a special Thanksgiving service at *their* house and asked us to come—bring whatever food we planned. But Dale darling, I—I don't know now. Will it bother you that they're in the place we once called ours—the house we lost?"

"Only for their sakes," Daddy said.

* * *

The first norther of the year blew across the plains, gnashing its teeth and screaming in no uncertain terms that Thanksgiving would be a bitterly cold "hog-killing day" in Texas—which is where it chose to stay until it had blown itself out.

"I'd planned to go in the wagon," Daddy said uncertainly. "But with this wind screaming like it's complaining of a knife in its chest, we'd freeze stiff. I don't know now. We'd better reserve what gasoline's in the car in case of an emergency. What can we do, ladies?"

The ladies were spared a difficult decision.

Jake parked his overhauled Model A Ford in front of the house and pulled Mary Ann out with him. "Run for it!" he yelled, bracing himself against the wind.

Packing Mother's sweet potato pies, baked beans, casseroles, and persimmon breads along with freshly churned butter and a wide variety of marmalades into the car, they hurried along through the blinding dust. Conversation was out of the question. The wind howled a monologue.

A large crowd had assembled and left the comfort of the open fire to greet the Dale Harringtons. In the excitement of seeing old friends, absence of the host went unnoticed at first.

Grandmother elbowed her way to them, hugging them breathlessly close and telling them all how good they looked. She herself looked lovely—exactly, Marvel thought, like a ripe peach. The reason for her glow followed close at her heels. Grandfather—and Marvel had never seen the man looking so fit. It was hard for Marvel to keep her humility listening to his high praise—harder still when she saw he meant it.

"Marvel, you've always had the potential of being a real beauty, but it's a reality now. Let me look at you—um-*hmmm*," he said approvingly. "A real beauty, classic beauty—the kind that's born in the soul! And I hear such wonderful things about you and your achievements. Held your own among those who'd put you down if they could. I know them all—know 'em too well! Good for you! Grandfather's right proud of you!"

"It isn't *that* bad," Marvel smiled, leaning her head against his shoulder affectionately.

Oh, the wonder of it all: the dearly familiar faces, smiles, and embraces...spicy smells...crackling of the fire—adding up to love, genuine concerned love. Problems seemed to melt away. Could it be that nothing was wrong after all?

Wistful thinking, she realized at the sound of Auntie Rae's voice. "Can't we slip into the kitchen, Snow—now, this minute?" There was no mistaking the urgency in her voice.

When Marvel turned, Mother and Auntie Rae were gone. In their place was Mary Ann. "Quick, into my bedroom before the other cousins see us. You must hate me and you have every right. It's inconsiderate to ignore you like I have—keep secrets when we promised not to."

Mary Ann had hold of Marvel's hand and all the while was pulling her forward. Once inside the bedroom, her cousin pushed aside the mountain of coats, sweaters, and mufflers piled on her bed. Then, patting a lace on the hand-crocheted bedspread, she motioned Marvel to sit beside her.

"Somebody'll interrupt, so I'll make this short. You just have to forgive me. It's not easy, tattling on your own father—and I love him. Oh Marvel, I do—just like you love Uncle Dale—"

"Don't cry, Mary Ann," Marvel said softly, wiping away Mary Ann's tears and pushing back her wealth of midnight curls. "I've been worried, not angry. But talk quickly. I *have* to know!"

Mary Ann lowered her voice and confided her guarded secret, her shame. It was her father, her idol. Everything was wrong. People looked down on his work. He'd tried to buy a radio of their own on the installment plan...turned down flat. WPA workers were a poor risk, they claimed. If he'd try getting himself a *job*, people suggested. Bank held a second mortgage on this house. Frederick Salsburg, well, nobody had seen hide nor hair of that swindler...and the bank would foreclose—already had word. And Uncle Worth had lost faith in himself completely, couldn't face it, and oh, Marvel, he'd taken to *drinking*.

Dinner was called. There was little time for more talk. But Marvel took time to say, "Mary Ann, listen! *You* can make all the difference—you and Auntie Rae. Tell him how much he means to you—how important *you* think he is. Stand by and this I promise: *God will help!*"

When they went out Daddy had found Uncle Worth. Red-eyed and puffy-faced, he clung to Daddy like a child.

✳ ✳ ✳

"This place feels like Tummy Tucker's icehouse," Daddy said through chattering teeth, once they reached home safely. "I'll get a fire going. Wow! Got smoke in both eyes. Wind's blowing right down the chimney. There, that's more like it—damper was shut."

"Ooooh, feels good already," Mother said, rubbing her hands to get her circulation going. "How's everybody's appetite? Still stuffed?"

"Not too stuffed for hot cocoa," Marvel told her. "I'm glad for this Thanksgiving break. Here's hoping it'll be warmer by Monday."

"We'll listen to the news. Could be something about this sudden storm," Daddy said, squinting as he fanned the uncooperative fire. "If you'll take over, baby, I'll go take care of the livestock. And Snow, you know what I'd like? Some good hot grits when I get back."

"Gladly, honey. You'll need something to warm your insides. I'll make it over the fireplace. That woodstove would burn the house down in wind like this. We don't want *that* kind of fire—"

She stopped short, eyes locking with Marvel's in fear. The moment passed and she began talking—too rapidly—about putting in a lot of homemade cheese. Another of the projects lying ahead of her was teaching ladies the skill. Why, hers was every bit as good as the hoop of surplus Mrs. Sutheral had brought for comparison then distribution.

"How on earth would we manage without those faithful old cows?"

"We won't have to, Mother, if feed holds out—water, too, of course. Bossy and Daisy will calve soon—too soon if this kind of cold keeps up. Good stock, those Jerseys. I look forward—well, it's a dream for now. Good, there's Daddy!"

Over big bowls of rich, cheese-laced grits, they reviewed the events of the day in what Daddy called their own "fireside chat," beginning with the end of the day and gradually working backward, all knowing why: the dangerous ride home—good that they started early and had no car trouble. Not another car on the road—good thing Jake changed bulbs in the headlights, got dark so early. Say, that food *was* something. Who would guess there were hard times other places?

When the small talk dwindled, Daddy asked openly how much they knew about his brother, other than his pitiful appearance. Mother gave her account, then Marvel. Daddy's came last. Mother and Marvel listened with fascination, for this was the most revealing of all.

Uncle Worth had been in the garage, pretending to work on the car. Weak argument, with all that company around—hiding out, of course.

"Let's talk about this, Worth old boy," I said. "Sort of down on your luck? It helps to be reminded of what you know already—that you're not alone. What seems different in your case?"

At first, Uncle Worth had been sullen, unwilling to talk. Then he'd denied any wrongdoing. Daddy kept hammering away until he wore through Uncle Worth's protective armor. Called him an armadillo, Daddy said, and that did it. Then came the remorse, the chest-beating, the self-hatred.

"Here's what's different in my case. I couldn't face facts. You can. Buying a house when I can't afford so much as a radio on installment. I'm no part of a man—except a heel! Just a crawling, groveling idiot—worse, I have no brain at all. How did I think I'd pay for a house? Going to be a banker in a bank that's not built, probably never will be. Banker! I'm a WPA worker, a loser, a laughingstock—a stupid dreamer."

" 'There's nothing wrong with dreaming,' I told him, and he said there was when a person refused to face the truth and *lived* in a daydream."

Marvel, feeling the fingers of the cold wind probing the cracks of the walls, sensed a warmth ringing her heart. Dale Harrington, the one who saw himself as the black sheep, had taken on a new self-image.

"Oh, I'm proud of you, darling," Mother said, her eyes shining. "I got the pick of the litter, of course! And you'll never know how you've helped Rae. But go on, I'm dying to hear the rest."

Daddy grinned a little self-consciously, but Marvel felt that she could see him growing taller, taller, taller as he spoke. He'd asked Worth if he had talked with their father. The idea terrified Uncle Worth and he had begged that his father not be told. Not their brothers either—their brothers in particular.

"Sooooo, we compromised. I'd say nothing to the other boys with one provision: He would have a talk with our father and tell him how he felt and for goodness' sake, about his broken dreams."

Mother set her bowl aside and put her slender hand over the hand of the man she loved. "You did your part. The rest is up to Worth. If only he'll keep his promise," she sighed, obviously thinking of her favorite sister-in-law.

"Will? *Did!* Make that past tense! My brother's too down-and-out—too hard on himself for me to risk another failure for him. I simply marched him up to our father and said, 'Worth wants to talk.'"

Before Daddy finished his story, the three of them were laughing—a beautiful ending for a beautiful day. As Mrs. Sutheral had put it, this might be their shining hour, and Daddy was the star.

When Uncle Worth poured out his story to Grandfather, the expected recriminations did not come. Instead, Alexander Jay Harrington, Esquire came close to driving his ornate cane right through that hardwood floor in his fury. Squaring his shoulders, he forced Worth to meet his eyes.

"Foreclose? Why, that little upstart! Of course you mean Cohane. Ever notice how the newest member of a fraternal organization is always the one to blackball the next candidate? That's insecurity—a form of snobbery all its own. Why, I gave Lije Cohane a mundane job when—when I opened that bank. Yep, I sure owned it. A lot about your old man you young fellows don't know! Work was my life, all for my family—a mistake, I guess. Not fair to push you the way I have—"

"Don't, Father—that hurts. We—we're the ones making mistakes!" Uncle Worth had protested.

"Well, let's stop the whimpering around and teach that young sprout a lesson he's not apt to forget. I see he's good at forgetting backgrounds. And I'm just as good at reminding him! Get yourself bathed and shaved—yep, you're going with me. And I give you my word that there'll be *no* foreclosures! He's in for a dressing-down here and now. It's one thing for a man to be bossy with his offspring, but when it comes to outsiders—Well, they'd better get ready for a good caning!"

The wind gave a wild shriek, reminding Daddy to tune in for the news. It was not good. This blizzard could last for days.

Coming this early in the year probably spelled a long, cold winter—unfortunate.

The announcer was right. And the winter following would be worse. But the three huddled in the drafty shack had no way of knowing. For now, they were listening with interest to the comments regarding the president—first in amusement that they concerned his "fireside chats," which Daddy had called this wonderful time together for themselves, then in anger and eventually fear. Losing faith in our leader was dangerous.

> What we're experiencing is mild, so far...never know what the future holds, naturally. Down in along the Ohio River, a million people needing flood relief.... The Year of High Water...everything swept away... with all too many states seeing their very land swept away by cruel winds...folks suffocating in spite of dust masks...farmland gone while city folks are buried under tons of black dust...some declarin' it's the end of the world...praying to the Good Lord for just one more chance. Can't happen here, you say? It can—and it may. Here this! It struck Amarillo like a cloud of black smoke *just last night!* Blame is placed on everything—including our president.

Mother and Daddy looked at one another and then at Marvel. Despair was written on their faces. Listening was more important than talking.

The radio crackled and snapped with static as the wind tore through the elements ruthlessly. Daddy fed the fire in a fruitless effort to drive the cold from the drafty room.

"Here," he said at last, handing both Mother and Marvel afghans, "let's play we're papooses. Oh, there goes the radio. Good!"

> Under the circumstances, it's better for Mr. Roosevelt that the election's over. No landslide as it was and undoubtedly would be worse for him now. I guess some of these mind readers who swindle patients out of their precious few dollars just for lying on a couch and probing their brains like gypsies read palms

would say we, as a nation, have ourselves a need to blame somebody or something for any misfortune. Now we're blaming one segment for not turning out at the polls and another for herding in ignoramuses and tellin' 'em how to vote. Civil War's over but *not* done with...bringing in all those poor blacks....Funny thing though...some of FDR's most loyal supporters were Negroes, *Eastern* ones and "corn-fed" ones from the Midwest...marched en masse down yonder in Tennessee...while down yonder 'cross the line in Mississippi they're still living in blackness—no pun intended, ladies and gentlemen—virtually disenfranchised by custom and that all-fired poll tax!

Well, he's in...for better or for worse...out after Communism, lurid grafters...and ready to enter the ring and do battle with the Ku Klux Klan. Sound dangerous? You'd better believe it...dark, dark days... from dust...starvation...grime in the factories... and *war clouds on the horizon....*

The radio faded out. Daddy whispered, "They can't take away our right to pray. Thank You, Lord, *for this day.*"

36

The Whisper of Eternity

The darkness of the world's problems faded when Marvel reentered school. Her heavy schedule kept her too busy for thinking of anything other than assignments, completing them all on time, and managing to get from one class to the other on time.

As the days flew past, it was easy to see that her teachers were impressed with her work. That brought no particular satisfaction. Marvel needed no recognition, just knowing that she was keeping up while others fell by the wayside was enough. She took no pleasure in their failure. Quite the contrary. She was encouraged only in knowing that someday, somehow she would be able to be the Good Samaritan they needed.

The days shortened. It was dark when she left home and dark when she returned. But it was light enough to make observations along the way, to take note of the land and its sad condition, and the needs that must be met in the rural areas. Either the county agent had failed to get into the backcountry or the farmers had refused his help. At any rate, the land was unterraced. The loose soil, dry in spite of the cold, was an accident just waiting to happen. Already dust was piling at the ends of rows and heaping against sagging fences. With so much land under cultivation, there was little grazing land—not enough to feed the gaunt cattle. Their hollow eyes looked sad, as if they foresaw their fate. The mules—poor critters—could hardly be expected to do the work expected of draft animals. Their coats were mottled from loss of hair. Their rib cages showed their skeletal frames, while their bellies were bloated from a diet of Johnson grass and pitifully inadequate amounts of grain soaked overnight (so one of the students told her) to "make 'em feel fuller."

Marvel sighed when she heard that. *If I corrected him,* she thought, and certainly she wouldn't, *and said, "The adjective 'full,' has no comparative degree, full is full," I would mean it both ways.* Neither of which he would understand....

Teachers were talking midterm exams already, even though middle of the school year came after Christmas. Either the idea was to motivate or threaten. Marvel felt secure in all except geometry. So what if she had to take one exam? She would still make the honor roll. She was at the top in all other subjects. Certainly, she was doing outstanding work in English. Spanish came easy. Fascinated by history, she had won the heart of old Mr. Stringfellow who, nearing retirement, needed a few stars. Surely everybody needed to be well-informed in civics, examining the Constitution and knowing our rights and how they must be protected. One would suppose that all students, children of the Depression that they all were, took a healthy interest in economics... how hunger of the poor and greed of the rich had led to World War I and could lead to World War II. She poured her heart out in the required term paper. As a natural result, the civics teacher had praised her highly and written along the margin: "Excellent! What a background you must have. Any plans for your future yet?" Domestic science was a pushover, a welcome relief from the heavier subjects.

Then came the staggering news: "Any student failing to achieve an A average in *all* subjects will be denied the right to an exemption in any one or more other subjects. An able student will perform equally well in all areas."

Marvel read the school bulletin first in dismay. Surprise turned to anger—an all-consuming fury which, she realized later, had been kindling within her for a long time. How dared they! Such thinking was unworthy of adults trained in matters of the mind. That all men were created equal had nothing to do with learning ability or opportunity—not even the so-called "equal rights." All one had to do was open one's eyes. That took courage, of course! And certainly it had nothing to do with aptitude. Someday, she thought fiercely—

Then, inhaling deeply, she willed the fury away for now. *Now* meant that Marvel Harrington could and *would* redouble all efforts in geometry. She was *not* equal to the high achievers in that area and never would be. But there were ways of compensating. Sadly, that would serve only to reinforce the teachers' faulty thinking. But the situation pushed her into a corner. Didn't society do the same?

Ironically, Mr. Phillips, who was a page-by-page teacher, did not postpone the proposition to be demonstrated by every student—admittedly the most difficult of all concepts—until last. One turned the page, and one did the work—without exception.

"Boys and girls, we have reached the Pythagorean theorem," he said crisply. "Come prepared tomorrow to prove the Theorem you see stated here: 'The square of the hypotenuse of a right triangle is equal to the sum of the squares of the other two sides.' Class dismissed!"

Marvel stared at the page. This—why, this was impossible. The problem which began with the statement Mr. Phillips had read occupied the entire page. The burden of proof lay in the hands of the students. And the proof required the use of algebraic equations! The symbols wavered then blurred. Oh no, she mustn't cry. The time and energy tears took would find release in another way: *work!*

But try as she would, Marvel was unable to master the concept. Daddy scratched his head and did his best to help, then gave up. It had been too long since his plane and solid geometry classes—even trig. Valuable? There had been no retention when a man couldn't so much as help his daughter.

"But give me tomorrow, sweetie," he said suddenly. "I'll figure it out—maybe even find you a shortcut."

"Oh Daddy," Marvel said gently, "you're Mr. Wonderful. But no—no shortcuts. It has to be like the book shows, exactly. Using a shortcut in math—even if it were a better way—would be a sacrilege. Like looking for a shortcut to salvation, he said once. And Daddy, the man meant no disrespect. Perfection is next to godliness."

And we don't HAVE a days' grace, she wanted to add.

The day following, when there were no volunteers to demonstrate the problem on the chalkboard, Mr. Phillips was angry. Although he kept his voice at its usual pitch, Marvel took note of the thin white line where his lips used to be. It was no surprise when he announced a pop quiz for the next session.

"You will *all* volunteer! I will *not* tolerate further procrastination. Have those pencils and your wits sharpened. Tomorrow you will prove more than a problem. You'll prove your ability to remain in this class!"

Reluctantly, Marvel shared the doomsday proclamation. Dale Harrington was enraged—as much at himself as the situation. It was unfair—downright criminal—and he'd tell the man so if the wind hadn't grounded the telephone lines.

Subdued, he turned helplessly to Marvel. "My attitude's not helping, honey. Daddy's sorry. Is it so important making that honor roll? Our future's not at stake!"

Maybe it was. But aloud Marvel said, "Don't worry, Daddy, I'll make it, that I promise."

Daddy groaned. "How?"

"Memorize it—sit right here like Abraham Lincoln and work by the light of the fire until I know it by heart. You know—like a great concert pianist who uses no music, just *sees* every note!"

It worked. With one hour's sleep, Marvel was halfway down the page, relying on perfect recall, when forced to stop the next day.

The principal, who had walked quietly up and down the aisles during the one-problem test, stood in front of the room to order that all students lay down their pencils. "This is disgraceful," Mr. Phillips said with distaste. "I'm ashamed of this class. One student, *one* has the formula! Marvel, will you stand, please!"

She dared not disobey the command in his voice. But this was terrible, something to be avoided like—like *Elmer Salsburg*! First, hot color had stained her face. Now she paled beneath it with only two circles of color standing out garishly. Quickly seating herself, Marvel wished she were a million miles away. Whatever else the man said fell on deaf ears. Escape was foremost in her mind. She felt exploited.

But when the bell rang, she was detained—twice.

First by Amanda Cohane. "How you pulled that off right under that watchful eye beats me! I'll see that Mr. Phillips knows you used notes. Cheating—yes, you're a *marvel*, all right," she hissed.

"Marvel, yes, *Harrington*. The last name may mean even more."

The other girl cringed. The name was not one she wanted to hear.

Then Mr. Phillips stopped Marvel to say, "No further classes. Gives you needed time."

Telephone lines were repaired and Mary Ann called that night.

"So much to talk about I don't know where to begin," her cousin said excitedly. "Oh yes, I do—of course, I do! Grandfather and Daddy went in to see that awful man."

"Elijah Cohane?"

"That's him. Well, they took the wind out of his sails, I'm tellin' you! He'll not be foreclosing, you can bet your life on that! Our grandfather even told the banker he'd be better at his job with a little more experience—you know, experience like ours! Can't you just see Grandfather waving that cane like it was the nation's flag and saying, 'Be good for that wife and daughter of yours to know what half soles feel like!' Marvel, I can't help but wish those two knew."

"They know."

✳ ✳ ✳

Christmas brought a blinding snowstorm. Roads were impassable. The Harringtons decided that since they would be unable to be with the family, this would be an ideal time to meet at the old church building and at least get acquainted and offer a Christmas prayer on Christmas Eve.

The turnout was surprisingly good. And, with the windows boarded up because of broken panes, the old potbellied stove took a bit of the sting from the bitter cold. The dilapidated piano (left to fall to ruin by the last singing school "ages ago") was out of tune but responded as if it were happy to be useful again under Mother's skillful fingers.

Oh, how they all sang! *That* they could do and do well, thanks to the training they had had as children. There was thunderous applause when Daddy shared news of the new hymnals and promised visits by the well-known Stamps Quartet—yes, in person!

Carol after carol they sang in voices loud, clear, and pure. Marvel noted that they looked heavenward, with eyes closed throughout, as if it were a sort of prayer. Trials and tribulations shrank to nothingness as they praised Christ the living Lord in song. And her own heart lifted on the wings of those songs. There was a whisper of eternity.

She, Mother, and Daddy walked home hand in hand, humming, "I need to hear the Christmas story"—in sweet simplicity.

"Let's have Fanny and her family tomorrow," Marvel said.

37

Three Free
Days

Excused from exams, Marvel enjoyed three free days.

"I feel so free!"

Daddy laughed. "Maybe you won't when you see all this slave driver you call 'Mother' has outlined for us!"

He grinned wickedly at his slave driver, who stuck a pink tongue out at her husband. "My slave here helped me plan. We're hoping for a magic garden, you see. We saved some seed, even from last year's poor crop. Then I answered an ad in the *Farm & Ranch* magazine Mrs. Bumstead lets me read. Sperry's Seed Company offered me *free* seed—oh, all kinds: okra, squash of all varieties, radishes, English peas, pole beans, limas. Oh, *everything*!" Mother's eyes were like twin stars.

Marvel grew excited with her, with one reservation. "What's the catch, Mother? They don't *give* those seeds away, do they?"

"They only required that I sell a dozen packages."

"That sounds good," Marvel said slowly, hoping her mother wasn't getting her hopes built up for a fall. "But there's so little money that I wonder—I'm thinking of our own allotment."

Immediately she was sorry. Daddy needed no reminders. But he took no notice. In fact, it was Daddy who took up the conversation.

"Oh, she's some businesswoman, my Snow White! Why, nobody can resist that sales pitch. Next thing you know, Sperry's will be trying to hire her! Go ahead, honey, tell the good part. What are you waiting for?"

"An opportunity!"

Daddy waved his white handkerchief in surrender. Even then, he could not resist teasing her. "Go on, here's your chance to confess your sins."

Mother giggled. "I sold every package at our songfest! At five cents a package—well, what better Christmas gift? Sooo, what about it, family? Want to help me plant a dream—or what's the legal term for harboring a criminal, Marvel? Your father and I aren't speaking!"

"Aiding and abetting," Marvel laughed, entering into their banter.

And so they planted a dream....

Mother and Grandmother chatted daily now that the telephone lines were in working order again. The church was coming along beautifully, Grandmother said proudly. And wouldn't it be nice when Snow and Dale could get services organized out there?

Yes, it would. Brother Greer was scheduled to come soon, real soon. The reverend gentleman came during Marvel's time at home. Not only did he come, he came in the company of the Stamps Quartet on tour out of Dallas.

Of course the building wouldn't hold the crowd. Almost crazed with eagerness to hear and to participate, people from miles around flocked in on foot, in wagons, and a few in cars of ancient vintage. Last of all came the young men on horseback, perhaps out of curiosity. Maybe they were responsible for ripping away the boards covering all the windows. At any rate, the open-air windows provided for dozens of heads of those determined to be a part of the audience.

Brother Greer took advantage of his captive audience, and catching them when emotions ran high was to the soft-spoken minister's advantage. Timing was everything. Yes, all readily volunteered, they would welcome church on Sunday. Sunday school, too—not just for children but for grown-ups as well? Well yes, more learning would do them all good. Had to roll out come daylight anyway, what with milking to do. That rooster wasn't worth the grain he consumed except as an alarm clock. Critter didn't know about Sunday being a day of rest. Still—

"I see some concern," the elderly gentleman said. "Go right ahead with your questions. We want everybody to be at peace with the arrangements."

Mr. Bumstead, whose wide middle came near to stretching from one initial-carved pew to the other, stood. "I'll act as spokesman, expressin' what most seem to be wantin'. Seems like Sunday school and church in the mornin' then preachin' again on Sunday evening—we're guessin'—well, seems like that's a heap of churchin'."

Those in attendance agreed.

"So what's chances of havin' singin' on Sunday nights?"

"I'd say very good—very good indeed! At least, we're hoping for that," said the stranger in a dark suit (all local men wore older work mackinaws). "Of course, I have no voice—not the kind of voice that votes! I only *sing* the Lord's praises."

The bass of the Stamps' Quartet!

His words might as well have been Lincoln's Gettysburg Address, for the night would live forever in the history of their church organization. *The world will little note, nor long remember what we say here. But it can never forget what they did here.*

Grady Greer remained in the neighborhood for the three days Marvel was at home. Later his trips would be periodic. He would come out to preach and teach, bringing some of the deacons along now and then. Yes, they would use the original board, of course. After all, ordainment—much like appointment to the Supreme Court, as Brother Greer saw it—was for life. Oh, and Marvel would be pleased to learn that her Grandfather Alexander Jay Harrington, Esquire would serve as chairman as always—that is, as soon as construction was a little farther along, and before there was mention of pay. Culverville's Baptist was sponsoring reconstruction of the sister church in once-thriving Pleasant Knoll. Well, and his weathered face had creased in smiles, didn't it follow that they should pass the good deed on—naming this church as their *brother*? The convention would help, too.

But for now, Brother Greer would be glad to accept the Harringtons' invitation. Crowded quarters? "Just wait 'til we all get to heaven. By the way, I hope the new hymnals will include some of the grand old hymns such as 'When We All Get to Heaven.'"

Still humming the beloved melody, he turned to Marvel, his face still glowing with last night's success.

"Right cozy here—and this will give us a bit of coveted time to review answers to questions you asked so long ago. You *do* have some free time?"

She laughed. "Free to serve the Lord!"

He nodded, pulled a crumpled page from his pocket, and read her questions back to her: "What makes the Bible special?" "Why is Jesus the only way to get to God?" "What is Christian conversion?" "What is the 'plan of salvation'?" "How do I become a Christian?" "Gift? Grace? Don't high morals count—and what of my good works?"

"Good questions—all of them, and the list goes on and on. As I recall," Brother Greer said slowly, "your main concern was to be better prepared to answer both Christians and non-Christians who ask questions and seek truths or more information, right?"

"Right, sir. But there are agnostics, even atheists, who go farther than doubting and even deny the very existence of God. Oh, how they scare me!"

"They scare us all, honey. But what can we do with the scoffers—those who goad us, taunt us, not to find answers but to put us out of business? Well, this is one business that's not going to crumble, Depression or no Depression! God's work will live forever through young people like you."

"Oh," Marvel objected, "don't put a crown on my head. *Don't!*"

The elderly man of God patted her hand gently. "In my dotage, I guess, but still able to answer some of your questions. So the Good Shepherd's not ready to declare me ready for glue! I'll respond here and now to one question only: your last one. When you meet up with one of those hecklers—scoffers who would dare laugh in the face of God—remember what Jesus said to do. Shake the dust off your feet and leave the rest to the Lord."

All the way through their talk, Marvel had seen a gleam in the eye of this wise man. Now he shared his plan. As he talked, her heart almost burst with joy—joy of fulfillment. To think that she, just plain Marvel Harrington, could be an instrument in the minister's plan—as were her parents, she was to find a bit later.

The plan, Brother Greer said excitedly, was to begin regular Wednesday-night Bible studies as a time for meditation and discussion—not of lofty, scholarly, hard to understand issues, but of everyday problems, situations all could relate to, matters of the heart. Of course, they would wait until school closed. Meantime, he would instruct Marvel, and hopefully her father and mother, too, as it was his prayer that they would serve as teachers in the Sunday school. He paused dramatically.

"And your questions are both challenging and inspiring—the very topics we will work with in these midweek meetings!"

Mother and Daddy walked in just as the minister finished.

"Good timing, both of you. I need to share my thinking. I want to retain this fervor the first meeting held, but the building's in sad shape. Suppose you could organize a group of volunteers to help get it a little more respectable, if I'm able to scrape up the funds? I have a source—well, that's *my* problem. Dare I hope, Dale, that you'll do the recruiting?"

"I'll do what I can. Sure!"

"Common sense tells me I'd best not push my luck, but this tuckered-out heart won't listen. So here goes. How about serving as superintendent of the whole kitkaboodle: repairs, spreading the word about the forthcoming prayer meetings? What's more, you'd make a fine superintendent of Sunday school, pro tem, until the group feels more comfortable."

He needn't have hesitated to ask. Daddy certainly didn't hesitate to accept. Without bothering with a formal *yea*, Brother Greer said, "An election later—everyone needs to feel a part of the body."

There was a lilt in Daddy's voice—a lilt which echoed in Mother's. "What are we calling this church, pastor? I'm sure you have that planned, too?" she half-teased.

But Brother Greer was dead serious. "Sure enough! I was coming to that. Has to be a 'chapel' in the name, following along with tradition, as I see it. Didn't I hear mention of your selling seed?"

"Well," Mother hesitated, as if fearing he was in on her husband's game, "yes—but—"

"Any flower seed? Specifically, morning glories?"

"Heavenly Blues!"

"Wonderful—exactly right. Just wonderful! See what your ladies think about 'Morning Glory Chapel.' Heavenly Blues—oh, bless my soul!"

Marvel turned away to hide her amusement. In his dotage? Why, their longtime friend was all but jumping up and down....

Time was passing. All too soon the three "free days" would draw to a satisfying close. But there was one more project in the making.

It was Annie and Ruth who brought the news. It had to wait until Marvel could give them warm hugs, say how much she regretted their decision to drop out of school, and catch them up on activities there.

"My offer to help on the basics still stands, and the on-the-job program's going great—providing you'd prefer going that route next year?"

The girls hung their heads in embarrassment. They didn't want to go at all, they said—just wanted to marry prosperous farmers and—

(Prosperous farmers? Just where did they expect to find *those*?)

Red of face, Annie and Ruth blurted out their other desires. "And raise a Christian family!" Annie finished, to which Ruth added, "That's why we're so interested in preparin' in you'all's classes. Now, that kind of learnin's real appealin'. Tell us more."

Marvel outlined the plans quickly. Mother, still excited, reminded the girls that they'd be very much involved, their mothers having bought seed. "'Morning Glory Chapel,' lovely name isn't it? And we'll surround the place with our 'heavenly blues'!" Her enthusiasm was contagious.

They wished they could talk longer, but they had to spread the word. Mr. Bumstead's truck was going to haul fresh beef to the cannery. Farmers couldn't afford more feed so would butcher . . . sharing with all.

"Mother, we can't. That meat's not safe," Marvel said desperately when they were gone. "You should see the pitiful critters. We can go without meat—use our cheese, eggs, peanuts, peas. Like Archie's dad said, 'Motley herd—ain't fitten' fer th' buzzards.'"

"Right—" Daddy muttered. "One day there'll be government inspection."

38

Strange Thing About Journeys

Schedules were changed completely for the remainder of the year. The change gave Marvel a short study period. Instead, she asked to be allowed to enroll for debate. Without hesitation, the principal referred her to Miss Robertson. The English teacher gave instant permission.

"In fact," she said thoughtfully, "I wanted a chance to speak with you concerning the county meet which is just around the corner, considering all else we have to do. Your records indicate," Miss Robertson said, picking up her glasses to check the folder before her, "that you are well-versed in public speaking."

"Yes, ma'am."

"I would like to have you try out for the declamation contest. Of course, we would have local tryouts here in school, winner to represent Titus County. Winner at county level in the senior division will go on up: district, state, and one day there's likely to be a United States contest. Right now we stop with state—and we've never had a winner for Texas. Which does not concern you, my dear. I'm only dreaming aloud. Ever dream, Marvel?"

"All the time! A dream to me is a daring adventure, a journey which can carry me far—" she stopped, suddenly embarrassed.

Miss Robertson's pale, almost colorless eyes, probed Marvel's blue-black ones. "You are destined to see them come true. But I have to say that unfortunately you'll be in the *junior* division."

"There's always next year," Marvel said.

In the end, she was to enter other contests: the picture-memory contest (due to no great interest in painting but to learn to appreciate the arts), and the essay-writing contest (she was a gifted writer and planned to do more of it no matter what else became her lifework). She would enter them and win them, becoming a sort of legend to be remembered and held before those to follow as an example as one who had, against all odds, put Culverville High School on the map! The trophies were on display in a glassed-in case—right where they belonged, as far as Marvel was concerned. They did nothing, made no contribution—just sat there in idleness... corpses of youth now dead..., for some....

Strange thing about journeys. The traveler cannot foresee the detours, and certainly not the destination. But for those who dare dream, that journey leads onward and upward—heavenward where it all began... to reach that final star. But traveling was enough for now.

* * *

Marvel's schedule for the second semester allowed for a more relaxed time with the domestic science class since she did not have to be in such a rush to get to geometry. She and Miss Ingersoll (who, at 36, was to be married and eagerly planning every last detail of her dream house, therefore concentrating the course accordingly) had become good friends earlier as the instructor was pleased with Marvel's preparation, thanks to Miss Marlow's dedication. Now the two of them grew even closer because of their mutual love of homemaking and all that went with it. The class had an opportunity to apply that which they must master—largely theory mixed with what one might call a combination of chemistry and math: what minerals and vitamins were contained in each food, how to balance meals and count calories, and exactly how to stay within a very limited budget when there was virtually no income... meet loans... allow for emergencies... yet *save*.

In the required portfolio, Marvel drew plans for a house according to scale (thanks to geometry!), landscaped it, and decorated the rooms (using original designs for wallpaper and woodwork from a watercoloring set Miss Ingersoll had tactfully placed on one of the worktables). Then arranged the furniture she hoped to purchase one day in imaginative ways: making use of the views, concentrating on the spectacular sunrises and sunsets for which east Texas was noted, grouping around both the native-rock fireplaces in her blueprint, and arranging seating space around the planned piano where family and friends could sing or engage in conversation.

Miss Ingersoll called each of the girls up for a private conference at her desk after she had reviewed the portfolios. "I am overwhelmed, Marvel." Sincerity filled her voice. "In fact, I would like to keep this for myself and use some of the ideas were I not reasonably sure you will be pursuing one of the many careers outlined here."

"You may have it—with my compliments."

"You don't plan to go on in any one of these fields then?"

"No, ma'am."

"But it's so obvious your heart was in it. I do have two questions, however."

Marvel smiled, unaware of the faraway look in her cobalt eyes. "My heart *was* in it," she said. "Someday, a long time from now, I envision building that house, restoring the land I love, when I return to the lost land of my childhood from wherever life takes me—"

Miss Ingersoll leaned forward, her voice dropping to a carefully low pitch, "Then you *are* of the Harrington stock: bankers, landowners. And obviously, you're speaking of the original place, the vast acreage where the old mansion once stood. That answers one of my questions. I wondered on reviewing your work why the house was so very large. As I recall, the beautiful old home was destroyed by fire."

"Under strange circumstances," Marvel said bitterly. Immediately she could have bitten her tongue off. But there was no *un*saying words. In her usual controlled voice she said, "You had another question, I believe?"

"I see that you made no mention of how you would finance, but in your case the land is there for you already. Unmortgaged?"

At Marvel's nod, Miss Ingersoll said briskly. "This is a necessary question, although it may sound personal. You made no mention of securing a loan. It is rare in these days when one has the funds—"

"I understand. And certainly I do *not* have the funds. In fact—"
Marvel stopped short. Miss Ingersoll was a dear person with a
job to do. But her job description did not require her students to
disclose family matters. For one foolish moment, she wondered
just what this lady would think if she blurted out the truth: 30
dollars to stretch over the entire year . . . land failing to produce . . . and food dwindling so fast that they were on the verge of
hunger!

Lifting what Mother called "that Harrington chin," Marvel said
quietly, "I won't be needing a loan when I restore it all!"

Her words were bright with conviction.

"Thank you, dear Marvel. You are my inspiration. *Next!*"

After completion of their homes, the girls needed to know how
to manage them. The course was thorough, including how to
plan balanced meals and serve them attractively, efficiently,
while observing all the rules of etiquette. It was an art to follow
all the rules, Miss Ingersoll emphasized, but all was lost unless a
hostess could put her guests at ease—whether one served a
formal meal or invited a few to pop corn.

And she required that, beginning from scratch, each girl must
plan a menu, invite guests in, cook the meal, and serve it under
her watchful eye. Marvel would remember forever when her turn
came to demonstrate. The dining room of the cottage she filled
with armloads of wild plum branches strung with snowy-white
blossoms. The white linen tablecloth and white tapers gave the
look of purity and simplicity. For the first time she thought of
Mary Ann's wedding dress. She must call her cousin that evening, tell her all about her success, and ask a million questions. . . .

The evening, however, was taken up by an organizational
meeting Daddy had scheduled at the church. Mother was as
excited as Daddy, but gave Marvel the option of going along or
remaining at home to study. Everybody would understand, it
being a school night.

"Does that include the Lord?" Marvel had laughed. "You *know*
I need to be there since I plan to teach Sunday school."

Her parents were pleased. But they seemed pleased about
everything these days. It was a taste of glory—being in charge,
their first opportunity to be leaders.

"Strange feeling," Mother said, her lovely eyes almost fev-
erishly bright, "but you know, I feel as if I'm preparing for

something. Oh, my hands are full with the church, the women's group, and," she grinned at Daddy, "our scratching out a living like *The Little Red Hen*. But it's something else, as if—" she seemed to be sorting out thoughts as well as words, "as if I were preparing for the future."

"Sure thing," Daddy said, obviously undaunted by reference to scarcities. "We, my darlings, are laying up treasures in heaven!"

All went well—so well that the next steps dominated the conversation: what to do and how to do it, every detail planned so far ahead that plans stretched into the summer. Wouldn't it be fun to announce well in advance that the initial prayer meeting would be a real celebration? Oh yes, yes. Hold an ice-cream social. Even call it a Little Red Hen supper. "Who'll bring the sugar? "Who'll bring the milk? And, for goodness' sake, don't let those cows go grazing on bitter weeds!"

Marvel had never seen her parents so excited. They were almost slaphappy with joy. Who in the world said Christianity wore a long face! Caught up in their childlike enthusiasm, she found herself relaxing. Until then, she had been unaware of the tension which had become a part of her. Setting priorities was no easy matter.

Take the matter of calling her favorite cousin who was also her best friend. By the time that call materialized, Marvel had come to see herself in an entirely new way. Surprising, to say the least, and admittedly not at all unpleasant....

"Girls," Miss Ingersoll said matter-of-factly, "we have new houses standing empty, just showplaces until they're occupied. By whom? You, of course—you, your husband, and your family—"

There was a bit of tittering, even a giggle or two.

"Stop the silliness—all of you! It's a normal way of life, and I am endeavoring to prepare you. Finding the right man to spend the rest of your life with, someone whose children you can be proud to bear—yes, we *will* get into all that a little later. And I must caution you in advance to be prepared for opposition to this part of the course. They'll say you're too young, too immature to study such matters. But I consider it appropriate—in fact, essential—considering that two of our junior dropouts are married already and one of them is pregnant. I have full cooperation of the school board. But as I said, that part will come later. First comes your own personal hygiene—and yes, *appearance*. As a hostess, you owe that to your *guests*. As a young lady, you owe it to *yourself*. It follows, of course, that as a wife, you owe it to your *husband*—later, as a mother, to your *children*."

It was hard for the girls to restrain their excitement as the teacher outlined the procedure. One by one, they would stand before the group for constructive criticism. While the girls' role would be strictly helpfulness—making the most of each good feature and compensating for the problem areas, she as instructor reserved the right to protest vocally the tasteless, overdone use of color, make-up, and jewelry. Why, some of them looked like signboards, she said.

"This is no game, let me assure you! It very well may be one of the most important steps you have experienced. And rest assured that I expect results. Your grades depend on that!"

Her last statement had a sobering effect. The evaluation was handled with dignity which gave the girls needed confidence. Marvel, who had shrunk into a knot of fear inside at the beginning, found herself participating and enjoying it all. When her turn came, she forgot herself and paraded objectively before the group.

"Where did you learn to walk like that?" one of the girls asked. "No book on *your* head. Why, you walk like a queen!"

Marvel's smile was one of radiance born of unshed tears. Her mind had gone back to Grandmother Riley's training, and she was overcome with a wave of homesickness to see her. Even news would help.

But what were they saying? Did she wear rouge? It didn't look like paint, but nobody ever had natural color like that. Why, her cheeks looked like June apples. No (they answered their own questions), it wasn't rouge! That was easy to see when she blushed and the color deepened.

"Of course, Marvel's coloring stands out doubly because of her fragile white skin. With a complexion like that you could wear any color, Marvel, although the pastels you choose enhance it," Miss Ingersoll said.

Choose? Marvel wondered what the reaction of this group (most of whom were "city kids") would be if she said, "I choose to wear whatever surpluses the home demonstration agent or my previous home economics teacher brings."

There *was* one suggestion. Wouldn't Marvel's hair be more becoming if the part were changed from the middle to a high side part? Maybe diagonal?"

"Let's experiment," Miss Ingersoll said, and proceeded to draw a comb through Marvel's sun-bright hair. Then, brushing the bangs back, she exclaimed, "Look at this, girls!"

Little "kiss curls," they said excitely. And what a beautiful forehead—too bad to hide a round forehead like that with bangs!

The teacher fluffed Marvel's hair in place, then suggested that she look at herself in the dressing room's long mirror. "Oh, one thing more. Let's use just a wee bit of Vaseline on your eyelids. There—makes those blue eyes shine even more!"

Looking at herself was like meeting a stranger. Mother had always said she was beautiful, but she had never believed that for a minute—never cared, actually. The change was subtle, but it was there—outward or inward was of no consequence. She glowed.

"Tell me *everything!*" Mary Ann demanded when Marvel called that night.

Marvel needed no encouragement. She told excitedly of the church, her schoolwork, and the recent make-over she had received. Then, in spite of Mary Ann's squeal of pleasure and wheedling to hear more, Marvel refused. "Please," Marvel begged, "I want news of *you*. The whole family, sure—but you and Grandmother especially have been on my mind."

The family was as usual pretty blue, not used to making-do like her and Marvel's folks, poking fun at the president's saying, "Wear it out, make it do!" something they'd been doing for years.

"Your grandmother's fine—missing you but finding pleasure in the company of our grandfather! Me? Oh, I love this house, love it, and so does Jake! We want to stay here forever and ever. Can you understand that?"

"Silly girl! Of course, I can. That's how I feel about this place. You know—oh," she laughed, "not this *house* forever, but here on this land. It's *home*: Texas, the land of the bluebonnets. Only they've quit blooming until there's rain. Then those seeds which have slept a thousand years will bloom out in all their glory."

"My goodness, you sound like they have souls!"

"Sometimes I think this whole country has. Restored as it should be, it sounds like the new heaven and new earth—the New Jerusalem."

"Oh Marvel, I can't say things the way you do, but that's how I—we—feel about Pleasant Knoll. Couldn't it be a part, too?"

Marvel laughed. "I don't make such decisions, Mary Ann, but we are all a part of each other. It's well-named, the heartland of America, and to think that Texas is a part. What a wonderful heritage."

The two were silent for a moment in a kind of awe. Then Mary Ann burst out, "Oh Marvel, I loved all you told me—all about the dream house—*everything*. But remember the words of that lady. You *do* need a someone to love, help you plan, share. We want to start our married life right here in this house. Oh, I'm glad it's ours!"

"It's all settled—I mean there's no chance—" Marvel was unable to say that name. She wished she'd made no mention, created no doubts.

But it was not she who created them. Somehow she knew before her cousin found a voice. "I—I think so. Still it scares me—"

"*What* scares you?"

"Oh, it makes no sense. He's supposed to be in that special school. But I wonder. . . . There's talk—and he's crazier than a loon. Be careful, be awful careful—and don't laugh!"

Marvel wasn't laughing.

39

Unwelcome
Attentions

It was one of those false spring days in late March when the sky was almost clear. The wind held its breath as if it, too, suffered from the exhaustion of a long, raw winter.

Days were lengthening and Marvel was able to see just how shabby housing was. Even the better houses had fallen to ruin. And how thin the ground which farmers were harrowing had become. Housewives were uncooping baby chicks and allowing mother hens to ramble with their new families in search of food. It was almost unfair, she thought, when there was no grain for their empty craws, but chicken was a staple for the family dinner table. Beef was in short supply, and fish—once so popular— were hard to find. Black people of the bottomlands engaged in what they called "hogging" the mudholes (a method by which they dragged a net or ducked kinky dark heads below the surface while probing the mud for fish with their hands—bare, shining bodies bobbing up and down like ebony corks on fishing lines). The few catfish they garnered were half-dead from suffocation and tainted with an unpalatable "muddy" taste. Of course, they found crawfish occasionally. And sadly, they encountered one of the most poisonous snakes in North America, the copperhead, called by them the water moccasin. Nobody knew how many had died of the viper's lethal bite, as few knew their wretched plight. Someday...

On this particular day, Daddy called the county agent early and shared his enthusiastic plans for planting watermelons on all the terraces between which Daddy had used his last commercial fertilizer (furnished by the government because the barnyard manure was no longer nourishing) and planted cotton prayerfully. He had to have enough yield to pay back the 30 pieces of silver!

He had been very excited when Marvel left to catch the school bus. Mr. Inman was bringing seed for experimentation. Would he go along? But of course! The idea was sound, come to think of it. They'd try vetch, hoping for a late rain as it didn't take kindly to dry-land farming, and use oats as a "support crop." Oats would be a good grain feed for livestock, and the vetch, if it received water, would be dandy for hay. If not—well, being of the legume family, it would feed nitrogen into the hungry soil.

Poor Daddy. Little could he foresee how fruitless all his efforts were. The melons would thrive, bloom, and bear fruit—only to be destroyed by a lost gaggle of roving geese. "If only they had taken their fill. Poor devils are bound to be hungry. But now so are we! The simpletons drilled holes in every single melon with those probing beaks, then moved on to the next one. Not a melon remains—not one!"

The oats and vetch did well, too, only to be declared "soil depleting" by the government—meaning no promised parity payment. But he could not know the future, any more than Marvel knew what this day held for her—two experiences she would have run away from, had she but known. And to neither was there a clear-cut solution.

A gentle breeze had risen by the time Marvel reached the bus stop, giving no hint of the mischief reserved for later in the day. The breeze discovered the wispy little curls Marvel's newly-styled hair now revealed at the top of her forehead, then moved on to ruffle the tender green leaves of a hickory nut tree. When the bus lumbered in, the wind was waiting to turn the cloud of dust the vehicle created into harmless miniature whirlwinds. Mr. Newland detained her at the door.

"Miss Marvel hon, I been wantin' to ask y'all a big favor. *Rest of ya'll shake uh leg, git goin', back uv th' bus like always, hear?* Set yourse'f down. I brung a goose pillar fer ya'll hopin' you'd set on the' platform 'long side me 'n take roll call, seein' as how ever'body knows Miss Marvel." The driver's words tumbled out hurriedly.

Marvel sat down quickly to be out of the way. She would have much preferred not to do this, but Mr. Newland needed help. And she did know all the students—which was what he'd meant, she was sure.

"Yes, I'll help you," she said, taking the notebook and pencil he offered.

Marvel set to work marking an "X" beside the names of those who had boarded the bus first. The remaining students she would check when the time came. Archie's father was talking all the while, of course—one of the several reasons she'd had reservations.

"We're gonna have uh better seat fer y'all 'n fer th' others, too, come nex' year. This ole bus is gonna shine, man! Th' boy's a-comin' home. Thought that news'd tickle yore ears! Anyways, that's th' good part—but—" he pushed the old felt hat, its discoloration and sweat-stained headband tattling its age, back from his brow, "they's uh bad side—like always. Our Archie's gittin' kicked outta CCC's. Oh, not from bein' uh bad boy. Ain't nothin' bad 'bout 'im 'n them bigwigs reckons th' same, good at ever'thing. Problem is soon as I git workin', they figger th' boy don't need s'port me'n my ole lady, 'n they don' give uh tinker's— sorry, but ya'll know what! But we'll manage, our Archie 'n me, Miss Marvel."

Our Archie! She found the phrase disturbing, but could think of no kind way of making it more clear. Instead, she said, "I'm sure you'll be able to manage. You're both resourceful. But, Mr. Newland, please call me Marvel—no need for Miss. Oh, good morning, Martha. Is Joe a little late—not sick we hope?"

"No'm, my brother's got to plow. Looks like this winter's over—least our pa's thinking so. Course, he's been known to be wrong. Kept saying all winter it would rain for sure. Well, it sure enough didn't. Fish have plum forgot how to swim! Oops!" the girl grabbed at her skirt the wind had whipped up.

The wind was rising then? The fact concerned Marvel. If only it would hold off until Daddy could get his seeding done. She breathed an inward prayer, only half-hearing Mr. Newland's monologue.

Good that he had the auto repair shop going. Business was increasing just as he'd predicted. Folks couldn't buy new cars, so they had to make the old ones do. After all, Mr. FDR would be right pleased knowing that, what with all that talk about sending relief to Madrid—that was in Spain, wasn't it? Seemed like those foreigners were always fighting.... China and Japan, have a look at them! And those Japs seemed a little huffy at us, too—didn't know why. But one thing was certain, real comforting, too, 'specially for parents with boys well-trained like CCC's trained them. But when the president made a promise, he kept it. Sounded like music to parents' ears hearing that strong voice say, "Our boys will *not* be sent overseas!" Had to wonder, of course, why some colleges started that military program again—ROTC, wasn't it? So glad our Archie's got better sense than getting into a mess like that—wasn't about to go to college...not even back to high school.

Some of the matters overseas concerned Marvel as well. She had heard it mentioned over and over in the news reports, but never discussed it with her parents. There were more pressing matters here at home.

Miss Robertson made a surprise announcement in English class, one which was to have a great impact on all it affected, Marvel in particular.

"Boys and girls, please pay special attention as there is no time for repeating. All who were exempted from midterm examinations are involved in a concentrated reading program in hopes that some, ideally all, will decide to enter the field of literature. I have the list of eligibles here, but you know who you are. Since we want you to have all the reading experiences we're able to make available, the principal and I have arranged for you to see *Alice in Wonderland*, now playing at the Star Theater. Free of charge, of course. A bus is now waiting to take you as the production is about to begin, so you may consider yourselves dismissed. Please do not loiter. It is a lengthy story. I have alerted your other teachers. Unfortunate that we did not know the exact date until this morning and were unable to arrange for return transportation. You will need to be back on time as your bus will be waiting to take you home."

Marvel had no particular desire to see the picture. The story held no special appeal to her. She'd often wondered why it was considered a classic. The concepts seemed too difficult for children to fully comprehend. And most adults surely would view the characters as childish. It might come as a shock to Miss

Robertson to read a book report reflecting a divergent point of view. Certainly, Marvel differed greatly from the generally accepted viewpoint.

Liking the story had nothing to do with the matter. This was an assignment. And so Marvel hurried out as directed. No loitering, Miss Robertson had said. Furthermore, she indicated that the principal knew of the plans—had helped formulate them as a matter of fact. Why then, today of all days, did Mr. Phillips choose to detain her in the hall?

His eyes were like burning coals in the semidarkness as she drew near. It was easy to see that he was angry. She knew a momentary fear. Was there a student enrolled who did not stand in awe of Mr. Phillips? He had a way of commanding respect without speaking.

"Marvel," he said briskly, "will you please step into the girls' restroom there for me? I've had reports of smoking in there!"

She breathed a sigh of relief. He trusted her!

"Yes sir," she said, hurrying through the swinging door. The room was vacant.

"No one is there, Mr. Phillips," she reported.

"Is there a smell of smoke?"

"No sir—none I could detect."

"Thank you, Marvel. You are a fine girl."

Her heart was singing as they reached the theater. All else was blotted from her mind. She would *enjoy Alice in Wonderland*— She had failed to take notice of the wind which was swinging the canopies over the downtown stores, shredding them free of the fringe which edged them. And, once inside, all sounds blended in, losing their identity in the process, with the earsplitting rumble of the giant pipe organ as an overture to the show. The music was not what she would call soothing. And the dank air was heavy with perfume—said to be loosed to mask offensive odors resulting from overcrowding an unventilated room. And it was hot. Overhead fans would have helped.

But the overstuffed leather cushions were comfortable after the long, jolting ride on the school bus, and nobody was saying, "Hurry, *hurry*, HURRY!" In that atmosphere Marvel let her mind drift back to the memory of bygone days when, with her family, she attended cliff-hanging matinees... sitting on Daddy's lap and (undoubtedly to the irritation of those sitting around them), having him read the dialog flashed across the screen. Now that she thought about it, those may have been her first reading lessons... the kid in the three-cornered pants, bright-eyed and eager... watching every word from her perch on Daddy's knees... listening to the drone of his voice until her lids drooped, as they were drooping now. It was easy in this near-hypnotic stage to imagine things. But in an unexpected flashback, something recorded in her subconscious surfaced and then faded. Did she or did she not see a second pair of eyes in the shadows of the school hall this morning? Somebody who had been in the restroom and left?

She did! Of course! They belonged to Amanda Cohane. Marvel had heard that the faster crowd smoked. But at school? Could anybody be foolish enough to risk expulsion, perhaps denied the right to graduate?

The show began. It was no better and no worse than Marvel had expected—just longer. It seemed to have dragged on for hours when it stopped short, catching the White Rabbit in mid-hop.

An air of apprehension hung over the room like a cloud as the pale man (looking paler now) who had collected their complimentary tickets stepped hurriedly forward to stand on the stage, facing his young audience. The manager?

"Sorry, folks, but there's a terrible storm making it essential that you seek safer shelter than this building can offer. We urge you to hurry back to the high school—brick building—and there is a basement, whatever your teachers plan. They've been in touch. Please remain calm in your exit, first row leaving first. I'll supervise your leaving this building. One more thing: Avoid power lines because of the cyclonic winds, and steer clear of other buildings as a funnel-shaped cloud is hanging over the area. *Quiet!* Some have volunteered—business men—to transport you safely. Accept any ride offered! Now, row one! Row two, prepare—*wait your turn in back!*"

Visibility was reduced to zero. Marvel's eyes stung painfully as, clutching her skirt with one hand and making an unsuccessful effort to push her wind-whipped hair from her face with the other, she braced her frail body against the wind's force and made her way to where the curb should be.

Once there, she was pondering what to do when a long, shining black car drove up and stopped directly in front of her.

"I can haul six—get in quickly!" a male voice ordered and reached to clasp her arm.

Marvel squeezed close to the driver and, without looking into his face, reached out to pull the next person in line to take the space beside her. The driver pulled away from the curb, negotiated the turn at the first intersection skillfully, and picked up speed with considerable risk. Her riding companions, awed by the storm, the automobile, or the *Alice in Wonderland* production (or frightened by them all), said very little during that brief ride to school. The driver said even less—or did he speak at all? Marvel was to wonder later.

For now, she was speechless. Her mind was on the powerful storm in progress. Was this the big wind she'd heard so much about—the one plaguing several surrounding states and that had struck the Texas Panhandle already? What would this do to Daddy's farm, his dreams? Surely both would be caught up and swept away. Today of all days—

Then suddenly they had reached school—and relative safety. The other riders alighted hurriedly and, pulling any garment they could loosen over their faces, made a mad rush for the building.

Marvel moved to follow, murmuring a polite "thank you" as she slid toward the door. But the hand of the driver was too quick. Reaching across her lap, he grabbed the handle of the door, catching her completely by surprise.

"You stay!" he hissed.

And then she knew. *Oh, dear God. Please, what do I do?*

Marvel knew without looking up that it was Elmer...Elmer Salsburg. And she was *trapped*!

"I must go," she said in as normal a manner as her voice could muster. "The bus is waiting. I will be missed."

"Ahhh, but I have missed you, too. What makes you think I would let you go now?"

"Because," Marvel said, hoping to have hidden her distaste for what she was about to say, "I've always hoped there was something of a gentleman hidden behind what others see." If only the motor weren't running—

"But not *you*, Miss Queen of the Cotton Rows? *I'll* show you what's behind what others see! Get your eyes off the ignition. Go ahead—scream. Nobody's going to hear you in this wind. A perfect day—all to my advantage—and there's no way to escape that easily!"

"Escape? I am not your prisoner."

"Oh yes, you are—just as I am yours. You are so innocent. We belong together. I should be angry with you, but you can meet that debt in other ways." This was stupid, melodramatic, childish—but dangerous.

"You're talking nonsense. Either you let go of my arm or—"

"You'll jump out? Oh no, you won't!"

And with that, he pressed down on the footfeed and, without switching on the headlights, sped toward the highway.

She tried pleading with him. It did no good. He enjoyed having her beg, as she had begged in that storm cellar.

"Oh Elmer, that was a long time ago. I *must* go back. Elmer, look out, there are other cars out there. We can't see—we'll be *killed*!"

"Then, consider the options. Say we can be friendly, *very* friendly."

"Never—*never*. I'd rather *die*."

"That can be arranged!"

With those words he sped ahead. There was the wild blast of a car horn. "Turn around—turn around this instant! Turn around, or I'll tell all I know about you. You wouldn't want that, Elmer."

For a moment he wavered, considered. Then, whatever reservations he'd had were pushed away.

"You're bluffing," he said and pressed harder on the accelerator.

Then Marvel made a mistake. Losing her composure, she gasped, "Listen, you've got to— Oh," helplessly, "you're crazy, *crazy*—"

"Don't *say* that word. You, you—I'll teach you—"

And with that his hands left the steering wheel and, without reducing the speed, he grasped her throat, choking...*choking*...*CHOKING*....

Whether Marvel planned what happened next or it was an accident caused by the writhing of her body in its struggle for breath, she would never remember. She only knew the outcome. Her right foot pushed his foot from the gas pedal. In his frenzied effort to regain control, he mistakenly jammed on the brake—hard.

There was a wild screech of brakes as the vehicle spun to face the opposite direction. Elmer's head jerked backward, then fell forward crazily. Was he knocked unconscious? Or (*Oh, dear Lord, be merciful!* her heart cried out) was he *dead*? God would have to help her.

Instinctively, Marvel grabbed the wheel, reaching over his limp body to steer—hopefully, dodging other cars, if anybody else was irresponsible enough to brave such a storm—and avoiding the graveled shoulders of the highway.

In what seemed an eternity, the ghostlike outline of the school building loomed out of the gloom. And simultaneously, Elmer regained consciousness, his first breath an oath.

Marvel turned off the ignition and leaped to the safety of the ground, running blindly toward the building as fast as her legs could move. She was shaken, exhausted, and in a state of shock. But nothing could drown out the hateful voice behind her.

"I have a score to settle with you—remember that! If you continue to reject me, you'll pay a price—you and every member of your royal family." Then, ironically, the madman changed, using a tone that was even more frightening. "Come back, dear cousin, can't you see I've changed?"

Changed? Did bad breeding *ever* change? As for his black soul, God alone could take care of that.

She'd learned only one thing for sure. Certainly, they had all known there was something wrong with him—dreadfully wrong—but now she *knew*. Her stepcousin was hopelessly insane. The white uniform? That of an inmate, of course... and he'd made several successful escapes. If he made another, her life was in danger....

Then suddenly she ran headlong into another human being. Her first thought was that somehow Elmer had managed to run past, head her off, and she was about to scream when she realized her mistake.

"I'm sorry," both of them murmured at the same time and, in spite of the situation, managed a laugh together. Male laughter—so the one with whom she'd bumped heads was of the opposite sex?

"Are you all right?" he asked with concern. "I was hurrying—"

"As am I," she managed, rubbing her eyes in a futile effort to see. "But yes, I'm all right except—" she rubbed her forehead, "except for a pumpknot—"

"Something we'll share in common, I suspect. You're in a rush—"

"Another thing we have in common," she called over her shoulder.

Did he call after her? It was easy to imagine anything in such a wind. Undoubtedly the "Wait!" had been a figment of her imagination—a protective device the mind used to blot out the terrible memory preceding.

The very fact that the quick exchange between two strangers blinded by blowing sand and debris could soothe her jangled nerves was rather amazing. He was entitled to a "thank you." Out of the question, of course, Marvel thought with a half-smile as she rushed down the shadowy hall. She hadn't so much as seen the face behind the words. But the voice she would always remember. It spoke of character. . . .

Where was everybody? In the basement? Gone home? Having no idea of the time, Marvel felt herself growing frightened again.

And then there were voices . . . muffled and low . . . a brief conversation between two girls—two girls obviously thinking they were alone.

"Quick, give me your notes before Mr. Hawkeye catches us. I skipped out on that silly movie, and here I am caught having to make a book report."

"Sure, sure. I've gone through it, as you ought to know," came the whispery reply. "Someday I'll clean out this bag. Oh, here they are—cost you a cigarette, Amanda."

"Oh, you're always bumming a smoke. Come out with it, tell your folks. They won't care, mine don't. Thanks, Kate Lynn."

Amanda Cohane! Copying Kate Lynn Porter's work. Marvel had thought more highly of Kate Lynn. The doctor's daughter seemed nice. As for Amanda—well, never mind that. How was she, Marvel, to slip past without being detected?

But it was Amanda who spotted *her*.

"You heard?" she said, as she approached Marvel.

"I heard."

"And you're going to tattle?"

"I have no reason to report what I overheard, Amanda, but—"

Marvel was going to say that she must rush. The bus would be leaving, if it hadn't gone already. But the other girl mistook her meaning.

"Oh, please don't say anything, Marvel. It's against our code, you know—the people who count around here, the crowd everybody tries to be a part of. And I can do so much for you. I hear you've hit it off with one of the football players—and you'll be wanting to join us girls on the pep squad. I can fix it. Deal?"

So now Amanda Cohane was offering a reward for her silence. A knot of disgust formed in the pit of Marvel's stomach. Why bother to correct the silly statement about her knowing a football player? It was none of this shallow girl's affair.

"Thank you," Marvel said coolly. "I'm unable to participate in the rallies. I have to catch the bus, just as I must attempt to do now. Excuse me, please."

"If you're trying to get even, I'm sorry I said anything about the geometry problem. And I didn't mention it to Mr. Phillips."

"It would have been obviously false," Marvel said over her shoulder. "But what's to be gained by my reporting what I overheard? You're only cheating yourself. I hope you learn that someday."

Another enemy or another friend? It made no real difference when the world outside was being blown to bits. . . .

* * *

It was good to sit in back of the bus in the evenings since no roll-taking was necessary. From this vantage point, Marvel could see the damages of the storm, which were considerable. Twisted limbs blocked the roads, and travel was slow. Oh, if only the wind had spared the farm . . . not stole away Daddy's fields of dreams. . . .

40

Voice in the Wind

The storm had moved on when Marvel reached home.

Mother and Daddy ran to meet her with outstretched arms. This morning seemed a million years ago. Being reunited made for a joyous reunion. They had been so worried about Marvel's safety, as she had for theirs. And the hull of a house was a welcome sight. How could it have survived such a blow?

"A miracle," Daddy admitted as the three of them set to work on the evening meal. "We were spared from the worst of the storm by the power of prayer. And I'll tell you, there were plenty praying! Fanny came running with Hezzie—the preacher-man as they call him—bringing up the rear, every one of the bottomland folks in between—all scared out of their wits. Well, we all were. And huddled together here, we watched that funnel cloud— actually witnessed its touching down—"

When he seemed overcome with emotion, Mother took up the report. "We could see buildings—or, at least splinters—twisting and whirling. And us not knowing if there was human flesh up there made us sick. I—we—*all* of us vomited. Oh, let's don't talk about it. We have too much to be thankful for, like," she tried to smile, "Fanny's using the *front* door—too scared to run around the house. Dale darling, do you feel like making the coffee now?"

"The coffee should have my strength!" he grinned.

At supper he told more. The tornado touched down in Texarkana...hit another small town he'd never heard of. Then, just as it seemed to be losing its punch...boom! Gathering force it struck Oklahoma, another tragedy to add to their list of disasters, then whirled into Kansas where it sucked up the remainder of damaged grain...gone...all of it...as well as the loose soil. Human life? Who knew? Last news report said all lines of communication were out, as were their own here....

Marvel sucked in her breath. "But our soil was spared? The terraces worked? Oh, Daddy..."

This was no time to tell them about the events of her day—and certainly not about Elmer. That he would surface again she had no doubt. Not knowing how or when was taking its toll. His evil presence hung over her night and day. Already he'd robbed her of delights in small things, replacing them with fear: sitting alone on the front doorstep to listen to the mellow notes of the whippoorwill down in the bottoms...watching the luminescent flash of fireflies in their earthly galaxies as they soared up to lose their identity among the twinkling stars...inhaling deeply the scent of dried flowers which had managed to retain the fragrance of their youth...and watching cautiously the bobbing of the swamp lanterns, the mysterious balls of gas which formed when conditions were right, nobody knowing when. But the promise (or threat) was there.

The lights which Marvel had found exciting were now a threat. And only now could she understand the fears and superstitions of their neighbors in the bottomlands. They were right. The "devil" would return.

* * *

Repairing the telephone lines took much longer than usual, damage was so far-reaching. Mother reported daily that she'd tried again to reach Grandmother or Auntie Rae with no success. Marvel, buried in a schedule which seemed to grow weightier with each passing day, was kept from checking on conditions in Pleasant Knoll. She'd seen none of the students from there this semester. Their schedules were differing, unfortunately. How could one get so involved?

And she was destined to grow more so. Miss Robertson, pleased with Marvel's report on the film, suggested that she write book reviews for the local newspaper. It would be good publicity for the school, and good experience for her. And,

Marvel would be pleased to know, she would be excused from further instruction in grammar plus giving her extra credit. "You'll be finishing your junior year at the head of your class," Miss Robertson said with satisfaction.

Marvel was supposed to feel complimented, she supposed. And in a way she did. However, she had sought no reward—just a good foundation.

She smiled and thanked the teacher, little dreaming what the favorable response to the reviews would lead to. When the small school newspaper began on an experimental basis, Marvel was invited to do a special column, all the while preparing for county meet....

Then, the night before they were able to make contact with the family, an unexpected event took place: unwilled...unscheduled ...*unwelcome*!

Virginia Thomas and Marvel had been in the same civics class the first semester. In the new scheduling, Virginia sat behind her in the study hall allowed to Marvel as a prep time for her newspaper copy.

Both girls were busy with little time for chatting, just a nod. Marvel was surprised on this particular day when Virginia interrupted her work by poking her with the eraser of a pencil. With her mind still occupied with the story she must complete that day, Marvel half-turned and raised a quizzical eyebrow.

"Note for you," the other girl whispered, "I'm appointed messenger."

"Note? For *me*? I don't understand."

"Maybe if you read it—" Virginia sounded a little impatient.

Marvel accepted the folded paper, murmured an apology, turned to face forward, and spread the mystery letter on her desk. She read it in disbelief, shook her head a bit to clear it, and read it again.

My dear Marvel: They tell me that's your name. I have tried unsuccessfully numerous times for a proper introduction without success. This note is difficult for me as I am not accustomed to writing girls I don't know. I dared only because I very much want to meet you, having admired you from a distance for so long now. My only plea for your understanding is to remind you that we have met—just a chance meeting, of course. Shall we say you just "blew into my life"? You've probably forgotten, but I remember. And remembering gave me needed courage. However, if you do not answer, I'll know the worst—that you are offended by my being so forward. Hopefully, Titus.

The note sent shock waves coursing through her being. Offended? No, to be honest, Marvel admitted to herself, she was excited in spite of herself. But she mustn't be. Why, this was ridiculous. So why was her hand shaking? There was no choice but to ignore the note.

"Excited?" Virginia whispered, unable to restrain herself any longer.

Marvel turned slightly, moving her head from the supervising teacher's view while feeling irritation at herself for slipping around. She'd seen the other girls being so devious, so silly...still...

Just one question, she promised herself. "Who is this person?"

Virginia stifled a snicker. "Who *is* he? Where've you been, kiddo? Your admirer's only the most sought-after boy in this school, captain of the football team, *plus* being an honor student. Are you kidding? You didn't know? He's in my chemistry class. Shhh, here comes the spy!" she spoke rapidly, "I'll take your answer—"

"There'll be none."

Marvel heard a gasp from her friend—and felt a little heartsick herself. It was the end of a friendship that never began.

For the remainder of the day, mixed emotions churned within her, making it difficult for her to concentrate. It was good to hear the dismissal bell ring.

Only during the long, punishing ride home on the bus did she dare come to grips with her emotions. She, Marvel Harrington—the sensible, mature, driven-by-ambition young lady—was behaving like a schoolgirl. An outsider could have looked into her flushed face, studied her shining eyes, and told her the truth—that what she felt was normal, natural, and good. But there *was* no outsider because Marvel held her secret close. It belonged to her—her alone.

She was afraid to answer the note—not offended. Afraid of the emotion so new to her—afraid of herself. And afraid to look her dream-come-true in the face. So fragile was that dream that it might shatter like spun glass once she saw its human form.

For now she knew that somewhere, buried down deep inside her, lay the unacknowledged desire to meet the owner of that pleasant masculine voice heard in the windstorm. And now she avoided it, preferring to create this person in her imagination. Why then did she feel that almost uncontrollable desire to weep? "Titus—oh, Titus," she whispered to the face she had never seen....

The telephone was ringing shrilly as Marvel opened the front door of home. Mother answered excitedly, "Mother!" and then talked in guarded tones. Dale Harrington and his daughter looked at each other wordlessly.

Marvel wanted to talk with Mary Ann, but Mother's conversation was surprisingly brief. They would know the rest tomorrow, Saturday.

Saturday? Yes it was, and Marvel had forgotten. Eager as she was to hear more of what Mother would report, she brought her mind back to order. Here was obviously another family crisis. How fickle of her to allow her mind to wander to such trivia... too late now to reconsider and respond somehow to the voice in the wind...a small matter....

"...and so," Mother was saying, "Father Harrington will be coming out for us...church was destroyed. But why is *Frederick* calling us together? Something is very wrong...."

41

The Fall

The Harrington family was estranged from Frederick Salsburg. All members agreed on that point. Marvel wondered what changed Grandfather's mind, made him weaken and honor his stepson's request for an audience.

"Request? *Plea* is more like it," Auntie Rae told Mother. She had called shortly after Grandmother to explain that the family would meet with her and Uncle Worth. "And we are in the dark completely," she said. "We simply can't imagine what's in the wind."

The wind. They lived by the wind. Instead of checking clock or calendar, this part of the world checked wind velocity and direction. Refreshed by a night's rest, it had gathered strength on the day of the dreaded meeting and seemed to be blowing from the four corners of the earth. Some would say it was a bad omen; others, that it was testing the endurance of mankind—perhaps carrying a particular grudge against all bearing the Harrington name.

But why speculate on the ways of nature—*or* mankind?

No amount of speculation could have brought an insight on what Frederick Salsburg sought. Alexander Jay Harrington, Esquire was to say later that he believed God Himself must have been surprised. . . .

Everyone seemed to arrive at one time—including Frederick: A new Frederick, broken, old, defeated. Marvel stared at this stranger in dismay. And the most amazing part was his sincerity—

no act, no play for sympathy. All bluster was stripped away, leaving a skeleton of shame.

Emaciated emotionally as the man was, he continued to dominate the scene. More curious than concerned, all others were silent.

He attempted to stand, found himself too unsteady, and asked for a chair. Immediately he began to speak, not meeting their eyes.

"It was good of you to come—more than I deserved. I—I can't ask for your forgiveness, only your understanding. You see, for the first time, I need *your* help—" he raised a trembling hand as if to detain what he expected to be a departing audience. "Don't go—I beg—don't go. I'm not looking for a handout or support of the family name. It's too late for that—too late for me. If somebody'll just bring Brother Greer—let him hear the lamentations of a fallen man."

"I'm here, Fred," Grady Greer said gently. "Try to relax. I believe I'm speaking for the family in saying we'll listen and do what we can."

The whole sordid story spilled out then before an audience stricken dumb. If the lurid account was true, why did he dare reveal it—and to them, of all people? They were soon to find the answers.

Frederick Salsburg's life had been one of deception. He hated them all, envied them at the same time. He coveted all their possessions as well as what they *were*: a stock with breeding he lacked. He'd have lied, stolen, swindled, *killed* to rise above his lot... which is just what he did! But the taint was always there, the bad blood, the predestination to hell! *No, no, the reverend was not to stop him. At least let him purge his dark soul by confession.* This, too, was a plea.

It all began with the loss of his mother, at which time he had been beset by fears in place of tears. There was money and it belonged to him—not to some other man she might choose to marry. He'd stolen a lot of the fortune, hidden it away... and yes, that was the source of his wealth: a coffer to which he added great sums by every means possible. But it was never enough to wipe away his hatred, his jealousy, and envy—all of which so warped his mind that nobody would ever be able to convince him this did not reflect in the birth of marked offspring, crippled and demented. Again he had failed! While their children were normal, healthy, and intelligent— Oh, they couldn't imagine the torture!

So he continued to punish them, but never as much as he punished himself! His wife turned away from him, his son's mind became more twisted, and all the while he was passing this sick hatred down to his son—the son Satan gave him the power to hypnotize. Yes, hypnotize into carrying out his every spoken word—even seeming to read his secret thoughts.

"But here's the one and only place where I can plead innocent. I didn't know—I didn't know," he groaned. "But that doesn't excuse me. What reason would you have to forgive me when God Himself has turned His back?"

"Frederick—Frederick, listen to me!" Brother Greer cried out. "God doesn't turn His back. Listen!"

"I will *not* listen. This has to be said—*now*. Can't you see you're talking to a dead man?"

A gasp of horror went around the room. But Frederick Salsburg did not allow time for words. "The next is worse but can be spoken faster, now that you have the background." His voice was flat, lifeless.

"I tried to be a good father—as if I could, as if it would have changed things. Nothing worked. Elmer overheard a terrible quarrel between Pauline and me—heard me say I wished she were dead, and you know the rest. And the fires—all of them, yes—and all my fault—the evil power of suggestion! And where is he now, this demon forged in hell's furnace? He was never in any academy. That idea came from trying to match your record, Dale. I *had* to succeed where one of the Harrington sons had failed—if only in your sight. You know, *pretending* my son made it and my stepfather's did not—"

"My son didn't fail!" Grandfather said loudly. "He *chose* not to go."

In the midst of all this dark nightmare, a bright light! Grandfather was defending his son. Daddy had the approval he had needed for so long.

"*Chose*, beautiful word," Frederick's voice was sad. "Elmer never had a choice in his life—because of me. And I lied about Annapolis. He had no opportunity. Never could have qualified anyway."

"But why, Frederick, why?" Uncle Worth asked him. "Was it so necessary for Elmer to look good in our eyes?"

Frederick Salsburg shook his head as if to clear it. "Yes and no. The truth is that I was forced to get him out of here, and in a hurry. Elmer was just a step ahead of the law, and I arranged to have him committed—"

"To an asylum?" Mother's voice was no more than a whisper.

An institution where he could receive help, where all would be kept in strict confidence. But now, the ugly truth was that Elmer had slipped through their fingers so many times, always leaving a string of crimes behind, that more drastic measures had to be taken.

"Like?" Daddy asked. "What did you do, Fred? We'd have helped."

"Oh, don't pour salt on my bleeding wounds," his stepbrother groaned. "I'd quote a Scripture if I had the right and say, 'Don't turn the other cheek'! You're heaping coals of fire on my head this way. *Like?* You asked—okay, like agreeing to have him committed to another institution—one of solitary confinement, a place reserved for the *criminally* insane. Either that or face a long drawn-out trial, a conviction. We all know he's guilty, and Elmer's an adult now. There could be capital punishment. He's not much of a son, but I'm no father either and—" he slumped forward and gave way to dry choking sobs, "we—we love each other—"

"Of course you do!" Grandmother said briskly and walked to him with a quick, lively step. "Now you look here, Frederick. Remember when I came for Polly's funeral, declaring to be a member of this family? Because in my heart, I am! I want you to know that, no matter what you are or may not be, what you've done or failed to do, doesn't alter one thing. That's love. And love comes from God, so stop denying that! If there's more to this sordid tale, get it off your chest. I'm hungry! Beans and ham hocks—you could use a square meal!

The atmosphere lightened. Grandmother was a love. And Marvel suddenly felt consumed by it. Everything was coming together for her—*everything*: earthly love, spiritual love, old things made new, and something more which bound them all together in a sacred completeness.

The man she'd once called Uncle Fred obeyed the Grand Dame (Grandfather's new title of address). Keeping Elmer hidden away had cost him his ill-gained fortune. At least he'd done one decent thing, he claimed defensively. His bundling Elmer away had protected the Harrington name. Maybe they would understand, he pleaded. No charge for keeping his son where he was now, so he could manage financially, but he wouldn't be around long and he needed reassurance that they'd protect Elmer... see that he was taken back if somehow he managed to escape again... not report him to authorities....

There was a murmur of yeses.

Brother Greer walked over to Frederick and placed his arm firmly about his shoulders. "Now son," he said quietly, "there is such a thing as returning good for evil. God took care of that, but He can't take care of your problems if you hold them inside. Isn't that what you actually need help on—your *real* reason for drawing us all together?"

"Partly," Frederick admitted. "Only I don't know why, when it's hopeless. When God had turned His back on me."

"God doesn't turn His back on any of us—sinner or saint. Because of your wrongdoing? Nonsense! We've all fallen short of the glory of God, Paul tells the Romans. And that would include us Texans as well! You've just chosen to go your own independent way, become self-willed, indifferent, even rebellious... and *you* have separated yourself from *Him*! Now, and I'm speaking to all in this room, can't we help this man who's dying physically and spiritually cross that gulf and get back to his Maker while there's yet time? I charge you—are you able?"

Grandmother quietly picked up her violin, tucked it beneath the still-unwrinkled chin, and drew the bow expertly across the strings. Could anybody fail to recognize the beautiful old hymn?

Apparently not. Someone hummed softly. And then softly they all sang the words: "Lord, we are able, our spirits are Thine...."

Frederick Salsburg was weeping openly now—the cleansing tears of genuine sorrow. But doubt remained in his voice.

"I—I just don't understand. God called me once, I think, and I gave money—"

"But not your heart. That's what He wants," Grady Greer said. "Surrender the heart first, and He'll show you His plan. There's no way to purchase a ticket to heaven, Fred. The only way is through His Son, our Savior. He's knocking at the door of your heart. Let Him in—He'll lead you across that gulf. You've confessed your sins to us. Now, confess them to God, apologize to Him as you have to these wonderful folks, and we'll all pray with you. He'll come into your life as He promised. Then roll up those sleeves, good brother. He'll put you to work—you'll never be unemployed again! Now then, we'll all kneel—"

When Frederick Salsburg rose, the transformation showed. He wore a glow. "I know the plan! I'm to build back that church!" he said with a shout of joy.

42

"Stars Fell on Alabama"

At home there was an unending flow of talk centering around the Salsburg miracle. Unbelievable...sad...heartbreaking really that the Harringtons didn't know years ago—maybe things would have been different. Now, with this terminal illness—yes, cancer—it was too late to form the warm relationship that could have been theirs.

"Well, it's never too late with God," Daddy said in summary.

"Thankfully," Mother smiled. "And we'll do what we can, darling."

Marvel made no comment. Inwardly she knew she could never love this man any more than she could conquer her fear of his son. But she could not *hate* them either. God understood that and would ask only that *His* love be shared with Frederick and Elmer Salsburg. He had given her peace through this experience, let her witness firsthand the change when the human heart surrenders without condition. All her studies with Brother Greer made sense now. God would reveal His plan for her life in His own time—just as He told the persimmons when to mellow and let go of the parent tree. Meantime, she could borrow from their patience.

There was visiting—relaxed, warm, and revealing—after the Salsburg miracle. Mother and Daddy found much to tell each other afterward about Grandmother and Grandfather and their pursuits (in work, yes, but—Daddy grinned—of one another!).

Sure enough? Sure enough! They were the talk of the town, those two—the Squire and the Grand Dame!

"Well, that mother of mine hasn't lost that daring, that love of adventure which I did not inherit. I need roots: the love, warmth, and sense of security one finds in a home!"

"One?" Daddy said with a twinkle.

"Three!" Mother corrected quickly. "That's us, *the three bears!*"

Daddy said his father had regained his vigor, too—thanks in part to Mother Riley. "And part," he said slowly, "to feeling in charge again. Strange isn't it, how things work out—that Frederick, after all their mutual distrust and disliking, loathing actually, could be the one to give him a sense of importance?"

"We never know. And something else! Imagine that the very man whose son torched the church would be the one to finance rebuilding—that is, after the storm destroyed their efforts. Such a shame."

"A shame about the whole town—one disaster after another. I'm still wondering how the worst of it left us relatively unharmed."

"Prayer."

Speaking of which reminded Mother of her prayers for the heavenly blue morning glories. "Honestly, Marvel, I do believe they're crossed with Jack's magical beanstalk! They're touching the roof and budding. You *must* see them. Oh, I'm so excited!"

"We never would have guessed," Daddy teased and went on to speak of his brothers Joseph and Emory. Good to see them again. Still having it rough—rough enough to have considered seriously picking up stakes and making a move, particularly after hearing from Alex, Jr. that he'd found the land flowing with milk and honey out on the coast with Jake's Uncle Russ. But last night's gathering brought back the need for family."

"I'm glad to hear they came to their senses! *No* moving!" Mother said.

"No moving," Daddy said. But his voice lacked her conviction.

That was when Daddy said, as if noticing Marvel's silence for the first time, "You haven't said a word, baby, and your eyes look as if you're in another world. Something troubling you?"

Marvel jumped. "Just listening with interest," she said, meaning it and not adding that the part about being in another world was true, too. What would they think if she said, "I've met a very special boy—at least, I met his voice"?

Foolish? Of course it was foolish. Why then did her hand reach anxiously into her sweater pocket to be sure the note was still there? It was. Her hand tightened around it as if it were a trophy.

Marvel had wanted to share about this with Mary Ann. But no! There was nothing to share . . . nothing at all . . . and never would be. And if there were? She would not have shared anyway. This secret belonged to her—her alone. It was as if the dream was a bit of fragile glass, and sharing it with someone else could cause it to fall to bits. But this was less than a dream—just a memory undreamed of. . . .

✽ ✽ ✽

At school Marvel found the schedule changed for the day. To her surprise there was to be an assembly the first of the year. The principal had some announcements, another student told her. Then—believe it or not—Mr. Phillips had agreed to allow time for a sort of pep rally (usually an after-school activity) and group singing.

"What about classes? And where do we sit? I've never attended an assembly in this school," Marvel said a little anxiously.

Her informant shrugged. "Me either. Play it by ear, I guess. Mr. P. will ride herd! The auditorium'll be packed like sardines. Sit anywhere—on your fist and lean back on your thumb if you have to."

She didn't have to. Marvel went in early instead of detouring by the girls' room for "primping," and found her study-hall desk unoccupied. It was near the front and afforded a good view of the platform.

Mr. Phillips' announcements were brief, to-the-point, and delivered without a smile. Those he reserved for deserving moments, and this was strictly business.

School wasn't out, which might come as a surprise to some, he said crisply. There was much to be accomplished, and loiterers, beware! All students were expected to keep their grades up, maintaining a high average as well as living up to the highest of moral standards if seniors hoped to graduate. One misconduct or one failure in achievement would disqualify that candidate. And juniors expecting to advance to senior status for the next school year must meet the same standards.

"A final word of warning," the principal said, his dark eyes panning the audience and managing to force every eye to meet his gaze, "do not overload your schedule and try to slip by. And those new to Culverville High will need to know that there will be no celebrating, other than the socials planned by your teachers, no skip-school day, and above all, no dances—in school or in private homes! Expulsion will be the price you pay—expulsion for the remainder of the school year, without chance of promotion for the following year. Be forewarned!"

In so crowded a room one could expect stuffiness—certainly in this auditorium where nobody would dare open a window without permission. Marvel suspected the air was tolerable here because no one breathed to use up the oxygen. All sat silent, straight and flat as paper dolls.

There was mention of honor rolls, the county meet, and one final assembly for the purpose of distributing letters, ribbons, and loving cups earned. Then, nodding permission to someone in the front row to replace him, Mr. Phillips advanced to the sidewall where, with arms crossed, he stood, his watchful eyes on the entire student body for the remainder of the assembly.

"Dutch" Harper, whom Marvel knew only by name, introduced himself as the pep squad leader, made a pitch for new members, named a date for tryouts, and then invited the present members to join him onstage.

As they demonstrated yells and songs, Marvel spotted— among others she had met—Amanda and Kate Lynn. Neither girl seemed bothered by the principal's warnings. Apparently they were above the law, belonging to the "right group" as they did, and having parents who considered themselves among the socially elite. It was sad, in a way.

Something clicked in Marvel's mind. Barbara Hutton, the Woolworth heiress—referred to in newspapers as the star-crossed darling of cafe society—was not the only "poor little rich girl." She must have known money and what it could and could not buy would cost dearly and that many would be cursed by it, considering the lines of her prophetic poem written when she, too, was in her teens:

> Why should some have all
> And others do without?

> Then why should men pretend—
> And, someday, women doubt?

The sound of a male voice, made harsh by a megaphone, jarred the auditorium. Dutch called loudly, "Now, let's have a little fun. Hit 'er, Miss Yukon! Use the *loud* foot-pedal. And the rest of you take your cue. First, a hobo song—"

The French teacher nodded and singing began, gathering volume as those without radios picked up the words to the lyrics:

> All around a water-tank,
> Waitin' for uh train—
> I'm uh thousand miles away from home,
> Singin' in th' rain...

"And now—

> The object of my affection
> Changes my complexion
> From white to rosy red
> Every time she holds my hand
> And tells me that she's mine!"

How long had it been since she'd sung anyway? Marvel had forgotten how much fun it was just to let go, relax, enjoy the moment, and enter that other world Daddy mentioned. Now all too soon, it was ending.

"And now, with a word of appreciation to our principal for allowing us this time-out for fun—that's it, give him a hand, folks! Hey, that's enough! We're about to close with one last song—a new one you're sure to like. Listen to the words and tune, then join in:

> Moonlight and magnolias,
> Starlight all in your hair...

"Got it? Here goes!

I never had in my imagination
A situation so heaven-ly—
A fairyland, where no one else could en-ter,
Just you—and me—dear—
We lived our little drama,
We kissed in a field of white—
And stars fell on Ala-bam-a
Last night!"

Caught up in this strange, new world, Marvel felt something inside her explode. Stars of a million colors fell all around her. Her heart turned a cartwheel and then raced furiously. Mercifully it slowed, but continued the singing. The explanation came then.

She was going to write to Titus, a boy whose last name she did not know and whose voice she had heard only in the song of the wind.

Easier said than done. What did one say when longing so much to meet another, yet fearing? Knowing that her words could open a door or close it? Weren't both steps improper: writing to a stranger or failing to answer a letter? *Please Lord,* her inexperienced heart begged, *don't let me sound too forward, just polite and friendly.*

Dear Titus: You are right (she began). A letter to a person you have not met is hard to write. I want to acknowledge your note, however, and to express appreciation for the nice things you said. Yes, I remember our chance meeting that windy day. Until we have a proper meeting, I suppose we can call it our "blind date." Sincerely, Marvel Harrington.

Marvel had finished the note but had no time to correct or rewrite when Virginia Thomas stopped by her desk and, pencil between clenched teeth and chin holding an armful of books, she began rifling through the one on top of the stack. Marvel, taking advantage of the unscheduled meeting, folded the note quickly and dropped it between the pages where the book had opened. At that exact moment, Virginia shoved another note onto her desk. From *him*? There must be some mistake.

"What's the matter? You two 'ave uh fallin' out—er sump'n?" the other girl sputtered, pencil still intact. "Lovers' quar'l—hmmm?"

"No—oh, no. Nothing like that!" Marvel answered breathlessly.

The bell rang and Virginia rushed away, leaving Marvel to savor the moment of anticipation—longing to read the note, while fearing to. Suppose he apologized, said he regretted writing, and told her to forget it? Then her having answered would be an embarrassment, a terrible mistake. In fact, it was anyway. Oh how *could* she have written such bold words? *Blind date.* How tasteless—tasteless and misleading—written by a girl who had never dated once in her life....

Unable to cope with the contents, she dropped his note into her clutch bag and hurried to class; and, forgetting the changed schedule, arrived at the wrong one! The silly mistake caused her to reach the proper class five minutes late. Disgusted with herself, Marvel determined to get herself under control. It was no use. Better by far to risk reading the note in class and have it over and done with, so life could go on.

My dear Marvel: Since you did not answer my first note, I should apologize for writing it. I had no right and realize too late that I was out of line. Yet, here I am daring to write again and ask that you overlook my lack of good manners. Will you pretend it never happened and let me arrange for a proper introduction—*please*? Hopefully, Titus.

Marvel felt a surge of relief. Their notes would have crisscrossed. No more apologies—and who needed an introduction? They weren't strangers. She hardly heard the dismissal bell. Virginia reminded her when, with palms up, she tossed still another note her direction. A single line: "Stars Fell on Alabama!" it read. And it was signed *T.*

43

A Perfect Stranger

In every child's life there comes a day which portends the future. Its full meaning is revealed years later somehow—in a glance remembered, a touch, a smile, or a flashback as the adult's mind aimlessly thumbs through the pages of life's memory book.

For Marvel Harrington it was the day she said "hello" to a stranger who was no stranger at all. At least, it seemed so in retrospect. But the elements of her character were already there. She was a warm and caring person—characteristics which served as a magnet to those who knew her, in spite of her natural reserve. Ironically, she was to learn later, the admirable blend of those qualities served to make her more vulnerable....

When Marvel reported to the organizational meeting for the school newspaper, she was surprised to find Mr. Angelo, instructor for the business opportunities class, in charge. She was even more surprised when the bespectacled man (who, in spite of supposedly impaired vision, seemed capable of boring a hole through the wall, so steady was his gaze) used her first name in his greeting.

She responded with a shy smile and murmured, "I am pleased that you remember me. We only met at enrollment, and now school's drawing to a close."

Mr. Angelo was studying her face. "But I've seen you and heard of your accomplishments—like to think I played a small part, not that I did. I *will* want to speak privately with you sometime—an idea I have."

More students pressed through the door, and Marvel sat down to help clear a passageway. The teacher explained the format, distributed schedules, made a pitch for his class by half-promising those who did exceptionally well part-time work with the local newspaper, and left the group on their own—each to write a sample news item.

There was a mass exodus. Marvel, supposing she was alone, decided to take advantage of the quiet time. Picking up a pencil, she set to work at once, removing herself mentally from her surroundings.

Deep in concentration, Marvel felt rather than saw the presence of another in the large but somewhat shadowy room. Light footsteps said the other occupant must be another girl, probably leaving.

"Someone turned the light off," Marvel said without looking up. "It's hard to see. Would you mind?"

"Yes," a deep, pleasant male voice said softly, but the single word echoed in the stillness as if spoken in a tomb.

Uneasiness gripped her. Here she was alone, and what if? No, *no*! Elmer Salsburg was no longer a threat, but—

The tall, lithe figure came striding toward her. He had pulled out a chair, straddled it with one fluid swing of his long legs, and sat facing her, chin resting on folded arms—while she sat frozen.

It happened so fast that there was no time to escape. And then, foolishly, she did not wish to.

In those few seconds Marvel took a sweeping glance and learned a lot about this intruder. His eyes, gray really, had a way of looking dark when focused on his subject. His nose was the right length, neither too long nor too short—and definitely patrician. The most expressive part of the interesting face was a firmly chiseled mouth. It was easy to imagine the humor it could portray and equally easy to see that it was more accustomed to thoughtfulness that went along with his eyes.

At the moment, however, the lips seemed to quiver slightly—as if he, too, was uncertain. Immediately she relaxed a bit.

Marvel realized that she, too, was under scrutiny. The lifted eyebrows above his thoughtful eyes were quizzical as if he was wondering how he would be received. She waited for him to speak, explain himself, tell her what brought him here—maybe disclose his name.

She didn't have to wait long. "I was about to suggest leaving the light off—keeps it cooler. Hello, Marvel!"

"Hello, Titus," she said simply, naturally, as if they met daily. "You knew?"

"Of course. I knew your voice—though we're strangers."

He nodded. "Well, some might say so. Do introductions make friends? Then okay, strangers—but wait!" Titus stood up, unfolding his limbs with the same ease he'd demonstrated in sitting.

Oh, don't go, Marvel pleaded silently.

But he wasn't leaving. Instead, he bowed comically from his middle.

"Miss Marvel Harrington, I believe?"

She laughed and he joined her. "That is correct," Marvel said.

"Then I have met my *perfect stranger,*" he said almost reverently.

A harsh ring of the bell signifying an ending of the period shattered their small world of discovery. They were back in the mundane world of school schedules. With a difference! It was no longer mundane.

"May I walk you to class?" he asked, gathering up her books.

"I would like that," Marvel said without guile, "but I have domestic science. It's a long walk to the cottage."

"I enjoy walking, and I have a study hall this period. Let's go!"

Marvel matched her stride to his as, bracing themselves against the wind, they hurried along together. Never once did conversation lag.

"So I finally met the girl I'd heard was so elusive—a Harrington!"

"Would the name have made a difference?"

"Of course not! But I *am* intrigued by your first name. Maybe that's what I fell in love with first—"

Marvel, having given up any attempt to control her windwhipped hair, turned to look at Titus. She considered herself tall, but he was some six inches taller and it was necessary to look up to meet his eyes. They looked dark as they had in the classroom. A little fear clutched her young heart—not so much of Titus but of herself. It was a new feeling, one with which an inexperienced heart cannot cope.

"Surely you jest," she said above the wind, striving for lightness.

"I am new at this, Marvel, but I would never jest about matters of the heart." There was a ring of sincerity in his young voice.

"Then let's talk about—about *other* matters. Do you realize I don't even know your last name?"

"I'm sorry! It's easy to remember: Smith—just plain Smith."

They rounded the last corner and she talked quickly. "But there's nothing plain, as you term it, about *Titus*. Is the name from the Bible, Shakespeare, our county—or what?"

"All of them, indirectly. But actually, it was my mother's maiden name. So you see," he laughed, "I bear a name with a background, too. But you haven't told me how you came to be *Marvel*—it's so right. You never could be a Martha, a Maggie, or well, anything else would be wrong."

She told him in the short time remaining how her father had chosen her name, now calling her "Miss Marvelous," and how close they were.

Titus nodded sadly. "I can see that—and I envy you. That was denied me." He told her then that his mother had died at his birth and how his heartbroken father had named him in her honor. His father had died shortly afterward, leaving his sister, eight years older, with the responsibility of his upbringing. Someday he would repay her.

"Oh, here we are. So we met in the wind and we part in the wind. Good-bye, my perfect stranger."

44

Double Identity

Marvel felt sometimes that she was two people as the air softened with springtime. She remained the studious, high achiever with the same goals. Nothing could change her heaviness of heart at the desolation of the land and the plight of its people and the burning desire to help those in need—with her parents at the top of the list. The other person inside herself felt a lightness of heart. She had entered a world of enchantment where all things were beautiful and all life's conflicts resolved, removed. In this blissful world no evil existed, only good—this land of perfect environment, this Garden of Eden. And all of humanity knew love, true love....

It was most confusing. In which world did she fit? Both? One thing was clear: She could never let go of either. The two worlds had sliced her heart through its middle, each taking a half.

"I wish the door of opportunity could be widened even a crack to let more people through," Marvel remarked to her parents. She told them then about the business opportunities class and what it offered.

Mother and Daddy agreed that it was a start. But she could tell that their minds were occupied with the here and now, and it was easy to see why. Gardens were late, probably would need replanting, and the cotton offered little promise. The stand was poor, and the plants which had managed to survive were spindly and tinged with yellow—a sure sign of malnutrition. In sad contrast, the thriving Bermuda grass, still struggling to regain its claim to pasture, triumphantly spread wide its hearty stolons and colonized everywhere.

"But the corn is green," Marvel said brightly, in hopes of diverting Daddy's attention from the failing cash-crop cotton. She, too, wondered how he would repay the bank. Amanda's face floated before her and seemed to settle where a colorful center-piece should rest on the breakfast table—only Mother's flowers were dying of thirst. Desperately, Marvel erased the vision and rushed on, "And the watermelons are up. Look, Daddy!"

He looked the direction her finger pointed and gasped. For there came Fanny and all her faithful little followers, hoes over their dark, exposed shoulders, and singing as only they could sing:

> Pow'r, pow'r, wond'r workin' pow'r
> In de blood, in de blood,
> O'de lam'...

Bless them. Coming to help Mr. Dale "outta de grass," they said.

Marvel hurried off to school, glad—so glad—to see Daddy happier today. Miracles still happened, and they sometimes came in black. . . .

Titus met her at the bus and took her books. Only then did she miss her lunch sack. Nothing to complain about when two-thirds of the nation was without food completely. Of course she could enjoy a sandwich at Flint's Drugstore like the town girls did every noon, if she had a dime. Those girls would never know what going without really meant, Marvel decided. Just yesterday she had overheard Amanda telling Kate Lynn that her mother had decided to cut her allowance, and had said that a trip to the beauty shop every week was unnecessary. A finger wave should last two weeks—except for special occasions. Kate Lynn sympathized.

"Something bothering you, Marvel? You've hardly spoken," Titus said.

"Oh, no—nothing—nothing at all," she smiled up at him. "And I speak from the heart."

Titus stopped. "Wait a minute, young lady. Are you poking fun at me—me and that theatrical pitch I made the day we met? I *was* trying to impress you, so I guess I deserve it."

"Impress me? You did a fine job, Titus. Now, is something bothering *you*? This is the first time you've come to the bus."

"Oh, the man is bold!"

"I'm not complaining."

Titus' hands tightened around Marvel's book, but he reached out and touched her only with his eyes. And she was back in her other world.

"I came to tell the news—good news, if you are as pleased as I am. Our newspaper group meets today, but I've heard in advance—" he said as they walked on together, the sentence teasingly unfinished.

"Titus Smith, *tell* me. Tell me this instant!"

"Yes, Miss Marvelous. As you wish. I met Mr. Angelo in the hall and he couldn't wait to say you and I are to be in charge of the publication: editor-in-chief, big cheese, whatever." The gray eyes were black again with excitement, an excitement Marvel shared. "Said we—you and I—turned in promising papers. I think *he* thinks we're candidates for those newspaper jobs."

"Oh, but we're not. I mean *I'm* not. I just want the experience!"

"Same here. There goes the bell—gotta shake a leg as sis says— But Marvel, here's the catch. We'll have to spend more time together."

"That's a *catch*?" she asked breathlessly.

"Oh, Marvel!" The way he said the two words made her heart sing. "It's great. But our schedules are packed, so I thought maybe we could share our sandwiches at noon?"

"O mercy me!" she mimicked Grandmother, causing Titus to laugh. "No sandwich today—the morning at home was a little confusing—"

"Which creates no problem. Will you be my guest for lunch, Miss Harrington?"

"Yes, Mr. Smith," Marvel almost sang the words. "Meet you here at the stroke of 12. Now, the books quick. I gotta shake a leg!"

His laughter followed her down the hall.

At noon the two of them sat cross-legged beneath a giant oak with folded newspapers for cushions, a sheet of notebook paper for a tablecloth. Titus broke his sandwich in half, peeled and quartered an apple, and laid out two large chocolate cookies.

"Do you say grace?" His voice was low and serious now.

"Always," she said, her voice shaking a little. They were so alike it was unsettling. "Could we just close our eyes and listen to the rustle of the leaves? People think I'm strange as it is."

"Same here. Good idea—we don't listen enough. Ever think the Creator's voice can come through the trees He created? What makes me think you'll understand when others wouldn't? Only I'm saying stuff I've never said to others, feeling it's okay."

"It's okay," she said with her head bowed and her eyes closed.

"You're beautiful," he whispered. "Now, that prayer. I have some things to tell the Lord privately."

Over the quick lunch they talked newspaper talk. Mr. Angelo would expect them to be well-prepared. A part of that preparation was getting to know each other. They decided, then agreed that they knew each other already. It was more like meeting an old friend, each word confirming what they knew in advance—a kind of déjà vu.

That was the first of many shared lunches—and shared feelings, confidences, and *selves*. The noon meetings, like his walking with her to domestic science class, accompanying her to and from the bus, and working together on the newspaper during the appointed time became routine, one requiring no discussion.

That they were an item never occurred to them. They were too engrossed in one another to take notice of the inquisitive eyes that followed them. They were simply Marvel and Titus, moving in their own private little world, while preparing themselves for the world beyond school and how to serve where they were needed. Their views, so parallel, were pure and untarnished. Never once did they fault humanity for its sad condition or place blame for their own somewhat deprived youth on the shoulders of society, criticize their schools, or claim their destiny was predetermined by their bloodline. They could be what they wanted to be. Weren't they heirs of the Lord? They'd laughed over that one, saying there was no question about it. They were in His "will"! And democracy guaranteed their freedom, too. How could they lose?

On several occasions one or several of the other football players sauntered over to stand momentarily beneath the cooling shade of the oak. Always they greeted Titus as "Cap" and always they lingered to ogle. Titus cut short any further advances by introducing Marvel with just the right amount of possessiveness in his voice. *How could they lose?* Oh, they couldn't, they couldn't—unless they lost one another. And that was unthinkable, Marvel would tell her private self. They *belonged* together. With that, she'd slam the door on the future....

"You're so gracious," Titus said after one of those introductions.

"Actually," Marvel said with a coquettish smile, "I suppose I should be flattered."

"Nobody could do that!" he said with a kind of fierceness. "You are so—so different—so completely charming any compliment would be sincere."

"You are very kind," Marvel said demurely, feeling suddenly shy.

"I wish—" Titus hesitated and when he spoke again, she knew his words took a different direction. "I wish I knew what you're thinking."

"That it is time we were going," she said, getting to her feet.

The sun had grown hot and Marvel felt a regret at leaving the shade. Did she miss the comfort of its comparative cool or the security of its seclusion, shielding them from the rest of the world? The thought made her sad. Time was going too fast. The wind was sweeping it away.

"You're too quiet again," Titus said.

Marvel nodded. "I was thinking—wondering how you came to go all out for all the sports. I've no quarrel with it. It's just that I can't see what part it will play— Do you plan a career?"

"Of sports?" Titus laughed. She loved his laughter. "Oh, I enjoy it in a way, but it's one of the stairsteps we've talked about. Hopefully, I'll receive some letters—hard work but worth it. Kind of an honor, I suppose. But what I have in mind is the scholarship they'll earn for me."

As they fought the wind toward the cottage, Titus told her his plans. The scholarship would pay his tuition, and he had promise of part-time work—would Marvel believe in the state capital? A friend of the family was a representative, aiming to be governor one day, so deemed it wise to choose aides from the various towns and communities. Of course, the scholarship carried with it a commitment to play college football—nice, he supposed, but what a schedule!

"Congratulations, Titus. I'm sure you'll get the scholarship. It's based on more than your ability to play the game. They can't be blind to your other qualifications: You're ambitious, hard-working and—and deserving. But—"

"But?"

"You want experience, preparation—not in sports—so?"

Titus understood her reservations. "So am I going into politics? Yes Marvel. Yes, I am. At least I hope to."

When she didn't answer, he went on, "And you're wondering how getting into the political arena can be of help. Somebody has to get us out of this mess, help us avoid getting in deeper—and, *God forbid,* ending up in war."

"Oh, Titus—"

"I know—I know—it's hard to think about. But if we're all isolationists or just *politicians*, you know, trying to make a name for ourselves—but what's needed is some good old down-home religion— Don't laugh."

"I'm not laughing," Marvel said softly, wanting to add, "I'm trying to keep from crying."

To avoid tears, she told him about her father and his unfulfilled desire to play baseball, about his hope to hold onto the land which he loved so dearly, and his plans to organize a team out in that rural area just for fun, diversion. And goodness knows, it was needed.

"I'd like to meet your dad."

"You two would get along famously. And you'd love Mother."

Titus studied her face closely, a look of something akin to hunger in those darkened eyes. "Do they know about me?"

No, you're my guarded secret, Titus. Only one did not say such things. And so Marvel shook her head as if hoping to do something with her wind-tousled hair. They were nearing the cottage, and Marvel was almost certain that several pairs of curious eyes peered from the windows—among them Miss Ingersoll's. She lifted her chin, proud to be seen with Titus.

"Well," he said with reluctance, "end of the trail for me, I guess. They're going to steal you from me. But there's tomorrow!"

Yes, oh yes there was tomorrow—a lot of tomorrows—and she savored each moment with a kind of sadness beneath the wild happiness in her heart. It was like—like storing up memories for the grave....

* * *

Marvel hoped that her preoccupation with Titus did not show. She looked in the mirror often, half-expecting to see stars reflected in the blue of her eyes. If they were too bright or her rosy cheeks had paled, all would notice. Mother would say she looked exhausted, that she was overdoing. Mary Ann would say she'd lost her mind, while Grandmother would say she'd found it. And Fanny would say she was bilious.

The thought of Fanny reminded Marvel that she was to make a children's garment as a final project in domestic science. Mother had remnants of cotton fabric to share in her home demonstration class today, Saturday. Beforehand, it would be nice to have the pink print. Wouldn't it be lovely against the ebony skin of Fanny's baby boy? Rompers, oh, how sweet—and she'd done nothing to show appreciation to Fanny for rescuing the cotton. The scraps of red ribbon the girls would love made into bows for their prized pigtails. Better measure him—babies grew fast.

Mother and Daddy were pleased, especially when Marvel suggested that she and Daddy look over the crops on the way to Fanny's.

"The watermelons look good, Daddy. Oh, look how they're growing!"

"Should have some ripe by the Fourth. Better eat our fill. There'll be no market," Daddy said, defeat echoing in his every word.

"Oh, I wouldn't say that!" Marvel said brightly. "He—uh—a friend of mine says there are some refrigerated cars now and freight trains are bringing in melons from south Texas. Their supply should dwindle about the time ours are ready to ship. Everything needn't depend on cotton!"

"The loan does. Our cattle are mortgaged. We could lose them all."

"But not the land!" His grin was her reward. Marvel renewed her vows. *I'd make any sacrifice—ANY—to pull us out of this.*

And yet, deep down, there was a conflict within her. It seemed a little unfair that this world of harsh reality should rob her newly discovered one of its glow. She almost dreaded coming home where her other world would be laid to ruin. And then she'd feel guilty...ask God's forgiveness.

45

Trophies

Suddenly there was an atmosphere of frenzy at Culverville High. Both Marvel and Titus found themselves caught up in it. Trying to meet all the teachers' goals while keeping up with extracurricular activities took its toll. It robbed them of precious time together.

They took to note-writing again, to the pretended aggravation of their messenger. After all, Marvel Harrington and Titus Smith were "names" now—important people on the campus. And she, Virginia Thomas, was a part of an unfolding drama.

Virginia delivered the notes with a flourish, hoping obviously that others were watching—except the teachers, of course. Mercy! That would spell trouble for the three of them. Once her eagerness to show off led to an unpleasant encounter with Amanda Cohane.

"That little snip saw Titus hand me this note, and you know how clumsy I am. Well, she saw me drop it and would you believe made a dash to get it? Even opened it, the sneak, then made out like she was going to look for the name so she could return it. I can't stand her," Virginia confided. "But I gotta warn you, she's out to get you. Watch out."

"What seems to be the problem?" Marvel asked innocently.

"Jealousy—just plain old green-eyed jealousy what with his being on the football team and being a big track star, and eyes only for you! Still, she packs a lotta weight, you know?"

"I know."

Virginia bit her lip. "She's trouble, her overstuffed papa being on the school board and all that. And there's no better trophy in her book than shagging in the captain of our football team. So maybe you two better bury the hatchet."

"In each other!" Marvel said, furious at mention of Amanda vying for Titus' attention.

"Wow!" Virginia whispered in awe. "You two *are* serious."

Marvel decided then and there that she would take advantage of every possible moment to be with Titus in person—preferably alone. She took to running out to the field where he was practicing for the county meet just to see him, walk back with him, hear his voice.

There was the added bonus of watching the rippling muscles of his body demonstrate in the bright, late-May sunshine the strength she'd felt but never had the opportunity to witness.

"Do you realize I've never seen you play in a game?" she asked.

Titus was wrapping a heavy towel about his sweat-soaked body. His hair, usually so disciplined and glossed by brilliantine, now hung boyishly over his high forehead. He had never looked more beautiful.

"I wish there were time to fix that," he said, his voice a little sad, as it always was when time was mentioned between them.

"I couldn't have stayed anyway—the bus, you know," Marvel said with regret. "But," she strove for brightness which was so much a part of her, "we've made each moment count."

Titus shook his hair from his eyes, squinted, and playfully pulled it back. "Let's shut out the world and all its rumble—don't I wish? Well," he slowed a little before darting in for a shower, and she slowed with him, "I'd say we've come to know each other better than most couples do in a year or two years—maybe in a lifetime. Think we'd ever get it all said—even in a lifetime?"

"We don't have to worry that one through—believing in an afterlife as we do. 'Bye, bye, we have to shake a leg, you know!"

"I'll never hear the end of that," he moaned. "Sorry I can't meet you at the bus."

"I understand," she called happily over her shoulder as she ran to her next class. Sorry? Oh no, he mustn't be sorry—not about *anything*. He'd called them a *couple*. She whispered that word over and over.

Later that very day Marvel was to encounter Amanda in the girls' room and it was good to hold the word carefully as a shield.

And, admittedly, it was to her advantage to have had Virginia's warning.

Since meetings with Titus were fewer, Marvel made a point of looking her best. Students had five minutes between classes. That offered a needed opportunity to dart into the girls' room, gloss her lids, fluff her hair, or wipe dust from her shoes.

The moment she opened the door, Marvel knew someone was smoking—regretful, but none of her business. The principal might or might not be aware. In a way, he was better off not knowing, considering that Amanda's father was on the board of trustees. It could put his job in jeopardy. Mr. Phillips was ethical to a fault, and right would prevail over personal need. Marvel respected him too much to put him in that position. Never once in her thinking did it occur that she could be wrong in assuming that Amanda was one of the offenders.

And she was right, of course. Cigarette in hand, the banker's daughter sauntered to the mirror and said to Marvel's reflection: "Here to report, Miss Harrington?"

Marvel spoke with a calm she did not feel. "I report only to newspapers," then added pointedly, "and they want only what is *news*."

Amanda was livid, eyes liquid fire, face paling so that her over-red lipstick stood out garishly. "Don't get cute, Miss Paragon of Virginity!"

"And what would *you* know about *that*?" Marvel said coolly as she walked out in deliberate serenity.

Outside, Marvel lengthened her stride and hurried to the bus to take her place beside Mr. Newland. Hopefully she looked, but *he* was not there.

He, too, had noticed that Titus no longer walked with her. "Ain't seen yore beau of late. Somethin' wrong?"

The blunt question smacked of hope—a hope which Marvel expected to dispel immediately. "Just busy," she said, beginning to check other students in as they boarded. "And Titus is *not* a beau, Mr. Newland."

"*All aboard?*" he called loudly before telling her eagerly that Archie was home. Good to have the boy, but felt bad that his own job took Archie from the three-C's. 'Course he was settin' up shop and all.

"That's good," Marvel said absently, eyes on her list.

Taking that as encouragement, Mr. Newland went on to tell her how Archie appealed to the young ladies since he had all that fine training—sort of military-like. He'd gone part way on one of the bus runs, and by chance Annie and Ruth had been at the mailbox. Well, both of them went for him—swooned, absolutely *swooned*, they did—"

It was easy to see Mr. Newland's disappointment when Marvel said she was glad to hear it, adding that both of them were nice girls, and that either would be fortunate to have Archie return their attentions.

And that, she decided, took care of that.

* * *

County meet was over and done with—almost. There would be an awards assembly as promised, but nobody knew when. Consequently, Marvel was at the domestic science cottage when the principal saw fit to announce that students were to assemble at once in the auditorium. She was enjoying a trophy more meaningful than a ribbon or loving cup. Miss Ingersoll praised the pink rompers highly.

"You sew so beautifully," she said, "but then, you do everything so well. You'll be a wonderful homemaker when you change your mind and decide that marriage has a place in your life. Didn't I see you with a young man the other day?"

Marvel's glow gave her away, but she was unaware that her happiness showed when she said simply, "Yes, ma'am, Titus Smith."

"I thought so. He'd be Lucille's young brother. I had her in class—lovely girl. Oh, back to the sewing. The girls make formals, you know, in their senior year. I'll look forward to seeing yours."

"It'll be blue," Marvel said dreamily, pushing away the question of how she would afford the kind of fabric a formal required. It was a year away yet.

"Oh, it *has* to be blue—so lovely with your eyes. The formal's not as impractical as it may sound. The girls use them for graduation, you know, wear them beneath their robes. Caps and gowns are compulsory because some are unable to buy nice dresses. Usually the girls go out for ice cream or cokes to celebrate. The gowns are off then."

Miss Ingersoll didn't suspect the truth then—that Marvel Harrington was among the "some" who could not afford such finery?

Titus met the bus that day. Bright-eyed with excitement, he almost ran in his rush to tell her that she'd missed assembly. How terribly unfortunate and unfair! He could have burst with pride, he said, when her name was called time after time: declamation, debate, picture-memory, *everything*—and then his and hers together. They were given full credit for putting out the first newspaper, called perfect examples. And, oh wait, she especially was honored... owner of the county paper was there to recognize her, so handed *him* this to give *her*.

The bus was waiting. "Titus, quickly—what about *you*?"

Hurriedly he lifted his right leg and spread his class sweater over his knee in display. It was covered with letters, pinned on crookedly for her inspection.

"Oh Titus, the scholarship—you got it. How *could* you wait to tell me—spend all that time on trivia?"

"Your honors are not trivia! And what we did together—"

"I'm proud of that part, but the scholarship means everything. Now you can go on to college—everything. Oh, I'm so excited I could—"

Mr. Newland was looking their direction, hurrying her with his eyes.

"You could *what*?" he said, clutching the sweater and blocking her way.

"I could talk forever! Oh Titus, I *have* to leave, so congratulations, d—" Marvel stopped quickly, horrified at what she'd been about to say. Before he could answer, she'd hurried to board the bus.

She wouldn't look back, she *wouldn't*. But she did.

Titus was standing with the wind in his hair and the sun borrowing light from those gray eyes, now dark with astonishment—and expectancy. She would always remember him that way....

✳ ✳ ✳

Mother met her wringing her lovely hands in despair. "Wild geese at *this* time of year—disoriented and lost, I guess. Oh look what they did to the watermelons—our only hope. Every melon ruined—gone—"

Daddy joined them, pointed at the terraces, and she knew Mother was right: Melons riddled with holes, maize sawed off at the roots, gardens dead of thirst. Oh, what was the use? It *was* hopeless. Marvel felt an overpowering weariness as the desperation of the old world closed in once more to blot out the brightness of the newly created world her young heart had discovered. She was tired...tired...tired—too tired to try to get her parents' attention, tell them about today's trophies—or even remember the letter Titus had handed her.

46

The Heart of the Matter

Marvel had hoped that the pace would slow after the county meet. If anything, it picked up speed. A kind of desperation ringed her heart as the end of school drew closer and she and Titus were denied planned time together. Just how she could bear being totally without him come summer, she refused to think about. He would be gone, while she—who knew?

But they were trapped and there was little they could do about it. Titus was tied up with countless meetings: counseling periods in preparation for entering college, meetings with some state dignitaries who outlined his responsibilities at the state house. And yes, he must come on this summer for orientation, working out in advance to help make the football team the best ever. (It jolly well better be, they implied, if he expected renewal of that scholarship!) Plus he had countless class meetings to plan the program for graduation, be fitted for caps and gowns, take pictures. Then naturally, so teachers told him, the yearbook would be his responsibility with his background in journalism.

Marvel found herself equally involved. Juniors must take this test and that one in preparation for their senior year. Miss Robertson wanted to plan Marvel's schedule well in advance, leaving time for participation in all literary events. Marvel realized, she was sure, that she'd be in the senior division and maybe going to State? *State?* Miss Robertson must have been surprised at Marvel's sudden enthusiasm. Why, that's where Titus would be. Oh, she had to win, and they'd meet in Austin. Just wait until she told him! She must arrange time.

But how? Miss Ingersoll, swamped with closing the books on another year, was also working on private matters: her wedding! Marvel *would* help her, wouldn't she? Projects to check in and out, evaluate—and then the teacher would desperately need her to assist with grading the final examination papers. Marvel *was* exempted? Yes, Marvel was.

In her daily note to Titus that day she indicated that there was something special she wanted to share. The possibility of failing to win at local, county, and district, disqualifying her for State never once occurred to Marvel. In their bright new dreams, anything was possible.

Marvel's note crisscrossed with Titus's note to her, as was so often the case. And the contents were somewhat the same. He needed to see her, he said. He had an idea that simply would not wait.

Then during the day one of the most unexpected things of Marvel's life happened—undreamed of, unheard of, unbeliev-able, *impossible*!

She, Marvel Harrington, the "girl from the sticks," was invited to serve as one of the six usherettes at graduation! The invitation was delivered in such an offhand, businesslike manner, and from such a totally unexpected source, that it was over and she had breathlessly agreed before there was time to consider what it involved.

Mr. Angelo, of all people, simply leaned over her shoulder in the study hall to whisper in her ear: "Marvel, I've been asked to serve on a committee to select usherettes for the graduation ceremony. It would please me to have you in the group. Will you think about it?"

Think? "Oh, I consider it an honor, Mr. Angelo. Thank you, sir."

Marvel hardly heard the man say she would be needing a formal. She could only think of playing a special part in Titus' graduation.

He was excited as she was at the news: both the possibility of her coming to Austin and, more immediately, "graduating" with him. Both of them had meetings cutting short their conversa-tion. But parents were sponsoring a junior-senior party—no teachers—so would she like to go?

"I wish I could offer to come after you, but," Titus spread wide his long fingers, "no car. I'm sorry."

Marvel shook her head. "Don't apologize. I really wouldn't want to go anyway. Oh, I'd *want* to, but—"

"I understand—and I agree. If you've heard that things sometimes get out of hand, you've heard right. And I don't want you exposed to that. And me, well, I can't afford chances."

"Absolutely not. You must graduate, and see me all decked out."

In what? For the first time it occurred to Marvel that she did not have the proper clothes. With that realization, her heart sank. This—why, this was to have been the greatest moment of her life. And just moments ago she'd been concerned about that silly party and the real reason she'd had to refuse to attend. She had overheard the girls from town discussing the affair, saying that they would wear silk sports dresses. Well, Marvel had no silk sports dress. In the end it didn't matter. But this did!

The bell rang, thankfully. Marvel had been squeezing back tears—tears which would never be shed because of what Titus said in parting.

"Okay, that settles that. I think we understand each other. Soooo, Miss Marvelous, we'll have a party all our own. The other's to be a picnic—and we'll have our private one. This one's on *me*!"

It was a memorable picnic, poignantly sweet because of the swift-flying time. Marvel was waiting beneath the shade of their private oak when Titus hurried to join her. He was carrying an enormous watermelon—the kind she was sure would split from top to bottom with a *pop*! once it was pierced by a knife—as if eager to show off its sugary-red goodness and share the natural goodness of its great heart.

She was right. There was such a loud report when Titus thrust his knife into the rind that both dodged to avoid the expected shower of sticky juice. That started the laughter. And it continued as they stuffed themselves on generous half-moon slices, juice dripping down their chins and forcing them to lean over the grass to keep the syrup from covering their clothing.

"Oh, yum-yum, this is absolutely the best watermelon I ever in this world tasted," Marvel said as she finished a third slice.

"Fun? This is one of the melons I told you about—the ones from south Texas. A friend of my sis brought her two right from the refrigerated cars. She'd taken care of the whole family when they came down with flu. That's Sis for you, always doing for others. You two would like each other. You'll meet her one of these days."

"Lucille, isn't it?" Marvel asked, remembering Miss Ingersoll's comments.

And that led to a discussion of their respective families. Marvel told the sad story of Daddy's watermelon crop and then the faltering cotton, the dead garden—and the dying hope. Titus expressed sympathy and understanding. Things were tough for him and his sister, too, although they could have been different— very different. His family had owned a lot of land, too, back in Titus County's youth. But there was no way the two of them could hold onto it. The irony of it all was that the purchasers knew from the beginning it was oil country, and took advantage of their ignorance. Pretended to be digging a well for needed water and hit a gusher! The wrong people were oil barons.

"Life's hard to understand sometimes," Titus said pensively. "I seem to have a lot more questions than answers."

Marvel agreed. She told him then about her sessions with Brother Greer and all about Morning Glory Chapel. But she must learn *patience*. She told him about the persimmons then.

He watched her face intently. "You've never told me exactly what your plans are. There'll be so many opportunities for you."

"I don't really know," she said slowly. "I've prayed for an answer, but it hasn't come. God seems to prefer keeping it His secret. Meantime, I'm preparing myself every way I know. Remember what Paul wrote to Timothy: 'Study to shew thyself approved unto God.'"

"'A workman that needeth not be ashamed, rightly dividing the word of truth'? Yes, I remember." He grinned then. "But I'm remembering some of Paul's other advice to his friend about shunning 'vain babblings.' I'm afraid I babble too much."

"You don't babble!" Marvel defended. "And I can't imagine your using profanity. That word's used in the same verse."

"Nope! But the guys do, and our coach should reprimand them and just ignores it. But *I* make my objections heard—see that we have a prayer, too. Are you laughing?"

"I am not! I'm pleased, Titus. Why do you keep thinking I'd laugh?"

"*Others* laugh, but you're not others. But I pray anyway. Not that we'll win necessarily, just asking God's protection, His guidance. Oh, there goes that bell. And us with all this melon. Quick, I have to take this carcass to the receptacle. Tear the heart out. The heart's a terrible thing to waste."

Tear the heart out. Marvel was to remember those words forever. *Tear the heart out of their beloved state,* a part of the heartland of America. *Tear the heart out of her parents,* as this drought had done. *Tear the heart out of HERSELF,* when she said good-bye to Titus. For this would be their last truly private time together. . . .

On her way home Marvel remembered the letter from the newspaper. A check! In her surprise she almost dropped it. The jolt of the bus would not allow her to read the entire letter, so she let her spirits soar. The money meant the blue dress for graduation—for Titus!

47

The Blue Dress

The evening meal was somber. Mother made a feeble attempt at conversation, but Daddy wasn't interested in the home demonstration meeting devoted to bread-and-butter pickles and buttermilk doughnuts. And there was nothing new in Grandmother's daily call. He had talked with all his brothers, and they'd reached some decision for the future—just tentative, but *something* had to be done.

A glance from Mother cut short his disclosure of details. They both seemed upset, so this was no time to share the news of special recognition from the county newspaper—no time to mention school at all. Her parents paid little attention to her activities these days. Didn't they care anymore? Marvel wondered. Then she scolded herself inwardly for such foolish thinking. Of course they cared! In fact, it could be that her education was at the root of the developing tension.

The walls on this house were paper-thin—so thin that voices went through them as if they weren't there. And now Marvel was recalling one conversation between Mother and Daddy. Their voices were pitched low but grew louder with feeling, then stopped short and silence took over.

"There's no way to turn, Snow. You've got to face it. We simply can't 'stick to our bush' as you like to call it."

"Stop it—I won't listen. If you mention moving one more time—"

Daddy's voice was cold when he said, "What do *you* suggest?"

"You *know* my feelings. Marvel's schooling comes first. I will *not* have her moved around the way I was. Is that clear?"

"Very," Daddy's voice was fierce, "and something else is clear now. How could I have been so blind before? I'm beginning to think it's this disgraceful shack you're afraid to leave—*anything* you can call a *home*. It comes before me, our daughter, our welfare. Why, it's a sickness." Daddy's voice had risen, and now it lowered but was still full of anger. "Anyway, that doesn't answer my question, which was what we're going to do!"

Mother's voice was broken, her phrases jerky. Wait the year out, she'd said. Something would break for them, and if not—well, they could consider moving back into town. Marvel would be eligible for the bus then.

Daddy had groaned. "And what would that help? No house, work—nothing. How could you have forgotten that's what brought us here?"

Now Marvel sighed in recollection and the fatigue closed in again. *Stop it*, she willed herself. *Stop it or you'll be sick and miss graduation!*

Jumping up from the table, she excused herself and, leaving her food untouched, escaped the prison of her mind by switching on the radio. Maybe there would be some news. She'd lost out on that.

Instead, there was a baseball game on the air! "Oh Daddy, come on in when you're finished. This is the first time I've heard sports on the news. Just saw reports in the *Dallas Herald* in the school library—hurry! It's your league—American, wasn't it?"

"Yes, American, honey," he said, but made no effort to join her.

Marvel gave up after awhile. There was studying to do, if she could concentrate. And her own reference to a newspaper served as a reminder to look at the small (she was sure it was, while wondering how she came to receive money at all) check and read the accompanying letter. It would explain.

She stepped onto the creaking porch for needed air. The wind had gone to bed, and the rising moon looked as big as Fanny's washtub and just as polished. One good thing about dust: It made for more beautiful sunrises, sunsets, and rising moons. Looking at the liquid gold of that giant moon and listening to the poignant music of the cricket songs, Marvel thought with regret how much she and Titus had missed: the moonlight walks, the languid hours of lying on fresh-cut grass in companionable silence just meditating on the stars hung in the heavens by God's own fingers—something this Depression could never touch.

Then she was back in the other world below those twinkling stars, jolted back by the one word she heard repeated in the kitchen over and over like a broken record for the Victrola: loan... *loan*... loan....

It was then that she knew, she supposed later—even before stepping into the square of lamplight the window let outside to read her letter.

> Dear Marvel Harrington: You are to be congratulated on the numerous awards you will be receiving today. According to all reports from your school, you are a very deserving student. We will be expecting great things from you during your senior year and even greater accomplishments upon your graduation. The staff here extends a cordial invitation to you to continue to share with us your talents, also an invitation to talk with us regarding employment in later years providing your choice of career is that of journalism. Since we have failed to furnish you with needed materials throughout the past year, may we offer this modest honorarium to cover the costs? We regret that present circulation and advertising do not allow us to pay you on a regular basis. Please know how deeply we appreciate you and the fine job you have done for us. We remain in your debt, as do our readers. In deep appreciation, A. Thomas Corey, Editor.

Marvel reread the letter, her heart thrilling to its every word. If only Titus were here to share the message he'd delivered! Oh why had she neglected to open the envelope? But of course she knew why.

Picking up the check, she read the figure and gasped. How had they known—oh, how could they? Because she knew now without question how the 30 pieces of silver would be used!

Dale and Snow Harrington stopped talking when their daughter reentered the airless kitchen—airless, as if all the oxygen had been sucked up in desperate gasps between angry words. In their bitterness and unaccustomed hostility, they had become withdrawn again: bent on "keeping up appearances," no longer sharing, no longer a family, no longer, Marvel thought sadly, "the three bears."

"We're out of debt!" Marvel said simply, laying the check on the small table between them.

"What on earth—how— Oh, *Marvel!*" Mother burst out.

Daddy stared at the check in disbelief.

Marvel, forcing a smile, laid the letter beside the check.

"See?" Mother was clapping her lovely hands. "I *told* you something would happen to change things, that we were worrying too much!"

Daddy looked at her strangely before turning to Marvel. "I can't take this," he said and his voice was that of a broken man. "I'm head of this household. I'll find a way to provide for my family."

"We're that family, Daddy: Mother, you and I. And does it really matter who pays when there's a pressing need?" Marvel said gently.

"She's right, Dale. We have no choice. You want this land—"

"The land's not at stake, Snow, it's the cattle," he said thoughtfully. "But you two are right. There's no choice. The cattle are our living. All right, Miss Marvelous. I surrender—providing it's a loan!"

Marvel shook her head. "It's no *loan*. I have come to despise that hateful word, so I'm more than happy to buy it! Now, can't we be happy?"

The light was back in his eyes. But the glow inside her was extinguished. She'd vowed to make any sacrifice—no matter what the cost—to help. But that was before the blue dress. Such a small matter, really, and yet so great. The dream would have cost very little, but giving up carried a high price tag: *the heart.*

* * *

Miss Ingersoll held her final exams early. Grades must be turned in well before graduation, she explained to Marvel, as she handed the first stack of papers to her. And with them came a surprise invitation to lunch that day, a week before school was to end.

"We'll go to the old Smith Hotel—that's where I usually eat as they serve a full-course dinner at the noon hour. That way I can snack in the evenings—a pattern I'll have to change," she laughed, "when I'm a married woman. A word about this place," the domestic science teacher said as they neared the hotel. "It's a historical landmark, in sad need of repair, and the same applies to its clientele, but they'll love *you*. Most probably know your relatives—as they know your friend's."

"Titus?"

"Titus Smith, yes. The place belonged to his grandfather at one time. Here we are, and I promise you the food's delicious."

It was. And the elderly people seated around the white-linen-spread table rose to greet them warmly. Miss Ingersoll was right about their interest in the new guest—probably, Marvel surmised, the first really young person with whom they'd come in contact for a long time. She answered their questions politely, but did not allow herself to be drawn into long conversations. That was regrettable. They needed to exchange their older wisdom for younger outlooks and enthusiasm, another area in need of change. The possibilities kept widening for her when they should be narrowing, preparing to focus on a life work....

Right now, she was Miss Ingersoll's guest. While the teacher appreciated the help she was giving, Marvel was almost sure that the invitation carried with it another purpose.

"The food's lovely," she commented, turning to face her hostess.

"I always eat too much. More fried chicken, Mrs. Holcomb?" With the platter safely out of her hands, Miss Ingersoll continued. "And I suppose each person has a story to tell you about the Smiths. But I'll add a bit about the younger generation: Titus and Lucille. I grew very close to her in class and felt so sorry for her, although she never complained. She's had a hard life, but her future looked bright—to me."

Miss Ingersoll paused to study Marvel's face. She wondered why.

"Lucille's work resembled yours, and I encouraged her to go into interior decorating. Then, having no money, she up and made an unfortunate marriage to an older—much older—man. She may have thought he'd give her the fatherly care missed in childhood. It didn't turn out that way."

When she paused, Marvel took the pause as a signal to show interest. "What happened?" she asked.

"Nothing good! He's practically an invalid: gassed in the world war, lost a leg, a lung, and some say his senses! He does receive a disability check which covers the rest of that barny old house—one Lucille settled for so she could see that Titus could live with them and stay in school—all the things she missed."

"She accomplished her goal," Marvel said softly, laying aside her fork.

"Not quite!" Her tone told Marvel that they were coming to the point. "You see, she was compelled to put aside her own dreams of the home she decorated but Titus keeps saying, 'Someday it will happen.' Oh, I hope nothing interferes with Titus's promise. He wants that home for her."

"Nothing will stop him, short of death. I hope her dream comes true."

Miss Ingersoll made no secret of her pleasure. Had she thought Marvel would stand in the way, come between him and his promise to his sister and himself? She obviously didn't know him very well.

"Now," Miss Ingersoll said in a voice that betrayed her with-that-settled attitude, "I heard in teachers' meeting that you were to be one of the usherettes?"

"Yes, ma'am—much to my surprise."

Miss Ingersoll nodded. "Too late for you to make that blue dress with rehearsals *and* graduation next week! But I've racked my brain trying to remember names of girls, if any, who made blue formals. Then in a flash it came to me: Erlene Gilbreath! And she lives somewhere in your neighborhood. I took the liberty of calling her just in case, and she knows you! She insisted that you stop by."

Erlene Gilbreath—certainly. Marvel had caught only glimpses of the older girl, a lovely blonde who used too much makeup but appeared friendly, what little she knew about her. Her brother Claud was a senior. She knew his name only through checking it off in the roll book. Claud boarded before she did, so what was to stop her from getting off just this once with him? Surely there was a shortcut through the strip of woods and she could get home on time.

* * *

The dress was so beautiful it stole Marvel's breath away: a soft, ribbed silk about the shade of the heavenly blue morning glories. And oh, what it did to her eyes! The style was just right—not extreme, the way she'd feared it might be. The becomingly girlish bertha was demurely concealing in front, stopping just at the hollow of her throat, then it dipped stylishly in back in the new "suntan" style, but conservatively. (Miss Ingersoll would have seen to that!) The bertha-style collar was edged with a pleated ruffle repeating the one at the ankle-length hemline. And no style could have been more becoming. The princess-fashion divided in the middle with a wide belt of self-material which emphasized Marvel's hand-span waist. And Erlene insisted that she take with her a single strand of her grandmother's pearls to match the great pearl buckle on the belt.

"Oh—oh, Erlene! It's a dream come true," Marvel whispered in awe when she saw herself reflected in Erlene's full-length mirror. "You'll never know—never, never what this means. And," Marvel admitted a little sadly, "there's no way I can repay you."

"Forget it," Erlene said a little gruffly, waving the matter away with her highly polished nails. "You're doing me a favor, kid, in wearing the dress. I'm looking at *myself*. I—I never graduated, you know."

"I'm sorry. So the dress has never been worn? I *am* sorry."

The other girl was no longer bluffing. The pale-blue eyes looked sad. "The biggest blow of my life— But you know the rules: flunk one subject and you've flunked 'em all. I tried hard to get out of geometry, but there's no hole to climb through in Culverville High—no avoiding the dictator called Phillips. Well, I washed out like I knew I would. He threw out that nightmare—something about the square of the hypotenuse—"

"The Pythagorean theorem. Oh Erlene, we *all* have trouble with that, but I have an idea. Just listen to me—please?"

Without waiting for an answer, Marvel explained how many students had come back to school and finished under the new program ... about the new job opportunities class ... and, most importantly, her secret method of solving the geometrical problem which had kept Erlene from graduating.

"Come back," she begged. "I'll be there to help you. Hear this!" And, closing her eyes, Marvel recited the troublesome theorem in its entirety. "You owe it to me," she insisted as a clencher, "in exchange for using your dress."

"That's cheating," her new friend insisted, "but I surrender. And now *I* can't thank *you* enough. And yeah, I gotta cut down on the makeup!"

Mrs. Gilbreath brought in lemonade, inquired about Marvel's family, and then invited her to ride in with them for graduation. Too bad her parents couldn't go, too, but the church would be packed, allowing only families of graduates to attend. And since their Claud squeaked through...

Oh well, there was always next year.

But for now, *this year! This year with her beautiful blue dress*...

48

Destiny of the Heartland

Daddy was listening to the radio now. Marvel was glad but would have preferred that he had not tuned in for the early-morning news on rehearsal day. She had awakened with a sense of excitement tingling throughout her body, only to have the light of that excitement extinguished by the harsh headlines: *Senator Huey P. Long Is Dead, Gunned Down by an Assassin's Bullet!*

Marvel gasped. Mornings allowed for no loitering. But, in horrified shock, she dropped to the corner of her bed, letting her clutch bag slide to the floor—not wanting to listen, but knowing that she must.

> The former populist governor, known as "the king-fish," hails from Baton Rouge, Louisiana, 52, was a political giant...controversial for sure...but why, we ask ourselves, must he die in his prime...be shot dead in the state capital? And nobody knows who the assassins are...or if we can attach a grain of truth to the conspiracy theories abounding in this time of confusion and fear....Can we trust those sworn to guard us...protect us...those we trust in a world like this? While this reporter's referring to the sugges-tion that bodyguards may have done this dastardly deed, he wishes to point out that nobody, *nobody* in that stinking sumphole called the political arena is safe in the very place so desperately in need of a dry

cleaning! Small wonder we can't find decent men out there where any breath inhaled carries with it no guarantee of exhalation.... It's dangerous... and our hands are tied.... How can we help?

The reporter had more to say, sketching out his version of the personality of the late Huey P. Long. He was saucy, brash, and full of a certain boasting joy, but nobody risked the Populist senator's wrath! He had the tongue of an adder, and his quotable insults, born of rural wit, would live on: "That man would milk his neighbor's cow through the cowlot-gate"... "Git out there and drag in the black vote, bearin' in mind that even a buzzard's pure white till he's half-grown." So, good people, he made his mark... just dangerous out there.

All Marvel could recall clearly as she ran the distance to the bus were the words of warning: *dangerous in the political arena....*

Oh Titus, why must you choose that route? Why... WHY?

News of the assassination remained in her mind as Marvel seated herself at the back of the auditorium where usherettes were to receive instruction for tonight's ceremony. It was almost as if she'd been there to witness the terrible tragedy. The world was so big and yet so small. What happened to one happened to them all. It took love...

A love that the others who were to serve with her tonight had never experienced yet, according to their meaningless chatter. If they'd so much as heard the news, they gave no indication. It was so hot, they complained, and they hoped there would be large electric fans in that stuffy, old church... and how long would this thing last today? They had hair appointments and a million other things to do....

Marvel looked around, seeing exactly the faces she would have expected to see: Amanda, Kate Lynn, D'Anna Coolige (an attorney's daughter), and two other smartly dressed girls she hadn't met, both obviously members of the "in"group. The fact that she was the only outsider did not bother her. In a few minutes she would see Titus—that's all that mattered. Already the grads were rehearsing, Mr. Angelo explained, but first, instructions on their behavior and mode of dress for the evening. Theirs were the first faces guests would see. They were representing the school, hence, chosen with utmost care....

And then they were in the shadowy church. A feeling of serenity stole over Marvel, as if a voice from the high, arched ceiling were saying to her heart: "Be still and know that I am God." Harsh winters were past, hot-breathed winds rendered harmless, and cuts and bruises inflicted upon her healed without leaving a scar.

And then she was looking into the eyes of Titus, seeing there an understanding of her feelings, a touchless kind of touching which said he felt the same way. It was only a moment in passing as those graduating matched steps with partners in practiced march to take their appointed places in the front pews. How tall he was, how straight!

When there was a break, Titus hurried to where Marvel stood by one of the stained-glass windows. "Out to the grass?"

"Out to the grass!" And there on the freshly mowed lawn, Titus stretched out full-length to lie facing her, his left hand supporting and lifting his face to look into her eyes. "How you doin'? Or isn't the wisecracking question, 'How's your head?'"

Marvel, sitting cross-legged, her pleated skirt covering her knees, smiled. "Not our language, but I'll answer the same way. I think the proper reply is 'Bettah!'"

It was his turn to smile. "But I'm not much on slang, or silly banter, really. I like our language 'bettah'!"

Marvel nodded and their faces turned serious. "We'll be excused to go home on account of needing to be here early. Our time's so short."

"Too short. We're leaving so many dreams unfinished—" she answered.

Titus rolled onto his tummy, never losing contact with her eyes. "Maybe dreams are never finished. I don't know. Have I ever told you, Marvel, about my aspirations here—for this very church where we'll both have graduated? I want to come back and see that it's not torn down in favor of some newfangled building with no character, no past, no memories of its own."

"I understand," Marvel whispered. "The church has a special place in my heart, too—now."

"My only regret is that we're not marching down the aisle together," Titus whispered quickly, having seen Mr. Angelo's motion to reenter.

Marvel jumped to her feet, her heart pounding in her ears, drowning out the wind, draining her strength, stealing her sanity.

What would he have said and how would she have answered if there had been more time? It was the first personal remark he'd made—if it *was* personal. *Don't read too much into it*, she willed her heart. "Be still...."

But something hung over them, something unsaid. And at the risk of Mr. Angelo's disapproving glance, Marvel burst out: "Oh Titus, please tell me—did you hear the terrible news?"

"About the senator, yes! And it shows the terrible need. We must go. Don't fret, Marvel. Never was it so true, 'Now's the time for all good men—'"

"'...to come to the aid of their country!' I know," she said a little bitterly. "Must you be so dedicated?"

"Yes," Titus said miserably. "Yes, I must. Neither of us has a choice."

* * *

Marvel grew more and more excited as the hour approached. The night would stand out forever in her memory, as one remembers a beautiful dream. Reality faded and she was hypnotized by the unfamiliar smell of hothouse roses, the soft glow of flickering candles, and the gentle strains of an organ, carefully concealed behind streamers of blue and gold—the class colors—now swaying gently in the breeze of electric fans. From the moment of Mr. Angelo's invitation, another world beckoned. And now she entered that third world, different from the other two, and Marvel let herself be caught up in its spell.

The music dropped yet another octave as ribbon-barriers were ceremoniously lifted and guests allowed to enter. Marvel escorted them down the carpeted aisle dreamily aware that she would have failed to recognize friends or family from Pleasant Knoll, were they there.

A loud peal from the organ, and the processional began. The graduates passed her, all looking disappointingly alike in their oversized blue-and-gold caps and gowns. And then it was over.

Forcing her eyes to focus, Marvel glanced at a copy of the programs she had been handing guests. The speaker was to be the Honorable O. Marcus Bradford, a retired chaplain in the United States Navy, the bulletin told her. Following his address, graduates would be presented by the principal to the superintendent who would offer congratulations. In finale, diplomas would be awarded by the president of the Culverville Board of Education, Mr. Elijah Cohane. Of *course*, Amanda's father...

"I wish," said the speaker, "that together with your diploma, we of another generation could place in your hands a safe and secure world, a world whose inhabitants dwell forevermore in the harmony of peace, friendship, and love. But, my young friends, I am afraid I must disillusion you—tell you that there is no such world. Once there was. Bear with me as I read of its beauty, its perfection."

Colonel Bradford opened his Bible to the book of Genesis and read the story of the Creation. There was a pause. And then he returned to the present.

"There are those who fault the preceding generation but, while we contributed to the sorrowful change, it all began before we were here. It reaches back to the fall of Adam and Eve who, in their disobedience, were banished from that one perfect place, shut off from the tree of life. Try to imagine if you can their despair, their regrets, wistful longings to escape this world of darkness and go home. How different things would be if only they had a second chance!"

Leaning down, this stranger who had captivated his audience said in a confidential tone, "Ever feel like that—hmmm? First, denying any wrongdoing, then rebelling, and at last, trying to regain favor by vowing that it will never happen again? Of course, you have—as have all who passed this way before you. But what happens? What happened to *them*? Did Adam and Eve guard those things over which they were given dominion, care for that land of perfect environment? You know the story. If not, just look around you and see beginnings of a wasteland.

And it would grow worse, he warned, and *worse*, and WORSE. Until at last nothing remained—and then the end of the world, as man had known it. Plants would die first, then animals, and, finally civilization...

The end of the world—such as man had known it? Marvel sighed. It was a sad story. There was a longing to get back—back to the world of her childhood. No, farther, just as this magnetic man of God had said. A longing to get back to a world she'd never known gripped her heart. And miserably she realized that to-night was the end of *her* world, an imagined one—a world of earth-perfect environment filled with the moonlight and magnolias that she and Titus had never been permitted to share except in song.

Colonel Bradford came back to this beginning as Marvel had hoped. She should have known he wouldn't leave that other world shut off from them, made inaccessible, with this world hopelessly locked out.

"But all beginnings must have an end. So, taking a giant step with all the explorings between, let's go to the final book, back to the tree of life once guarded by the flaming sword. Is there a way for us to cross that gulf which separates us from that land of perfect environment? Yes, we *can* go back home—back to that land of love, for God is love!

"But meantime, we are not to lie at the foot of our crosses, do nothing here in this world. Heretofore your destiny has lain in the hands of former generations. Now the destiny of the heartland lies in yours. So go in peace, complete your exploring—and come home!"

49

World of Tomorrow

The third world had faded. The stirring words of the Commencement address continued to ring in Marvel's ears, as she guessed they always would. But she was back in a world of reality—a world where a noisy din of voices replaced music, where hothouse flowers grew limp and wilted once the doors opened to the hot wind, where candles were snuffed out with its breath and their glow replaced by the harsh white glare of incandescent lighting. And where it was entirely possible to stand alone in a crowd as Marvel stood now, waiting there on the entrance landing—waiting, watching, and praying as the minutes ticked away.

Titus was much in demand. All his team would be gathering around him, saying the things one says in parting after a warm relationship. Girls would be hovering close, giggling and wanting memory books autographed by the school's football captain. There would be teachers...perhaps family demands...other friends...and a need to check in the cap and gown for next year's grads. Would he find time for her? And the Gilbreaths would be leaving when Claud was finished.

Streets were lined in these days of failing economy with ragged men shamelessly begging. Always their plea was the same hopeless, "Mister, can you spare a dime?" Her own heart was a tin cup of dwindling hope: "Mister, can you spare a minute?" But minutes were as scarce as coins now.

"Marvel?"

"Titus?"

Now they were back at the beginning, and, simultaneously, the end.

"My sis planned a little get-together of her friends, so there's no time."

There never was. Marvel nodded hopelessly.

"I wish she'd known you—that you could have come and shared watermelon again."

It wouldn't have been the same. Both of them knew that.

"Or," Titus said a little desperately, "I wish I had a car. This is no place to say good-bye."

No place was right—unless more was said. Time was running out.

"You're too quiet," he said, trying hard to recapture the mood of their short past. "You haven't spoken a word."

"No," Marvel said. The one word was all she could manage.

Titus glanced over his shoulder, checking, she was sure, to see if someone was waiting. There was a ragged intake of breath when he turned back to look into her eyes. His own gray-now-black ones were filled with unmistakable pain—pain she longed to hear expressed. Only then could she share her own, as they had shared all else. Must parting be like this? How could she cross the gulf into his world until the door was opened? The closeness they'd felt was gone—lost forever—

"It's been nice—wonderful's more like it." Past tense.

"Yes."

"So—good-bye, Marvel."

"Good-bye—good-bye, Titus." Another wordless sacrifice.

Marvel turned away, paused, then lifting the skirt of the beautiful blue dress started down the high flight of concrete steps, gripping the rail for support. *Say something—anything—just call me back....*

One step. Two. On the third step she stopped. And both of them turned at the same time.

She'd only intended to wave in parting, Marvel told herself afterwards. And Titus undoubtedly realized that he should have walked her down the steps, that he'd been thoughtless—rude—

But there were no words to explain away their running toward each other and meeting when he was one step above her, then clasping hands as if, once touching, they could never let go again.

"Marvel—"

"Titus—"

And then they were both talking at the same time, words spilling out foolishly, neither hearing what the other said. Finally, with a shared laugh that wiped away all threatened tears, they slowed down.

"My sister's probably waiting."

"And so's my ride."

"Let 'em wait," Titus whispered. "I *can't* let you go like this!"

"I didn't want you to. Good-bye's not the right word for what we've shared—"

"And will be sharing in the future. I *am* coming back, you know. Will you—just promise me you will—be here."

"I'm not going away," Marvel said, her heart singing a melody while a million stars sang with it. The world turned upside down, then righted itself. And everything made sense.

They were breathing rapidly, talking rapidly, forgetting to unlace their hands.

"I never did ask you, Marvel, if there's anybody else."

"You didn't need to."

"No." He was open, sincere, sure of himself. Theirs was a world of security, filled with friendship and love. But they were not in it alone. There were others—the others they must rescue before it was too late.

"Are you thinking what I'm thinking—that we never found time to talk about ourselves ... not really?" Titus's voice was filled with tender meaning.

Marvel sighed. "Except what we could do—*must* do—to help restore hope. But Titus, that *is* about us. What we *are*. Well, isn't it?"

She looked up at him, unaware of the appeal in those great blue eyes, sparkling with tears that would never be shed. And so his groan was a surprise. His deep young voice should lilt with laughter.

"Oh, mercy me!" he tried to grin. "That doesn't tell how beautiful you are—how you outshine all other girls—especially tonight, the night that belongs to *us*!"

"Thank you," she said demurely, then with more feeling, "oh thank you, Titus!"

Yes, the night belonged to them. Let others say what they would, think what they would, *do* what they would. The two of them shared a secret—the secret of arriving back home where they had started from, after leading others to rediscover that God created the earth round.

It was then that the two worlds of Marvel Harrington came together to make one...softly...silently and without the pain of collision. The dreams were back. Ahead stretched the rolling hills of velveteen pasture, dotted with sleek, soft-eyed cows... acres and acres of gardens for sharing with all who passed by...and a flower-starred yard with a gate swinging inward through which all could enter. None would be barred, for there would be no assassins, either of body or character, and no more sorrow or tears. Then Mother would have her home and Daddy would have his land in that beautiful world of tomorrow. It would all begin this summer when heavenly blue morning glories covered the little chapel and Bible classes began for *all*—race, code, creed, color forgotten.

That would be the world of reality then, the world of glad tomorrow. But always it would be painted with memories of this night, touched with moonlight and magnolias, a world into which they could always retreat.

"We won't exactly be pioneers, you know, just carrying on with the hard-bought freedom our forefathers fought and died for."

The sound of Titus's voice almost surprised her. Marvel had drifted so far ahead in her thinking. Now they were back to their heritage.

"I know—but does it matter? We're not looking for recognition, money, or fame—just results. Both out there—and right here at home."

"You always understand—and it's good. Our thinking, I mean. Anybody claiming there's plenty of room up there on top hasn't taken geometry with Mr. Phillips, looked at triangles or pyramids—"

Marvel laughed softly. "It all comes back, doesn't it? We'll do it *our* way. You go, I stay. Mission fields are everywhere, even in the cotton fields. But it all takes time, more than *we've* had. Time and patience others don't seem to know about—"

"They don't know about persimmons like we know—"

They stood for a moment, not wanting to part.

"Will you write to me, Marvel?"

"You know I will!"

Somewhere in the distance, as if by design, the Salvation Army band struck up a triumphant marching song:

> For me it was in the gar-den He prayed: "Not My
> will, but Thine,"
> He had no tears for His own griefs, But sweat-
> drops of blood for mine
> HOW—MAR-VEL-OUS! HOW—WON-DER-FUL!
> And my song shall ev-er be:
> HOW—MAR-VEL-OUS! HOW—WON-DER-FUL!
> Is—my Sav-ior's—love—for me....

Neither of them could speak, but Titus lifted a forefinger and brushed a little truant curl from Marvel's forehead. "Marvel— my Marvelous—"

Two impatient blasts of car horns, and they parted. But this time Titus was humming the hymn softly, "How wonderful, how marvelous..."

And happily, Marvel's heart hummed with him.